JASPER SPRINGS OMNIBUS
VOLUME TWO

BOOKS 4-6

EVIE RILEY

Jasper Springs
Series Omnibus
Volume Two
Books 4-6
Copyright © 2024
Evie Riley
ISBN: 978-1-77357-733-3
978-1-77357-734-0
Published by Naughty Nights Press LLC
Cover Art By Willsin Rowe

GRAYSON

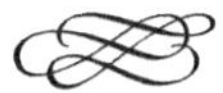

AN MM FRIENDS TO LOVERS
ROMANCE

Grayson
An MM Friends To Lovers Romance
Jasper Springs
Book Four

Copyright © 2024
Evie Riley
Second Edition
ISBN: 978-1-77357-720-3
Published by Naughty Nights Press LLC
Cover Art By Willsin Rowe

**A weekend of glamping.
A little too much wine tasting.
All inhibitions forgotten.**

Grayson Sanderson can't escape the pressure from his parents to find someone to settle down with, especially with his sister's impending nuptials on the horizon. Despite his successful life running a bridal boutique, Grayson can't seem to find his own Prince Charming.

When a series of unfortunate events force Grayson to room with his sister's best friend's brother on the bridal party's weekend wine trip, Grayson finds himself in uncharted territory.

Henry Markell can't seem to catch a break anywhere. When his sister invites him to come along to her friend's bridal party weekend for some well needed luxury and relaxation, Henry thinks his luck is changing.

Until he discovers he's sharing a dome with the sexy and mysterious Grayson, who is more than out of his league. But Henry can't help wanting things he can't have.

Will Grayson give in to his dreams? Or will Henry's notorious bad luck get in the way once more?

Readers seeking a friends to lovers romance with forced proximity set in a cozy little town may find this story ticks that mark. While Grayson and Henry will have cameos in future stories, each book in this series can be read as a standalone.

CHAPTER 1

GRAYSON

I SHOULD HAVE KNOWN that the offering of freshly poured coffee and scones would come with strings.

I mean, after all, this was my sister we were talking about.

"Please, Grayson, do it for me..." she whined, batting her long eyelashes at me, pouting like she used to do when we were kids.

I looked out the window of the cafe, sighing in exasperation because I knew I would inevitably give in. Because if I didn't, I'd never hear the end of it from her, my mother, and God knows who else. But that didn't mean I was going to go easy.

"You know I don't really care for the *bar scene*," I said, my voice firm. But that never swayed Giselle.

"We have a month until the wedding, Grayson. Don't get squeamish now when we're in the home stretch."

I scoffed at her remark. "Excuse me for having *standards*, Giselle."

She crossed her arms, raising an eyebrow at me. "Impeccably *high* standards, might I add. You haven't even had a date in what? Three years?"

I bristled at her words. It wasn't like I *couldn't* get a date. Honestly, I knew if I wanted I could just swipe right on about anyone I fancied, but truth be told, there was far more pressure on me to "pick the perfect match" since I'd come out to my parents.

Which was Giselle's fault entirely.

Not to mention the dating scene, especially in this town, wasn't exactly the most private. When you lived in a small town like Jasper Springs, and your family was one of the most well-known, everyone and their brother was up in your business.

Including meddling, pain in the ass siblings.

"It's different for me, and you know that," I said with a sigh, knowing my fate would be sealed soon enough.

To my surprise, my sister's gaze softened, her lips frowning slightly.

"Oh, Grayson, I didn't mean——"

"I know you didn't, but the fact of the matter is you know mom and dad hold me to a higher standard now."

"Like they didn't have high expectations for me? And Aaron?"

"Aaron's father is the CEO of a high-end realty company. There was never any doubt they'd love him," I said, wanting to veer away from this uncomfortable conversation.

I loved my sister, and she was one of the sweetest, most empathetic allies I knew. But regardless of how understanding or big her heart was, she'd never really understand my station. The oldest sibling, the one our parents expected would lead this family into the next era with a bunch of crotch dumplings, a total Betty for a wife, with a seven figure stock portfolio and a house in the Hamptons.

And I'd shattered all their dreams of the perfect American family when they'd found out I was gay, in the worst way possible.

Caught red-handed with my tongue down my sister's high school ex-boyfriend's throat.

Talk about a scandal.

Our families knew each other well, and Cody and I just happened to be working at the same suit store at the time, and he and my sister seemed to be civil enough that inviting him and his family to the summer shindig was a no brainer, and it just sort of... happened.

After several martinis at the family bbq.

In the pool house.

Where we'd forgot to lock the door amidst nearly half the population of Jasper Springs, because we were drunk. But we'd been fucking around for weeks at that point.

Needless to say, the whole debacle was a nightmare, and when push came to shove, Cody clammed up and sang the tune of "He came on to me. I'm not gay."

I was forced to come clean and tell my parents the truth, much sooner than I'd wanted to.

Of course, I'd planned on telling them... eventually. When I found Mr. Right, and knew he was the one, so they'd never question me or my choice, but now...

Now my parents were looking for any reason to remind me of my bachelor status, my eternal singledom after what had happened with Cody.

"I'm sorry," I said, shaking my head as I dispelled the unforgiving, awful memories. "I'm just... All this wedding stuff is getting to my head, I think."

My sister squeezed my hand softly, forcing

me to look at her pleading eyes, her sympathetic face.

"Does that mean you'll come? I promise it'll be fun. We've been so hell-bent on planning, I think we could all use a drink and some tunes, don't you?"

Damn it.

"Always a bridesmaid, never a bride," I said, flashing her with a smirk as I pulled my hand away. "Perhaps I could settle for *one* drink. But that is it! I swear, I—"

Giselle's smile brightened as she nodded in response. "Seven o'clock at M's Place. Don't be late."

CHAPTER 2

GRAYSON

THE AIR SMELLED like stale nuts and beer, and I couldn't help but wrinkle my nose. I didn't much care for bars in general, but bars like M's Place were below even my lowest standards.

I didn't begrudge anyone for owning their own business, but the place could have most certainly used a more sophisticated Queer Eye to spruce the place up and make it more comfortable.

It didn't take long to find my sister and her wedding party, being as her laugh was like a dolphin call all on its own.

I made my way through the sea of folks, hot,

sweaty bodies clamored together to watch one another drone out tone-deaf songs on stage.

I swear to god if someone sings Taylor Swift, I will lose my shit.

Casually, I strolled over to their two high tables pushed together.

"Grayson, so glad you could make it!" Mia said, coming over to give me a hug. While Giselle and I may not have run in the same circles, we spent a ton of time together outside of those circles, which meant sometimes there was overlap.

I hugged Mia, my gaze settling on the remainder of the party around the tables. Giselle's neighbor, Julie, and her friend slash florist, Taylor, her fiancé Aaron, the best man, Riley, and the most nauseating couple I'd ever met, Lacey and Lane.

Mia's earthy brown eyes sparkled in the low light as she smiled, pulling away.

"Yeah, well, I didn't really have much of a choice, now did I?" I whined, and everyone chuckled.

Giselle rolled her eyes, just as our server came to our table with a platter full of waters. My eyes widened as I recognized the man, if only from passing events.

"Hey, Henry! I'm so glad you could wait on

us tonight!" Mia said as she squealed with excitement at her brother.

Henry smiled affectionately, the corners of his lips turning up with, no doubt, practiced politeness.

His chocolate brown hair fell haphazardly into his amber eyes, his hand placed delicately on his hip as he greeted us.

I didn't know the man well, and the last time I'd truly seen him was at Giselle and Aaron's engagement party nearly four months ago.

He looked different, dressed down in a pair of jeans and a black *M's Place* shirt with an apron tied around his waist.

For some reason, my cock stirred as my gaze settled on said waist, on the slender, toned muscles of his arms that his tight uniform shirt only drew attention to.

"Henry," I drawled as his gaze caught mine.

"It's Grayson, right?" he asked as he tapped his pen against his book.

"It is," I said, shaking my head and dispelling all the weirdness that had somehow managed to set between us.

"What, uh, what it'll be?" he asked, his tone casual, all business and no play.

"I'll have a gin martini, with extra olives, please," I said, leaning against the table, if only to try and stifle the erection that was forming in my pants from the sheer *sight* of this man.

The last time I'd seen him, he'd been dressed in a basic blue blazer and dress pants, dark hair slicked back like he was going to a school dance or something.

I'd thought he was cute then, like a little fish out water. He stood out like a sore thumb among the rest of the three hundred and fifty guests at the engagement party, but he'd also hung back.

I, of all people, understood being anti-social. Especially when you were being dragged to a wedding event against your will. So, I'd done the most noble thing I could do, and left him alone to his devices. I knew I much preferred if someone left *me* alone, but alas, being the brother of the bride and part of the wedding party had its disadvantages too.

"Coming..." he said, his voice cracking for a moment as he pulled at his collar. "...right up," he said, turning away from me, but not before I could see the flush of pink in his cheeks.

My gaze fell to his perfectly shaped ass in those tight blue jeans, and I had to admit, it looked divine walking away from me.

I broke away from the preferred sight, if only because I didn't want to seem like a total creeper.

Mia threw her arm around me, forcing me to look up, noting Giselle caught my gaze and raised an eyebrow at me.

"Tonight is going to be the best night ever!" Mia drawled as Lacey, Julie, and Giselle raised their water glasses in salute, and I was remiss to raise my own.

But when in Rome, one should do as the Romans do, right?

CHAPTER 3

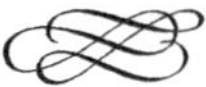

Henry

I set my sights on my sister and the other members of Giselle's party from behind the bar as I gathered waters for the table together, watching with perhaps a little bit of fear of missing out.

My sister, Mia, and Giselle had been friends for years, so it wasn't like it was unexpected that Giselle would have asked her to be a bridesmaid. What was unexpected was how Giselle constantly opened the invitation to me to join her and the wedding party at events that were deemed for the wedding party themselves. Like tonight, they had all decided they needed a "night out" and had decided to come to M's Place for the monthly Bar Bingo and Karaoke. Giselle texted me, as well as my sister, inviting me, but unfortunately I'd been called in to work due to a last minute call off. Which happened to be the very place they were going.

How embarrassing that I couldn't hang out with everyone because I would be the one *serving* them.

But I guess, in a way it was like I was still part of the group... even if I couldn't really hang out because I was working.

The party themselves was a decent size, and I recognized a few other individuals at their table, even though I knew they weren't part of the main party. Taylor, the local florist, and Giselle's GQ-esque brother were also in attendance.

Though from my understanding the older Sanderson sibling was both elusive and single. Not that either of those things should matter to me, but it was nice to know I wasn't the only one who liked to keep to themselves in this gossip-ridden town.

While Mia and Giselle were practically joined at the hip in their younger years, they were also a few years older than me, which meant when they were giggling over heartthrobs and having sleepovers, I was still playing video games and building Legos.

To be frank, I wasn't part of the *it* crowd, and I didn't spend a lot of time over the Sanderson's. It wasn't even until Giselle's engagement that I'd met her older brother for a millisecond before he was being pulled away by their mother for something.

Still, I had to respect the man for doing his own thing and staying out of the mouths of the Sunday Susans who loved to dish over who was romancing who.

I headed over to the table, if only to say hello and get their orders started, but between the bar and the hightop, something changed.

It was like the closer I got to them, to *him*, I could feel this magnetic pull, like the planets were aligning or some shit.

I shook off the weird feelings as I set my tray down, dispersing the drinks. Mia threw her arms around me, Giselle squealed in excitement, Aaron and Riley entangled in some deep discussion about hockey, and Lane and Lacey were, of course, entranced in one another's eyes as usual.

Which left Julie and Grayson as my focal points.

Heat enveloped me as I caught Grayson's steady gaze, and I couldn't help but meet it.

At the engagement, he'd looked rather dapper in his expensive suit, every bit the well-to-do bachelor, but in the low light of M's Place, dressed down in a pair of tailored chinos and a dark blue button down, his dark hair swept back like some teenage heartthrob from those old magazines, I couldn't help but gape at his features.

His perfect jawline, plush, pouty lips.

Deep, rich hazel eyes that reminded me of autumn sunsets over the lake.

God, he was beautiful.

And like an idiot, I'd only realized I was staring when I heard the tail end of Julie's drink order. I quickly recovered, thankfully, and continued around the table, making eye contact with everyone except the man whose stare was burning a hole in my back at the moment.

Finally, when I could no longer ignore the hot older brother of my sister's bestie, I turned to face him with dignity, but I was weak.

I was barely able to form a coherent sentence around the man, apparently captivated by his dreamy sunset eyes, and the way his shirt clung to his form like a second skin, drawing attention to his toned arms, his strong form.

Somehow, I'd managed to take the man's order without flatlining completely, though I hightailed it back to the bar like I was being chased by fucking zombies, if only to get a breath of air, regain my sanity.

What the hell was wrong with me?

It wasn't like I'd never met or seen the man before, but somehow…

Somehow, this felt different, like we were both meeting again, as someone new.

And I wasn't sure how I felt about that.

Thankfully, Giselle and her party were true to their word. They'd come to let loose, and boy did they let loose.

As I loaded up the empties from their second and third round of drinks, Mia grabbed me by the arm.

"And just where do you think you're going?" she asked with a giggle.

"To the kitchen to drop these off…"

"Play with us," she said as she waved her bingo dabber at me.

"Oh, I don't know if I can, I—"

"Oh come on, Henry, surely you can just tell your boss your unruly customers forced you into it, and the customer is always right," Giselle said with a smirk as she slid a bingo card over to me.

My gaze caught Grayson's, who just shrugged as he drank gracefully from his glass.

"Best not to deny them. They are ruthless," he said, shaking his head to dispel some stray hair that had fallen out of place.

My gaze settled on the way he wrapped his pillowy lips around the large olive, the sight of his tongue along the green skin eliciting my cock to attention.

My mind was apt to wander at the sight, images of those lips wrapped around other things pushed forward in my mind as I wondered what said lips would feel like against mine.

I'd never been a person to deny fantasy, but then again, most of the places I'd worked left little room for attractive men and steamy fantasies to begin with.

It wasn't like I didn't have a selection here, in Jasper Springs, but I also didn't have the best luck when it came to most things. And I had even worse luck when it came to men. The thought of my ex threatened to rise up, but I shoved it down quickly.

I didn't want to think about the past, and certainly not while I was at work.

While my sister had worked at the same job for the last seven years, I was still looking for that adult career. You know, the one where you get up everyday, punch in, do your thing. The job that might be boring, but was stable.

After getting let go from my last job, I'd had zero luck finding something that paid as well, but I knew waiting tables would be enough to get me by until I'd found something else.

Still, Jasper Springs may have been a lot of things, but it certainly wasn't lacking attractive men who were most certainly out of *my* league.

Grayson slowly sucked the olive, using his teeth to pull it off the toothpick, and I felt my heartbeat quicken. My cock voiced its own opinion by twitching against the inside of my pants, and I was more than thankful my most inappropriate erection was hidden by my damn server apron.

I gulped as I forced myself to break his sensual stare, if only because now was certainly not the time to get all hot and bothered.

"Just one game," Mia pouted.

I sighed, looking over my shoulder at Max, who seemed to be chatting up someone at the bar at the moment, which meant she too was distracted.

Maybe one game wouldn't hurt.

"Sure, but uh, just one game," I said as the host called out the first number, B-6.

I marked it immediately as grunts and yes's surrounded the space. I noticed Grayson had not moved. Instead, he looked rather uninterested in his game.

With every number called, I neared closer to

Bingo, eliciting squeals of excitement from my sister and the other party members.

Except Grayson that was, who looked at my card with a scowl.

"G-54!" The host yelled, and my sister yelled "Bingo!" faster than I could comprehend I'd won.

I'd... won!

Maybe my luck was starting to turn around.

CHAPTER 4

Henry

I'D FINALLY BEEN LET GO CLOSE to twelve-thirty. Giselle and her party had already left, and my last table was on their way out. I counted my tips, which did not include my bingo winnings, if only because I didn't feel right claiming them being as I was an employee and on the clock. Instead, I'd let Mia claim them.

She was more excited about the bingo than I was anyway.

"Can you restock the soap in the men's room before you go, Henry?" Max yelled at me over her shoulder as I undid my apron, folding it up and tossing it underneath the bar.

"Yeah, of course," I answered, not even thinking twice about it.

I'd just finished replacing the empty package when I heard the faintest groan from the stall at the end of the men's bathroom.

Panic flooded me because honestly, even though I'd heard stories about the patrons who had a little too much fun, I hadn't had the pleasure of encountering one myself. After all, I'd only been working at M's Place for a couple weeks. Less than a month. I really thought I'd have more time before I had to peel a drunkard off the floor.

I cautiously approached the stall, gently swinging the door in, since it was apparent it wasn't locked. My eyes widened to see Grayson, knees propped up, head leaning against the stall wall, a fresh sheen of sweat on his brow. Despite the fact he looked more than wasted, something about the way his hair was all disheveled, the way he carelessly hung his wrist off his knee, he was still GQ-level hot.

Who looks hot when they are wasted? No one!

"Hey there, Grayson... you, uh... gotta get up, buddy."

Grayson opened one eye, his gaze scanning over me with disdain as a cough escaped his throat.

"I don't have to do shiiiit." He pouted, taking in a deep breath.

I carefully knelt down, getting on his level, forcing him to look at me.

"Bar's closing down, you can't stay here..." I said softly as I pulled out my phone, queuing up Giselle's number.

Grayson's hand stopped me in my tracks as he grabbed mine. My gaze met his and he shook his head.

"Don't... call... my sister."

"I wasn't going to," I lied.

"Bull fucking shit, Henry. This isn't my first fucking rodeo," he growled.

"I was calling you a cab..." I said, switching gears.

Grayson laughed. "I don't need a cab, I have the Porsche."

His sweaty palm against the back of my hand didn't move, and I contemplated what to do.

"You are not driving anywhere under my watch, Grayson."

Grayson scoffed, but he didn't argue.

"You'd look pretty in my baby, baby," he crooned, and I couldn't help but blush. Even if his compliments were the babbles of a drunk man.

"So fucking pretty..."

I could have just left him there, went and got Max and told her he was being a pain in the ass and wouldn't listen. Her tone alone could make a grown man cry and I had no doubt she could whip Grayson into submission easily.

And then I could go home, and Max would take care of everything, and...

But something in the look in Grayson's eyes, amidst the drunken glaze, I saw something else, something that pulled at my own heartstrings.

It was the look I'd had when I felt like I couldn't catch a damn break.

So, I did exactly what I should not do. I slid my phone in my back pocket, and I reached out to help him up.

"Okay, well, this train is leaving in five minutes, so you need get up."

To my surprise, Grayson actually listened to me, rising to his feet. I stood, reaching out to stabilize him, and he fought me off initially.

"I don't need—" Grayson bristled in my grasp, stumbling in the small space, but I caught him, my reflex almost instantaneous, as if I rescued drunk patrons on the regular.

"I need your keys," I said as I settled my hand around his waist. I half expected him to flinch, but instead he eased up at my touch, relaxing against me as if his body couldn't protest quite the way his mouth did.

"My left pocket," he breathed, and I carefully slid my hand in, my fingers wrapping around the warm metal keyfob.

I took slow, measured steps, if only so he could keep up, garnering a look from Max as we stumbled side by side toward the door.

CHAPTER 5

GRAYSON

THE FAMILIAR WHIRRING of my car door locks sounded in my ears, mingling together with the warmth of Henry's palm against my back. I could feel his heat through the silky fabric, and something about it made me feel relaxed. Relaxed enough that I wanted to curl against said warmth, but I was far too drunk to garner the control I wanted.

I'd fucked up. Royally. That was apparent. I said I'd stop for just one drink, but one turned into two, two turned into three...

It wasn't that I wasn't having a good time, but watching my sister and her fiancé, and even Lacey and Lane—the most annoying couple on the face of the planet—I couldn't help but feel like a fuck up.

Why couldn't I have a boyfriend who was head over heels for me?

Why were the men in my life always too afraid to come clean about who they were or just looking for a fuck around guy?

Why did I always fall for men who would shove me under the bus the first chance they got?

Was I that much of an asshole?

Henry helped ease me into my passenger seat, my head rolling back against the headrest. I groaned as the self-loathing thoughts permeated my brain. His hand slowly slid across my waist as he fastened me in. I couldn't help but stare, with him up so close, noticing the finer features of his perfect, almost innocent looking face. The urge to reach out and run my hand through his dark hair was prevalent, and just as I moved to do so, he pulled away and I dropped my hand. He patted my seatbelt with approval, before shutting my door. It seemed like forever, the moment of pause between his shutting my door, and him getting in the driver's seat, and I half wondered if he had changed his mind, and decided he was going to leave my drunken ass here.

When he folded himself into the driver's

seat, I couldn't help but notice the curve of his ass fit nicely, almost as if he was made for it.

As if he was made for me...

I shook the hazy thoughts from my brain, resting my head against the headrest as I closed my eyes, my intoxicated thoughts making themselves known despite my best intentions.

"Do you ever just feel like... like everyone else is on some set path that you don't have access to?" I said, completely not expecting Henry to respond to the words of a drunk asshole like myself.

"Yeah, I, uh... feel like that a lot, actually," he said quietly. For a moment, we just sat there in the silence, and it was... nice.

But my idiotic mouth wanted nothing more than to fill the space.

"It's just, this wedding... it's... it's exhausting." I sighed, opening my eyes. Upon doing so, I noted Henry was staring at me, his hands gripping the steering wheel.

I raised my eyebrow at him in question, noting the blush that crept into his cheeks.

Blushing Henry in the front of my Porsche was not a bad sight.

In fact, it only aided in my inebriated thoughts of fantasy as I imagined myself straddling his lap, my ass backed up against the steering wheel, grinding myself against him.

Biting those perfect lips and watching those cheeks pinken from my touch.

My cock twitched its approval of such a situation, but I was also dizzy and did not think I could make the move with enough sophistication at the moment as the room was still spinning.

"I can imagine, being as you're actually in the wedding party," he said.

"That's not... that's not what I meant." I sighed. "It's exhausting having to watch my *younger* sibling get her happy ever after, when I can't have the same thing." I forced myself to look away from the beautiful man in my car, if only because I feared with the uncharacteristic vulnerability I was expelling at the moment, I would fall over the edge and dive into *woe is me* territory.

Poor little rich kid, boo fucking hoo.

I did not *pout* over anything, or anyone for that matter. I was Grayson Sanderson. I was an absolute fucking diamond, and I knew my worth.

Henry spoke up, his voice even and smooth, like hot chocolate.

"I know the feeling. Not because of my sister. I mean, it's like everyone else I know is off getting married and having kids, and buying houses, and I'm just like... I just want a stable job and a boyfriend and like, maybe a cat or something, you know?" Henry said, letting out a sigh.

I turned to look at him, feeling an almost magnet pull, a kindred spirit of sorts. I did know. I knew exactly how it felt to be the black sheep, to be the one off the beaten path. Or maybe it was the several martinis I'd had, making my stomach flip.

Either way, I had the strangest feeling that maybe, just maybe there *was* someone who understood me for once. And that was tempting. Too tempting, to fall into hope.

"You're easy to talk to, you know that?" I said, feeling my heart catch in my throat.

Henry coughed as he broke my gaze, turning on the car.

"We... we should probably get you home," he mumbled as he backed us up, and headed out onto the road.

My shoulders slumped as he looked away, hiding from my words. I got the feeling pretty little Henry didn't get praised enough where it mattered.

Fucking pity.

"You, uh, do you still live at home with your parents, or..."

Shame fell over me immediately at his question, even though it wasn't meant to be derogatory in any way.

My sister had moved out with Aaron pretty much as soon as they'd graduated. I'd moved out too, for a few years, but after mom had hip replacement surgery, I'd moved back to help her out around the house, and just never left. Even though I knew I could anytime, if I wanted.

Maybe I was waiting for the right man to come in and rescue me like a sad princess or something.

God, what is fucking wrong with me?

I meant to say 'yes' like a normal person, but instead all that came out of my mouth was, "I don't have a home," like I was some bridal vagrant.

"Well, how about you stay with me then? For tonight, I mean. It's late, and you can figure out your next move in the morning?" He rushed the words, and I watched his jaw tense while he stared on at the road.

If I didn't know any better, I'd say he was flirting with me, but I knew the truth.

He was just being a Good Samaritan. Any man would have done the same, right?

CHAPTER 6

HENRY

GRAYSON WAS HEAVY AGAINST ME, but I was no weakling.

Though if lifting trashed patrons becomes a thing, I might have to start going to the gym more.

I fumbled with my keys at the door as he leaned against me, his face pressed against my neck so close I could feel the heat of his breath on my skin. The sudden warmth against my flesh caused goosebumps to rise on my arms, and the way Grayson squeezed my waist, the way he *sighed* when he breathed me in, was a form of intoxication all its own.

What the hell is wrong with me?

I shoved the odd feelings down as I jiggled

my key in the lock, the door opening finally, and I squeezed his hips back.

"Come on, big guy, let's get you settled," I huffed as we ambled through the doorway. I flipped the lights on, kicking the back of the door to close it with a soft thud.

"You smell good," he murmured, and I couldn't help but roll my eyes.

"It's not me, it's my Glade Plug-In," I remarked as I led him over to the couch, depositing him there.

He fell with ease against the couch, leaning back against the cushions like he was truly as exhausted as I felt.

He leaned his head back, his lips parting, another sigh leaving him that caused my damn cock to twitch. Without my server apron to hide behind, I silently cursed, thankful he was staring at the ceiling instead of me.

I knelt on the ground, taking my time and easing his shoes off, the leather smooth against my skin. I set them aside, readying to lift his legs onto the couch when I noticed he was staring at me from above, a dark gleam in his eyes that froze me in place.

"Wh... what?" I asked, worried I'd somehow done something wrong, or that this was the moment he was finally going to upchuck.

"You're just... you're fucking beautiful, do

you know that?" he said, his words slurred and hazy, but awe-filled nonetheless.

My eyelashes fluttered as I tucked some sweaty, stray strands of hair behind my ear.

I shrugged off his flirtations. After all, he was drunk. Everyone looked pretty with martini goggles.

But in the morning, when he'd see me with my bed head and my Star Wars pajama pants, I doubt he'd think I was beautiful.

I was average, at best, and I was okay with that.

Except at that moment, I wanted to believe his drunken words. I wanted him to see me sober the way he did drunk.

Why, I had no clue, but it didn't change the fact of the matter. Come morning, Grayson wouldn't remember a thing he said tonight.

And he'd go back to his life, and I'd go back to mine.

"Thanks, but, uh, I think that's your martinis talking. Now, let's get your legs up here," I said as I lifted his legs up one at a time, settling them on the couch cushions, reaching around his waist, if only to situate him so he was elevated enough against my couch pillows that if he did decide to upchuck everywhere, he was less likely to destroy my couch.

And more apt to destroy his shirt.

Which was soft, and warm, and...

Grayson leaned up as I settled him, and I turned to face him. Our faces were just mere inches away, and this close, I couldn't help but notice underneath the scent of gin and olives, he smelled like musk and cedar, hints of orange and pine meddling with the alcohol that was like a hit to my system.

I breathed him in for a moment, appreciating the sight of his dark eyes and lashes, of his perfectly pouty lips.

He leaned closer, his lips hovering just a breath from mine.

I paused only for a moment before turning away. I didn't go around kissing hot, wealthy, intoxicated men. I did have morals, after all, and as badly as I wanted to kiss Grayson—to know if his lips would feel as soft as his shirt—I knew I shouldn't.

But that didn't stop my cock from protesting otherwise.

"Okay... all settled," I whispered as I slid my hands out from underneath him, stepping away. I reached over him, grabbing the blanket that was draped across the back of the couch and quickly unfolding it, covering him in haste. I needed to get as far away from this man as possible, if only to quiet my stupid cock with a mind of its own.

"Henry..." he groaned as I backed away.

"Good night, Grayson," I said, before turning away and running to the safety of my bathroom like a god damned coward.

Only when I was alone, in the sanctity of my bathroom, did I let out a sigh of relief.

I turned on the water for the shower and adjusted the temperature to my liking.

Steam coated my bathroom rather quickly as I disrobed, stepping into the small space and letting the hot water soothe me, washing away the weirdness that had transpired moments ago.

Grayson tried to kiss me.

Because he's drunk, Henry. Not because he's into you.

Bracing myself against the tile, I closed my eyes as I fantasized someone like Grayson could ever be into me.

That *he* could be into me. Images flooded my brain about what he would taste like, the texture of his lips, the salt of his sweat on my tongue.

His swollen cock in my mouth.

Fuck, fuck, fuck, don't go there, Henry.

But it was too late, my cock had already voiced its opinion on the matter, and there was only truly one way to get the thoughts to leave. I groaned in guilt as I wrapped my hand around my shaft, the friction a most satisfying sensation.

I leaned into my hold, slowly rocking my hips forward, building a rhythm. My palm was wet and warm, and the slide of my cock against it elicited a deep groan out of me.

I wondered about those perfect, pouty lips of his, and what it would feel like to press my mouth to his, what his mouth would feel like along my skin, biting and sucking my flesh at all my sweet spots. Beneath my ear, on my neck.

And most certainly, I wondered what his lips would feel like wrapped around my cock, his tongue licking me clean of the precum that was currently coating my hand and shaft.

I thought about that dark look he'd given me as I knelt before him, my hands around his ankles.

I fantasized about him *commanding* me to *take care of him.*

I came without warning, grunting in guilt and relief, leaning my head against the tile, watching the ropes of my release circle the drain, round and round.

My breathing started to even out as I tugged the last remainders of my release out of my softening cock, and I knew I needed to put Grayson Sanderson as far out of my mind as possible.

Because this... this wasn't some romance novel.

This was life, and the truth was that aside

from Giselle's wedding, I'd probably never see Grayson again.

Right?

I finished cleaning myself, turned off the water, and climbed out. Wrapping a fluffy towel around my waist, I used another to quickly dry my hair. I grabbed a clean pair of sleep pants and slipped them up my legs, pulling a t-shirt on over my head.

Finally dressed, I slipped out of my bathroom to check on Grayson before heading to bed myself, noting that he was passed out, snoring away. I noticed however, the blanket I'd given him had fallen to the ground and he was now sleeping on his side.

I sauntered over quietly, doing my best as to not make a peep and wake him. Slowly, I knelt to pick the blanket up, carefully laying it over him. I gently tucked it in the back, taking a moment to appreciate the beauty of his slumber, like a freaking weirdo.

He looked so peaceful, so content. It was envious.

"Good night, Grayson," I whispered, even though I knew he couldn't hear me.

And when I said good night to him, I promised myself that it would end there.

The fantasy, the hope.

Come morning, everything would go back to normal, the way it was supposed to be.

I slipped into my bedroom, beneath my sheets, and let my own wave of exhaustion take me under.

And I dreamed of wild, amber eyes, and pouty lips, and wedding bells in a forest full of pine.

CHAPTER 7

Henry

The sound of clanging and crashing stirred me from my sleep. For a moment, I panicked until I realized exactly what was the cause of the crashing. Or rather who.

I rubbed my eyes, and scraped my fingernails over my scruff, slowly ambling through my hallway to the kitchen. Sure enough, I found Grayson opening and closing cabinets, my kitchen in a little bit of disarray, but not as disheveled as the man in front of me.

His shirtsleeves were rolled up, and his hair was a bit messy, no doubt from sleeping on the square pillows.

"What are you doing?" I inquired, my voice still slightly groggy from my abrupt awakening.

Grayson stopped his tirade, turning to me slowly, eyes appraising me as if *I* was the one who was daft.

"I can not find any espresso in this god forsaken place," he said with poise, shaking his head as if it were quite obvious. "This house needs, espresso. I need—"

I casually opened the cabinet nearest to me, the slender one that didn't fit much in it other than drink mixes and of course, coffee. I grabbed the brown paper bag of freshly ground morning roast that I'd purchased a few days ago.

I could feel Grayson's eyes on me like a hawk. I casually set the bag down in front of him on the counter, meeting his gaze.

"What is this?" he asked, though he didn't look at the coffee. Instead, his gaze was fixed on me, on my lips. I couldn't help but smirk up at the towering man.

"Espresso." I deadpanned.

"This—" Grayson said as he took the bag from my hands, opening it to sniff it and frowning. "This is *store bought* coffee."

"Caffeine is caffeine, either you want it or —" I remarked as I snatched the bag back, heading over to the coffee machine.

"I suppose in a pinch, it will do." Grayson

mewled, almost as if I'd caused him a great deal of trauma by offering him a fresh, hot cup of coffee.

It didn't take long for me to throw a pot together, and I continued on my morning routine, opening the fridge and gathering my supplies for breakfast. Eggs, bacon, bread...

"Do not feel as if you have to do this on my behalf," Grayson said as I set the ingredients down, setting up my skillet and turning the burner on. I tossed some bacon in, letting it sizzle.

"Aren't you hungover? Hungry?" I asked as I cracked the eggs into a second pan.

Grayson casually leaned against my island, crossing his arms. I could feel his gaze on me like a laser beam; hot, holding me in place.

"Please, I am not some amateur, Henry. I am a professional. I do not get *hungover*. Not anymore."

"I don't think that is the selling point you seem to think it is," I said, realizing I sounded kind of like an asshole. I usually wasn't so loose lipped around people, but Grayson didn't feel like most people. It was far too easy to just say what was on my mind around him, and that was dangerous.

The last thing I wanted to do was piss him off, even if it was only because I didn't want him running to his sister and complaining, and for the wedding itself to be awkward because I had slipped up and said something stupid.

"Yes, well, my *selling points* have not been a problem for most people," he bit out, like a bratty child.

I don't know why, but his attitude made my cock twitch, and a grin erupt on my face.

Maybe I need the coffee more than he does.

I turned the bacon once more as the coffee pot beeped. Naturally, I took my time, grabbing some mugs and setting them down, pouring the coffee while breakfast cooked.

"Cream?" I asked as I opened the fridge once more to grab my french vanilla store brand creamer.

"Fuck..." I heard him curse, and I turned to look at him as he ran his hand over his face, shaking his head.

Maybe he still felt off from last night...

"You okay?" I asked as I set the bottle down.

Grayson nodded. "Yes, I'm fine, I just..."

"What, Jasper Springs Market ain't good enough for you?" I asked, raising my eyebrow.

Why the fuck did I just say that?

I never was this brash, this upfront with anyone!

Grayson flipped some dark hair out of his eyes, the motion drawing attention to his slender neck, his perfectly sinuous shoulders, his toned, pale arms.

"I mean... yes. To the cream. And two sugar cubes," he said poignantly.

I couldn't help but laugh as I opened the slender cabinet yet again, pulling out two slim cane sugar packets.

"Well, hopefully this will be good enough. I call it 'deconstructed sugar cube'," I said, flashing him a smirk as I passed him the packets.

He took them out of my fingers, his long ones brushing mine in transfer. His touch was soft, warm, and I liked it.

Stupidly, I wished I could hold onto it a little longer, but I knew I needed to put all those thoughts—about him, about me, and whatever weird tension had somehow built between us—out of my brain.

I hurriedly finished up with the coffee, sliding him his mug as I manned the stove. I tossed the bread in the toaster oven, and for a moment with everything going, I paused to take a sip of my coffee, noticing once again Grayson was staring at me.

"I should go," he said, though he made no move to set down his mug. In fact, his hand gripped it tighter, and I could see the steam wafting in the air, contrasted by his shirt.

"You should eat something first. Can't let you go on an empty stomach, after all."

"If you insist," he said, straightening his posture as if he was challenging me to a dual or something.

I gripped my own coffee, letting the warmth spread from my fingertips.

The toast popped up, breaking the odd tension, and I set my coffee down, gesturing for my guest to sit at the island, amidst the mess he'd made as he tore everything out of my cupboards looking for his beloved *espresso*.

"Order up," I said as I plated his food.

Something passed between us as I stood beside him, only inches away. I set his plate in front of him, but his gaze held me still like I was truly the prey, and he was a vicious hunter.

My cock stood at attention, liking the heat of being on the spot as he pinned me there with his dark, amber gaze.

Bad idea, Henry.

Bad, bad fucking idea.

Just walk away now and no one gets hurt.

Especially you.

I swallowed harshly as I backed away, if only to break the spell that had formed between us. Maybe Grayson wasn't the only one hungover.

Hungover on pretty rich boys who smell like heaven and look like a goddamn wet dream sitting in my kitchen.

"Thanks," he said as I slid him a fork, going about to fixing my own meal.

We ate in silence. Awkward, charged silence. Thankfully, Grayson ate his breakfast and sucked down his coffee rather quickly, and before I'd even finished my own cup of coffee, he was walking toward the door.

"Well, this has been lovely and all, Henry, but I believe I have overstayed my welcome," he said.

"Grayson, wait..." I said, feeling a bit like an asshole. I didn't want him to stay, but I also didn't want him to leave.

Grayson stopped just before the door, as I caught up to him.

"I just... don't want things to be weird... between us," I said, trying to articulate something I barely understood at the time.

He narrowed his gaze at me, furrowing his eyebrows. "Why would anything be weird?" he asked.

I closed my eyes, realizing how stupid I must have looked. I'd assumed maybe, just maybe, he remembered an inkling of what had happened, how he'd tried to kiss me, but assuming from his reaction, he didn't.

Or he did, and he just didn't care. Either way, I knew I was obsessing, and I just needed to let it go. I needed to let him go.

"Oh, uh, nothing, I just..." I sighed, giving up as I opened the door. "Do you need a ride?"

Grayson held up his car keys. "You drove my car here, remember? As I said, I have overstayed my welcome. You have been most hospitable, but I will not burden you further," he said with a slight, polite smile.

I nodded in understanding. "Oh, yes, of course. Okay."

I'd be lying if I said it didn't bother me. A part of me, a sad, lonely part had actually wanted the excuse to drive him back, if only because for some reason, I liked being around the man.

Not to mention his leaving would mean the momentary excitement would dissipate, and I'd be back to my normal, boring life.

Punch in, punch out.

Go home, alone.

Maybe I really do need to get out more.

I held the door open for him and he stepped through, stopping halfway. The motion put us rather close together, close enough when he turned to me, I could see the flecks of gold in his amber eyes. Feel his hot, bacon-scented breath on my face.

Instinctively, I leaned in closer, almost as if pulled by an invisible force. Like he was too hard to resist, and I knew I should.

"Goodbye, Grayson," I said, my voice a dark, breathy whisper. My gaze fell from his sunset eyes to his pillowy, pouty lips.

"Goodbye, Henry," he whispered, his tongue darting out to lick his lips in a motion that made my damn cock throb.

Think unsexy thoughts, Henry.

And with that he just... left.

He left me standing halfway in the hall of my apartment complex, hot, hard, and wanting.

Some people in this life are just lucky, people like Grayson.

But I wasn't a lucky boy.

I would never have the things I wanted, because what I wanted was well beyond my means, beyond my pay grade, beyond my reach.

And as I cleaned up the mess Grayson had left, I vowed to put him and all thoughts of him to rest, once and for all, for the sake of my own sanity.

CHAPTER 8

Grayson

I sighed as the incessant beeping from my phone echoed in the empty air of my humble abode.

I wasn't usually home at this hour of the day, but the corporate gods had decided to grace me with a three days off in a row this week.

I was still skeptical if Caroline and Sven would be able to hold down *Shimmer*, the bridal boutique I'd been working at for the last ten years.

Truthfully, I loved my job, I really did. I enjoyed every aspect of previewing the dresses and the wedding pantsuits too. I enjoyed styling women from all walks of life, and watching them completely come undone when they set their eyes on *the one*. When they saw themselves for the first time in that perfect gown, when they realized everything they knew was going to change.

Hell, I even loved dealing with the drama behind the desk, and gossiping with my co-workers. I knew how to manage *Shimmer.* What I didn't know how to do, apparently, was manage my fucking life.

I still couldn't believe I'd been such a lush the night prior, and not only that, I'd made a gigantic fool of myself in front of Henry, which shouldn't have bothered me as much as it did.

For some reason I cared what he thought. But thankfully, another rampant *ding* pulled me from my pity party, and I prepared to gloat in all my glory, expecting Caroline to message me with sad emojis because she was utterly incapable of running the show without someone telling her what to do.

And Sven is about as useful as a bag of rocks.

Very pretty rocks, but I digress...

Only, when I opened my notifications, I saw it wasn't my ill-fated co-workers who were messaging me with pleas to save them. It was my sister.

Honestly, I still don't know which would have been worse.

I sighed indignantly, knowing it was best to respond to her.

Apologies, I was out and only just got back. What's up?

Giselle tapped away quickly, sending me the eyeballs emoji.

And where were you at the tender hour of 9am on your day off?

A part of me debated lying to her, but I also knew better than to try and keep anything from my sister. She could smell a fib a mile away, even through text. So I shrugged, bit my lip and just let the cat out of the bag. It was better that way, at least then I could control the narrative.

If you must know, the martinis landed me on Henry's couch last night.

I waited for the onslaught of her words, and sure enough, she fired them off without haste.

You what? I thought you had a ride... you said... wait, you didn't...

I rolled my eyes.

Please, I'm not that easy, Giselle!

I texted her back. *I did nothing of the sort, and Henry was a complete gentlemen. A perfect prince charming. Drove me home and put me up for the night.*

I paused, wanting to say more, which was odd.

I never really felt the desire to spill *all* my secrets and feelings to my sister. Usually, I only gave her the bare minimum of information, but it seemed after Henry's home cooked breakfast... and the close proximity against his door... I was feeling uncharacteristically off. Maybe I was still drunk.

Well, hopefully you won't be too hungover to join Aaron and I for dinner tonight.

I fell back against the couch, the cushions squeaking. The memory of Henry's soft couch cradling me threatened to erupt in my brain, but I pushed it away.

Now was not the time to grieve over such things.

Just you and Aaron? I asked, twisting my lips in suspicion.

Every Sunday, up until Mom had her surgery, rain or shine, we had family dinner. And even if I didn't want to admit it, when I was living on my own, it was always nice to come home at least once a week and catch up with my sister, and devour my mom's delectable desserts.

But those dinners were a thing of the past now, and my sister seemed to want to pick up the torch, which shouldn't have bothered me, but...

Being over at Giselle's was like stepping into the world I wanted, but knew I couldn't have. And as much as I was proud of my sister for all she'd accomplished, and the life she and her groom-to-be had built, if my parents were in the room, I'd never hear the end of it.

The tiny little digs at my job, at my perpetual singleness, my perpetual failure to launch.

Mom and Dad are coming too, duh.

I leaned my head back on the couch cushion, debating how to answer. It wasn't like I didn't see enough of them already, but going over for dinner was a level of self-inflicted trauma I wasn't sure I was up for at the moment.

My sister must have taken my pause for urgency, because she tapped out two texts in rapid succession.

Please, Grayson... it would mean a lot to me to have all of you here.

It'll be just like old times, I promise.

Leave it to my sister to lay on the dramatics. Maybe it was her pleading, maybe it was because for a moment I dared to hope it *could* be like the good old days.

Before I'd embarrassed myself and my family.

Before I knew I'd be alone forever.

I'll have to get back to you a little later. I'm in desperate need of a shower right now.

It was a shitty response, but I was getting too

close for comfort. And I really *did* need a shower.

I meant what I said to Henry. His hospitality was more than spent, and I didn't expect to start showering at his place and walking around it like I lived there or something. No, as far as I was concerned, he'd done his part, and I needed to take care of myself.

But I'd be lying if I said that I didn't find some sort of twisted satisfaction in the way he took my shoes off, the way he covered me, making sure I was comfortable.

The way he *took care* of me.

The memories flooded me, hazy as I remembered how close he'd been to me. The heat from his breath warmed my skin, and his lips looked so deliciously plump, the desire to suck on them, to kiss them was like a living breathing entity all its own.

And for a moment, he looked at me with the same hunger, the same desire, and I leaned in just a fraction...

Fucking hell.

I peeled myself off the couch. Maybe my sister was right; maybe I was that easy. Pump me full of a few drinks and I'll fall to my knees for prince charming.

But there wouldn't be any falling on any

knees. Not now, and certainly not in my future since I'd probably fucked that up too.

I waltzed through the quiet house, until I'd come to my bathroom, relishing in the privacy. My father was religious about his job—I guess the apple didn't fall far from the tree there—and my mother spent most of her days volunteering at the local Jasper Springs Library.

Until four thirty, I had the Sanderson estate all to myself.

Sliding into the shower as the hot steam filled the room was a welcome relief.

Instantly, I let out a groan, letting the water rush over my chilled skin.

My memory was hazy at best, but I could still remember that look Henry gave me, the way his gaze fell to my lips, how his Adam's apple bobbed just before he'd parted his lips.

Before he'd walked away.

My cock stood at attention almost immediately upon his memory, and I sighed in defeat.

That wasn't what I came here for.

But I was alone, and I was hot, and I knew the release would feel good. And after the night —and awkward morning—I'd had, I wanted to feel better.

So, I closed my eyes as I wrapped my hand around my cock, slowly stroking my shaft as I let my mind wander.

I let Henry's image fill my brain, of him on his knees before me, hands undressing me. Only this time in my vision, he didn't stop at my shoes. This time he painstakingly took his time, unlatching my belt, unzipping my pants...

Fuck.

My cock twitched at the thought of Henry and his long fingers playing at the buttons of my chinos, unzipping me.

Wrapping said fingers around my swollen, leaking head.

A deep, unrelenting grunt escaped my throat and I snapped my hips, picking up more rhythm, thrusting my cock faster into my fist, as I let my fantasies take flight.

I imagined his fingertips brushing over my slit, gathering my wetness before sliding those pretty fingers into his perfect mouth, where I could watch him lick and suck my precum off his coated digits.

And then I imagined kissing him, letting my tongue roll over his, biting, sucking at his bottom lip like a goddamned lollipop until I could taste myself. I imagined his wet cock sliding against my own, hard and slick, erupting over the both of us.

I nearly slid against the tile as my orgasm pushed forth, the sound of ecstasy leaving my throat a strained, deep sound that was some-where between a moan and a plea for mercy.

My cock pulsed, throbbing as I came and I tried to catch my breath.

It felt like forever until I'd gone soft, until I'd come back down from whatever dimension my astronomical orgasm had taken me to. Water ran down my face, down my arms and chest, washing away my fantasies like the sins they truly were.

CHAPTER 9

Grayson

When I'd dressed in clean clothes, I felt a fraction better, but there was still the matter of my stomach. While Henry's impromptu breakfast had been good, it was nearing noon. I checked my pockets of my clothes from the previous night, expecting to find my wallet, but it was not there. Panic flooded me as I retraced my steps, trying to remember where I'd put it or if I'd left it in my car.

It seemed to be missing from my house entirely. It wasn't in the kitchen, or the bathroom or... I rushed outside and pulled open the car door, a quick check of my glovebox revealed that was certainly not the case. I trudged back inside, pressing my fingers to the bridge of my nose as I tried to force the memories to reveal where I'd left the damn thing.

My eyelashes fluttered as reality rushed over me, because I knew it would cost me—in ways that had nothing to do with my wallet.

Because the truth was, the likeliest of places my wallet probably was, was at Henry's house.

But I couldn't just show up at his house hours after leaving like some crazy mother-fucker. That would be far too stalker-ish.

So instead, I pulled up my text, and sent my sister a text.

Do you happen to have Henry's number?

True to her nature, my sister let me stew a moment before answering, which only meant this truly was going to be a bargain.

I do... But why do you need it?

I cursed as I tapped out my response, knowing full well I was at her mercy.

Because I think I may have accidentally left my wallet at his house.

Giselle texted me a string of judgmental emojis, complete with a kissy face.

I think someone is smitten.

I sighed in repose.

It's not like that. It's just an honest mistake, and I'd like to get it back.

A string of emojis burst on my screen, followed by her response.

I mean, that's like the oldest play in the book, Gray.

She wasn't wrong, it was rather cliché, but it wasn't like I'd *planned* to do such things. I could scheme just as good as anyone else, but I'd never stoop to such basic ploys to land a man. I had other charms for that.

Sure enough though, my words did not dissuade her from wheeling and dealing.

I'll give it to you if you promise to come to dinner tonight.

I grit my teeth, but I knew I would say yes. Especially if I wanted my wallet back.

Fine.

And when she sent over his number in a flash, I knew my fate was sealed.

CHAPTER 10

Henry

The last thing I expected to get during my day of adulting was a text from Grayson. For starters, I'd never given him my number, but that didn't mean it wasn't accessible.

A part of me dared to get my hopes up, thinking maybe, just maybe...

But my thoughts were quickly shut down when I realized he'd messaged me because he'd left his wallet at my house.

Of course.

I finished putting my groceries away, and headed over to the couch, sliding my hand behind the cushions, and sure enough... a hard, smooth bulky object met my palm. Wrapping my fingers around it, I pulled it out. The Italian leather was cool to the touch.

My timer on my phone went off, telling me I needed to get my ass moving if I wanted to make it to the cafe to grab lunch before my shift started.

Are you able to meet me at Jasper Springs Cafe?

I slid his wallet in my pocket as I set about to grab my keys and head out the door. I'd just made it to the car when he answered.

When?

I texted back quickly.

How about twenty minutes?

His response came just as fast.

Yes, that would be great.

I tossed my phone in the cup holder, turning on the radio with an exaggerated sigh. For some reason, my nerves were getting the best of me. It wasn't like it was a date or anything. I mean, the guy was literally just coming to retrieve his wallet. But there was a part of me—a hopeful, wishful part—that dared to think maybe it could be more. Maybe... just maybe, we could grab a coffee and have lunch like two normal friends.

Friend.

I didn't like the taste of that word on my tongue, but Grayson wasn't really an acquaintance either.

I shoved the thoughts down as I drove off for

the cafe. Maybe I was just having an off day because of everything that had transpired last night, or that weird tension that had formed between us this morning on my doorstep.

Whatever the case was, I needed to focus on the task at hand. Lunch, wallet delivery, and making it to work on time.

CHAPTER 11

Henry

The cafe itself was bustling at this hour, since it was the preferred lunch stop for most of the nine to fivers due to the fact that they had phenomenal sandwiches, as well as their delicious bottomless coffee. Not to mention they were *fast*.

I noticed him first, leaning languidly against the windowpane. I paused for a moment, taking in the sight of him. He couldn't see me from where he was standing inside, my small Toyota hidden by the oversized SUV in front of me, which gave me the guiltiest feeling. Like I was being a total creeper, but I couldn't help it.

With the light pouring in, lighting up his

dark hair and features, in his business casual slacks and button down...

He looked positively dreamy.

Snap out of it, Henry!

I sighed as I headed toward the cafe, my stomach growling with a hunger that went far beyond food.

The bell jingled as I opened the door, and was assaulted with the incredible scent of fresh, percolating coffee and garlic bread. I sucked in a deep breath of the wonderful aromas and headed over to Grayson with quickening strides.

"Hey," I said nervously, causing him to look up from his phone. His dark gaze settled on me, the corners of his lips turning up in a polished, genuine smile.

"Hey," he said, flashing me with a smile.

Sweat had already started to bead on my skin and my stomach decided to protest its indignities at that moment, turning his precious smile into a frown.

"You, uh... want to get something to eat?" he asked awkwardly.

"I mean, I'm sure you have a busy schedule, so we should probably just—"

"Tell you what, you give me my wallet and I'll buy you lunch. It's the least I can do after acting like a fucking asshole last night."

His words settled on me, and I wasn't sure how to feel about his offer. In my experience, people usually weren't just... nice out of the kindness of their hearts. At least not to me, anyway.

But I never let that stop me from being who I was. From helping people or giving parts of myself away.

Though what I had to offer a man like Grayson was beyond me, I still couldn't begrudge him for trying to make amends, even if it was just because he felt guilty.

What kind of man would I be if I denied him the chance to placate his well-groomed conscience?

I slid my hand in my back pocket, if only to make sure I still had his wallet, the whole reason for the meeting, after all, which I did.

"I mean, that's not really necessary..." I said as I handed him his wallet.

Grayson took it from me, his fingers brushing the backs of mine. The smooth, warm feel of his skin against mine sent a jolt through me, fueling my goblin brain once more as I wondered involuntarily what his body would feel like against my own.

Naked.

Before I could even stop myself, my cock sprang to life, and I pulled away.

"I insist," he said as he waved me toward the line of people at the register.

Caught between a rock and a literal hard place, I didn't want to be rude.

But I was also acutely aware of my current situation, and didn't want to upset the already delicate balance between Grayson and I.

And I really *was* hungry.

Damn it.

"Fine," I said, as I all but raced him to the line, keeping my sights trained on the menu if only to try and focus on unsexy thoughts.

Grayson came up behind me, and I could feel his warmth. My overactive imagination immediately wanted to dive off the deep end into more highly inappropriate thoughts, and it truly was a struggle to remain vigilant.

Fuck me sideways...

Just as the line moved, I did too, deciding I'd keep my order simple. Just a coffee and a smoked gouda and ham panini. It was my usual order.

"That's it?" Grayson raised an eyebrow at me.

I shrugged, not wanting to appear as judged as I felt.

What's wrong with a coffee and a panini?

"I like to keep it simple," I said, feeling on the spot.

Grayson nibbled his lips, his gaze darting from me to the cashier. "I'll have a prosciutto caprese melt with a bowl of tomato bisque and one oversized cinnamon roll."

Judging from Grayson's stature and shape, I truly wondered where the hell he was going to put all that food. I wasn't the most in shape man in the world, but I would have bet my bingo winnings he was one of those health-food nuts who spent a lot of time at the gym

"Something simple, and sweet. To say thanks," he said, flashing me with a smirk that only made my insides rush with warmth, and my cock spring back to life.

Save me now!

It would appear that my prayers would be answered, as that was the moment my sister texted me, the loud and obnoxious ringtone going off like a siren in the otherwise cozy and quaint cafe. Grayson chuckled as I snuck away to the counter to retrieve my *simple* order, while he paid.

I hurriedly silenced the text, noticing some of the looks from other patrons who must've been utterly disturbed by the loud screeching Stewie from Family Guy sound that played every time she messaged me.

Once I'd settled myself down in a seat and set my tray down, I pulled out my phone, hiding my own embarrassment behind the lights of my bright display.

Did you get your schedule yet?

I stare at my sister's text, debating if I should answer. Technically, I wouldn't get the schedule until I went into work, but she didn't know that.

I could very easily just tell her I wasn't available for the weekend trip she'd been *begging* to come on with Giselle and the rest of the party.

As if he could read my mind, Grayson sat down with his tray of food, his smooth voice penetrating my thoughts.

"You look like you've seen a ghost," Grayson said, and he took a sip of his coffee, crossing his long legs.

I looked up from my phone at the fine specimen in front of me, and for some strange reason, I divulged the truth.

I seemed to do that a lot around Grayson. Drunk or not.

"It's my sister, she's... been up my ass about this damn Wine Fest trip coming up."

"Giselle's trip?" he asked, looking slightly confused.

I nodded in response.

"I wasn't aware you were invited to that," he said, and I couldn't deny the words bit. I knew he wasn't trying to be rude, but his shock at the admission only cemented my suspicion that I just wouldn't fit in.

"Well, it's not like I'm going or anything," I said defensively. "Lord knows, I wouldn't fit in with all of you yuppies anyway." The words fell out of my mouth before I could stop them.

Grayson's eyebrows furrowed, and he had the audacity to look *hurt.*

Like I was the asshole.

Maybe I was. Maybe that was my curse in life—to be a grumpy, lonely old asshole struggling to find his happy ever after because everyone and everything was too good for him.

"I see," was all he said, as he picked up his tray. "I just remembered, I have a meeting in about fifteen minutes. Guess I'm getting this to go," he said, and my heart splintered.

I would have bet my last dollar there was no meeting, and I'd just single-handedly detonated the one chance I might have had.

Stupid, Henry!

Fuck!

I watched as he gracefully approached the counter, as the employees packaged his sandwich, and as he walked out the door without so much as looking at me or waving goodbye.

And suddenly I wasn't so hungry anymore.

CHAPTER 12

Henry

All day I'd stared at my phone. At the conversation I'd started with Grayson. Our meeting at the cafe was gnawing at me.

I hadn't meant my words to sound so harsh, but perhaps there was some truth to them. It was probably apparent to anyone with eyeballs that we were in stark contrast. While my sister and I had both grown up in the same house, with the same parents, she'd always been starstruck by the finer things in life. It was her mission to be *one of them*, and being besties with Giselle exposed her to such things. Gave her opportunities purely because she'd aligned herself with the upper echelon.

Though to be clear, she wasn't some wealth-chaser who was happy to lap up scraps or anything. She fit in that world just as much as Giselle and her brother did.

Everyone in Giselle's circle was like her. They had everything.

Love, money, nice houses, good jobs.

A weekend in the mountains "glamping" with my sister and her preppy friends, sniffing wine I couldn't pronounce, did not sound ideal to me.

But maybe that was the point.

Maybe I needed to leave my comfort zone and put myself out there.

I hovered my thumb over the screen on my phone for only a moment before my co-worker, Andi, passed me, jostling me from my trance.

"Cara just sat your table five," she said as she started throwing a side salad together.

I sighed, shoving the phone back in my apron pocket. "Thanks," I murmured, exiting the kitchen and strolling over to the table.

But the moment I left those doors and set my gaze on my table, I wanted to run right back.

Because sitting alone, looking like a goddamn snack of revenge, was fucking Grayson Sanderson.

Well, better get this humiliation over with.

"Can I, uh... get you something to drink?" I said as I forced myself to stand tall, look him in his deep amber eyes, and act as if I hadn't just completely made an ass out of myself earlier.

To my surprise, Grayson only looked at me with a gaze that was a mix of dark and inviting, and apathetic.

"Fancy meeting you here. Again," he said.

I crossed my arms involuntarily as I regaled him. "Well, this *is* my place of business. But you already knew that."

God what was wrong with me?

Why do I just have to worst fucking word vomit around this man?

It's like he's a curse or something!

Grayson twisted his perfect pout, shrugging. "Perhaps I just needed a drink after a long day."

I sighed in defeat. "Let me guess, gin martini with extra olives?"

Grayson smirked, a dark chuckle escaping his lips.

"Heavens, no. I wouldn't want this to turn into an episode of Groundhog Day."

I actually laughed.

Like an idiot.

"Well then, what it'll be, *Grayson?*"

"Perhaps I shall keep it simple with a rum and coke."

"Noted," I said as I slowly backed away, making my way to the bar.

"Whattaya need, Henry?" Max asked as she wiped the bar down again. She was meticulous about constantly wiping it down and I wasn't entirely sure it wasn't out of boredom and not some undiagnosed OCD.

"Rum and coke." I said, taking a moment to breathe.

She looked from me to Grayson before raising an eyebrow. "Isn't that the guy you escorted home last night?" she asked with a grin.

"It's not what you think, I promise."

Max laughed. "Better not be. I ain't running an escort service, sweetheart."

I rolled my eyes. "Besides, I already put my foot in my mouth," I murmured as she slid me the drink.

"Too bad, so sad. Hey, those days you put in for, you got 'em."

My blood chilled.

"I... what?" I wasn't entirely sure I heard her correctly, and my panic button was already at an all-time high.

Max cleared her throat, obviously taking my shock as I didn't *hear* her. And instead she all but *yelled*, "Those days for the big wedding trip this weekend. You got 'em. Go spend the weekend with your friends and make sure you have a glass on me!"

My cheeks flushed and I hurriedly grabbed Grayson's drink, caught between the devil and the deep blue sea.

I all but threw his drink at him because I was so agitated over everything that happened.

It truly was the worst fucking day ever.

"Should probably tell your boss you're not spending your time with a bunch of yuppies," he drawled as he took a sip. "I thought about mentioning it to your sister, but..."

I huffed indignantly. "Are you legit blackmailing me into going on a trip?" I asked, my neck aching from all the whiplash.

I watched as he sipped his drink, his lips shimmering with fresh moisture from the alcohol.

Lips that looked far too tempting...

No, Henry!

I watched as he slid his hand in his pocket, pulling his phone out, and I panicked.

Sue me.

I lunged for his phone, not needing him to tattle on me like a grade-schooler to my sister of all people, my stupid, senseless jabberings.

The motion pushed his chair back, pitching me into his lap haphazardly, our faces only inches from one another. He gazed down at me, raising an eyebrow, his smirk more than amused.

Up close like this, the heat between us was undeniable. I should have known then that I would be a goner when it came to Grayson. The man knew just how to press my buttons.

I fought to regain my composure, knowing there were multiple eyes on us. Including Maxine's.

"Do not say a word about this... to my sister."

"Or what? Hmmm? What will you do, Henry?" He grinned, and I realized he liked this.

He liked playing with me and my emotions.

Because he truly was an asshole.

And I was at a disadvantage, and he knew that.

"Giselle and Mia will be so happy to hear you are coming," he taunted as I righted myself, brushing off my apron with a huff.

The prevalent *need*, the desire, to do as this man said was like someone had lobotomized me.

I'd never wanted to *obey* someone's demands —albeit outlandish demands—so badly.

Maybe there really was something wrong with me.

As I delved into a spiral of madness, Grayson spoke.

"Someone really should mop up that spill," he hollered over me at Maxine. "Poor old Henry could have been sorely injured," he said with a wicked grin.

Abruptly, I turned away, leaving a chuckling, smug Grayson in my wake.

What had I gotten myself into?

CHAPTER 13

Grayson

I swear the Kardashians had nothing on the Sanderson's. Because as I sat in my sister's dining room at her table, next to my mother and across from my sister and father, I was about ready to lose my shit.

It seemed the sole rum and coke I'd had to loosen up my tense nerves had not been enough. Because I'd barely been at her humble abode for an hour before our mother launched into her alcohol-infused interrogation.

As if living under the same roof wasn't enough turmoil.

You can leave at any time, Gray.

But I was truly a glutton for punishment, it seemed.

And running away to the kitchen hadn't been enough of a clue that I didn't wish to have the conversation.

"All I'm saying, is you're pushing forty, Grayson. You should be settling down, laying roots, not—"

I set about to fixing a drink, a martini. Perhaps I could drown myself in olives and gin and none of their words would hit me.

"I'm perfectly content with my life the way it is," I lied.

My father—a man with the utmost impeccable timing—must have had nothing better to do, because as soon as I'd poured the liquid, a waft of cigar smoke poured into the room.

"Your mother has a point, Gray. How can you sell happily ever after if you don't subscribe to the newsletter yourself?"

I shook my head as I gripped the glass tightly. My gaze settled on my sister, who was leaning against the entrance to the kitchen, her eyebrows furrowed.

She mouthed, "Sorry."

Yeah, I bet she was sorry. Sorry that our family drama ruined her prize pot roast dinner.

Not sorry that she'd suckered me into the

seventh circle of hell dressed up like Martha Stewart.

"I don't need to be a delusional romantic to have a sense of purpose, but I don't suppose you would know anything about purpose considering your own commitments," I drawled.

"What the hell is that supposed to mean?" he said as he narrowed his eyes at me.

"Nothing," I said as I all but shot back my drink.

"Perhaps you should go easy on that, Gray," my mother said, hiccupping from her own round of liquid courage.

The same liquid courage that spurred her to bring up my skeletons in the first place.

I pulled the shaker from her, turning my back.

"I only learned from the best, mother. Isn't this how one is supposed to deal with meddling, pain in the ass family?" I shot my father a look, raising my eyebrow at him. His jaw tensed, but he didn't say anything. Instead, he only puffed on his cigar like an angry old man.

"Gray..." my sister called out, but I'd had enough.

I stormed through the kitchen door, out to the covered deck, traipsing over to the fire pit Aaron was lighting.

The door slammed shut, and within seconds, I heard my sister's voice.

"Aaron, baby, can you give us a minute," she said softly.

Aaron looked between us, then at the shaker in my hand. He shrugged, kissing his fiancé on the cheek as he headed indoors. "Whatever you say, sweetheart."

When the door slammed once more, I knew we were truly alone.

"Have they sent in reinforcements?" I said as I popped the top off the shaker. I hadn't even bothered to pour it in a glass.

What was the point?

Giselle took a seat next to me, setting her hand on my thigh. "They just want to see you happy, Gray."

"I am happy!" I yelled, but Giselle did not flinch.

"I think we both know you're not. You're afraid."

I scoffed at her.

How dare she!

"I am not afraid of mom and dad..."

"Afraid of change, I mean," she said.

I didn't like the way her words made me feel, so instead, I ignored her, focusing on my drink left in the shaker instead. "Change is inevitable," I murmured.

"It is. And it's a good thing, you know."

I looked at her with softness, her round face, her pristine eyes. She'd always been such a positive ray of sunshine, a believer in the most whimsical of things.

The exact opposite of me.

My parent's words reverberated in my head, acting as if my age was some expiration date, and if I didn't lock a man down in the next two years, I would be an old maid.

Or an old butler, technically.

"It's okay to not be okay, Gray. It doesn't make you a failure."

"Is that what your therapist tells you, sweetheart?" I asked, and the minute I said it I regretted it. Apparently, I just couldn't stop saying the wrong thing as of late.

"Grayson..." she moaned as I slammed down the cocktail shaker, getting up and putting some distance between us.

"I think I've overstayed my welcome," I said, sliding my hand in my pocket.

"Grayson, don't—"

"I'll be fine, Giselle. Don't worry about me," I said, needing to get as far away from her and my pain in the ass family as I could.

It wasn't like I lived *that* far away. I was practically right up the road.

In the solitude of my Porsche, I was finally

able to breathe, to let out a frustrated breath before turning on the engine.

CHAPTER 14

GRAYSON

I'D HAD every intention of driving home, but somehow, some way, I ended up in the parking lot of M's Place. And I just sat there, staring at the faint glow of the sign against the dusk, watching the doors like somehow they would have the answer. Which clearly didn't make any sense.

Maybe my sister was right. Maybe I wasn't fit to drive. Maybe I should just relax my seat and take a nap until this fucking existential crisis disappeared.

I'd just about settled on reclining when I heard a knock on my window. I jumped up, noticing Henry on the other side.

Was I hallucinating?

I hurriedly rolled the window down. Against the oncoming night, he looked warm and inviting, chocolate brown eyes and shaggy hair blowing in the wind across his tan face.

His perfect, kissable lips parted just the slightest to tease my already sensitive psyche into oblivion.

Fuck, he was *pretty*.

But the warmth radiating from his gaze, from his fucking aura, settled something inside me I couldn't quite put my finger on.

"Hey," he said softly as I gaped at him like a lunatic.

This is becoming a habit.

"Hey," I said, not sure what else to say. I felt on the brink of something, like at any moment my cracks would split and I'd never be able to piece myself back together.

And Henry must have sensed it too, because his eyebrows furrowed as he leaned into my window just the slightest.

"Someone said there was a guy in a Porsche just sitting here, like casing the joint. They wanted to call the police, but..."

Henry swallowed, his gaze flashing to my lips.

"I kinda had a feeling it might be you, and told Max as much."

My gaze drifted to his lips, his jaw. The curve of his arm as he leaned against my driver side door.

"You covered for me?" I asked, my voice breathy, desperate.

I hated it.

Henry cracked a smile. "Yeah, I, uh... guess I did."

"Oh," I said, like an idiot. Completely dumbfounded by his presence.

"Bad night?" he asked softly.

I leaned back against my seat. "You don't know the half of it."

I watched Henry's lips twist, listened as he tapped his fingers on the outside of my car door.

"I, uh... can give you a ride home. You look like you need it."

I sighed, rolling my eyes as I looked up at the ceiling. I didn't really need it. Two drinks wasn't enough to put me under, but I couldn't deny Henry's offer made me want to say yes, if only because I selfishly wanted him in my proximity. I liked being around him, talking to him.

What was happening to me?

I wasn't usually this... this... messy.

"You're working, I—"

"Give me five minutes," he said firmly, pointing at me with his finger like a teacher scolds a child. "Don't move."

I held my hands up in mock defeat. Something about the tone of his voice, the firmness of it, made my blood rush and my damn dick twitch.

Not now, buddy!

"Yes, sir," I drawled as I watched Henry walk away, his dark jeans accentuating the delicious curve of his perfect ass.

A man could get used to a sight like that.

Focus, Gray!

I'd only just shut my eyes, when I heard his voice again.

"Get up, sunshine," he said as he opened the door for me.

For a moment, I stared at him, against the sunset, lit up like some angel.

I'd never been one who liked to be bossed around or told what to do. Too stubborn, too overly confident, too bold. But something inside of me flipped a switch as I listened to Henry without so much as a protest.

Maybe I really am spiraling into chaos.

Hello pre mid life crisis...

I slid into my passenger door, letting Henry in the driver's seat once more.

"I'm taking you home this time," he said as he turned to look at me with an appraising gaze.

I sighed as I brought up the maps feature on

my car, watching his gaze fall as he realized home was as easy as a few clicks.

"You could have told me that yesterday," he mused as he pulled out of the parking lot.

"Yesterday, I was a bit... under the weather."

"Mhmm. And what are you today, because you're certainly not above it," he bit out.

"I'm... in the middle of a rather unsettling storm," I said sarcastically.

"Something wrong? You wanna talk about it?" he asked, his voice shaky for some reason.

I turned toward him, taking in the sight of him in my driver's seat, his long, toned arms, the way he grabbed my steering wheel. The way his hair shimmered with streaks of gold as the dying sunlight poured in through the windows.

"A lot of things. But it doesn't matter," I murmured, feeling far too vulnerable and guilty for my own good.

The closer we got to the wedding, the more I seemed to be unraveling.

It seemed like no time at all when we'd finally come to my humble abode. The driveway was still empty, which meant my parents were likely still at my sister's.

Whatever the case, I was glad for the moment at least to have the house to myself, if only to wallow in my sorrows and guilt. Alone.

Before I could open my door, it swung open

of its own accord, and I looked up at Henry once more as he offered me his hand.

I wanted to take it.

I wanted to set my palm in his, feel that heat that seemed to brew between us when we touched. But I was also agitated and annoyed, and instead, I pushed it away, opting to get myself out of my car.

I wasn't some damsel in distress, or a passenger prince, thank you very much.

Henry stepped back, giving me a wide berth to stroll up the driveway toward the door. I didn't expect him to follow me.

But I didn't dislike it either.

We stood on the steps of my porch for a moment, my keys in my hand.

"Do you... want to come in? For a drink?" I asked plainly. I was aware that we were rather close, though I couldn't remember how that happened. Henry stood so close, it would have been easy to reach out and wrap my arms around his trim waist, would have been no trouble at all to slide my fingers through his hair and kiss him like my heart and my opinionated dick wanted to.

But the memory of the previous night reared its head yet again, making me remember just how I'd fucked myself with such behaviors before. I didn't want Henry to think of me as some asshole who got drunk and went around making out with hot guys.

I mean, sure, I'd had my fair share of that, but Henry wasn't just some guy. I wasn't sure what he was really at the time. I could barely process my own feelings, let alone the sparks forming between Henry and I.

"I shouldn't, really, I—"

"Not a drink, drink. I mean, like a... hot tea or something?"

Good God, what was wrong with me?

Had the martinis gone to my brain?

"I mean, I probably should get going. You're okay and..."

"Henry..."

"I should go," he said as he turned away, and I watched him once more like a tall glass of water, held just out of my reach.

And only then did I realize how thirsty I was.

Henry

"Okay, so the only thing we're missing really is snacks," Mia said as she ticked off more items on her list.

While I traveled much lighter than my sister, there was a part of me that still felt like an outsider. For starters, some of the wedding party were bringing their significant others—Lane and Lacey obviously came as a pair—not to mention my sister and her boyfriend, and of course, Giselle and Aaron. Even Julie was bringing her beau of only three months, Marcus. Riley, Aaron's brother was even bringing his co-worker!

Not only would I be spending the weekend

—which I couldn't get out of now, because Grayson had taken it upon himself to tell my sister and Giselle that I was indeed coming— with my sister and her well-to-do friends slash party members doing yuppie stuff I had no experience with, but I was going to have to see Grayson all weekend.

Which should have been a good thing, considering the man was like Grade A Certified Eye Candy, but it seemed like every time I got near him, I lost my damn brain.

I couldn't stop thinking about the other night. The night he showed up to M's Place, looking lost. When I drove him home—for real, this time—and how close I was to kissing him on his front porch.

Or when he'd smirked at me at the cafe prior to that, teasing me for being *simple*.

Or when he'd tried to kiss me when he was drunk, or the fact I seemed to have no filter around the man.

"I'm sure there will be enough food to feed an army at this thing," I said as I zipped my suit-case. I probably could have gotten away with just a duffel, but I liked to be prepared, espe-cially if we were going to be staying outdoors in tents. The mountains were usually pretty cold at night.

I'd been camping a few times as a kid, mostly summer camp.

While I wasn't the biggest fan of the woods and hiking, Mia and Giselle said this was *glamping* and not actually camping, but I still didn't want to take any chances.

At least, if all else failed, I knew how to pitch a tent and start a fire. Besides, it was just a weekend. Surely, I could survive a few days in the mountains with my sister and her friends. I'd survived worse.

"Oh, I'm sure there will be, but sometimes it's just nice to have your favorite comfort snacks after a long day of drinking or hiking, you know?" Mia said as she nudged me.

"So just how many bags of hot fries are you bringing then?" I teased.

Mia rolled her eyes. "Obviously the family size bag will be enough to keep me satisfied all weekend," she said, and she stuck her tongue out. "I can't believe we leave tomorrow morning," she said, her lips turning up into a genuine smile.

It was my turn to roll my eyes. "Yup, thrilled."

"It's going to be amazing, Henry, I promise. You're going to have so much fun!" she squealed. "Maybe you'll even meet your own prince charming!"

I sighed as I rolled the suitcase to the side of my couch. "I doubt it, but I'm glad one of us is optimistic," I grumbled.

"You don't give yourself enough credit, you know that, right?" she said as she took a seat next to me, her perfectly highlighted hair bouncing as she did so.

I sighed, knowing the conversation that would follow, and I knew I didn't want to talk about my perpetual singleness.

"Not everyone is your ex," she said softly, and my shoulders fell.

I knew my sister wasn't trying to pry or be a pain in the ass. She genuinely wanted me to be happy, and was my biggest cheerleader in life.

I wanted those things too, but...

"I'm a thirty-one year old man waiting tables at a dive bar, renting an apartment, and I don't even have a fucking goldfish, Mia. Pretty sure I'm a low man on the totem pole."

Mia frowned, her gaze sympathetic. "You never know, maybe you'll meet a Richard Gere type and sweep him off his feet," she teased.

"Please. You'd look much better in a Vivian dress than I do," I shoved her with a laugh, trying to ease my way out of the conversation with compliments. But my sister saw right through me.

"That may be true, but you are a thirty-one

year old man who has a heart of gold, who makes enough in tips to afford your rent and then some, and goldfish are a pain in the ass. You have to, like, clean their tank every forty-eight hours or something or they stink to high hell," she said with a grin, and I couldn't help but laugh.

"All I'm saying, is you are way too hard on yourself. Let up a little. Maybe go into this weekend with no expectations, and just... see what happens. For once, don't try to predict the outcome. Live in the moment, Henry."

Her words sunk in, melting my cold heart and resolve just a fraction.

Maybe she was right, maybe I was too hard on myself.

Maybe I did need to just... let go a little bit.

Three days.

I could relax for three days, right?

CHAPTER 16

HENRY

"FUCK!" I yelled as panic laced through me. I banged my head against the steering wheel as the dying sounds of my engine echoed in the air.

Of all days for my car to kick the bucket, the morning I was supposed to leave for the damn trip was the day my car decided to say, "Eff you, Henry, we're through!"

It would be just my luck.

I sighed as I called my sister, my stomach twisting, already knowing she would be disappointed, but also, that she probably would just think I'm trying to get out of the weekend altogether.

"Hey Henry, what's up?" she answered, and I could hear voices in the background. She wasn't alone.

"I'm not going to be able to make it," I sighed, waiting for the scolding.

"What? Why? I thought—"

"My car won't start. Like, it won't kick over. At all... I'm going to have to call Triple AAA or something, regardless, but it doesn't look like I'm leaving my driveway. Unless, you're able to pick me up—"

"I can't. I dropped my car off for a recall yesterday and I'm riding with Giselle and Aaron. I'm sorry." She sighed in disappointment, and I felt like the worst fuck up on the planet.

"Does he need a ride?" Giselle's voice shimmered in the background.

"Yeah, his car won't start," Mia said.

"Grayson's driving up by himself. I'll call him, see if he can pick him up."

My blood chilled.

No, it fucking *froze*.

Here lies Henry, frozen like a popsicle.

"That's really not necessary, Mia, I—"

The incoming buzz of a text ominously pulled my attention as Mia asked, "What did you say?"

I swiped up to see Grayson had texted me, "Pick you up in twenty minutes."

I swallowed harshly as I answered Mia.

"Grayson just texted me." The words felt like both a balm and a curse.

"Oh great! I'm so glad that worked out! See you soon, brother!" she said with excitement before hanging up the phone.

I watched with bated breath as the silver Porsche crawled into my parking lot, as the tinted window to the driver's side slid down with ease to reveal Grayson's gorgeous face, his hair swept back with only a few strands falling free in front of his sunglasses.

"Someone call an Uber?" he said with a smirk. His gold watch glinted in the sunlight as he gripped his steering wheel.

Fuck, he was so hot.

Perhaps I was right. Perhaps this was a bad idea all around. Perhaps I could pretend to fall ill. Maybe event faint.

I sure felt like I could as I stared at him in all his GQ-esque glory.

"I don't remember requesting the X model," I said as I dragged my suitcase up the hill. Grayson met me halfway, taking my suitcase from me in a gesture that surprised me. His warm hands against my cold, steady grip was a welcome contrast.

"Well then, today must be your lucky day," he said as he tossed my suitcase in the back of his pristine trunk.

Seriously, whose trunk is that clean?

It's suspicious.

I watched as he slammed it shut, the corners of his lips pulling up into a smirk, before sighing in defeat as I sulked toward the passenger side door.

I attempted to open it, but it wouldn't budge.

With an exasperated sigh, I turned to see Grayson approaching me lazily, reaching his hand out to brush mine away, the feel of his fingertips against the back of my hand sending a chill racing up my spine.

Beep beep.

The mechanical whirring of the locks unlocking sounded and Grayson opened the door with the lightest tug.

"After you, Henry," he said, his voice dark and inviting.

"Thanks," I said, as I crawled in, letting Grayson carefully shut the door and assume his rightful spot in the driver's seat.

CHAPTER 17

HENRY

THE ENTIRE WAY to the Brideshead Mountain Resort was complete and utter torment.

For starters, I couldn't stop staring at Grayson the entire ride up—not that there was much else to look at—and I'd already heard Mumford & Sons at least twice in the trip via the satellite radio station, and in my opinion, once was enough.

And clearly, even though I was more than capable of holding a conversation with a hot, annoying asshole, I had apparently lost my last marble, because I found it hard to talk about *anything* but the elephant in the room.

Or more like the elephant trunk in my pants.

I was no stranger to instant attraction, but never in all my years had I been this worked up over just being within close proximity to a man like I was with Grayson.

Not even when I was with my ex... which should have been a clear indicator to me that Grayson was *not* like anyone else.

On the planet.

It was like one touch, one look, was all I needed and *BAM!*

Instant boner.

Which only led me to feel even more insecure and on the spot.

Kill me now.

I glanced at the display as I shifted in my seat yet again, trying to get comfortable and not draw attention to my damn cock.

Think unsexy thoughts...

A feat that was damn near impossible when I was sitting next to the hottest man alive.

The maps on the dashboard showed we were still about an hour away from our destination, and I couldn't help but groan.

It was going to be a long freaking weekend.

CHAPTER 18

GRAYSON

AFTER THE VALET had taken my car, Henry and I waited for the shuttle alongside the rest of the party, awkwardly.

I'd tried my best to make the ride pleasurable, putting on relaxing music, stirring up conversation, but I'd be lying if I said it was meaningless chatter. Honestly, I was intrigued by Henry and his attitude. Despite our sisters being friends for years, he was truly a mystery to me, but every time I asked a question, Henry either didn't answer, or he answered me with short, curt responses that felt somewhat... personal.

Perhaps he's just in a mood over his car.

After all, an engine that wouldn't start could

be a sign it might be time to get a new car. Though I wasn't the best mechanic in the world, I knew that sometimes things were salvageable even when it seemed like they weren't, so I decided to send a message to my car-enthusiast uncle as soon as we touched down. Perhaps he could fix Henry's automobile woes, which would help.

But I won't say anything until I've got confirmation from uncle Bob in the first place. This weekend is supposed to be fun, after all.

While I'd stayed at the Brideshead Mountain Resort before, I hadn't stayed in one of their *glamping* domes, which were still relatively new to the resort. The shuttle to the *glampgrounds* was more or less a small van, decked out inside with modern furnishings. Sleek, oak tables with cup holders and a shared cooler stocked with everything imaginable, it was part RV part party bus, and I was only marginally concerned our glamping domes would be just as tacky. Riley, Aaron's preppy teacher brother and his fellow teacher assistant, Cadence, who he'd brought as his plus one, were jabbering on about his latest trip to Italy with his students, Lane and Lacey were enthralled by the existence of one another again, making moon-eyes at one another, while Julie and her date were involved in some deep conversation with Mia and my sister. For a spacious shuttle, we were all somewhat crammed.

Henry squeezed his suitcase between his legs, crossing his arms.

When we'd finally arrived at the "check-in", it was nothing more than a rustic cabin with a wooden post out front that read *check in*. The post itself was covered in flowers and vines, and the air was a tad bit on the chilly side, but it was only after ten in the morning.

We all piled off the shuttle, dragging our luggage in various states of excitement and involvement. I followed up close to my sister, if only because I wanted to get into my dome and just relax. Have a bit of calm before the storm of planned activities that would undoubtedly transpire. Lord knew my sister probably booked a hiking excursion without giving us all ample time to rest and recharge.

Not all of us functioned with the same amount of energy she did.

When I got to the post, behind her, her shoulders tensed.

"What do you mean you don't have the room? I called ahead of time, with the total headcount... you're *supposed* to have room for twelve people!

"It wasn't mentioned anywhere in our reservation that you wanted two single domes. The reservation says…"

"What's the problem?" Aaron asked as the others filtered in behind us.

I could feel Henry like a ghost behind me, his presence like a magnet, drawing me to turn around and take in his beautiful face, but I had to remain vigilant.

I was not so easily swayed by an emotionally unavailable, bratty, beautiful man.

Was I?

"They don't have the two singles I reserved for Grayson and Henry."

I felt the tension rise like a mercury thermometer behind me at her words, and I couldn't help but sigh.

It seemed I'd fallen into a bout of bad luck lately where Henry was concerned.

At least, at the time it felt like bad luck, but now…

Now, in hindsight, I could see it was the exact opposite of bad luck.

It was fate.

"You said you have six doubles reserved, correct?" Aaron asked. The concierge nodded, smiling, but I could see the terror behind their eyes. I knew that look well, as my co-workers often wore it when a Bride came in to try her dress on, and the wrong dress had been delivered... because *someone* had typed the wrong thing into the system when it was ordered.

And as a fellow sales guru, I knew just how to placate the poor woman currently worrying she'd be pulled into the manager's office over this.

"Y... yes, but I'm afraid I don't have any single domes available this weekend because of the—"

"Wine Fest," Giselle sighed.

"Henry can stay with me," I said, causing everyone to turn and look at me like I'd grown three heads.

"I mean, it's the logical solution. They already have six domes, and everyone's got a roommate, so..." I shifted my stance, feeling the heat of Henry's gaze. "Just add another mattress or whatever. I'm sure you can do that, right?"

The concierge's shoulders sunk as she shook her head.

"Unfortunately, I can't. As I said, all the doubles and queens were booked out a month ago, and your Rustic Romance Party Package included only suite domes, which all come equipped with one king."

At her words, I caught Henry's gaze, the shock in his eyes as evident as his tense jaw and flushed cheeks.

"Is... is there any vacancy back at the hotel? A cancellation maybe?" he squeaked.

"I'm afraid not, sir," the concierge gently said, and Henry sighed.

"I promise not to steal the covers if you promise not to snore," I taunted him. Henry only had the audacity to look away from me, but I didn't miss the stain of crimson in his cheeks.

I really was a glutton for punishment.

"Well, I guess that settles that then..." Giselle said, looking back at me for a moment.

"Big brother always has a solution, doesn't he?" Aaron said with a wink.

I rolled my eyes as everyone let out faint laughs.

"Uh huh. One less crisis we have to deal with this weekend," I said, nodding at Henry, adjusting my sunglasses. "Now, can we please get our keys or whatever and get to these God forsaken domes? I'm tired and I'm fucking starving."

CHAPTER 19

GRAYSON

THESE FOLKS WEREN'T KIDDING when they said *dome.* The gigantic, hexagonal glass dome looked like some cross between a spaceship, a greenhouse, and an AirBnB.

And it was entirely exposed, in the middle of the woods. You could see *everything.*

The attendant who shuttled us to our domes walked us up to the front entrance, and tapped the keycard reader before handing us both our individual keycards. "Now as long as you have this on you, as soon as you come in contact with the door, it will unlock."

"It's so…"

"Open." Henry said nervously.

"Oh, the glass is solar powered. Once the sun starts to go down, the windows turn to shade, which is why we have these—" The man motioned to two lanterns out front on either side of the dome, which were not lit. "Wouldn't want our guests getting lost in the woods in the middle of the night." He chuckled.

"Right," Henry said with a sigh.

"Each dome has its own hotspots with ample WiFi, and is equipped with all the amenities of home. There's four outlets, two on either side of the bed, plus two extra outlets in the kitchen, which includes an espresso machine and a microwave."

"This is not camping," Henry uttered as he stepped inside, looking up at the glass ceiling in awe.

"That's right, sir. This is *glamping.*"

"You got that right," I said as I strolled in, setting my suitcase down on the left side of the bed. I watched as Henry slowly walked around, touching the sleek surface of the dressers and countertops like they were made of gold.

"I'll give you time to get settled. The itineraries will be delivered each morning of your stay with the lists of pre-booked activities. Meal times will be in the courtyard, which is about a ten minute walk from your dome. Since you are a party, this section of the woods is reserved and private to just you and your party. Should you wish to make your way back to the hotel, you can call for transport, or it is about a twenty minute hike downhill to the resort itself."

I nodded as the attendant backed away, leaving through the door.

"If you need anything, and I do mean *anything*," he said, his gaze flashing to Henry with warmth, "My name is Cam, and I'm only a phone call away," he said, pointing to the in-dome telephone on my nightstand.

"Thank you, Cam, that'll be all," I said dryly as I dismissed him.

When the door closed, I turned to see Henry already unpacking, his suitcase sprawled across the sleek, shiny wooden floor.

"Henry," I said as I approached him cautiously.

He looked up, his face devoid of any emotion. "Yeah?" he grunted.

"I know we haven't..." I started, feeling at a loss for how to express what I wanted to say.

It seemed the moment I came near Henry, I lost all my faculties.

But I needed to try, if only because I didn't want the weekend to be awkward.

Or the wedding.

A truce needed to be called.

"I think... we may have gotten off on the wrong foot," I said.

Henry sighed as he set his clothes out neatly on the bed in careful, organized piles.

"Grayson... we don't... we don't have to do this."

"Yes, we do," I said firmly. "I know I haven't given you the best impression of myself. I'm just... this wedding has me coming undone at the seams," I said as I set to unpacking my things on the opposite side of the bed.

We both worked in tandem.

"Aren't weddings supposed to bring people *joy?*" he asked sarcastically.

I smirked. "Apparently for some, it breeds stress."

"And you are part of the one percent that gets stressed out by weddings?" he asked, turning to arrange his clothes in the dresser. I watched as he did so, noting the slender curve of his arm, the way his shirt rose just enough to show a sliver of skin.

My cock sprang to attention, and I groaned in defeat.

Maybe this was a bad idea.

But what other choice did we have?

The last thing I wanted was for my sister to start out her weekend on a sour note and be miserable the entire time.

"I sell wedding dresses for a living, if anyone knows the stress of weddings, it is me."

"That's an interesting career choice. I would have pegged you for a stock broker or an accountant, or something."

It was my turn to stock the dresser as Henry waltzed over to the kitchen.

"How judgmental of you," I taunted.

Henry turned to appraise me with his gorgeous brown eyes, looking me up and down like I truly was some prize pony, and my cock twitched at the sight.

Never in my life had I wanted someone to *like* me, not the way I wanted Henry to like me. His gaze, his approval, his *praise* was like a drug I didn't know I needed.

"Me? Judge you?"

"You did call me a yuppie," I said, brushing some stray strands of hair out of my eyes as I finished up with the dresser.

"I didn't..." Henry sighed, and we both stood there, a mere distance apart, staring at one another like it was some sort of standoff.

"I'm just... not good at... this." Henry huffed, taking a seat in one of the rustic, cream-colored chairs adorned with a shellacked wooden frame. He set his face in his hands as he let out an exasperated sigh of his own.

"Good at what, Henry?" I asked, truly piqued.

"I've never been good at... fitting in with people. Mia... she's always been a chameleon. She can adapt to wherever she is, whoever she is with. And this life... this... traveling and brunch and lake houses and spa retreats... she's a classic. She fits in. But I don't, I—" He sunk into his chair, and I watched his shoulders fall.

"I don't have anything in common with anyone here. With you," he said sadly. "I'm so out of my element."

Oh, that's what this is about.

I pulled up a chair opposite him, crossing my legs. "Henry, look at me, I want to tell you something," I commanded, and to my surprise, he did just as I asked, without refusal.

So he can be a good boy when he wants to be.
Noted.

"What?" he asked, his lips parted just the slightest. Between his perfect pout, his innocent chocolate eyes, and the look on his face, I knew I was a goner.

Because I'd never felt so *compelled* to let my secrets out, the way I did when I was with Henry.

"I don't fit in either," I whispered.

Henry shook his head. "You're just saying that. You—"

"I'm the literal black sheep in my family, Henry. They *expected* me to be the one to run off into the sunset and have three point five children with a house in the Hamptons and an admirable stock portfolio. But what they got was a son who prefers cock, with a praise kink, who's done nothing but consistently disappoint them, who works a high stress job just so I don't have to be home and be hounded by my parents about what a damn failure I am."

Henry's eyebrows furrowed and he rubbed his knees. "Grayson, I—"

"It's fine. I'm *fine* with my choices in life. I've accepted that those things aren't for me," I said, feeling strangely vulnerable with the onslaught of baggage I'd just unloaded on Henry.

It was like I had word vomit or something.

Except, I *did* want some of those things.

I wanted Prince Charming to come in and sweep me off my feet, but I'd accepted that probably wasn't going to happen.

"All I'm saying is, maybe we both shouldn't judge a book by its cover."

Henry nodded, pursing his lips. "Right. Fresh start."

"Fresh start," I said, just as a knock on the door pulled my attention away.

I rose from my seat, careful to hide my sudden erection as I walked to the door.

Cam stood there, with a cream piece of paper. He handed it to me like it was made of lava.

"What's this?" I asked dryly.

"This is your itinerary for the *evening*," he said with a grin.

I grabbed the paper, letting my gaze rove over the fancily printed sheet.

Lunch in the courtyard in thirty minutes.
Spa Soak and Reflexology at 1:30.
Walk at three pm.
Dinner in the courtyard, served tableside.
Smores & Campfire following.

I let out a sigh of my own as I dismissed Cam once more.

"Thank you, Cam," I said, all but shutting the door in his annoying face.

"What was that all about?" Henry asked.

I turned to see him removing his shirt, headed for the shower. I swallowed harshly at the sight of him, his exposed, tanned, trim chest.

I'd been with plenty of muscle in my day, but there was something about Henry's understated tone, the softness of his hips jutting out from his jeans, that made my already sensitive cock ache with desire.

I shifted my weight, my attention pulled to the beginning of moisture already starting to pebble at my head.

Fuck me sideways.

"Just, uh, our itinerary for the evening. Lunch in the courtyard in thirty minutes," I said.

Henry nodded as he disappeared through the door to the shower, which wasn't large by any means, but it was frosted glass, and therefore, at least it gave enough privacy that I wouldn't have to suffer the sight of a blurred out, naked Henry taunting me and my stiff, leaking cock.

I turned away, grabbing my cock through my chinos as I cursed. Knowing Henry was only a mere feet away, naked was not helping matters.

The sound of water hitting the tile was like a lullaby, and I briefly looked over my shoulder. I couldn't see him from where I had migrated to, on the edge of the king-sized bed, which meant he couldn't see me either.

But I still felt a sense of shame and guilt as I unbuckled my belt, unbuttoning my pants. Considering anyone traipsing around outside would have quite the voyeuristic show if they decided to look in. Thankfully, a quick scan of the windowed perimeter was enough confirmation that Cam was indeed gone, and no one else was in sight. Still, the idea of someone—particularly a hot, naked someone I was a mere distance from—catching me with my swollen cock in hand, thrilled me more than I care to admit.

For God's sake, if I didn't take care of my unruly cock, I wouldn't be able to think straight. Especially when Henry came out of his afternoon shower.

All wet, tanned, and...

I let my body fall back onto the bed with ease, pulling my cock free. I glanced once more to make sure Henry couldn't see me, and I couldn't see him. I could see the edges of the shower in my vision, the rest of it hidden by potted plants and a rather modern looking partition.

Checkmate.

My feet planted firmly on the ground, my chinos around my ankles, I slipped my hand around my sensitive shaft, using my fingers and thumb to spread the warm, sticky precum over my head, thrusting my hips up against my palm as I began to stroke myself. Despite the fact I couldn't see him from this angle, my mind filled with images of Henry and his soft hips, his tanned chest.

His pouty, perfect lips.

I let my imagination wander, drawing the lines of fantasy once more. It didn't take much, as the thought of Henry in the shower, with his own hand wrapped around his cock, was all I needed to cum, hard and fast.

I slid my hand over my head, if only to minimize my mess and hide the evidence of the shameful self-love session I'd just engaged in with the object of my desire mere feet away. The desire to groan in ecstatic release was prevalent, but I didn't want to draw attention to my guilty masturbation session.

I struggled to catch my breath, to keep my moans stifled down deep inside, as I stuffed my softening, wet cock back in my boxers, hurriedly heading toward the kitchen—complete with a sink—and washed away my sins, just as the tinkling waterfall sounds diminished, and the sound of the shower door opened.

That was fucking close.

I nonchalantly zipped and buttoned my pants before turning to see Henry, towel around his waist, water gleaming on his bronzed skin, dark, wet hair falling in his beautiful eyes, and I was more than thankful I came already.

Because I was certain if I hadn't, I would have right there.

Henry truly was a sight for sore eyes.

"Are you... showering before lunch or—" His cheeks pinkened as his gaze roved over me.

I shook my head. "Well, seeing as how we are down to fifteen minutes, I say probably not.

Cam said the courtyard is about a ten minute walk, so we should probably leave as soon as possible."

Henry nodded. "Yeah, of course. I'll be ready in a sex... I mean *sec*!"

He spun around, but I didn't miss the scarlet flushing his cheeks as I let out a laugh.

How he didn't know he was so very right indeed.

CHAPTER 20

Grayson

I let the water run over me, my hands braced against the stone wall. The heat and steam felt good, especially after sitting for the last few hours outdoors.

Not to mention, I was still overly stuffed from dinner.

Though after spending the evening mostly sneaking glances at Henry—who'd been avoiding me all night by talking to his sister and her beau—I was more than frustrated.

But I also had to remember that Henry didn't really owe me anything, and talking to people who actually knew him, well, was probably a sort of comfort.

But damn it if I wasn't jealous.

I wanted to be the center of Henry's attention.

That wasn't like me, at all. I didn't chase after men, nor did I throw myself at their feet.

But I would have thrown myself over the fire pit and roasted my ass like a marshmallow if it would have caught Henry's attention, which is why I'd taken it upon myself to leave the party early. Both me and my unruly cock had had enough taunting for one night.

Besides, it would probably be best to be by myself if only so I could take care of said frustrations and just pass the fuck out.

No doubt my sister had us scheduled for an early rise. Something I was *not* looking forward to.

Honestly, I barely registered anything except the sound of the water, and my own relief. I breathed much easier as I let out a deep groan, watching my release as it slid down the drain, along with my pent up frustrations.

I turned the water off, pulling the towel off the rack and wrapping it around my waist. In the dome, it was quiet, save for the melodies of easy listening jazz coming from my phone. Opening the door, I grabbed my phone, padding out of the bathroom, and almost stopped in my tracks as I laid eyes on Henry.

Who was in nothing but Star Wars printed pajama pants, on top of the bed.

Browsing his phone, but...

Panic laced through me as I wondered how long he'd been there.

What if he'd been there when I...

Or perhaps he'd been too engrossed with his phone.

"When... when did you get here?" I asked plainly as I headed over to my dresser.

Henry's gaze shot up to me immediately, his eyes darkening. "I literally just came," he said, his voice breaking into a cough as he shook his head. "Came in the door, I mean."

"I see," I said, watching his pink tongue dart out to trace over his lips.

A part of me wanted to drop my towel right there and really give him something to lick, because the unexpected heat that had formed in his gaze was driving me wild.

It was almost as if... as if maybe, Henry felt this undeniable connection too.

But I got the feeling Henry wasn't the type to take risks, so I needed to tread carefully.

"Any... anyway, I was just setting my alarm," he said hurriedly, keeping his gaze fixed on mine as I pulled out my boxers from the dresser. I made a point to hold his gaze as I dropped my towel, waiting to see if he'd take the bait

Henry bit his lip, swallowing harshly, but he didn't look. Not even a glance.

Though by the scarlet flush in his cheeks, he didn't need to.

Well, I'll be damned.

"Can you believe my sister expects us all up at the ass crack of dawn? It's absurd! We are supposed to be relaxing..." I said, snapping the band on my boxers until they smacked my skin.

Henry pulled his legs up, crawling underneath the covers as he looked away. "Yeah... right. Relaxing," he said with a sigh as he lay on his side, presenting his back to me as he touched the base of his lamp on his side, making the room darken.

And just like that, the spell was broken, and Henry had clammed up once more.

I sighed in defeat. Judging from Henry's reaction, I knew perhaps he felt *something*. I just wasn't sure if it was something he wanted to act on. Though why he would fight such feelings, I did not know, but I garnered whatever the reason was, it must be a good one. No one goes through life with walls like that unless they'd been shattered before.

Which made me want to find the man responsible for such atrocities and give him a piece of my mind.

"Goodnight, Grayson," Henry murmured as

I slid into my side of the bed, careful to leave an ample amount of space between us. A part of me wanted to pry, to press. To tell him it was okay, he didn't have to hide from me, but as I opened my mouth, I heard the softest sound coming from him.

Almost like a purr.

I watched the rise and fall of his shoulders as he breathed, his breath slow and steady, and the sound of his soft snores filling the quiet air. The light from my side illuminated him.

I didn't know Henry well yet, but I knew he deserved every bit of light and happiness this world had to offer, and whoever had made him think otherwise would get their just desserts.

Karma, and all.

Suddenly, exhaustion hit me and the sound of his soft snores were almost melodic, hypnotizing even. I couldn't help but smirk, knowing there was no use fighting the slumber I was about to fall into.

"Goodnight, Henry," I whispered as I touched the lamp on the nightstand.

CHAPTER 21

I CURLED CLOSER to the warmth that surrounded me. The air smelled faintly of lavender and sage, a most relaxing scent. I fell into that scent, into the pit of warmth. I hadn't felt so relaxed in a while, and certainly not since Grayson showed up the other night.

Grayson...

His name filled my consciousness, along with thoughts of his perfect lips, of his dark, inviting eyes, and that dead-sexy smirk he was always wearing. I shifted my position closer to the fire, groaning in satisfaction. I could feel the head of his cock brushing against my ass, and I let out a deep groan as I arched my back, seeking more of the friction.

My own cock was already alert and aware, no doubt reeling from my sexy dream state. Warm fingers slid over the waistband on my pajama pants, a leg threading through mine as he pulled me closer.

I didn't want the dream to end, but my alarm broke the veil of ecstasy.

I reached out instinctively to shut it off, and then I realized in absolute horror, I wasn't asleep, and I certainly wasn't dreaming.

My hand hovered over my phone as my gaze settled on a hand across my stomach, and I felt the vivid, sizeable hardness pressed against my ass.

"Oh my God," I said as I scrambled out of Grayson's hold, smacking my alarm much more harshly than I meant to.

"Oh my God, I am so sorry, Grayson. I—"

"Good morning to you too, Henry," he grumbled as I threw myself out of bed.

I quickly tried to readjust myself, embarrassment flooding me. I looked at Grayson, fueling up another apology, but all my speech left me when I noticed Grayson's gaze roving over me, stopping right where I was holding my—

"I'm not a... morning person," I stammered.

What the fuck?

Grayson laughed, the sound smooth and warm, showcasing his perfect teeth as he sat up, the covers sliding off of him to reveal his perfectly defined chest.

"Could have fooled me," he said, his gaze flicking back up to my reddening cheeks, then back to my hands still awkwardly shielding my noticeable erection from him.

"It's not... I didn't mean to—"

Grayson ran his hand through his dark hair. "Please, don't be embarrassed. We're both adults."

Yeah, single adults.

Who are supposed to be starting fresh!

And not making things awkward!

I was acutely aware that I was once again, making things awkward, but I couldn't help it. It was like my damn superpower or something.

I swallowed harshly as I looked back at him. "I need a shower," I mumbled. Clearly with all the blood rushing to my cock, my brain was not working at full capacity.

"Henry..." He sighed as he let his head fall back against the headboard.

I turned around, making a beeline directly for the shower, if only for the space to breathe, to process what had just happened.

Grayson and I... spooned.

Granted we were probably asleep when we gravitated toward one another, but still…

I'd awakened with Grayson's arms around me and his cock pressed against me, and I didn't hate it.

In fact, I kind of liked it, if I'm being honest, but I didn't have time for romantic revelations at six thirty in the morning.

I turned the water on, relieved by the crisp, cool sensation. I braced myself for the shiver, knowing it was most certainly what I needed to wash away all the embarrassment and the desire swirling inside of me like a hurricane.

I quickly washed my hair with the shampoo provided, which smelled like lemongrass and cedar and was actually quite invigorating. After I'd finally finished up, I grabbed my towel, and headed for the main room, doing my best to avoid staring at shirtless Grayson in his *boxers*, looking like an Esquire magazine spread.

But I was weak, apparently, because the moment I came out to see him, his perfect ass on display, standing there like a Greek Adonis staring at a paper in front of a literal cart of breakfast items, I froze.

Cue Henry Popsicle Mode.

"What—"

"Breakfast is served," Grayson drawled.

"Apparently, my sister had a spread delivered

to all our tents this morning," he said as he looked up from his paper.

"Oh, well... that's kinda nice, actually," I said as I turned my back to him, fishing out a pair of underwear, cargo pants, and an olive green shirt.

"No doubt to make up for the fact we are *horseback* riding at eight in the morning," he grumbled.

"Horseback riding?" I asked as I pulled on my shirt. I could feel Grayson's eyes on me, and I fought to turn around and meet his gaze.

"Did I stutter?" he asked, his voice dark and smooth.

I turned around, weak to fight my own impulse to find him only inches away from me. There I stood in my shirt and my fresh pair of boxer briefs, acutely aware of his disheveled hair, of his looming, sexy stare, and the visible outline of his cock.

How was this man still single?

He was quite literally, all the things fantasies were made of.

What flaw did he have?

Because as far as I could see or discern, there were none.

Grayson was confident, sexy, and more than sure of himself. But he was also candid and vulnerable, and mysterious.

He was everything a prince charming should be.

And he was so close I could touch him. That I could kiss him, if I wanted, and I wanted to, but...

Did *he* want me to?

Despite his flirtations, and his drunk pass at me the other night, he hadn't made a move to confirm such things. In fact, he'd only done the opposite and insisted on a "fresh" start. But then it seemed every time the curtain came down...

I wasn't sure if I'd purely imagined the attraction between us, or if it was something that truly was reciprocated. But I wasn't capable of voicing my wonders out loud when I didn't have a full grasp on the reality myself.

"No, you did not," I said, my own voice dropping an octave, my gaze falling to his lips.

All it would take is one small move. One step forward and I could slide my hand over his hip, or run my fingers through his hair.

One gentle tug and I could pull him toward me, toward my lips.

But I was afraid.

Of what I wasn't certain.

"Shower's all yours," I said, my voice steady as I flashed my gaze from his perfect pout to his intense amber eyes.

Grayson smirked as he handed me the itinerary, and I watched him walk away from me, sliding his boxers off just before he hit the door so I could get just the slightest glimpse of his bare ass.

While the move was careless, as undressing for a shower was a normal action, his move felt deliberate.

It was almost like he *wanted* me to see him, like he wanted to taunt me with his perfection.

Look at what you can't have because you're too fucking scared.

I grunted as I adjusted my cock, turning away from the sight in favor of breakfast.

The sun shone through the hexagonal windows like beams of heaven, lighting up the champagne flutes full of champagne and orange juice, no doubt, across the array of bear claws and croissants and pastries with fresh fruit.

I wasted no time as I dug into the cream cheese danishes and fresh strawberries, watching the light cast rainbow prisms on the inside of our dome as I waited for the bane of my literal existence.

CHAPTER 22

If you've never been on a horse before, nothing can truly prepare you for the experience. For starters, I was surprised at the sheer size of the horse before me, and the way he looked me in my eye, snorting and huffing, I couldn't deny I was panicking.

"Have you ever ridden a horse before?" Grayson asked as he came up behind me. I watched as Lane helped his partner up on her horse, watched as she threw her leg over the saddle.

Mia and Giselle spent a lot of time together as teens, and I'd heard the stories she'd told about Giselle's horse. I even remembered when she asked our parents for a horse for her birthday, which they clearly denied.

Though she hadn't bought her own horse yet, she regularly visited the barn where Giselle used to board her childhood horse, and once in awhile, I knew she would take a ride.

But I had no such experience, and therefore, I felt out of my element.

"No," I said with a sigh, turning to see Grayson's intense gaze roving over me once more.

"I can just... sit this out. Wait for you guys to come back."

"Absolutely not," Grayson shook his head, just as Mia came over to us, on her *horse*.

"I'm so excited for you!" she beamed.

"Don't be, I was just telling Grayson I think I'm going to sit this out."

"And I told you that is not an option," Grayson said, crossing his arms.

"What did I tell you about *new experiences*, Henry?" Mia said with a scolding glare.

"Yeah, well, some new experiences are clearly not for beginners."

"You do as I say and I promise you you'll be master of the saddle in no time," Grayson said, smirking at me with that delicious pout of his, stirring up all the desire and pent up frustration all over again.

"I don't have a choice, do I?" I sighed.

Grayson shook his head, his smirk widening. "Fast learner," he said as he motioned for me to follow him to the open stables where Julie and her date were getting ready on their horses, leading *my* horse to a spot that looked open enough we could have space for me to embarrass myself fully and probably fall off.

This was a nightmare.

"Okay, so first things first... the horse can smell your fear," he said as he looked at me.

"I'm not afraid—" I lied.

Grayson only had the audacity to raise an eyebrow at me.

"There's nothing to be afraid of. The horse is a gentle creature. He only responds to your insecurity, your fears. You are in control, and he will follow *your* lead. So, trust yourself."

I swallowed harshly as his words fell on me.

"If only it were that easy," I mumbled.

Grayson ran his hand along the horse's hide, until he came to the saddle.

"It is easy," he said as he patted the saddle. "When you have a good teacher," he said warmly. "Besides, once you're up there, on top—"

It was his turn for his cheeks to redden for once, but I wasn't entirely sure it wasn't due to the wind.

"Once you're holding the reins, you'll know what to do."

I watched Grayson adjust my saddle, like a true master. It was both shocking and interesting to see him in his element, doing something he was clearly passionate about. His confidence with the horse was much different than the Grayson I'd seen thus far.

"Now, step here," he said as he motioned for me to place my foot in the stirrup. "Set your hand on me if you need to steady yourself, and swing your leg over the saddle until you've found the stirrup on the other side."

I did as he requested, knowing everyone was waiting on me, and not wanting to hold anyone up. I pursed my lips as I set my foot in the stirrup, bracing one hand on his shoulder, and using the other to hold the handle of the saddle. I hoisted my leg up—rather ungracefully—just as he instructed, fumbling with the stirrup on the other side. But I managed, nonetheless, turning to look at Grayson, who was smirking at me again.

"Very good," Grayson said. "It's good to know you can be broken too." His tone was dark, gravelly, and made my cock stiffen just the slightest. Despite being uncomfortable, I was glad the saddle and my vantage point hid such things.

Before I could bite back at Grayson's sexual innuendos, he cleared his throat and left me to my own devices. Mia and her horse trotted over to me, as I attempted to grab my reins.

Grayson had been right, but I wasn't going to tell him that. Being on top of my horse felt... nice. The vantage point was pretty, but also there was a peacefulness I didn't know I'd experience. My sister tried her best to give me tips, and I tried my best to listen, but I couldn't focus entirely because the sight of Grayson—who was wearing tight, riding pants and a form-fitting long sleeve—was too much to tear my sights from.

I watched the way he mounted his horse, in one fell swoop, knowing he'd probably done this before a million times. But something about watching him felt like it was the first time. And I was captivated by the way he administered his control. How boldly he gripped the reins, his commanding voice.

He trotted up next to his sister, only looking over his shoulder once at my sister and I, his dark eyes commanding me the same way he did his horse.

Let me lead.

My cock and I were powerless to resist, and so I gripped my reins and followed Grayson into the woods like a lamb to the slaughter.

CHAPTER 23

HENRY

THE RIDE through the mountains was a lot better than I expected. Aside from the sound of the horses neighing and trotting, there was a serenity to the woods. Birds tweeting and chirping and small animals skittering through bushes. Our ride took most of the day, and I came to learn that the trail we were riding led us through seven waterfalls.

To say it was breathtaking would be un understatement, and I started to think perhaps my sister was right. Maybe I did need to just let myself *enjoy* things, rather than over think them. So that was exactly what I had vowed to do the rest of the day, and the rest of the weekend.

Just... enjoy the moment.

The relaxing air as my horse and I trotted through the woods, the beauty of nature. I even enjoyed talking to Aaron and his best man, Riley, a little bit about their travels and the places they'd been. The places I'd *like* to see someday.

Though it seemed as if the tables had flipped, because the more comfortable I became in my current environment, the more comfortable I got with the conversations and the people, Grayson seemed to do the exact opposite. Aside from his flirtatious training earlier, he kept to the front of the group, leading us with Giselle, but he was mostly quiet.

A part of me wondered if it was something I said or did, but Mia had informed me Grayson was usually quite stoic when he rode. I wasn't sure if sisterly DNA told her I was pining on the inside, or if she was genuinely just trying to pry about my feelings toward Grayson. She always did have a knack for pulling the things out of me I refused to tell anyone.

CHAPTER 24

I WATCHED the fire dance as we all surrounded ourselves around it. After a most delicious dinner of fire-roasted beef and vegetables that probably cost more than my luggage, we were served with an array of after-dinner drinks and fireside desserts. Where s'mores were a staple at all the campfires apparently, there were other desserts to choose from.

I'd always been a simple man, something Grayson taunted me about, of course, but even then, when I expected him to say something, he was rather quiet.

Perhaps he is just having an off day or something.

I sipped my warmed *Glühwein,* a concoction

Giselle told me derived from the Germans and was quite popular around the holidays, relishing in the sweetness of the mulled spices and the burn of the heated alcohol as it coated my throat and warmed me from the inside.

It truly was the best drink I'd had, and it was perfect to sip around the campfire in a copper mule mug amidst the chilly mountain air.

Thanks to the WiFi available in the glampgrounds, Julie was able to access her Spotify, and graciously provided us with a playlist that was probably as chaotic and unhinged as she was.

Seriously, I was not a fan of *Axe 2 Grind* or Taylor Swift, but I wasn't the one controlling the tunes.

The sounds of Willow and The Anxiety's *Meet Me At Our Spot* swept through the air, the singers crooning on about being hypnotized by the lights, and I couldn't help but look up from my current marshmallow sandwich, catching sight of Grayson lit up by the strings of outdoor lights, grumbling over his burnt marshmallow, twisting his lips in frustration.

I couldn't take my gaze off of Grayson, who sat more or less by himself, away from the rest of us.

I didn't like seeing Grayson like this.

Removed, quiet.

Alone.

Maybe it was because I knew what it felt like to *be* alone, maybe it was because Grayson had told me that he felt like an outcast too.

Or maybe it had something to do with the three glasses of *Glühwein* I'd had.

I assembled the rest of my perfect s'more and walked over to where he sat. Immediately, his gaze flashed up at me, and I could have sworn he looked surprised. I handed him my s'more.

"You look like you need this more than me," I said.

Grayson hesitated for a moment. "Is this a trick?" he said, narrowing his eyes as his fingers grazed mine, taking the chocolaty marshmallow treat.

"No trick. I just... noticed your marshmallow skills seem a little... beginner," I said, flashing him a smirk. Thanks to the wine, I felt a bit better than I usually did. I found myself just talking instead of trying to constantly figure out the right thing to say.

Or what not to say.

"Well, we all have our skills, it seems," he said as he bit into the s'more, the marshmallow caving and exploding as he groaned.

Same marshmallow, same.

I picked up his stick before heading over to the dessert cart that boasted all the ingredients for everything from s'mores to hand pies to banana boats. I grabbed some marshmallows, noticing how everyone else was in their own little bubbles with one another. Laughing, singing, dancing. Drinking.

When I came back to the lonely log that Grayson was taking up residence on, I slowly set to fixing his stick—and my own—with their prospective sweets.

"It's all in the wrist," I said, motioning to him as I held the stick, to watch how I turned my wrist and not the stick itself. "You want to make sure you get at least ten seconds on all four sides."

"A marshmallow does not have sides," Grayson grumbled, but his tone was marginally lighter.

I gazed back at him with a confident smirk of my own. "Everyone has sides," I said, realizing my error far too late.

Grayson's shoulders loosened, and I didn't even bother to correct myself.

How could I, when it seemed it was the right thing to say?

I handed him his stick and he took it from me with ease.

"All in the wrist, huh?" He cocked a smile.

The heat in his tone was like a spark to dry

kindling. Normally, I agonized over socializing like this.

Innuendos, flirtations, jokes.

But after a few drinks, and being near Grayson—a man who seemed to unravel me whether I wanted him to or not—I couldn't help but respond.

"As you said, we all have our skills, *Grayson*."

Did I really just say that?

Grayson let out a dark chuckle as he rose, heading for the fire to roast his marshmallow, and I followed. Taking my spot beside him, I didn't realize how close I was until I bumped his shoulder.

"Sorry," I said instinctively.

Grayson shifted his stance as he leaned closer to the fire, watching his marshmallow intently. "Trying to throw me into the fire now are you?" he teased.

I shifted my stance, bumping into him again, smiling at his tone before reaching out and gently turning his wrist.

The touch itself was warm, and not at all sexual.

I was, after all, just helping him with his sub-par roasting skills.

But something about the way his skin felt beneath my fingertips reminded me of the warmth of his hand over my stomach, of his body curled around mine, and I let out a small gasp. I brushed the underside of his wrist rhythmically with my thumb, and swallowed harshly.

I knew I should let go, but...

I didn't *want* to let go.

Grayson didn't move either. Instead, his gaze fell to where I held his wrist.

I gently turned it again, gazing back at the fire, watching as the white sides of the marshmallow turned golden with just the swiftest of motions.

"Not everything is perfect on the first try," I said softly, pulling back.

Grayson followed my lead.

I dropped my hand, nodding toward the perfectly golden marshmallow, which sported an even color on all sides.

"Some things take time," I said with a shrug, setting to roast my own marshmallow.

My stomach flipped, but I wasn't sure if it was from the alcohol, or the way Grayson was looking at me.

He assembled his s'more as I finished roasting my marshmallow. Pulling the giant toasted piece of fluff off of the stick, melted marshmallow spread along my fingers. I quickly tossed the sticky, melty confection in my mouth, licking my fingers clean, if only because I hated to feel sticky.

The sounds of Post Malone's *Circles* came on over the speakers, and I noticed the rest of the party had decided dancing was apparently a good idea.

Giselle and Aaron wrapped their arms around one another, lost in each other's eyes, and the rest of the couples followed suit. For a moment, it felt like I was witnessing something private, and the reality of my singleness spread once more.

I hadn't danced with anyone in years.

Five years, to be exact.

My gaze drifted to Grayson, who was staring into the fire like it held all the answers to the questions he didn't dare ask out loud.

I mean, it was a dance, right?

It didn't mean anything. When in Rome and all that...

"We should join them," I said without thinking.

Grayson turned to me, his gaze studying me. "What did you say?"

"I said, we should join them. I mean, it's just dancing, right? Fun shouldn't be something that is only reserved for couples." I shrugged.

I looked back at him in question. "I mean, unless marshmallows aren't the only area you're lacking in skill."

Why did I just insult him?

What the fuck is wrong with me?

I knew the answer to my thoughts as my head was currently spinning.

"That depends," Grayson smirked as he set his hand on my waist, pulling me closer into his hot, sexy vortex.

I slid my hands up his chest, resting them on his shoulders.

"On what exactly?" I asked, my voice unfamiliar, even to me, filled with a darkness I didn't know I was capable of.

Grayson's hand slid over my hip, resting at my back as he *gently* pressed his palm against me, coaxing me closer.

Pressed against him I could feel *everything*.

My breath caught in my throat as my own cock sprang to attention against the sizeable outline of his hardness.

"If you'll let me lead," he said darkly.

"Maybe that's what I need," I murmured, feeling lightheaded as he swayed us back and forth. I leaned against him, staring up at his dark eyes with wonder, drunk and under his spell.

I hadn't been this close to anyone in a long time, and the reality was slightly terrifying.

I could feel myself falling for Grayson and that scared me.

How was it possible to fall for a man I barely knew in only a matter of days?

My hand slid over his chest, over his heart, and somehow that made it real.

Grayson leaned his face down just the slightest, his gaze full of heat and confidence.

And suddenly, I was faced with the reality that I hadn't *been* with anyone in years, and my insecurities got the best of me. My heart racing, my throat tight, my cock aching for release, and sweat forming all along my body where he touched me, mixed with the fact that we weren't truly alone—and everyone could see us. I panicked.

I pushed away from Grayson, breaking our hold. "I can't do this, I—"

"Henry..."

"I'm sorry," I said, flustered as I did the only thing I could think of.

I ran.

What I didn't expect, was for Grayson to follow me.

Away from the courtyard, the woods were dark. The faint glow from the string lights cast just enough light I could see the tree I almost ran into. I stopped, dropping my hands to my knees as I tried to catch my breath.

"Henry!" Grayson called, and I stood, slowly

turning to see the disappointment on his face I knew would be there.

Why did I keep fucking everything up?

Perhaps I was cursed.

Cursed to be a perpetual cockblock to myself for all eternity.

"You are infuriating, do you know that?" Grayson growled.

My eyes widened. "Me?" I snapped back.

He ran a hand through his hair, his gaze dark under the shadows, his lips pressed into a thin line.

"Yes, you! You push me and pull me, only to push me away when I get too close. I'm tired of playing these games with you, Henry. Tired of wondering if you feel this too. Tell me you don't and I'll leave you alone and never ask again."

"This is not on me!" I hollered back. "You and your constant flirtations are maddening, do you know that!"

"Me? You're going to pin this on *me*? Are you insane?" he barked.

"Yeah, I am! Because you tease and taunt me, with your fucking pretty face and your killer body, and... your touch, and... but you don't have the fucking balls to actually follow through, and do something about it—"

Grayson grabbed my face between his

hands, crushing his lips to mine in a brutal flurry.

Every bone in my body stiffened as it took a moment for me to comprehend what had just happened. Almost instantly, I melted in his grip as some switch inside me flipped.

I slid my hands into his hair, gripping his silky locks as I parted my mouth, my tongue stroking his in a desperate attempt to find my footing, my grounding. Grayson's grip on my face was fierce, and I ground my hips against him, my cock desperate for the friction of his hardness.

Grayson groaned in my mouth as he thrust himself against me, eliciting a deep, satisfied sound to escape my throat.

And then he broke away, his labored breath the only sound I could hear.

"Am I being fucking clear now, Henry?" he growled, his grip on my face easing up slightly as he tried to catch his breath.

"Crystal, *Grayson*," I said as I slid my hands out of his hair.

CHAPTER 25

Grayson

"Great. Now that we've cleared that up, let's head back to the fire," I said, my voice softening, and I could hear the relief in it.

Henry gazed up at me with a mixture of understanding, and hope.

"I— I think I need some air," he said quietly. "I'm just, uh... I think I'm going to head back to the tent."

My heart broke, but a part of me understood. So much had happened between us, and it was apparent that up until moments ago, Henry hadn't understood I truly *wanted* him. And maybe I hadn't understood what that meant either, or the depth of it.

Maybe Henry wasn't the only one who needed space to process everything.

"Okay. Be careful," I said, my voice shaking. All I wanted was to stop him from walking away.

Because unbeknownst to Henry, he held my heart in his hands, and I was trusting he would not shatter it completely.

Henry nodded. "Of course," he said as he slid his phone out, queuing up his flashlight. And I watched him wander off, watched him leave, with my heart in my throat.

Once he was out of my sight, I headed back to the courtyard. It appeared that Henry wasn't the only one who had decided to turn in.

The only ones left at the campfire were my sister, Aaron, and Riley. Riley and Aaron were, of course, engaged in a deep conversation about something I had no clue about, and my sister was sipping her hot chocolate in front of the fire.

I took my seat beside her for the first time since we'd arrived back from our ride.

"So, that's what's had you all out of sorts lately," she nonchalantly drawled, not even looking at me.

I wanted to deny her allegation, but we both knew there was no denying it. Anyone with eyeballs would have been able to see the flames between Henry and I, especially after his dramatic exit.

Whether or not they would draw attention to it was still unclear, but for Henry's sake, I hoped they wouldn't. I got the feeling that Henry didn't like attention.

"It's complicated," I said, folding my hands in my lap.

Giselle scoffed, shooting me an *are you serious* glance.

"What?" I asked.

"What is this? An episode of *The Young & The Restless*? Relationships aren't complicated."

I sighed, opening my mouth to protest, but my sister stopped me.

"That's just a crock of shit explanation for when things aren't going the way you want them to," she said.

I stared into the fire, watching the ochre flames dance and change shape swiftly.

"Did you ever just... meet someone and the timing was off? Like... way off?" I asked quietly.

My sister slurped her hot chocolate annoyingly, making me wait for her answer. "Not everything is perfect from the get-go, Gray. Some things..." She looked off in the distance, her gaze settling on her fiancé, who was laughing with his best man, and I didn't miss the glaze of love in her eyes. "Good things take time."

Her words settled on me, making me think about this whole situation. I'd known of Henry for years, but it wasn't until the other night, that I really truly *saw* him. That night, I'd been an idiot and gotten carried away, and Henry had shown me his true colors. He was caring, and sweet, and easy to talk to, and I enjoyed being around him.

And he wasn't bad on the eyes at all.

But the reality was that we'd only really started to discover one another, let alone our undeniable attraction, and it had barely been two weeks.

Falling in love with a man in that short of an amount of time was impossible, wasn't it?

Was what I felt for Henry *love*?

It was, but I wasn't ready to admit that yet. If I was being honest, I fell for Henry the moment I looked at him in my car.

And then I fell for him again when he'd gotten a *simple* sandwich and soup, and again when he stood on my porch, gazing at me like I was some hero in a romance movie.

And there were so many moments after that too, and I got the feeling those moments would never disappear. If we went through with this—

whatever *this* was—I was certain there would be so many more moments to fall in love with Henry.

If he would let me.

"Yeah, well, good things also need their beauty rest," I said as I took her empty cup from her hands. Giselle looked at me with annoyance, but I shook my head. "It's getting late, and if I read the itinerary correctly, we have a wine festival tomorrow." I said, flashing her a grin.

"Gray..."

"We're going to need all the rest we can get if we're going to be drinking all day long," I teased.

My sister looked as if she wanted to press me further on matters that had nothing to do with wine, but she relented, admitting defeat for once.

Maybe she really does need a good night's sleep.

"Mhmm. Well, in that case, perhaps you should head to bed too. Some of us need more of a recharge than others," she nipped.

"What's that supposed to mean?" I bit back.

Giselle rose, smiling from ear to ear. "Well, I am the younger model..." she teased.

I shook my head. "The best wines, my dear, are the ones that have *aged* gracefully," I said with a grin of my own.

Giselle laughed. "Sure, whatever makes you

sleep better at night," she said as I rose. Giselle wrapped her arms around me, and I could not help but do the same. "Goodnight, Gray," she said softly, as she headed toward Aaron, who was putting out the fire.

CHAPTER 26

I DON'T KNOW why I was so nervous, standing on the precipice of the glamping tent. But my heart was racing as the automatic locks clicked, and I opened the door. Though the sight of shirtless Henry, laying on top of the covers, reading a book—with a handsome, shirtless man on the front nonetheless—settled every nerve in my body.

He did not look up at all, completely engrossed in his tale, and I cautiously approached my dresser. I stood in front of it, and even though I could not see him, I could feel the heat of his gaze.

I removed my shirt first, before tackling my

riding pants, which were doing nothing to quell the desire that had already started to percolate at the sight of shirtless Henry in gray sweatpants, reading a book.

Simple things, indeed.

I slid my pants off, turning to catch his deep brown eyes gazing at me over his book.

Shifting my stance, I smirked at him over my shoulder, noticing his gaze was fixated on my ass.

"See something you like?" I teased.

Henry's gaze flashed to mine, blinking only a few times before he tugged his book higher to hide the flush in his cheeks. But I caught just enough scarlet to know his rebuttal of "no," was a damn lie.

And for the moment, that was enough.

My sister had mentioned good things took time, and I knew Henry was a good thing.

Waiting wasn't easy for me, but if it was what Henry needed in order to feel comfortable with *this*, with me...

I'd wait as long as it took.

I took my time folding my clothes and setting them aside. The world outside us was dark, and the lights of the dome were not bright at all. In fact, the amber glow that touched everything made the dome itself feel far more intimate. It was almost as if we truly weren't in the middle of the woods. It was like our own private bubble.

I pulled down the sheets, sliding in easily as I lay on my side. I slid closer to Henry, if only to try and discern what it was he was actually reading, checking out the book cover.

"What are you doing?" he asked, fidgeting on top of the covers, but he did not squirm away from me as he had this morning.

"What are you reading?" I asked, and Henry's eyes narrowed as he clutched his book to his chest.

"I'll tell you under one condition," he said evenly.

I leaned on my arm, flipping my hair out of my eyes as I gazed up at him. From this angle, he looked positively ravishing. His dark hair was slightly messy, the amber lights casting a golden glow on his eyes and his natural tan skin. The light grey of his sweatpants contrasted with the softened edges of his hips deliciously. My heart raced, all the blood in my body pooling directly in my stiffening cock as the thought of being *underneath* this man ravaged me.

I wanted to see this man come undone, and I wanted to be his inevitable undoing as well.

I wanted to watch him writhe beneath me. I wanted to push him right up against the edge, to drive him as mad as he drove me.

And then I wanted to watch his face as he came, knowing the pleasure was all mine.

Mine.

"Anything," I breathed, far too desperate for my own ears, but I didn't care. I found the more time I spent in Henry's presence, I didn't care how I sounded, or what I looked like, or what I said.

"You have to *promise* you won't judge me," he said, raising his eyebrow.

"Of course, I won't I—"

"Promise!" he said seriously.

I rolled my eyes, showcasing my crossed fingers in surrender. "Scout's honor," I said.

Henry sighed, closing his book, setting it over his lap as he pulled his legs up to his chest.

"It's about this guy who buys a house and it's haunted," he said, gulping nervously.

"And..."

"And the ghost that haunts it is a really sexy gay ghost from, like, the 1900s."

The urge to laugh was apparent, but I had promised him I wouldn't. I pursed my lips. "That's... interesting." I said, keeping my expression stoic.

"I knew it, you think it's stupid," he said rolling his eyes. "I can see it in your eyes, you want to laugh."

I slid a little closer, and Henry didn't budge.

I slowly, deliberately pulled the book from his lap, looking over the cover and the synopsis.

"I don't think anything you do is stupid, Henry," I murmured as I flipped through the pages, stopping on a random page to skim it.

Henry's breathing increased, and I realized he was nervous.

A part of me liked to see Henry uncomfortable, liked to push his buttons in the way he pushed mine. So, naturally, I did just that.

I started to read a random page out loud, but soon came to the understanding I'd stumbled into a sex scene that was more than graphic.

"Oh my God, stop. Just stop..." Henry cried, covering his face with his hands.

I lowered my voice, making it dark and gruff, keeping an absolute straight face when I got the spicy bits, drawing out the groans and sounds if only to agitate Henry because I found it endearing how he blushed, how he tried to hide the obvious tent in his sweatpants—those things hide nothing—until I was certain I had him on the brink of madness.

"You are insufferable," he groaned in defeat. "An absolute menace."

"Well, if that's the case, I think that's enough bedtime stories for tonight, don't you?" I breathed out as I tossed the book on my nightstand, before sliding back to my side of the bed.

Henry shifted from his position on top of the covers, to underneath, cursing under his breath. "And you say I'm the one who's infuriating," he murmured.

This time I did laugh.

Henry shut the light off, and settled on his side of the bed, our breathing the only sound in the air.

We must have lain there in that bed for nearly twenty minutes, neither of us ready to fall asleep.

I noticed the shift in Henry's breathing as he tugged the covers over to his side, and instinctively, I moved toward him, giving up the fight. I cautiously slid my arm over his hip and gently tugged him against me. To my surprise, he didn't fight my touch, but instead relaxed into my hold, his breaths shaky.

"You are cold," I said, sliding my leg between his, pulling him back against my warmth.

"I mean, we are in the woods... It gets cold out here..." he murmured. He shifted in my arms as I fought the desire to let my fingers stroke his bare skin, trace lines over his soft edges.

To let my hands wander along the waistband and over his covered...

Henry sighed, turning in my grasp so that he was chest to chest with me. I could see him in the darkness, the only light that of the lanterns outside casting a faint fiery silhouette on him.

"Grayson... I..." His voice was soft, barely a whisper. Then, I felt the faintest touch on my hip. A familiar warm palm rested against my exposed skin, and a sigh of relief escaped him.

"We don't have to do anything you don't want to do, Henry. I need..." I sighed in defeat of my own. "I need you to know that, okay?" I whispered, even though there was no need.

Henry pulled himself closer. I could feel his hardness against me, spurring me into arousal once more.

"Okay," Henry whispered.

Just as I thought this would end the way it usually did—with Henry getting jumpy and fleeing the scene, I was surprised.

Henry leaned in and *kissed me.*

But this kiss was different than the one we'd shared earlier, in the woods.

That had been a rush. Wild, unfettered, and brand new. But the way Henry kissed me now, as his hands slowly explored my stomach, my chest, my neck, and even my face, was something so much better.

His lips moved slowly against mine, his tongue slipping into my mouth with ease as he carefully caressed mine, sucking on my lower lip as he thrust himself against me, eliciting a deep, contented moan to bubble from my throat that I was powerless to stop.

I ran my hand over his perfect ass, gripping it as I thrust myself against his rigid hardness. I slid my hand beneath his waistband, just enough to feel the warmth of his skin against my palm.

A deep sigh escaped him as I let my fingers stroke his skin.

"You like that?" I breathed, slowly and as gently as possible tracing lines over his hip with my fingertips. "You like it when I touch you like this?" I asked as I ran my fingers over his heated skin.

Henry nodded as he kissed me again. He bit at my lower lip, sucking the flesh into his mouth as his clothed cock *throbbed* against mine.

"Yes," he breathed.

I trailed my hand over his stomach, letting my fingers brush against the trail of hair, teasing him. I meant what I'd said, and I didn't want to go any further without Henry's expressed consent.

"You can tell me to stop, if it's too much," I whispered into his mouth. "You don't owe me anything," I reminded him. Though I hoped he wouldn't shut down what was happening between us, because it felt better than good.

It felt *right*... in a way it never felt with anyone else.

Henry's hand slid between us, and I half worried he was going to push me away, but instead, he leisurely slid his hand beneath the opening in my boxers, gripping my aching cock in his palm, squeezing just the slightest, and I shuddered with ecstasy.

The touch, *his* touch, was overwhelming.

"Henry," I groaned into his mouth.

"I don't want you to stop," he whispered, his thumb brushing my wet slit, spreading my precum over my swollen head.

"I just..." he breathed against me, his words full of hope, fear, and promise.

"What is it?" I asked, kissing him again. "You can tell me."

"I haven't wanted anyone like I want you... in a long time," he whispered.

"Fuck, Henry..." I moaned in defeat.

Henry wrapped his hand around my shaft, his warm palm squeezing me rhythmically.

"I want you too, Henry," I whispered, letting my lips travel from his mouth to his jaw, his neck.

With his free hand, he grabbed my forearm, pushing me lower. It wasn't much of a push, and

I found Henry's sizeable erection rather quickly. I let my fingers trace its length, marveling at the texture of his thickness, committing to memory the feel of his veins and the thickness of his shaft.

The sound that escaped his lips was something like a cry and a moan all at once. I ran my thumb across his wet slit, spreading it in the same way he did to me.

"Make... make me come... Grayson, I'm so..."

"You didn't say *please*," I said, my voice gravelly and dark, nipping at his lips.

Henry thrust himself against me greedily as he stroked my shaft, which was now fully out of its boxer prison. His hand wrapped tightly around my shaft and I ground myself against him, fucking his hand until the head of my leaking cock brushed against his rough palm.

Fucking hell, Henry likes to play dirty!

"Please, Grayson..." he moaned into my mouth.

I wanted to feel his skin against mine, but I also didn't want to ruin this perfect moment.

I quickened my pace as I stroked him, squeezing in intervals. His cock throbbed in my hands, swollen and thick, and I could only imagine how it would feel in my mouth, cutting off my airway.

Fuuuuck...

"Oh fuck, Grayson, I'm—"

I covered Henry's mouth with mine, knowing I was about to come too.

Henry collapsed into my kiss, his entire body melting as his hot, wet release coated my hand, sliding through my fingers. His cock pulsed in my grip, and I came with an unrelenting growl, thrusting myself against his hold as I spilled myself in his hand.

I kissed Henry with promise, with hope. We were both a hot and sticky mess, but it felt like everything was different, and a good different.

Like we'd finally crossed some invisible line and everything was going to change.

And as we lay there, in blissful post-orgasm ecstasy, tangled together, I had never felt such peace.

I only hoped that when we woke up tomorrow, that peace would still be there.

CHAPTER 27

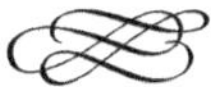

Henry

I curled into the warmth surrounding me, breathing in the faint scent of smoke mixed with an underlying lavender.

Grayson.

Immediately, the memories of the previous day, and night, came flooding back to me. How we'd woken up together just like this—tangled around one another like vines—and how scared I'd been because I *liked* how it felt.

The way his fingertips traced smooth lines along my skin, or how his leg fit perfectly in between mine.

A part of me still wanted to panic, to run to

the shower and gather my feelings so I could convince myself I *didn't* feel anything.

But as I opened my eyes, only to catch Grayson staring at me with a look that only made my insides melt and my cock twitch, I found resistance absolutely futile.

"Good morning, gorgeous," Grayson drawled, his voice still a tad bit hazy from his slumber as he gently kissed me. His palm against my hip was warm, but it didn't wander. Instead, it stayed frozen in one place as if he was panicking, as if he too, was nervous.

But I suppose that was my fault.

Grayson had more than called me out on my flighty behavior, at the fact that the closer he got, the more I pulled away.

But I couldn't help it. The last person I let get close to me...

He cheated on me.

The entire time we were together.

I knew it was irrational to think just because I'd had one bad apple meant the whole orchard was bad, even with the fact it had been years at this point since we ended our engagement and broke up. But the whole experience changed me.

Putting myself out there, trying to find someone else, even a rebound, just didn't sit right with me. I'd thought I loved my ex, and that was why I was so devastated, so affected.

But as I lay there wrapped in Grayson's warm arms, staring at his beautiful face, I wondered if I ever really knew love at all.

Because the way Grayson looked at me, the way he touched me... and the way he let his guard down around me... it was impossible *not* to fall in love with him.

The realization scared me, but it also invigorated me.

I leaned into his soft kiss, relishing in the taste of his tongue on mine, letting my hands travel over the solid surface of his chest, up his neck until my fingers tickled the edge of his hairline.

"Good morning," I breathed into his kiss.

My cock twitched as Grayson tugged me closer, thrusting his morning wood against mine with a deep groan.

Just as I contemplated a replay of the previous night, a knock sounded on the door, making me flush with fresh panic. In the daytime, the domes were like large windows, which meant whoever was at the door, could likely see us. My entire body rushed with heat as we broke apart, Grayson only smirking at me as he swung his legs out of the bed.

"I, uh..., think I'm gonna hit the shower," I

said, coughing, if only to try and dispel the insecurity I felt at the moment.

I stumbled out of bed awkwardly, thanks to the maddening erection that was more than disappointed that our morning interlude had been cut short. I wasted no time disrobing once I was behind the partition and the glass sanctity of the shower, turning on water. Though I opted for warm water only because it was rather cold in the dome. I'd barely had time to get adjusted to the warmth before the door opened to reveal a rather jaw-dropping vision of Grayson.

Completely naked.

My gaze dropped immediately from his gorgeous face to his dick, which he held in his hand, his thumb lazily stroking his head.

My gaze flashed up to his sexy eyes, to his smirk.

"Now, where were we before we were so rudely interrupted?" he said as he stepped into the shower with me.

I couldn't move.

For starters, the shower itself wasn't that big. Sure, it was big enough we both could fit, but we couldn't both be under the showerhead at the same time.

Not to mention, it was one thing to *touch* Grayson's dick, but it was quite another to see him stroking his own erection in front of me as he watched me with a lustful gaze that only made my cock throb.

Grayson must have read my silence as a lack of consent, because immediately his eyebrows furrowed, and he dropped his hand.

"Unless I just interrupted *you*," he said cautiously.

And that snapped me out of my daze for some reason. I hated to see Grayson disappointed, which didn't make sense to me at the time.

I took one slow step forward, then another, until I was chest to chest with him and his back was flat against the shower wall. The squeak of his flesh against the glass echoed in the small space.

I reached out, trailing my hand over his hip as I stared at him, hoping he could understand.

I wanted Grayson.

More than I think I could comprehend at the time.

"You aren't interrupting me," I whispered, watching as the water fell down over his skin in crystal clear rivulets.

Grayson slid his hand between us, his gaze fixated on mine as he ran his thumb over my slit before stroking me slowly. My eyes fluttered shut of their own accord as I tried to choke down the moan forming in my throat.

But it was no use. My head fell against Grayson's shoulder as my hips rocked forth and I thrust myself against his relentless hand, once more.

"Look at me," he said, his voice full of command, full of lust.

I opened my eyes, lifting my head as I did what he asked.

His amber eyes held me still, like a statue. The only sensation I was acutely aware of was the warm water slicing over my skin and the pulsing of my cock in his warm, wet hand.

My lips parted instinctively as I sucked in a breath, and Grayson *praised* me.

"You are so fucking beautiful," he breathed, releasing my cock.

I whined without thinking, missing the feeling of his hand wrapped around me.

"Such pretty eyes you have," he whispered, holding me still against him, our stiff cocks rubbing against one another. My head rolled back as his lips assaulted my neck, right over my erogenous zone.

I wrapped my hand around him, and he groaned, taking my lips with his.

"And these lips..." He groaned, breaking away to trace his fingers over my bottom lip, gently tugging at the flesh.

"I've been fantasizing about these lips for

days," he said, biting at my bottom lip in a way that made my fucking knees *buckle.*

My cock throbbed and I couldn't help but grind myself against him. With the way he was touching me, the tone of his voice... I couldn't help my sudden *need.*

My desperation.

I needed Grayson. I needed his order, his lead. I needed him to set me free.

With a shaky breath, I took his finger and slowly placed it in my mouth, taking careful precision not to gag myself—after all, that would be embarrassing—and slowly rolled my tongue around his finger, licking the tip of his finger, and groaning in slight exaggeration.

Grayson reacted just as I had hoped, cursing as he thrust himself against me.

"Such a little brat too," he huffed as he set his hands on my hips and turned us around, backing me up against the wall of the shower, water splashing and running down his back now. The chill of the glass against my flesh was a welcome contrast to the heat between us.

Grayson placed his hands on my wrists, spreading my arms at my sides as he ground his wet, warm cock against me.

I gazed up at his dilated eyes, his lips still swollen from kissing me.

"Grayson, I—"

His expression softened and he removed one hand from my left wrist, instead, using it to trace gentle lines along my jaw.

"Yes, baby?" he murmured, and I think my soul left my body.

"I w... want..."

"Tell me what you want, Henry," he said, kissing my lips gently. "Tell me and I'll give it to you."

There were a hundred things I wanted to say, but because I'm a damn idiot and socially awkward as fuck, not to mention I'd been perpetually single for five years, the words that flew out of my mouth were, "I need you to know I'm clean. Before, we do anything else." I squeaked.

Grayson smirked. "Is that what this is about? Because I can assure you my record is spotless."

"I just... I meant what I said last night. It's been a long time, and I... I should just stop right now, I—"

"Henry." Grayson's smooth voice pulled me like a magnet. "I meant what I said too. We don't have to do anything you don't want to do," he said as he gently let up from where he pinned me. His fingers slid softly through my wet hair.

His words settled all the panic inside of me.

Because I did want him.

I wanted him so bad, it hurt.

"I want this," I said as I kissed him, pulling his weight against me once more.

Between his kiss, his revelation, and his words, I was a goner.

And my cock was aching for release.

Which is probably why the next thing out of my mouth was shocking even to me, but I couldn't deny that Grayson made me braver.

"I want you, on your knees." I swallowed harshly, my gaze flashing to his as I focused on his amber eyes. I needed to look at him, or I was going to lose my nerve.

"W... with my dick in your mouth," I managed to get the last part out without passing out.

Grayson didn't miss a beat as he slid to the ground, taking my rock hard cock in his hand and making quite the show of licking off the precum that had formed on my head with his perfect, pink tongue.

Sweet lord, if he keeps this up I might not even make it into his mouth!

My legs shuddered as he took me in one movement to the back of his throat. A deep, unrelenting moan escaped me as my back arched off the shower walls, my hands seeking his wet, silky locks to grip, to ground myself. My eyelids fell closed as he rolled his tongue around my shaft, hollowing his cheeks, while I gripped his hair, pushing him down further, spurred on by ecstasy I didn't even know I possessed.

A part of me worried I was going to choke him, but before I could pull back, Grayson slid his hands up my thighs, grabbing my ass as he *pulled* me closer, until I could hear the faintest gag from him.

I came without warning, hard and fast, my legs buckling beneath me and the only thing keeping me standing was Grayson's deep groan as he *swallowed* me down.

I opened my eyes, hazily gazing down at him. The sight before me would have brought me to release if I had not already being in the midst of coming.

Grayson, naked before me, cock swollen and gleaming, his perfect pouty lips stuffed with my cock and my release *dripping* down his chin with saliva and shower water.

I eased my grip on his hair, trying to catch my breath. When he was finished, and I had started to soften, he stood, bringing me close for a rather sloppy, salty kiss.

I'd never tasted *myself* before, and certainly never on anyone else.

But I didn't hate it.

In fact, I found myself melting into his arms against the wall, my hands sliding in his hair once more as our tongues tangoed together.

When we broke away, Grayson laughed as he grabbed the shower gel, lathering his hands together, instructing me to turn around once more. His hands felt so good as he lathered my body, and the hot steam was relaxing. I almost felt like I could just curl up in bed once more and fall asleep. But that wasn't on the itinerary.

"We're going to be late for the wine festival," I exclaimed as all my faculties returned to earth.

"Oh hush. *We* will not be late. Everyone else will just be early," Grayson teased, sudsing my hair with shampoo.

I tilted my head back, running my hands through to wash it out, turning around once more to look at him, and do the same to him.

Maybe it was his use of the word *we*, or maybe it was just that I was accustomed to self-sabotage, but with my emotions and boundaries all over the place with Grayson, I felt a sting of panic.

"Um, Grayson... can I... can I ask you something?" I said, working up the lather of the shower gel across his solid pecs

"Anything," he said almost so softly, I barely heard him.

I got the feeling that Grayson wasn't the type to get soft and warm, and that made what I was going to ask all the more difficult. But I wasn't as quick to wear my heart on my sleeve, and I wasn't exactly a spontaneous, go-with-the-flow guy.

"Can we... can we just keep this... us... between us, for now?" I asked hesitantly, worried I was going to destroy this perfect moment.

But with my head back on right, I knew it was best to set firm boundaries now so my heart wouldn't be broken later.

I understood Grayson was attracted to me. Hell, he'd made that abundantly clear by that point, and I was more than open to exploring what was happening between us, but until I had a firm grip on *my* feelings, I wanted to keep things private.

Relationships are between the people *in* the relationship, after all, and when things don't work out, or something happens, it's a lot easier to control the damage.

I'd learned that the last time.

Something shifted in Grayson's eyes, but before I could discern what it was, he grinned that sexy Grayson grin, and nodded. "Of course," he said, switching me shower spots so he could rinse off.

I smiled in return, exiting the shower and grabbing my towel, feeling the best I'd felt in a long time.

Maybe this weekend wouldn't be so bad after all.

CHAPTER 28

HENRY

I TOASTED Mia with a glass of Rosé, some of it slightly sloshing out of my glass.

Grayson was animatedly telling a story about some weekend with his sister where they both ended up lost in a vineyard, the whole group roaring with laughter.

I watched him with drink-infused eyes, and my heart raced. Everywhere he went, he commanded attention, exuded authority.

I'd never been with anyone like him and that was as thrilling as it was scary. Because outside of the bubble Grayson and I had somehow built, I could see him the way everyone else did. And I could see how drastically different we were. But there was a spark within me that continuously burned, reminding me that the Grayson everyone else saw, wasn't the *real* Grayson.

Just like the me everyone else saw, wasn't the *real* me.

That spark, only made me want him more. It made me want to push and pull him, only to come undone under his command in private, pushed to my own limits. I wanted the Grayson who opened up to me, who was gentle and sweet when it mattered the most.

I wanted the sexy GQ model man who knew how to get me off with a *mere look.*

I wasn't one to drink usually, and I didn't think *tasting* would get me so off my rocker. The world was spinning, and the music was playing from the live band, and the sun was shining.

For the first time in what felt like forever, I felt *alive.*

As Grayson wrapped up his story, we all headed to the courtyard of the resort itself. Paved in stone with tents spread all across the field, it was a sight to behold. The resort was packed. With the wine festival being one of the biggest events of the year, apparently.

Thankfully, Giselle and her future husband had taken care of everything. I'd never had the chance to be on an exclusive, all paid vacation before, and though I'd offered to pay for my dome, Mia and Giselle thwarted my offering every chance I brought it up. After the fire the first night, I stopped, if only because Mia was getting exasperated at my insistence.

We all traipsed over to the picnic table in the center of the stone courtyard, the only one that was visibly empty due to the *reserved* sign on it. The girls threw down their purses in a flash as their dates settled with the boxes of the wine purchases everyone had made. "Come dance with me!" Mia said, tugging on Giselle's arm.

"I'll dance with you," I said, sweeping in to grab my sister as Giselle tumbled back into Aaron with a giggle.

"Come on, you lush," I teased as I hooked my arm in hers, pulling her up toward the dance floor.

"We'll be right behind you!" Julie called out.

When we finally reached the dance floor, my sister seemed to have forgotten all about her friend.

I spun her around and she laughed, throwing her head back in joy.

"Are you having a good time?" I asked.

Mia's smile was bright. "The best time. How about you?"

I couldn't help but return her smile genuinely.

"I can't remember the last time I had this much fun," I said as I spun her out and then back in to my arms.

And for the first time in my life, it felt like the sky was the limit.

CHAPTER 29

GRAYSON

THE RESORT WAS CRAWLING with people, but as far as I was concerned there was only one person I was focused on.

My sister and her friends continued to drink and converse, the sun beating down on us and everyone within the courtyard. I watched as Henry spun his sister around the dance floor, smiling like he didn't have a care in the world.

I liked seeing this side of him—even if it was because of the several glasses of wine we'd been *tasting*.

I knew somewhere deep beneath the surface, this was who Henry was. He just needed someone to remind him.

"Excuse me," I said to no one in particular, as I made my way through the crowd toward the dance floor.

"Wait for me, Gray!" Julie crooned behind me, but I wasn't concerned about her.

I wasn't concerned about anyone except the fine specimen in front of me, who was lighting up the damn room. I saw the way the women on the floor were looking at him, and even some of the guys at the picnic tables I passed.

Possession swelled inside of me.

Mine.

That one is all mine.

"Sorry to interrupt," I drawled as I approached a pink-cheeked Mia, who almost instantly backed away from her brother.

Up close together, the family resemblance was obvious. They both had the same eyes, the same perfect bone structure. But the dark hair and eyes on Henry were much more sultry than the dark hair and blue eyes his sister sported, not to mention his perfect, luscious lips.

Lips that I want to taste over and over again.

Lips that I want wrapped around my cock right about now.

"Oh, it's fine, Gray," Mia said with a hiccup, followed by a giggle.

Something sparkled in Henry's eyes as he

crossed his arms, his black polo making his golden tan stand out all the more.

"My dance card is full," he said brattily, turning away from me. But I could see the hint of a smirk on his lips.

So, Henry wants to play.

"Perhaps you can make an exception," I whispered in his ear, shifting just so he could feel my arousal against his thigh.

As expected, his eyes widened, flashing to mine, filled with heat.

The music was loud, and Henry looked back at his sister, who was now dancing with Giselle and Julie in a circle, the three of them laughing like little kids.

I slid my hand around Henry's hip, pulling him toward me once more. The band struck up their next chords, something about she'd tell them what she really, really wanted… a melody and words that were achingly familiar, but I couldn't quite place. The bass was thick, and it was some semi-dark electronic beat that sounded more like a heartbeat than a song. The woman crooned huskily.

Henry swayed his hips back and forth to the music, moving in tandem as I pulled myself closer, acutely aware that everyone could see us.

But I didn't care. I wanted them to see us. I

wanted everybody in fucking Brideshead to see what was mine.

"Everyone calls you Gray," he murmured. "Everyone but me."

I let out a dark chuckle.

"Is that what you want me to call you? Gray?" he asked hazily.

I hooked his chin under my knuckle, forcing him to look up at me. In his eyes, I could see a heat that was unmatched by any sun, any flame. I liked the sound of my name on his tongue, no matter how he said it. But something about the way he used my nick-name, caused every nerve in my body to short circuit.

"You can call me whatever you want, baby," I whispered drunkenly as I pressed my lips to his.

To his own inebriation, Henry did not fight me. Instead, he melted against me like butter, groaning into my mouth, making my already hard cock twitch with anticipation.

"Gray..." he groaned my name, swinging his hips to the music, his dark eyes flashing at me with lustful haze.

"Yes, baby?" I responded breathlessly.

"Is it hot in here, or is it just me?" he asked, his cheeks red with heat.

"Need some air?" I asked, running my

hands through his hair, feeling the heat of his flush.

Henry nodded as my fingers traced over his jaw, over his pout.

"Follow me," I commanded, squeezing his hand as I pulled him away from the dance floor.

"Where are we going?" he asked breathlessly.

I led him through the winding stone pathway, away from the noise, away from the drunken patrons and our wedding party.

Until I found just the place.

The underpass was much cooler, being in the shade, and it was also less populated. I pulled Henry to the side, into a darkened alcove, surrounded by potted plants and trees.

Henry's breathing was rapid, his cheeks still flushed.

"Gray—"

Before he could get the rest of the words out, desire took over, and I shoved him up against the stone arch.

"Do you have any idea how fucking hot you were up there? How many people were undressing you with their fucking eyeballs?" I nipped.

Henry ran a hand through his disheveled hair.

"Me?"

"Yes, you," I said as I took his face in my hands.

"Does that bother you?" he asked, his lips parted just enough to draw my attention.

Fuck, his mouth was so god damn perfect.

"You are *mine*," I said, gripping his hips as I thrust myself against him. "I don't like anyone else thinking they can have you," I breathed.

"I don't want anyone else," Henry said hopelessly.

"Show me," I growled.

Henry snapped my buttons like a damn powder keg, picking up exactly what I was throwing down.

"What if... what if we get caught?"

Well, that wasn't a no.

"You'll just have to be quiet then, won't you, baby?"

Henry slid his hand in between the slit in my boxers, his thumb brushing over my head swiftly. He kept his gaze trained on mine as I watched him slide down my legs to the ground.

I reached out, threading my fingers through his hair, licking my lips as I watched him take me into his mouth.

His tongue rolled around me and he lurched forward on his knees, forcing me into the back of his throat with a deep groan.

"Fuck," I cursed as his warm mouth cradled me. I tightened my fingers in his hair.

"You like that?" I asked, my voice dark and gravelly, gripping his hair and holding him to me, not giving him the chance to speak. But his grunts and groans were enough of a confirmation, as was the obvious bulge in his pants.

"What was that?" I asked, pulling him off of me so I could get a good glimpse at him. His perfect pout was swollen from kissing and sucking me, and his pupils were dilated beyond belief. He was the prettiest thing I'd ever seen.

"Yes," Henry breathed.

"Show me. Show me how much you want this cock," I spat, my words full of command, jealousy, and desire.

Make me yours, baby.

Henry didn't miss a beat as he took me down once more, sucking, licking, and rolling his tongue, deep, unrelenting groans of satisfaction emanating from his throat, vibrating through my cock.

"Fuck, Henry!" I cried, forgetting all about being quiet.

I didn't care if anyone saw us.

I wanted them to see.

Wanted everyone to know Henry was mine, and I was his.

I thought Henry swallowed every drop of

me, because all my senses disappeared the moment I came, erupting in his throat like a fountain.

When I pulled him up from his knees, intent on buttoning my pants, Henry surprised me by going in for a sloppy, wet kiss, his mouth full of my load.

I fumbled with my pants as Henry rubbed his hardness against me, unloading my salty release into my mouth.

God, he is perfect.

Like the gracious man I was, I accepted it without hesitation, swallowing it like a champ.

Henry's kiss was unhinged. The slightest gasp of ecstasy escaped him, and I knew.

He fell against me, into our heat-filled kiss, an absolute mess.

We were both an absolute mess.

But in that space of disaster we were a perfect storm. Henry was rumbling, terrifying thunder, and I was bright, electrical lightning. An electric, perfect match.

I pulled away, taking in the sight of him in all his glory.

"Fuck, that was hot," I murmured, sliding my hand over his ass and cupping his cheek in my palm with a squeeze.

"Yeah, you are," he whispered back.

The music carried above us, and I was

aware we needed to get back to the group. But I didn't care about the wine festival or listening to another one of Riley's dumb student stories.

A lazy grin spread on my face at his words, his genuine praise.

Fuck, I am.

I only cared about one thing.

"Mine," I whispered, kissing him gently.

"What?" Henry's voice was so soft I barely heard him.

"You're mine," I repeated. "And you're pretty hot too." I teased.

Henry looked up at me with glassy eyes. "You mean it?" he asked, his voice shaky.

I nodded, sliding my hand through his hair, gripping the strands once more and pulling his mouth to mine, my gaze falling on his. The world was a blur as I answered.

"Absolutely, baby."

CHAPTER 30

GRAYSON

THE SUN SHONE through the dome like the Heavens were parting or something. Gold, bright, and far too early for my liking.

I blinked furiously, filtering the light. My head was pounding, my stomach empty as all hell, grumbling away.

I rubbed my eyes and sat up, the covers falling off of me. My gaze traveled to Henry, who was laying flat on his stomach, the covers barely covering him, his bare, pale ass on full display.

For a moment, I felt at peace, watching the rise and fall of his back, until I felt the urge to pee. Throwing off the covers, I swung my legs out of bed, my cock bristling from the friction of the sheet.

Head pounding, and half-dazed, I made my way to the bathroom, when I realized that I was also naked.

Panic laced through me as I tried to recall the prior night's events, but everything was a blur.

A wine-filled blur, and I couldn't remember anything after a karaoke-infused dinner at *Lovers Lodge*, the main bar that was open for the after-events of the festival.

I remembered arriving with Henry and everyone else, but I had no idea *how* we got back to the dome, or if we...

"Oh fuck," Henry's voice alerted me as he called out, "Grayson!"

I finished my business, heading back to the main room, to see Henry looked as panicked as I felt.

His gaze settled on me, and I stood there before him, feeling the most judged I have ever felt in my life.

What... what happened?" Henry asked, his voice shaky, and all I could do was shake my head nervously.

"I... I don't know," I said honestly. But that was apparently the wrong thing to say, because Henry's eyes widened.

"What do you mean you don't know?"

"I don't... uh... remember. Do you?" I asked, frozen in place.

Henry's eyebrows furrowed with concern, and I could see his breathing increase.

"No," he said, his voice laced with anxiety.

"All I remember is singing karaoke, and dancing..." He ran a hand through his disheveled hair, swallowing harshly. And then Henry said the quiet part out loud, and that changed everything.

"Oh my God, did we..." His voice elevated, the panic more than evident.

This was not how I wanted things to happen, if they were going to happen at all.

The fact I couldn't remember did not bode well. Henry deserved more from me.

I took a step closer toward Henry, who was sitting in bed now, breathing rapidly. I reached out for him, if only to soothe his panic, and perhaps my own. His gaze flashed at me as he pulled away, breaking my heart.

No no no no...

"Grayson, answer me..." he said, his voice and his body shaking.

"I told you, I don't know. Everything is a blur. I—"

A knock sounded on the door, and Henry

shook his head, throwing his legs out of bed with full force.

"I need a shower. Don't come after me," he said solidly. My shoulders fell in defeat as I watched him walk away, and the entire world felt like it was crumbling.

How could I have been so fucking stupid?

Because I was drunk.

As I surveyed the clothes strewn across the room, I picked up my underwear from the edge of the bed.

The answer was more than obvious. It wouldn't be the first time I got drunk and took someone to bed, but Henry wasn't like everyone else. He was different. Delicate, even.

And I'd just signed a one way ticket to destroying the foundation of something beautiful, something epic.

"The one good thing to happen to me in years, and I fuck it up. Good job, Gray," I said to myself, sighing in defeat as I headed to the door. The Breakfast cart was sitting at my doorstep, with an itinerary, but no annoying Cam to be found.

Even the staff knows I'm a fucking idiot.

I pulled the cart in, grabbing the itinerary and scanning the activities for the day. My sister had planned a morning hike to the Brideshead Waterfall, complete with waterfall side dining for lunch, and a formal dinner at *Wildfyre,* a reservation only restaurant between our glampgrounds and the Brideshead Resort's main lodge.

My stomach rumbled with hunger, but when Henry came out of the shower, not even turning to look at me, or acknowledging me at all, I lost my appetite.

CHAPTER 31

Grayson

The hike to the falls wasn't as bad as I thought it would be, but I wasn't the only one who was hungover and tired as hell. Leave it to my sister, who had a liver made of steel, to book a mid-morning hike the morning after we'd been drinking for the majority of a whole day.

I sucked down some more water from the cooler on site, trying not to be a total creeper, but I couldn't take my gaze off Henry. I'd contemplated trying to talk to him, to apologize and tell him I was sorry, that I didn't mean for anything to happen...

I still couldn't remember exactly what happened, but all signs pointed to the obvious.

We slept together, and I didn't even remember it.

I wanted to remember it. Wanted to recall the feel of his body pressed against mine. I wanted to remember the look on his face as I inched my way inside him. I wanted to remember the moment he called my name, shattering around me.

But there was nothing. Nothing where those perfect memories should be, and I hated it.

But what was worse, was that Henry wouldn't even look at me. Instead, he avoided me like the plague and had taken up social inter-action with his sister and Julie instead.

The Brideshead Waterfall raged behind me, a force of nature. It was beautiful, and the moment itself a stunning one, but I couldn't enjoy it because I wished I could be spending it with Henry by my side.

"Henry giving you the cold shoulder over your drunk makeout?" Giselle asked quietly.

"What?" I nearly jumped five feet off the ground.

"Last night? The festival? You two could barely keep your lips off one another," she said with a smirk.

"I... don't remember."

"That sucks," she said taking a drink of her own water.

"Henry's such a reserved person to begin with. You, on the other hand…" She crossed her arms, nodding toward him and Mia who were laughing about something Julie said as she animatedly moved her hands.

"Drunk or sober, you're a total diva," she teased.

"I am not a diva," I snapped.

"You are the Susan Lucci of Jasper Springs, Gray. Dramatic as fuck."

I scowled. "Am not."

"All I'm saying is maybe you could learn a thing or two from Henry about slowing down."

My sister had no idea how right she was, and I despised that.

"Yeah, well, it was just a drunk kiss, right. Not like it means anything," I said.

Giselle pursed her lips. "It's okay to not be okay, Gray. We've all been there." Her words were sincere, but they only made me feel angrier. Worse.

"This isn't my first rodeo, Giselle," I growled, turning around to leave, running right into to object of my desire.

Henry's eyebrows furrowed, and I wondered how long he'd been standing there.

"Henry," I said softly, and he pushed past me.

"Excuse me," he said as he headed for the cooler, breaking my heart once more.

But perhaps I deserved such things.

Susan Lucci, and all.

CHAPTER 32

Grayson

After a dinner fit for a king, Riley and Aaron decided to hit the billiards. Even Henry didn't protest, which was probably a testament to his mood.

"Aren't you playing, Gray?" Julie asked as she chalked up her stick.

I shook my head. They'd divided into teams. Boys against girls. Henry's gaze caught mine, making me feel all the more aware of how shitty I actually felt.

"No," I said, shaking off his judgmental stare. "I'm, uh, going to go for a walk, let this food settle a bit," I said with a fake smile.

Julie nodded. "Cool. We'll be here!"

I turned on my heel, heading out into the air-conditioned hall. I wandered aimlessly through the main lodge, toward *Reception*, a small bar-restaurant that served pretty much only bar food and drinks, when I heard someone call my name.

"Grayson Sanderson!" The voice was as charismatic as ever, and I didn't even have to look to know who it belonged to.

I turned slowly to see Cody, my ex.

I froze in place as I took in the sight of him. It'd been years since our affair, but he didn't look any different, save for some lines and wrinkles around his eyes.

"Cody," I said in the flattest voice possible.

After all, the man was responsible for forcing my coming out, and our drunken tryst had become a badge of dishonor, casting my family as a main source of drama and gossip for weeks.

I thought we were doing the right thing, keeping our affair a secret. After all, no one needed to know our business but us, right?

I thought I loved him at the time, despite everything, and that what were doing was just.

But as I looked at him in the light of *Recep-tion*, I realized I never really loved him.

I was willing to take whatever I could get because I didn't think I deserved anything better than shadows and secrecy.

Which made me think about Henry.

We'd promised to keep whatever was happening between us a secret, but I'd slipped up. Maybe I did it on purpose.

Maybe I wanted everyone to know I was absolutely head over heels for Henry.

I'd never felt so strongly for another man in my thirty-eight years of life.

"What are you doing all the way up in these parts?" Cody asked, sipping a glass of whiskey. He motioned for me to sit, and I did.

"Giselle is getting married," I said evenly, testing the waters.

"I heard. We RSVP'd you know. The fam and I."

I nodded as a waiter came over to our table.

"Can I get you another, sir?" he asked, nodding to Cody's drink.

"Sure. And my friend here will have..." Cody raised an eyebrow.

"Oh that's not necessary, I—"

"It's a drink, Gray. Not a marriage proposal," Cody teased.

I debated what the right thing to do was, but I'd never been the best at making *good* decisions.

If I was going to go down in flames, why not let the whole town see I was on fire?

"I'll just have a martini, dry—"

"Extra olives?" Cody said, grinning wickedly.

I nodded politely at the waiter, wishing he was someone else. A hotter waiter, with dark eyes, and sinful lips, and a heart of gold.

"You know what, scratch that. I'll have a glass of the Kendall reserve, thanks," I said, feeling more than agitated at Cody's nonchalance. The waiter left, and I shifted uncomfortably in the wooden chair.

"Am I that predictable?" I asked, leaning back in my chair.

"You have high standards. Nothing wrong with that. You know what you like."

"Anyway, Giselle thought it would be a good *bonding* experience to bring the party up here to spend the weekend glamping. Well, the party plus some friends," I said quickly, acutely aware it sounded like I'd come alone. Why I cared what this asshole thought was beyond my comprehension at the time.

"Glamping? That sounds like the gayest shit ever," Cody drawled, leaning forward in his chair, bringing himself closer to me.

Once upon a time, I thought Cody was *it*. His preppy style, his bad boy charm.

I could more than see why my sister always talked about him when they were together, and after we started hooking up, I could more than see his appeal.

But as I sat there, talking to him, sharing a drink, I saw him for what he truly was.

A fuckboy.

And I had no time for fuckboys, not anymore.

I only had time for one person. One person, who I needed to tell how I felt.

"I need to go," I said as I stood up, and Cody did too.

"Always on the run, Gray. You haven't changed at all," Cody said as he pulled me in for a hug.

I accepted, if only because it was a polite gesture, and that's where I went wrong.

I'd misjudged Cody's intentions, apparently. Because when he pulled away from the hug, he pulled me in closer, and planted a wet, drunken kiss on my lips.

"Just like old times," he drawled sourly into my mouth.

CHAPTER 33

Henry

I watched Grayson leave the billiards, feeling like a complete and utter failure of a human being.

All day I'd ransacked my brain, trying to find even a shred of memory of what had happened between us, but there was nothing. I hadn't truly blacked out from drinking since my freshman year of college, in which my sister had to take my ass home.

And after that, I swore I'd never get black out drunk again, knowing the position I put myself in.

But I'd had a good time, up until my memory faded to black. The things I could remember—singing karaoke with Mia, Julie, and Grayson, sucking Grayson off underneath the underpass, tasting all the wine, dancing with my sister—I had meant what I said to Mia. I couldn't remember the last time I had so much fun.

I hated that I couldn't remember what had happened between us.

Casual sex wasn't something I did.

But I knew, despite having no memory of it, that was exactly what happened.

We fucked.

There was a sliver of a chance that we might have just passed out, but I *could* remember making out with Grayson, among other things, so the leap was only logical.

And I'd be lying if I said I *didn't* want to be fucked by Grayson. Or that I didn't think about fucking him. Which was certainly a new development for me, being as I'd never topped anyone before.

But it wasn't the ninety-nine point nine chance we had sex that bothered me. What bothered me was that I had been careless with my heart, and with Grayson's.

I wanted to take my time with Grayson. I wanted to be sure he wasn't going to break my heart like my ex. I needed to *trust* him. I needed to know with absolute certainty that Grayson didn't just see me as a fun weekend, and was going to discard me the minute we got home. I needed to know Grayson saw me as more than just the younger brother of his sister's bestie, and I also didn't want things to be awkward after this weekend, with the wedding on the horizon and any other events I might see him at. After all, this weekend wouldn't last forever.

What was going to happen when we arrived home and went back to reality?

Would Grayson still want to be with me without all the romance and sophistication surrounding us?

When the reality wasn't all glamping tents and waterfall hikes and expensive wine?

I wanted more than anything to tune out the anxiety, the panic, and the negative thoughts that threatened to sour the best weekend I'd had in a long time. But I couldn't get my head out of my ass, and because of that, I watched Grayson leave, and I did nothing.

Mia nudged me from my internal prison. "Your turn," she said, her gaze soft, understanding.

I grabbed my stick, lining up my shot as I sucked in a deep breath.

Some things in life were simple. Like playing pool. The rules were understood, and there was a clear indication of what to expect when you played the game. I wished life was like that. Easy to understand, easy to play.

Instead, it was messy and chaotic. It was scary and thrilling, and beautiful and ugly all at once.

Crack!

The clacking of the balls sounded together as they dispersed, the eight ball going right in the corner pocket like I had hoped.

Giselle whistled in approval as Riley and Aaron high-fived one another.

"Damn, Henry, I wish my brother were here to see that. He's the best player when it comes to the game. I bet you could give him a run for his money."

Giselle said with a smile.

"I'd love to see that," Aaron said with a laugh. "Someone putting Gray in his place for once."

My blood chilled, my face expressionless at the casual mention of the object of all my desires.

Their words only made me feel worse.

Giselle took her spot, as Riley reset the rack. Mia settled beside me.

"Did something happen? Between you two?" she asked gently.

"Oh something happened," I murmured. "But, neither of us can really remember *what*."

Mia's eyes widened, her mouth forming an 'o'. "And that is a bad thing?" she asked cautiously.

I felt my shoulders loosen with defeat.

"I just... I don't want to be some casual... fling, Mia. I—" I ran my hand through my hair, feeling the heat of my skin as my words spilled out of me relentlessly. I was powerless to stop them.

"You like him," she said, her voice solid, matter of fact. It wasn't a question.

"Yeah, I do," I whispered, my voice shaky.

"So then tell him," she said as if it was the most obvious thing in the world. I sighed.

"I can't." I admitted.

"Why not? That man was pining after you all fucking day, and you can't even see it, can you?" She huffed.

"What?"

"You are so thick sometimes, Henry. Not everyone is a liar and a cheat like—"

"I know that, Mia," I snapped.

"Do you? Because it looks to me like you're living in the past with a ghost instead of living in the moment with someone who is obviously crazy about you."

"It doesn't matter," I sighed, fidgeting with my stick. "I fucked everything up, anyway "

"Then fix it," she said, as Julie called her to take her turn.

I watched my sister line up her shot, her gaze flashing at me before she struck.

The balls scattered across the green in all directions, and hers slowly crawled to a stop, in the middle.

I passed my stick off to Riley, not wasting another moment. "I'll be back," I said, leaving it at that as I trotted off in the direction Grayson had disappeared.

Anxiety still flooded me, but now it was met with something else.

Hope.

I'd been so focused on the fact I'd messed everything up, I hadn't even given a thought that maybe I *could* fix it. Apologize for my dumb behavior. Tell him I liked him.

Maybe even... loved him.

I stopped dead in my tracks as I set my gaze on him. He was standing up from a table, where he was with someone and they looked pretty chummy. The man moved to hug Grayson, wrapping his arms around him. Grayson wrapped his arms around the man, and then... and then he kissed him.

My heart shattered into a million pieces at the sight.

"Fucking knew it," I said, turning around on

my heel, only to hear Grayson call out my name.

Tears prickled my eyes as I headed toward the exit, toward the transport concierge.

"Henry, wait," he called.

I held my sob in the entire ride back to the glamping tent, my fist balled as I felt like crumbling. Just as we arrived, the rain started to pour, and I ran from the transport to the front step as fast as I could to avoid getting soaked.

I threw open the door of the dome, relishing in the silence of being alone and I let out a gut wrenching sob that was as desperate as it was painful.

"Fuck," I cried, slamming my fist against the domed windows. I tore away, headed for the shower, when the door opened, pulling my attention once more.

Grayson stood in the doorway, the lantern light casting a golden glow on him, his blue button down soaked, clinging to his perfect chest, his dark hair wet, hanging in his eyes like some Esquire Brand Mr. Darcy.

And I both hated and loved it all the same.

"I can't do this with you," I said, my heart beating so loud I thought it would echo in the room.

"Henry, please, it's not... it's not what it looks like," he said as he took a step closer.

Enraged with several years of pent up baggage, in his presence I came undone.

"Oh really, Grayson? You going to tell me he tripped and fell onto your perfect mouth, and you were giving him CPR?" I growled.

"He's... Cody's not important to me. Not anymore."

I let out a dark laugh. "Anymore, right."

"Henry, please, just listen to me!"

"Listen to you? Listen to what, your lies? You said I was *yours!*" I cried, my stomach turning in anguish.

"You promised!" I yelled, as several years worth of trauma unleashed itself on Grayson.

Grayson stepped forward, but I held my hand up to stop him. I worried if he got any closer, I might actually explode into a million pieces.

"Don't," I said shakily. "Just... leave me alone," I said through tears and sobs.

"Henry..."

"I mean it, Grayson," I said as I headed for the shower, not looking behind me. Because I knew if I did, I would see Grayson's heart breaking too.

And I'd know it was because of me.

CHAPTER 34

GRAYSON

THE MORNING WAS QUIET. Too quiet.

I'd spent the night tossing and turning, my body cold from the chill in the air. Henry slept curled up on the edge of the bed, far away from me.

It had been poor timing that he'd show up the moment Cody decided to be... well, Cody.

I'd pushed him away, but the damage was done. Henry saw him kiss me, and he must have thought...

Well, it was more than apparent what he thought, because the tears running down his face were enough to cut me to the bone.

I'd pleaded with him to listen, but he wasn't capable of listening. Seeing Cody and I set off some trigger, something buried beneath Henry's charming, sweet exterior.

Perhaps it was the very trigger that had kept him with one foot out the door, this entire weekend.

Whoever had hurt him... I wanted to wring their fucking neck. For tarnishing this perfect man who deserved the world and made him think he wasn't enough.

He was worth more than gold.

I needed to make him understand that as far as I was concerned, there was no one else, and the moment I saw him crumble before me, his voice full of pain as he cried "you promised," I knew there would never be anyone else.

Because I was in love with Henry.

I was completely balls to the wall, head over heels, soap opera style in love with Henry.

He showered and dressed without a word, packing up his suitcase. After wine check, we were wrapping up the afternoon with spa appointments, and then we'd be leaving.

It would be time to head back to reality.

A reality where Henry and I would part our ways.

Probably never to speak again, given everything that's happened.

"Cam's here," Henry said coolly, dragging his suitcase by the door.

"Right," I said, the tension between us palpable. There were so many things I wanted to say, but I couldn't find the words.

CHAPTER 35

I CLOSED MY EYES, trying to enjoy movements of the masseuse who was massaging my temples, but it was no use.

"You are tense," she said. "Relax."

"That is the point of a spa, you know," Giselle murmured from beside me.

Aaron was not a fan of the spa, and instead had opted for a classic shave at the shop below, while my sister, Julie, Mia, and I all enjoyed a mid-morning facial.

"Yes, well, it's been a rough weekend," I nipped, not in the mood for my sister's prying antics.

"What part was rough?" Julie teased. "You looked like you were enjoying yourself to me."

I peered at Julie by opening one eye.

"I don't see how that is any of your business."

"Does this have anything to do with why you left pool early and never came back?" Mia asked, and I grumbled as the masseuse held my head still, chastising me.

"Relax!" she barked.

"That is damn near impossible," I said, getting up from my seat.

"Where you going?" the masseuse asked, obviously surprised at my gesture.

"To the Jacuzzi. To *relax!*" I snapped, turning on my heel and taking off for a lounge that wasn't full of gossiping bridesmaids and a bride-to-be.

I ended up in the men's spa, disrobing so that I could soak in the Jacuzzi alone for a moment and collect my thoughts. I'd just closed my eyes when I heard the door open.

"Oh, I didn't realize you were in here," Henry's voice was soft.

I opened my eyes, my gaze fixed on him, his fingers playing with the tie of his fluffy robe. He had the audacity to look hurt. As if I was the one who had ruined him.

As if the very sight of him didn't cause my heart to race.

"You don't have to leave," I said.

"Are you sure—"

"Stay," I said, my voice shaking. One word.

I wanted him to stay, and I wasn't just talking about his presence in the spa.

I wanted Henry to stay *with me.*

But I could barely get the words out before his stomach rumbled. I watched his cheeks flush as he twisted his lips.

"Hungry?" I asked.

"I, uh... haven't really had much of an appetite today," he said cautiously.

"You should eat something," I insisted.

Henry disrobed, peeking over his shoulder at me for a moment before sliding his spa sandals off. I watched as he slowly walked over to the Jacuzzi opposite my side. Away from me.

Part of me wanted to rise and join him, to pull him into my arms and tell him I was sorry.

I was sorry someone somewhere made him feel like he wasn't enough.

I was sorry for compromising us both the other night.

I was sorry for sitting down in the first place with Cody, thinking he had changed, because I had changed.

But most of all, I was sorry for whatever

pain I had caused Henry, and I wanted to make it right.

I wanted to be the man to heal his wounds.

I wanted to love him the way he deserved to be loved.

But I said none of that, because the masseuse came in, setting her gaze on me with fury.

"Your time is up, Mr. Sanderson," she said, tapping her watch. The spa ran in fifteen-minute intervals, and I was well over my time.

"Understood," I said, rising from my pool, feeling the chill of the air from the shift in temperature. I grabbed my robe, tying it closed as I followed the woman out.

"Could you see that my friend in there, Henry, receives a charcuterie platter and a pastry assortment along with a selection of your finest teas and coffees, please," I said as I headed toward the locker room. "And, please, put it on my tab," I ordered.

The woman smiled pleasantly. "Of course, Mr. Sanderson, will there be anything else?" she asked as I stopped at the door.

"Anything he wants, of course. Tell him it's been taken care of."

CHAPTER 36

THE DRIVE HOME was thick with unsaid words. Grayson kept switching radio stations, until I finally relented, turning it off altogether. I supposed it was time to rip the band-aid off and address the elephant in the Porsche.

"I can't do this. This awkward silence. We need to talk."

"I couldn't agree more," Grayson said, not looking away from his attention on the road.

There was so much I wanted to say, but all I could settle on was, "I'm sorry I yelled at you."

Grayson's expression did not shift. "Yes, well. Cody has that effect on people," he murmured.

"Is he your—"

"Was."

Hope dared to blossom in my heart, but I needed to get things out. I could not be distracted by slivers of hope.

"I'm sorry too," Grayson said softly as the GPS announced a turn.

I glanced at the map screen, reading the ETA. Thirty minutes.

I only had thirty minutes left with this man who I was certain was holding my heart hostage.

I wanted to tell him he couldn't have it.

My heart.

Me.

But the truth was, he had it the moment he looked up at me from the bathroom floor of M's Place. I just didn't know it then.

But before I could even speak the words out loud, Grayson continued.

"I never meant for any of this to happen... like this." He sighed. "I never intended to hurt you, Henry."

Panic laced through me at his words, hope fighting for a chance to breathe.

But it would not win. Not that day.

"I never wanted things to be awkward between us," I said, my heart in my throat. "Some friend I am, huh?" I said, blowing out a defeated breath as I looked out the window. I couldn't look at Grayson, knowing the blow was coming.

"Is that what we are? Friends?" Grayson asked warily.

I couldn't look at him, nor could I answer him. Not when I felt like the harsh truth of reality would smack me in the face.

"Because if that's all you see me as, Henry, that's... fine, but..."

I sat up in my seat, scooting to the edge as I waited for him to continue.

A notification popped up on the map screen, the electronic voice calling "Text from uncle Bob, would you like to hear?"

"No," Grayson said coolly, turning onto the main drag into Jasper Springs.

I'd be home in ten minutes.

"But I'd hoped maybe we could be more than that. More than friends, I mean."

The air fell silent.

Every nerve in my body stood at attention, that hope blossoming in my chest like a bad weed.

I wanted to be more than friends, too, but...

But I needed time. Everything had happened so fast, and...

"I can't," I said as he pulled up to the parking lot.

I wanted him to fight. To take my face in his

hands and kiss me, like he had in the woods, and tell me I was a damn fool.

I wanted Grayson to rescue me from myself, but he wasn't capable of that.

I needed to rescue myself, first, from the ghosts that haunted me.

Grayson didn't do any of those things.

He only smiled softly, and said, "Okay. Just friends then."

I opened my door as Grayson got out, unlocking the trunk. I grabbed my suitcase as he tapped away at his phone absentmindedly.

"Thanks for... the ride," I said, turning to head down the hill to my apartment.

"Uh huh," he said as he leaned against his car in that graceful, seductive way that made my cock twitch.

I hoped I was doing the right thing, protecting Grayson.

Protecting myself.

CHAPTER 37

THE HOUSE WAS EMPTY, as it always was at this time of day.

While I relished in the isolation, usually, this time it was not what I needed.

What I needed was Henry and his perfect mouth, his presence, his understanding.

How had everything become so complicated, so fast?

I knew the answer, but I didn't want to admit any of it. Or my part in it.

I wanted to blame Henry and his obvious baggage. I wanted to blame Henry and his push me, pull me, brat attitude. But I knew Henry wasn't the *only* factor. I'd pushed, and pushed, but I hadn't told Henry the truth.

I'd hid the truth from myself by covering it up with steamy kisses, and tangled limbs, and drunk sex.

The truth was I was absolutely in love with Henry.

And he wanted to be *friends*.

The emptiness of the house echoed with my sob. I couldn't remember the last time I cried over a man, period.

But Henry wasn's *just* some casual fling.

I meant every word I said in that car.

I wanted more.

I wanted to lay in bed with Henry reading gay ghost porn, and I wanted to roast a million s'mores with him, and I wanted to watch him get all flustered trying new things.

I wanted to play push me, pull me until we both were so worked up we'd have to fight for dominance.

I wanted to dance with him at my sister's wedding, and kiss him under the stars until he couldn't breathe. I'd never felt like this about anyone.

I'd never fallen in love like *this*.

My phone rang, pulling me from my meltdown.

"You home yet?" Giselle asked when I

answered, and I sighed, wiping my nose with the back of my hand as I tried to stuff down my sobs.

"Yeah," I said, my voice shaky.

"You okay, Gray? You sound upset."

She didn't know the half of it.

"I'm fine, sweetheart. You guys get home okay?" I asked, trying to change the subject to anything else so I didn't fall into deeper despair.

"Yeah, we just got in. Aaron is meeting up with some friends tonight. I was actually going to call up Drew and see if he wanted to hang out now that we're back, I was thinking M's Place? You can join if you want..." she said, her voice full of excitement.

Just for once, I wished I had the positivity my sister had. That I could just enjoy myself like she did, flitting from event to event like a butterfly.

I sighed, "Yeah, okay. See you there."

CHAPTER 38

Maybe I was holding on to wishful thinking. Hoping that life would be like a romance novel, and I would show up to M's Place and sweep Henry off his feet. We'd kiss, and apologize for being stupid assholes, and live happily ever after.

But Henry wasn't there.

I stared at my martini, but I hadn't touched it, when Giselle bumped my shoulder. Drew — the famous Drew Axel who'd come back to Sweetewater and reconnected with my sister recently on his tour, and who was now dating her florist, of all people—and his beau were on their way.

"You haven't touched your martini," she said softly.

"Thought I wanted it, but I guess I'm not in the mood."

Giselle twisted her lips, and then she let out a bombshell.

"Did you know Henry was engaged before?" she asked.

My gaze shot up to hers, eyes widening. "What?"

"About five years ago," she said, stirring her drink.

I was floored. Henry never mentioned his ex, but I would have thought he would have at least mentioned being *engaged,* given our company, not to mention all the talk of weddings...

"No," I said dumbfounded. "I had no idea."

Suddenly, his being uncomfortable around the wedding party made a lot more sense. I closed my eyes as I realized I should have seen it. His fear of commitment, his apprehension to act on his attraction.

I can't.

Not I won't, I *can't.*

Because the person who hurt Henry was someone he must have loved very, very much. Enough to want to spend the rest of his life with them.

"What happened?" I asked.

"Apparently, according to Mia, the guy had been cheating on him. From the get go."

"For five years?" I asked dumbfounded.

Giselle nodded. "Henry found out because he came home early one night."

I let out a shaky breath. "He found them together."

Giselle nodded. "Broke off the wedding the day after, and he's been a lone wolf ever since."

Henry's tear-streaked cheeks and the anguish on his face replayed in my brain.

You promised.

You said I was yours.

The words fell out of my mouth, vulnerable and full of emotion.

"He said... he said he just wanted to be friends," I breathed.

Giselle offered me a look that said, "Are you serious?"

"He's scared, Gray. Can you blame him?"

No, I couldn't. Not now, not when I knew *why*.

"I mean, anyone with eyeballs could see you two are crazy about one another. Last I checked, friends don't kiss each other the way you do, drunk or sober," she said raising her glass to me.

"Hell, Aaron doesn't even kiss me like that," she said with a laugh.

I blushed at her insinuation.

What the fuck was happening to me?

"A word of advice? One Sanderson to another?" she said, much more serious.

I sighed. Knowing my sister, I'd get the advice whether I said yes or no. So, of course, I said yes.

"He just needs to know you're not going to bail when things get hard."

"I'm not——"

"Not everything has to be Susan Lucci, Gray. Love isn't always trays of pastries and charcuterie or extravagant resorts. Sometimes it's just the little things."

"Like roasting a marshmallow," I said dumbly.

"Like dancing along to the Spice Girls," she said sweetly.

"Or reading gay ghost stories,"

My sister raised her eyebrow, but she didn't press me.

Drew and Taylor walked through the door at that moment, Drew calling out for us, shattering the tense moment.

I knew what I had to do at that moment.

I'd been waiting for a prince charming of my own to rescue me, but what if I was the knight in shining armor?

CHAPTER 39

Henry

I STOOD in line with my sister, indecisive over what I was going to order for lunch.

It'd been nearly three days since I had gotten back from Brideshead. Three days, and a hundred unsent, deleted texts I couldn't find the courage to send.

I'd done everything I could, focusing on work, watching movies, I'd even started *running* on the outdoor trail with some of the other tenants from my building.

Nothing would erase Grayson Sanderson from my mind.

Which was probably why I leapt at the chance to grab something to eat with my sister.

Even if only for an hour or two, I could focus on something that wasn't my royal fuckup of the century.

The first man to come along since my ex, and I'd completely ruined everything because of...

Well, because I couldn't fathom how anyone would want me, when I wasn't good enough for him.

I'd been so excited when he proposed, all those years ago.

At the idea of forever.

I thought our love was the things dreams were made of.

But I knew then, standing there in the cafe, that it was all me.

I saw what I wanted to see. I saw a young, attractive man who was friendly enough in public, but who always had to "work late" or attend some function I wasn't invited to.

I never saw the signs he was cheating, because I truly believed he loved me.

Because I loved him.

Or rather, I loved the idea of him. A fiancé, a husband. Maybe even a father. And all those dreams fell apart the minute the truth was revealed. He never wanted me. He never really wanted to get married, he told me that night. He was doing it because it was just what was expected when you'd been with someone a while, and I seemed like a nice enough guy.

I'd closed myself off after that, because I didn't want to be someone's number two option. But in doing so, I became so closed off that I didn't even consider the possibility that I could be someone else's number one priority.

Like I said, I have the worst fucking luck.

"What are you getting?" Mia asked.

"Probably the same thing I always get," I said as we moved up in line.

That's when it clicked.

I looked at the menu, remembering the day Grayson and I met up—so I could give him back his wallet, of all things. Because he'd left it at my house.

He'd teased me for keeping my order simple, and then nonchalantly shoved a cinnamon roll at me.

Offering me more than just a dessert.

He was offering me a chance to try something new. A chance to break the same cycle, the same rut I'd been stuck in.

Big changes, start with small ones.

A lost wallet.

A cinnamon roll.

A horseback ride.

A kiss.

I looked at the menu differently after that.

"You know what, I think I'm going to change it up this time," I said. "I'll have the caprese wrap. And a cinnamon roll. With a cafe mocha, please."

Mia shrugged. "I didn't think you liked cinnamon rolls. You always said they were too sweet."

A soft smile tugged at my lips. "People can change you know," I said, feeling the weight of my words, as I thought about all the ways I *had* changed, just in these last few weeks.

With Grayson.

We don't have to do anything you don't want to do, he had said.

Granted, when he said it I knew he meant sexually, but I realized at that moment as I placed my order, that his words went beyond the physical attraction we shared.

This dynamic, bold, commanding man who was a natural born leader was more willing to defer when it came to *me.*

That depends, will you let me lead?

His words reverberated in my brain.

I'd never once considered that I was topping from the bottom, but I realized I was.

I pushed and pulled at Grayson, unsure of my footing, of my feelings. But nothing in life was certain.

Nothing except the moment we had in front of us.

And all that truly mattered was how we spent those moments. I'd spent them worrying, talking myself in circles and telling myself I wasn't enough for Grayson, instead of *allowing* myself the pure joy and happiness I felt when I was with Grayson to rule me and my heart.

"Have you heard from Grayson at all?" Mia asked as she finished her order, walking over to the counter with me.

I shook my head, all the truth converging on me at once. I needed to fix this. I needed to apologize, and I needed to make things right.

Because I didn't want to keep repeating the same thing over and over again. I wanted things to be different.

I deserved the chance to love again. I deserved happily ever after.

"No, I, uh... I think I fucked up, Mia," I said, grabbing my tray.

Mia blinked at me in confusion. "What? What do you mean?"

"I've been a fucking asshole to Grayson..."

Mia's gaze softened as she said, "Ahhhhh."

"Fuck," I cursed.

Mia blinked again. "You don't usually curse," she said as we took our seats.

"I know," I said, taking a sip of my mocha

latte. I'd never had one before, but it tasted pretty good.

New things.

New experiences.

New is not a bad thing.

"I just don't know how I'm going to fix it, but I need to."

"Just call him." She shrugged. "You think too much," she nipped.

"What if... what if I call him and he wants nothing to do with me? What if I blew it?" I asked, biting my lip.

Mia popped a tater tot in her mouth. "What if you haven't? What if your prince charming is waiting for you to come to your senses?" she said with a grin. A shit-eating grin.

"You know something I don't, Mia?" I asked, narrowing my gaze at her.

Mia puckered her lips, her grin mischievous. "Only thing I know is Grayson leaves work in about an hour. He should be home by five o'clock."

"And how do you know that?" I asked, a plan already forming in my brain.

"That's not important," she said, plopping another tater tot in her mouth as I slid my phone out of my pocket.

My fingers hovered over the letters of my keyboard nervously. I pushed the nerves down though, knowing they'd always be there. Until maybe, one day they wouldn't be.

New things, Henry.

New things equal new results.

Are you free tonight to meet up for some coffee?

I sent the text, letting out a deep breath as I did so. I expected to wait a while, after all it had been days since I heard from him.

But he messaged me back almost instantly.

Absolutely.

CHAPTER 40

Henry

I waited patiently with my coffee, watching the door. When Grayson appeared, panic spread instantly. But I shoved it down for the moment, focusing on the tall, hot as hell man in front of me, dressed in a nice suit.

I preferred the dressed down version of Grayson, but he looked like a damn wet dream in a suit.

My cock voiced our opinion rather loudly and I crossed my legs.

"You rang," Grayson said as he sat down, folding his hands in his lap.

"Do you want to get a coffee first?" I asked, nodding to the counter. There was no line.

"Are you offering to buy me a coffee, Henry?" he teased.

"I am," I said nonchalantly.

"Well, in that case, I shall keep it simple," he said as he rose from his seat, and I followed him to the counter.

"I'll have a flat white, please," he drawled, his tone smooth like the cream that would no doubt grace the top of his latte.

"I tried something new today," I said, breaking the ice as they handed him his coffee.

"Really?" Grayson asked, sipping his drink.

"I thought about something you said." I shrugged, leading us back to the table.

Grayson sat gracefully, crossing his legs and I sat beside him. He cast me a wary glance, but he did not move.

"What did I say?"

"Do you remember when we first came here? I came to give you your wallet back—"

"Ah, yes. How could I forget the beginning of our... friendship," he said cautiously, but I could see the spark in his eyes. The longing.

Maybe we could be more.

I want to be more.

"You teased me, about my *simple* order. Then you bought me a cinnamon roll."

"Yes, well, dessert is the best part of a meal."

"Change is hard for me, Gray."

I didn't miss the way his entire body relaxed, the way his shoulders fell, his eyes watered at the mention of his nickname.

The next words out of my mouth were the hardest, but I knew if I didn't say them, I'd regret it.

"But I know change is a lot easier with you."

Grayson let out a breath, taking another sip of his coffee.

"I don't like cinnamon rolls, though," I said, clearing my throat.

Grayson smiled wickedly. "Then we will simply find you a suitable replacement."

I focused my gaze on him, fully aware we weren't talking about dessert anymore. Which should have scared me but... it didn't.

Because I trusted Grayson.

I trusted him with my whole heart.

"Well, I mean... there is one dessert, I really like," I said, feeling a blush creep on my cheeks.

"What is that?" Grayson said, his fingers stroking the sides of his cup in slow motion. He shifted his legs, fidgeting in his seat as he cleared his throat.

At the risk of sounding like an absolute idiot, the words fell out of my mouth. "A good cup of coffee," I said as I raised my cup.

Grayson raised his in repose. "You deserve the best coffee there is, Henry."

"I already have the best coffee there is."

CHAPTER 41

THE CAR WAS silent and heavy with tension as Grayson turned it off.

It was now or never.

Six little words.

Six words that would bring about a change I knew there would be no going back from.

"Do you want to come in?" I asked, my words loud in the space between us.

Grayson looked at me skeptically, biting his lip. "Do you want me to?" he asked, his gaze full of hope.

Full of love.

I nodded. "Yes. I do."

Grayson opened the door without saying a

word, and I did the same. He walked me to my apartment, which felt like an eternity. We stood on my front step, and I fumbled with my keys, my nerves getting the best of me.

"Hey," he said, holding his hand over mine. "Nothing has to happen..."

I opened the door, his fingers sliding around my wrist as I turned the key. I gazed up at him, and I'd never been so sure of anything as I was in that moment that I loved him.

That as long as I had him, I could make it through anything. Even the hard, uncomfortable moments.

"I love you," I said, the words heavy in the air.

I opened the door, the both of us looking into the darkness.

Into the realm of uncertainty.

"I love you, and I want you to stay. I want you to stay with *me*. I know I won't always say the right thing, or do the right thing, and I'm not some polished, perfect—"

Grayson pulled me close, capturing my lips with his and we stumbled in the door. I kicked it closed as I fought to wrestle my arms around his neck, pulling him closer against me, needing his kiss, his tongue, his touch.

All of it.

I needed *him*.

"Oh, Henry," he whispered my name like it was a prayer, his lips and tongue caressing mine with so much passion, I felt like I would catch fire and spontaneously combust.

"I love you too," he whispered. "I've wanted to hear you say that for so long," he murmured, his hands traveling down my shirt, resting on the waistband of my jeans.

I could feel his hardness against my own, and the euphoria of his words shattered the last bit of my armor.

"But I didn't want to scare you away..."

I felt lighter, better, having said them. The truth couldn't hurt me anymore.

It could only make way for something better. Something brighter.

Because when Grayson said those words, *I love you, Henry,* I felt it.

I felt the truth, the weight of them, and in his eyes I could see he truly meant it.

He loved me.

Despite everything that had transpired, everything we'd done, everything I'd said...

This man loved me.

"You're mine," he whispered.

"Promise?" I asked, my fingers sliding up beneath his shirt.

Grayson picked me up, my body reacting instinctively to his hold as I wrapped my legs around his waist. His hands cradled my ass as he carried me to the couch, all but throwing me down on it.

I leaned back, taking in the sight of him, his vivid erection practically punching through his pants, dark hair falling in his eyes, lips swollen from kissing me. He grabbed himself, licking his lips and my cock twitched with anticipation.

"Promise," he said, his voice dark and gravelly, removing his pants.

I quickly hurried to free my own cock, my gaze trained on him as he slowly undid each button on his shirt until he was standing before me.

God, he was sexy as fuck.

And he was *mine*.

The notion, the reality as this man looked down at me, lazily stroking his cock as he watched me, was overwhelming.

After removing the remnants of my clothes, I lay there, waiting.

Grayson sauntered closer, his gaze never leaving mine.

Wordlessly, I dropped to my knees, my cock throbbing with need. I sucked Grayson into my mouth, wasting no time licking and nibbling, and laving my tongue all along his shaft.

Mine, mine, mine.

Grayson sunk his fingers in my hair and pulled me up by it. It hurt, but I liked it.

It felt cathartic almost.

The pain, the pleasure.

He kissed me, his tongue running rampant in my mouth as he thrust his cock against me. I could feel the warmth of his precum spreading along my shaft, and I shuddered with desire.

"No," he said, shaking his head, his hot breath on my neck like fire. "Let me please you, baby. Let me show you how much I fucking love you," he whispered huskily against my neck.

"O... okay," I said, his words registering.

His hand wrapped around my cock, pulsing, squeezing as he pushed me back against the couch, dropping to *his* knees. He opened my legs with a force that I swear could have popped my hip out of its joint. Grayson licked the inside of my thigh, tracing lines up to my shaft.

"You're going to do exactly as I tell you, do you understand?" he asked, the command in his voice evident.

The anxiety in me ebbed. Giving up control was not easy for me, but with Grayson... I knew I could.

He would make it all okay. He would fix the broken parts of me. I wanted him to lead.

I nodded. "Yes," I said.

Grayson smirked. "Good boy," he said, and

he swallowed my cock, deep-throating me in one swift move.

"Fuck!" I said, feeling my balls tighten, my orgasm already starting to form.

Grayson let up, removing his mouth from my cock, appraising me with a heated gaze as my angry cock throbbed with need. I tried to catch my breath. "Turn over," he said, his gaze darkening.

"What…"

"I said, turn over. Show me that pretty little ass of yours," he growled. "I want to taste you." His tone was all business, but there was a playfulness to it as well.

The faintest twist of his lips gave him away. "Unless… you don't want me to…"

I turned over faster than you could flip a pancake.

I absolutely wanted to, and my cock was in mutual agreement. I wanted things to be different this time.

I needed Grayson to understand how much I trusted him.

Grayson spread my cheeks almost instantly, and the onslaught of his tongue along my tight pucker, warm and wet, made me curse again. I braced myself against the couch, my legs tightening as he relentlessly licked me until I felt the faintest pressure.

I squeezed my cheeks, my thighs stiffening.

"You okay, baby?" he asked, his lustful voice tinged with concern.

I closed my eyes, arching myself back on his finger, taking a little more.

"Yes," I said, catching my breath. My leaking cock brushed against the cushions, the friction maddening.

I was so consumed with desire I didn't know if I needed to fuck my hand or be fucked. Maybe both.

"You like that?" Grayson cooed, sliding another finger in, stretching me, slowly, taking his time, letting me adjust.

I nodded as I let my forehead fall against the cushions. "Yes," I said.

I had the faintest feeling of déjà vu as my voice reverberated in my brain.

"You like that, Grayson?" I said as I slid my hand along his thigh, his legs forcing me closer, edging my cock against his entrance.

"Yes," he said, his words hazy and dark.

I gripped the back of the couch as memory spilled forth.

"Fuck," I said. I felt like the wind had been knocked out of me.

Grayson removed his fingers, his tongue probing me once more, and I cried out as another memory pushed forth.

"You're so tight," I growled, my cock pulsing as I bottomed out. I'd never heard myself like this.

I didn't know I was capable of such things...

Grayson gripped my hair, his legs locked around me like a vice, thrusting his cock against my abdomen as he cried out, bathing me in his hot release.

The emptiness I felt as I waited for him was maddening.

"Henry," Grayson's voice brought me back to the moment, and I could hear the wistfulness in it.

I turned to look over my shoulder, our gaze meeting, and I knew.

He remembered too.

"Please," I begged. I was so hard, it hurt.

"Grayson, please..." I forced the words out, the world spinning all around me.

Grayson pulled me back against his chest until he was fully inside me. The onslaught of pressure, of pain, was only temporary as he wrapped his arms around me, his right hand finding my cock, gently squeezing.

My eyes fell closed in ecstasy as he slowly dragged himself out, the pressure maddening as I waited for the fall.

"That's it," he purred, rocking back into me in a slow, torturous fashion.

"Yes," I said, leaning my head back against his shoulder. His thumb teased my wet slit as he snapped his hips against my cheeks, picking up the pace.

"Come for me, baby."

His words pushed me over the edge. I came hard and fast, with Grayson's name on my tongue.

Warmth spread within me as his erratic thrusts stilled, as he gripped my chin and turned my face to meet his lips, swallowing my ecstatic cries with his kiss. His mouth moved against mine with grace, with a sweetness I wanted to taste over and over again.

My favorite dessert.

"Mine," I murmured against his sweet, torturous mouth.

"Mine," he whispered in repose, his lips curling into a smile as he held me, my entire body and soul coming undone in his arms.

And only when Grayson let me go, did I realize I was finally whole again.

EPILOGUE

Grayson

I looked at Henry from the passenger seat of his brand new, fully repaired Toyota. While I preferred to see him behind the wheel of my Porsche, I also knew that if we were going to do this—have a relationship—I needed to let Henry drive the car sometimes. Figuratively, and physically.

"You sure about this?" I asked

Henry's shoulders loosened and he pursed his lips. He nodded. "Yes." His answer was solid, confident.

Ever since the other night—the night Henry finally opened up and let me in—it was like he was a different person.

Not as tense, not as scared.

I reached out to take his hand, squeezing it with support. "Okay then, let's go have ourselves a gay old time, baby," I teased.

Henry let go of my hand, opening the door, and I did the same.

It didn't take long to find Giselle, who was in the center of the room occupying three high top tables. The party was there, plus Drew and the florist.

"Hey guys, I'm so glad you could make it," Giselle said, giving us both warm hugs.

Henry hugged her back genuinely. "Hey."

"Aaron's angling for a rematch," Mia said as she hugged her brother.

"A rematch?" I asked, looking between them.

Henry let go of her, rolling his eyes. "It's nothing, just—"

"Henry scored the winning point that other night when we faced off in the billiards," Giselle shrugged. "I told him I'd love to see him whoop your ass in a game, and then when Aaron heard you both were coming..."

"What do you say, Gray? You up for a challenge?" Aaron cracked a smile over his beer.

I shot my boyfriend—God, I still felt my damn heart race every time I called him that—a dirty look.

"You think you can beat me?" I asked, licking my lips. I hoped Henry would take my bait.

And he did. Like the good boy he was.

He brattily flipped his dark hair out of his eyes, shrugging. "I know I can," he said.

Oh, it's on, baby.

"I will hold you to that," I said, as Aaron fist pumped the air.

"Yes! Gray's on my team!" he hollered.

"Then Henry's on mine, " Riley rebutted.

"I hate to break it to you, guys, but it looks like the table's taken," Julie pointed to the corner.

I could see a group of three men hanging out, not playing, but taking up the space nonetheless. Riley crossed his arms.

"Well, we'll just have to ask them nicely to move." Aaron shrugged, chugging the remains of his beer. "Or we'll have to challenge them. Winner takes the table."

"I'm down with that," Henry said, interjecting.

The smile that formed on my face was impossible to hide. I slid my arm around Henry's shoulders, pulling him close, my lips at his ear.

"Winner takes the loser in the backseat of

your car," I whispered, knowing it would throw him off.

Henry cast me a sly look. "I'm going to make you swallow that promise," he whispered back, grinning wickedly.

"I'm counting on it, baby," I said as he slid his arm around my waist, and we walked toward the billiards knowing we'd already won the game.

Because as far as I was concerned, there was no greater victory than happily ever after.

Thank you for reading Grayson and Henry's story.

If you enjoyed this book, please return to your favorite retailer and leave a review. Even a few words could mean the world to an author.

Continue the series with Riley's story, Book 5 in Jasper Springs!

RILEY

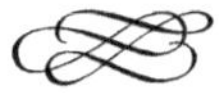

AN MM AGE GAP ROMANCE

RILEY
AN MM AGE GAP ROMANCE
JASPER SPRINGS
BOOK FIVE

COPYRIGHT © 2024
EVIE RILEY
SECOND EDITION
ISBN: 978-1-77357-722-7
PUBLISHED BY NAUGHTY NIGHTS PRESS LLC
COVER ART BY WILLSIN ROWE

RILEY

Secrets.
High expectations.
A truth revealed.

Riley Evans is counting down the days to his brother's wedding. If only he could find a date for the big day.

When a chance meeting during karaoke night finds Riley's plus one up for wager, Riley finds himself the winner in more ways than one.

Too bad his love game isn't as strong as his pool game.

A self-made OnlyFans man, Eric Olsen has built his entire life being the man everyone desires. Being Riley's date to the hottest wedding in Jasper Springs should be an easy win, but Eric soon finds himself desiring the sweet-as-pie art teacher.

If only he could come clean about his life and his feelings.

Will Riley break free from the chains of expectation? Or will Eric embrace his truth at the expense of losing the man he wants most?

Readers seeking an age gap romance with a little hint of D/s set in a cozy little town may find this story fills the bill. While Riley and Eric may have cameos in future stories, each book in this series can be read as a standalone.

CHAPTER 1

Eric

I CHECKED my watch for the second time in five minutes. The cafe was bustling at this hour and I couldn't help but wonder if he was here, some-where, looking for me.

Though, to be fair, I looked a lot different with my clothes on.

Maybe I should start bringing pictures of my dick to these meet-ups so people can identify me better.

I sighed, taking a sip of my coffee as I watched folks hustle in and out of the cafe. A couple of nonchalant stares and whispers from some women told me they either thought I was cute or they recognized me from my work.

Despite my audience being made up of

mostly men, I knew there were plenty of women out there who were into my performances, if only by the sheer amount of "I want to choke on this dick" and "fill me up Daddy" comments I received on my Daily Cum Shot threads from cock thirsty women subscribers.

I bounced my leg with anticipation, checking my watch again.

My blind date was now fifteen minutes late.

Or he wasn't coming at all.

I would bet it was the latter.

I wasn't ashamed of what I did for a living by any means. Though I'd learned to at least keep the "Hi, I'm Eric, you might know me from Only Fans as *XxPrinceAyricxX*" to myself until they at least showed up.

I could swipe right on anyone when it came to hooking up, but I wasn't looking for someone to just placate my sexual desires. If I wanted that, I could have anyone I wanted.

Call me crazy, but I wanted *more*. Sex might have been my job, and I wasn't lacking when it came to dick. What I was lacking though, was substance. I wanted someone to *love* me, and I'm not talking about the me that half a million people watched daily. I wanted someone who I could play video games and watch stupid gay movies with, but also someone who wouldn't bat an eye at eating sushi off my dick.

What can I say, I have priorities.

You'd think as a man who interacts with thirsty subscribers for a living, I would be more than fulfilled. But the truth was, every day I turned off my webcam, spent from my performance, and I felt empty as shit.

And the deafening silence of my townhome was not helping my mental health when everything screamed, "You are alone!"

Just once, I wanted to see someone else loafing on my couch, someone else raiding my fridge.

Someone else using my shampoo and shower gel.

I wanted to walk down the street with someone respectable, some modern-day prince charming with a cup of coffee, I wanted to wake up next to a man who wasn't going to leave after breakfast and never come back.

I drained the last bit of my coffee as my notifications went off on my phone one after the other.

No doubt the masses were all commenting their praise and dirty thoughts, as I'd only just posted my latest video an hour ago, right before I left for this blind date my friend, Julie, *insisted* I go on.

I found it easier to try and get to know a guy if I unloaded a round first. I wasn't one of those guys who could go multiple rounds when I was performing, despite my stamina training. Maybe when I was in college I could pull that off, but now, I needed a break in between, partially because it took a lot of focus and concentration —as well as training—to be able to perform at the level my subscribers required, and to get a good, full shot for the camera.

Which is why I only posted once a week now instead of the two or three times a week I posted when I started my OF.

I got up, headed to the trash to pitch my coffee as a text came in among the strings of OF notifications.

Buried beneath the "I want that all over me," and the "need someone to suck that?" comments, Julie's bright purple icon blinked at me.

I'm waiting...

I huffed a sigh as I texted her back.

Yeah, me too. Your mark never showed.

I casually strolled to my black Benz—the first big purchase I'd made after I switched from amateur camming to the big leagues and opened my OF. I'd worked my ass off—well, my cock off too—to have the things I did. My townhome, my car, my top of the line sneaker collection.

But once men heard *how* I'd made a living

for myself—despite the fact my job actually consisted of more than just coming on camera every day—their damn balls disappeared and suddenly I became a damn leper, and most of them just never called me again.

Julie typed away.

What? Are you sure?

I rolled my eyes as the car unlocked, picking up on the signal from the keys in my pocket.

I arrived ten minutes early so I could get my coffee, and just left. I waited for a half hour, Jules. No one approached me.

I'd even worn my "nice" blazer, the purple velvet one that made me look sophisticated, yet stylish.

It was easy to pick out a bright purple jacket amidst the muted tones of Jasper Springs's average population, which was why I'd chosen it.

I started the car, feeling defeated.

You didn't tell him about the OF, did you?

I hoped Julie had remembered to keep her mouth shut. Lord knew, when she got to talking sometimes, shit just slipped out.

Of course I didn't. You asked me not to. She responded, quickly adding, *I told him you work in social media.*

That was the understatement of the year.

My shoulders fell as anxiety crept in.

It was a small town, what were the odds they looked me up?

That maybe they already knew?

Slim, probably, but not zero.

I was careful to keep my public profile separate from my OF, but if someone really wanted to dig around, I'm sure they could find out what my *self-owned business* was.

Oh well. Another one bites the dust, I guess.

Guess I'm just chopped liver then. I texted back.

I'm sorry, Eric. Maybe something happened, do you want me to reach out and ask?

I considered her words as I pulled out of the parking lot.

The last thing I wanted was to appear desperate, even to Julie. If some asshole couldn't be bothered to show up, why should I beg for his attention?

But a part of me wanted to believe that maybe there was a good reason. Maybe something came up at work, or maybe they had to rescue a fucking cat from a tree or some shit. Anything.

But I was already over the situation, and I wanted to move on. I wanted to forget about being overlooked yet again, because I didn't want to go down the road of self-loathing.

What I wanted to do was to get a drink and

maybe find some hot piece of ass to take home and numb the pain of rejection for a little while.

Just for the night, anyway, since apparently that's all I was capable of landing.

No, it's fine. Don't worry about it, Jules. Thanks anyway.

I tossed the phone on the passenger seat, not even bothering to check her response as I sped toward M's Place.

CHAPTER 2

RILEY

I HATED FRIDAYS. For starters, every Friday was school spirit day, and no matter what the season, there was always a pep rally or a game, and catching up on the end of the week reports and tests while trying to balance curriculum planning for the following week was exhausting.

But today, I felt worse than normal because I'd fucked up entirely and forgot about the blind date ‚Julie—my brother's fiancée's bridesmaid and a long-time friend of mine— had tried to set me up on.

To be fair, I'd fully intended on showing up, but when my principal showed up five minutes before I was ready to head out with a stack of paperwork for me regarding my annual school art trip to DC in a few months, I knew I was done for.

My job always came first because my job, my students were my life.

Because I had no life of my own, not really. Sure, I hung out with my brother and his friends, my coworkers sometimes, but I wasn't anyone's first choice.

Because all my friends are either married or engaged.

I'd never had time for romance, and now, here I was an eternally single art teacher in his late thirties who couldn't even tell his boss *no* when I had a fucking date.

But I wasn't fast enough, because my blind date—who was supposed to be wearing a purple blazer—was nowhere to be found in the other-wise dead cafe, when I'd arrived. I needed a drink, and in this town there really was only one watering hole to go to that was openly queer friendly and actually had decent drinks.

M's Place was packed, as always. Normally, I despised crowds in tiny spaces, and M's Place was definitely a small space. Maxine somehow managed to squeeze a postage stamp size stage in between the bar and an alcove that was some hodge-podge mashup of pool, arcade games, and one of those weird antique Love Magnet Meter games from the fifties in between the thirty high top tables and ten booths, while making the place open and friendly and not claustrophobic. Which was a damn miracle.

It was probably fate that I'd run into my brother and his wedding party at the bar. Though knowing Giselle, she was fixing to make this a weekly shindig.

I sipped my beer as Julie nudged me.

"What happened with your blind date earlier?" she asked.

I sighed, running a hand through my hair. "I got held up at work, actually. Principal Weatherly dropped off a shit ton of papers regarding the trip and—"

"Shit, you missed it?" she asked, biting her lip.

"I mean, I went, but... he was gone. Can't say I blame him, you know. I was like, forty minutes late."

Julie pursed her lips. I shrugged in defeat.

Just as I opened my mouth, I saw Grayson— my future in-law—and his new boyfriend, Henry—Giselle's friend and bridesmaid Mia's brother—strolling into the bar arm in arm like they owned the damn place.

We'd all spent last weekend together in the mountains, but both Grayson and Henry didn't seem too keen on socializing with me. Well, I guess technically, looking back on the weekend, it made sense now, but at the time it felt like I just wasn't cool enough to join their little club.

To be honest, I'd always been like that. An outsider. My brother was always the popular one, and I was just the social outcast who preferred history books to keggers in the woods.

That's why I'd brought Cadence, my TA, with me to the weekend trip.

My brother, Aaron, and I got along just fine as long as the topic was sports related, or involved some sort of competition. Which wasn't hard when I worked for our alma mater, Jasper Springs High. Our football team, the Jasper Springs Otters had gone undefeated last year.

But I needed more than just someone to casually grunt and chime in.

Not to mention Aaron was the star quarterback when we were in high school, which was what?

Damn near twenty years ago now?

I smiled as Grayson and Henry arrived at our table and everyone made introductions. Julie excused herself to go to the ladies room, Giselle and Mia hot on her heels.

Henry's grin was enviable, and Grayson's natural air exuded a confidence that was also quite admirable.

I was genuinely happy they seemed to be happy, just like everyone else in Giselle and

Aaron's party, but I still felt a sting of jealousy being the only single guy in the party.

"Where's Cadence?" Aaron asked, pulling me from my thoughts.

"Probably having a better night than me," I said, wanting to avoid the question I knew was coming.

"She your plus one?"

"No," I said flatly, then taking a long drink.

"Why not? She seems nice. Not to mention she's got a killer rack," Aaron teased, nudging me. "Mom and Dad would love her..." he said with a laugh.

I rolled my eyes. He wasn't wrong, but he also knew pussy didn't do it for me.

My family always assumed I'd settle down, especially being in the line of work I was. Of course, I wanted to settle down too, but I didn't have the heart to tell my parents it wasn't with a woman. My brother understood the fact that I was as gay as a hot pink toaster, and he always told me I was being dramatic. That it wouldn't matter who I was with, that they wouldn't care as long as I was happy. But that was easy for someone like my brother to say. He was getting married to the daughter of one of the most well known families in Jasper Springs. Giselle was practically Miss Americana.

Aaron was more than supportive though.

Hell, he even tried to hook me up with a gay or bi friend once or twice. But those guys, they didn't want relationships. They wanted to fuck around, and while that had been fun in my college years, as a thirty-eight year old high school art teacher, I needed something more than just a guy with good deep-throating skills.

Who am I kidding?

Hell, I probably need that too, since my sex life is about as dry as the Sahara these days.

"Mom and Dad would love any woman I brought to the wedding, even if she was a lesbian."

Aaron laughed, shaking his head. "True. You have a point. But at this rate, you're going to have to hire a date for the wedding," he said with a laugh.

I rolled my eyes again. "You sound like my coworkers," I grumbled.

While my parents had not yet given up on the dream I'd meet the right woman, my coworkers were practically sending me singles profiles for men within a thirty mile radius or trying to set me up on blind dates every chance they got.

Just earlier in the school day I'd gotten into a debate with my classroom neighbor, Chris, about literally *hiring* an escort like my life was a

LGBTQ version of the Wedding Date or something.

"I'm just saying, the deadline fast approaches... and no one wants to be alone at a wedding," he said.

"I'm not *alone*. I'm the best man."

"You don't technically have a partner."

"And even if I did find a date in time for your wedding, it's not like they'll be up there with me," I reminded him. "For God's sake, I'm a glorified ring bearer."

My brother sighed, obviously deciding this conversation was a lost cause, switching gears, instead challenging Grayson and Henry to a pool match.

I sighed, my shoulders sinking. Perhaps I just needed a distraction. Something to take my mind off my impending singleness. Something to relieve some stress.

So I agreed to play with the boys, if only for a little while. It was a school night, after all.

"You guys wanna play?" Aaron asked the group of guys who were *sitting* all over the pool tables lazily enjoying their beers.

They were a small group of three, two of them some twenty-somethings who looked more 'bro' than man, with their hats on backward, their perfectly trim beards, and their flannels too tight fitting.

"Sure," the one in the front said, setting down his beer. The only one without a hat who looked older than twenty-one, brushed his hand through his dark hair, pushing up off the table with ease. While his friends sported the same buffalo plaid flannel, their unphased sexy leader sported a black fitted tee shirt that showed off his rather toned arms. His striking blue eyes glittered underneath the low light of the bar, and I couldn't help but think he was *hot.*

The kind of hot you dream about because you know you'll never have a chance of landing someone *that* sexy.

"Eric, you're on my team," bro number one nipped at Mr. Blue Eyes.

"Name's Aaron, this here is my brother, Riley, and that's my future brother in law, Grayson, and his boyfriend, Henry."

Mr. Blue Eyes smirked, grabbing his beer.

"Pleasure to meet you, boys," he said with a grin. "I'm Eric, these here assholes are my associates, Jordan and Sticky."

I furrowed my eyebrows. "What kind of a name is Sticky?" I asked in disgust. The man known as *Sticky* came forward, laughing darkly.

"My name is actually *Stanley, handsome,* but my subs call me Sticky," he said with a gaze that was more predatory than anything I'd ever seen. It made me uncomfortable.

"Yeah, cause you don't know how to keep your fucking hands to yourself," Eric snapped, and Sticky scoffed.

"You ain't never complained," Sticky retorted.

Eric passed me a pool cue and some chalk. "Don't mind him, he was dropped on his head as a small child. It's the brain damage," he said.

I took the polished stick from his hands, my fingers grazing his. "Noted," I said, relishing in the warmth, the smoothness of his touch.

"You suckers ready to lose?" Jordan taunted.

Eric smiled wickedly.

"How about we make this a little more interesting?" my brother said, as Jordan, Sticky, and Eric took their places.

"How so?" Jordan asked, nodding at us.

"Loser buys the winner a round of drinks," Aaron suggested.

Grayson squared his shoulders as he set the balls.

Eric smirked, his gaze roving over me.

"Famous last words, boys. Let's play."

CHAPTER 3

Eric

One game turned into two games, and because I'm a man of my word, I bought the new guys a round of drinks.

I had to admit, Aaron, Grayson, Henry, and Riley were all pretty good opponents, and it was nice to have a challenge for once.

Riley shifted his weight as he turned to me for a moment.

"So..." he started, and a part of me felt bad for the guy.

I could tell he wanted to talk, probably even flirt a little, but his Sunday School get up of a green polo and khakis and messy bronze hair was surprisingly not as much of a turnoff as it should have been.

Maybe I'm just all messed up because of earlier. Maybe I just need to fuck myself right again.

"If you ask me about the weather or sports, I will throw this beer in your face," I taunted him.

Riley blinked, his mouth agape. "Well, what would you advise I ask you about, Eric?" he said, crossing his arms, the pool stick held between his toned arms, making me think of other things. "Got any pointers on losing?" he taunted.

What are you like, five, dude?

I scoffed at his juvenile insult, though I couldn't deny it stirred a need to show this man exactly how to take a loss.

On his knees with my cock stuffed down his throat.

I shifted, if only to try and dispel the rowdy serpent in my pants.

"How about you ask what you really want, Riley?" I said, batting my lashes at him, my tongue sarcastic as hell.

Where did that come from?

Riley scoffed, shaking his head. "Forget it," he said.

It was Jordan's turn in our second game, when the girls arrived.

"Hey you..." I said when I realized Julie came with the group.

Julie's mouth fell open in surprise, as she glanced between Riley and I, our backs against the wall, separated by none other than an old-timey love machine game.

Seriously, who played those things anymore?

I thought they wiped them all off the face of the earth.

"Well, fancy meeting you here, Eric," Julie said, pulling my attention away from the tall, blushing man beside me.

I leaned in to hug her, catching a whiff of her perfume and nearly choking on it.

She pulled away with a grin. "I thought you'd be home nursing your wounds," she teased.

"You two know each other?" Riley asked, fidgeting with his stick again, running his hands up and down the length in repeated motion.

Instinctively, my body and brain jumped to sexy thoughts about what his stick actually looked like, and what a show it would be to watch him.

Sprawled out all over my bed, hand wrapped around his cock.

Riley was tall. I'd probably peg him at six two, but he carried himself with stature. My mama always said God let things grow until they were perfect, and at a nice old five foot nine, I supposed Sky Daddy knew to quit while he was ahead.

I might have been on the shorter side compared to most, but my cock made up what I lacked in height easily.

Still, I knew big dudes came with big sticks, and I was a size queen.

Plus, I was still peeved after I'd been stood up by my blind date.

"Eric, you're up," Jordan said, drowning his beer as he flashed his gaze at Julie.

"Why, hello..."

"Leave her alone, Jordy. She's taken," I said, flashing a wink.

Julie laughed as I lined up my shot, retorting some burn at Jordan that made the rest of the guys holler and Jordan curse.

Setting my gaze on my prize, I couldn't help but notice Riley in my field of vision. Or more accurately, Riley holding his stick in front of him, front and center to his dick, distracting me for the moment.

My own cock twitched as I licked my lips, trying to focus on the balls in front of me instead of the ones out of reach.

I'd been swiping right on matches for the last two years. On top of the fact I regularly shared my most intimate moments with half a million subscribers, I had a keen sense of gaydar.

In a nutshell, I knew when someone wanted to fuck me. At this point, it was like a sixth sense or something.

And the way Riley kept staring at me, it was more than obvious. Not to mention his conversation skills.

I would have bet the farm that he hadn't had a good lay in while.

Something about that realization made me feel both guilty and intrigued.

My phone buzzed in my pants pocket, no doubt my comments going off still. They'd be going off all night.

Until I posted my next video, to appease my thirsty masses.

I took my shot, watching as the balls dispersed, clacking against each other as they came together. The eight ball slowly rolled, knocking another ball into the corner pocket, causing me to curse.

"Damn it!" I said, pressing my lips together. I'd been too distracted by khaki-covered groins and the ever present buzzing of my phone against my ass to make a proper shot.

I totally missed.

"Nice try," Riley said tauntingly as he pushed off the wall, smirking at me. "Maybe you should aim for the ball you want to hit."

The sight of his lips turning up in the

corner, the way he cockily squared his shoulders as he sauntered to where I stood was a damn rush. Heat enveloped me as he nudged me aside with his hip.

How fucking dare he!

"Now, let me school you in how it's really done," he teased, positioning himself to take his shot.

I ran a hand through my sweaty hair. If he made this shot, that would be twice we'd lost. And I certainly didn't want to lose. Anger flooded me as well as a fresh current of desire, because his words only made me want to put him in his place.

Bent over the fucking pool table.

I hate losing.

I took a pull of my beer as Julie settled beside me, crossing her arms. Sticky settled on the other side of me, and we watched long-limbed Riley angle himself, bending over the table. His arms were long, toned and trim and drew attention to his fingers. I watched as he curled his hand around the base of his stick, which was not helping the current erection in my pants or my competitive fantasy about teaching him how to fucking aim for the bullseye.

I shifted my weight as I focused on my drink.

"See something you like?" Julie teased.

"I'm not sure yet," I said honestly.

Sticky nudged me. "What's there to consider? The guy's been staring at you all night."

"Yeah, well, staring is creepy," I nipped at Sticky. I wasn't sure why I felt so on the spot, so vulnerable. Maybe it had to do with the beers I was pounding back. I'd lost track after the third...

Sticky and Jordan were the closest things I had to brothers. I'd met them at an adult entertainers expo a while back, shocked to hell and back that they were both Jasper Springs natives like me.

In this town of bake sales and cookie-cutter families, it was nice to have people who weren't judgmental of what I did for living.

Because they were doing the same thing. Having friends who understood the ins and outs of the business, the work that actually went into being the object of so many people's desires, made my job feel a lot less lonely.

Except Sticky and Jordan were more than just friends. They were a package deal. They both were on the platform too, producing similar content to mine, except they did it together.

More like they did each other.

For the fans, of course, despite the fact neither of them were gay.

Sticky was... well, Sticky. I didn't think he had a preference for anyone as long as they had a hole and were willing to put up with his stupidity. We'd fucked around a few times over the years, but I always felt like shit afterward, which is why we'd stopped.

Jordan was as straight as Riley's pool stick. Or at least, he *insisted* he was. My guess was he was probably bi and he just hadn't come to terms with it yet.

They were both also eternal bachelors, like me.

Who happened to live together, and who happened to fuck once in a while...

Christ, even Sticky has someone to share shit with, even if he's just a fucking coworker who's not as straight as he thinks.

"Hey, Riley," Julie called.

Riley turned to look at us briefly. "Yeah?"

"Wanna sweeten the deal?" she asked.

Aaron, Grayson, and Henry turned to face us, Jordan looking up from his beer.

Oh no, this can't be good. I know that look..."

"How so?" Jordan asked skeptically.

Julie shrugged as she set her gaze on Riley.

"Uh..." Riley raised an eyebrow.

Julie smirked, turning to Jordan. "Well, you

see Aaron over there is getting married... and Riley here needs a plus one...”

Aaron laughed, fist bumping the air. “Yes! I’m so in!”

“What?” Riley’s face paled. “Jules... No...”

“If Riley scores this shot, *Eric* will have to accompany him,” she said, practically grinning from ear to ear.

Well, isn’t that interesting.

Julie cast me a wicked gin.

“And if we win...” Jordan grinned in return. “Loser has to pose for the Jasper Springs Hotties Calendar.” Jordan grinned. “Which I happen to, uh... do some work for.”.

He was the calendar’s number one model, next to that local firefighter who thought he was the next Brad Pitt. Dawson something or other...

“We’ll do it!” Aaron and Sticky called out in unison.

Fuck.

I wasn’t opposed to being someone’s plus one, and I’d be lying if I said I’d never been auctioned off before—that was for a charity event Jordan had gotten roped into—but the idea of accompanying Cinderella to the ball made my insides heat like an inferno.

Yeah, it’s probably the beer.

Riley shook his head, dispelling the hoots and barks, leaning closer, sliding his pool stick in between his fingers. Back and forth, back and...

"Fuck!" I said as I was literally smacked in the groin by the end of Riley's stick, my hardness now ebbing with pain as my balls stung.

Immediately, I covered my aching junk, knocking over the remainder of my beer and spilling it all over Julie.

"Oh my God!" Julie cried as Aaron and Co. screamed, "We won!" over and over.

"Fucking ay!" I howled, sucking in a breath as Riley turned, his eyes wide in terror.

"I'm so sorry, Eric. I—"

"Fuck you," I snarled as I attempted to breathe.

Julie laughed as she shook off the spill.

"I think that's enough for one night," Aaron said with a grin. "It's been fun guys, but I think our work here is done," he said.

"Aw, fuck..." Jordan said, grabbing his coat.

"What?" Sticky asked.

"We've got an hour left until—"

Neither of them had to say anything, since I knew what time they usually posted. While I was a once a day guy, my friends posted multiple times in a day.

Sticky pulled the keys from his pocket, sliding his hand around Jordan's waist, nodding to me.

"You good, bro?" he asked.

Finally able to breathe, I nodded. "Peachy," I bit out as the crowd started to disperse.

"Do you, uh... need a ride?" Riley asked cautiously.

"That depends, Riley Rabbit," I huffed. "As long as you don't have any stray sticks laying around to whack me with—"

"I'm so sorry, the stick just... slipped."

I flashed my gaze up at him, conflicted by both the steamy thoughts and the reality at hand.

Yeah, I bet it slipped.

Cheater.

"Looks like you have a date for the wedding, after all," Julie said with a wink.

Riley blushed, like a damn Sunday School teacher as he ran his hand through his hair.

Fuck, she was right.

Now I had to honor my word.

I grumbled as I flipped her off, and she just laughed, leaving Riley and I in her dust.

"I'm so sorry, Eric, I— Let me make it up to you," he said as I grabbed my purple blazer from the back of my chair.

"Fine," I said, tossing it over my shoulder. "Let's get out of here."

CHAPTER 4

My heart was racing as we walked to the car.

For starters, Eric was hot. The guy was most certainly above my grade level when it came to the dating pool. Plus, judging by his bold fashion sense and his flawless skin, I'd garner he was in his late twenties, which meant he was at least a good ten years my junior.

While he'd agreed to the terms of winning and losing—being my *date*—he didn't seem all that into it.

Or me.

And then on top of everything, I damn smacked the man in the balls—by accident, I swear—and now was trying to make up for my eternal fuck ups by at least giving him a ride home.

Maybe I'm just not cut out for dating in 2024.

I sighed in defeat, hoping that perhaps we could put this bullshit behind us, and maybe I could just tell him not to worry about the wedding.

I'd come up with some line or excuse for Aaron, and we could both just forget this whole thing ever happened.

I opened the passenger door to my blue sedan before he could do so himself.

I am, if anything, a gentleman, plus I did feel bad about hitting him in the balls earlier.

Eric's blue eyes sparkled in the parking lot light, surprised by the gesture.

"Thanks," he said, visibly swallowing.

"It's the least I can do," I said, waiting for him to take a seat before closing the door.

"Right," he said.

Within seconds, I was in the driver's seat, turning the car on without thinking.

The audiobook I'd had queued up prior to arrival blared through the speakers, which wouldn't have been a bad thing if it wasn't a damn *sex scene.*

Oh my God!

I tried to turn the app off on my phone, but it wouldn't budge.

"Shit!" I said as I fumbled for the right button to turn it off through the car speakers.

I took him into the back of my throat in one fell swoop until I couldn't breathe, his deep groan only making my own cock throb even more as he grabbed me by the back of my hair... "You take this cock so good, baby... just like Daddy likes it."

"I'm so sorry about this," I said, as I bashed my fingers against the display, trying to stop the most embarrassing moment of my life.

Yeah, there's no way this guy would go anywhere with me now.

Probably thinks I'm an absolute perv.

Fuck. My. Life.

Eric smirked devilishly as I finally managed to get the damn button to work and stop the dirty words from tumbling through my speakers. I looked at him, legs crossed with his velvet jacket in his lap, his head in his hands, thumb pressed to his mouth. He looked... amused.

"You seem to be doing a lot of apologizing tonight, Riley," he said, his voice dark and gravelly. "Your grievances are stacking up."

I couldn't help but turn scarlet at his tone, his words. "I know, I just..."

"Didn't think you were the audio porn type," he said with a raised eyebrow as I tapped my maps on the display.

"I'm not, it's not... it's not porn, it's literature," I defended.

Eric laughed. "Funny, historians say the same thing about the Marquis De Sade," Eric shrugged.

"Your address," I said bluntly, trying to steer the conversation away from where it was headed. Eric looked piqued, his grin deliciously provocative and his gaze intrigued. But I wasn't about to let a poignantly voiced sex scene carry us all the way home.

For starters, as I sat with my foot poised above the gas, I was acutely aware of all the blood rushing to my swollen cock, and the sight of Eric in my car, looking like sex on a stick combined with the lusty tones of my latest M/M smutty read, would be enough to crucify me forever.

I'd never live this night down in my own mind if I came in my pants like a damn teenager.

I was thirty-eight years old, for God's sake. Surely I could keep my dick in line for what, thirty minutes?

Eric shifted in his seat, his eyes dark with mischief. "You didn't say please," he touted.

I let out a choked laugh, swallowing my pride and my embarrassment as I implored him with my gaze.

"Please, Eric," I said softly, my pulse racing.

"Well, since you asked so nicely, and you are so keen on making up to me," he said as he leaned forward, tapping against the letters on the display, never looking at me once.

"But you should know for future reference, the correct answer is, 'Yes, *Daddy*.'."

My cock *throbbed* at his tone, his words, my mortification heating my body like a boiling pot.

Wait a minute... Was he... was he flirting with me?

"F... future reference?'" I asked as he hit the green 'go' button, a sly grin on his face.

I threw the car into drive as he sat back languidly.

"Well, I am a man of my word, Riley, and the deal was I will accompany you to your little firehall wedding."

I scoffed at the idea of anyone calling Giselle's taste mediocre, or insinuating her wedding at the damn Paradise would be anything but black tie, or little in any manner. But then again, Eric had no idea Aaron was engaged to the Blake Lively of Jasper Springs, and how could he? He'd gone to the bathroom when Giselle kissed Aaron goodbye, heading home with Mia.

Not to mention, I didn't even know if Eric was a Jasper Springs resident, since I'd never seen him before, and as a teacher in this town, I knew almost *everyone.*

"You don't... you don't really *have to,* you know," I said with a sigh.

Though the idea of showing up with Eric on my arm *anywhere* made my entire body stiffen.

He was absolutely gorgeous, and I had a feeling he'd look impeccable in a nice suit, with a tie...

Images pushed forth in my mind of him standing above me, cufflinks shimmering in the light as he gazed down at me, running his hand over his...

No!

Don't go down that road!

Not now!

I glanced at the address on the maps app, if only to bring myself back to the here and now, surprised to notice it was indeed within Jasper Springs. In fact, it was part of Jasper Springs Estates, which I knew was the higher priced condos that housed some of Jasper Springs's upper crust.

I was pretty damn sure CEO Weston Rhodes and that town celeb, Drew Axel, just moved there, if I'm not mistaken.

The place had been a hot commodity lately.

"Will there be cake?" Eric asked, with a slight laugh.

"I mean, what wedding doesn't have a cake?" I retorted.

"Will there be alcohol?" he continued.

"I mean, probably top of the line considering it's Giselle..."

"Will you be all cleaned up and pretty in a nice fucking suit?" he asked, and I felt flushed, nervous.

All cleaned up and pretty...

Did he think... wait...

"Yes..." I squeaked.

"Well then, sounds like it'll be quite a night, don't you think?"

I laughed nervously. "I, uh... guess so?"

I passed the sign that read *Jasper Springs Estates*, lit up by the small spotlights. In the darkness, it looked almost ominous.

I cruised down the road, looking for his address number, focusing on anything but him.

"There," he pointed to a sleek, gray condominium. The spotlights in the yard cast shadows on it, illuminating it vividly.

The car rolled to a stop, and I turned it off, opening my door as Eric moved to open his.

When I came around to his side, he was just shutting the door. He fell back against the car for a moment, his gaze flashing up at me.

"What the fuck are you doing?" he asked, but his voice wasn't angry. It was curious. He didn't move. Instead, he just looked at me in question.

"Walking you to your door, obviously," I said, shaking my head.

"You don't have to do that," Eric said, shifting his weight, holding his jacket in front of him like a barrier.

I leaned against the car, biting my lip as I looked back at him. There was something about him that called to my inner gentleman. His apprehension at my polite conversation, at my opening of the car door.

I wondered about the partners in his life who hadn't shown him such etiquette.

That was another reason I despised trying to date in this day and age. Most men were the epitome of *I can do it myself.* I'd been told as much before, which made me feel quite ancient, despite the fact I wasn't even forty yet.

"I know, but…" I swallowed nervously as I offered him my arm. "Humor me?"

He looked at my arm like I'd grown three heads, and for a moment I didn't think he'd take it. But when his hand grasped my arm, just the slightest, I couldn't help but grin as I pulled him away from the car, slowly guiding us up his sidewalk, the air crisp against my skin.

It wasn't a long walk by any means, and we

were on his porch within seconds. Eric dropped his hand, sliding it into his pockets for his keys.

I stood politely, waiting to watch him enter the door before I bounded back to my car, but he stood there for a moment in silence before he spoke.

"When's the last time you had fun, Riley?" he said, furrowing his eyebrows, forcing me to look at him in question.

"I beg your pardon?" I asked, confused by his question. It wasn't what I had expected.

"And I don't mean the kind of fun that ends with you home before midnight," he said, clearing his throat. "I'm talking about real honest to God, *fun.*" His voice came out dark and inviting, sending a chill snaking down my spine.

I wondered momentarily if his definition of fun differed from mine, almost sure that it did.

I paused, considering his question. I'd gone on the trip to Brideshead recently, but it wasn't what I'd call fun. I'd enjoyed myself, sure, as anyone in the beautiful expanse of nature with copious amounts of alcohol would. But I wasn't into drinking like the rest of my party mates, nor was I into watching everyone drunkenly make out.

I thought about the trips I took with my TA and my students every year. Last year we'd gone to Italy, and while I most certainly enjoyed myself, it was still awkward, at times. Mostly because I was the only single adult gay man on vacay, and engaging in any sort of romantic liaisons—or one night stands—was out of the question. My focus was on keeping my kids safe.

And sharing a room with my bestie slash coworker while also responsible for one hundred teenagers in a foreign country is not something I would call *fun* either. Not to mention, most of my free time during the year, and even in the summer, was devoted to volunteering for school events, programs, and curriculum.

I twisted my hands together, feeling the sweat overtake me. I wiped them on my pants, if only because the sudden heat as Eric stared at me was making me feel on display. I closed my eyes, and I sighed.

I could have told him anything, but instead I settled on the truth.

"It's been a while, I guess," I said.

Eric shifted.

"A while, huh?" he asked as he nodded at me, moving closer.

I looked down at the sliver of space between us. A part of me wanted to move closer, meet him halfway. To reach out and run my hands through his hair, and let myself have a little bit of *fun*.

To tease, to touch.

But I barely knew Eric, and I certainly didn't want to come off as one of those assholes who just took things without asking.

Eric clicked his tongue for a moment, before speaking. From this angle, I could feel the heat of his breath on my neck, the scent of whiskey and beer prevalent from his drinks earlier.

"Give me your phone," he commanded.

Every bone in my body, including the unruly one throbbing against my briefs stood at attention.

Because it wasn't what he said, it was *how* he said it.

With authority, with demand. It was the sexiest tone I'd ever heard a man use, and it made me want to drop to my knees on his fucking porch.

Maybe the smutty audiobooks were warping my brain.

Wordlessly, I drew my phone from my pocket, handing it to him. My hands were sweaty as he pulled it from me, his fingers grazing over my knuckles, sending fresh jolts of electricity racing through my veins.

I watched the light fall on his face, my heart in my throat. He tapped away furiously before handing me back my phone with a stoic gaze. I had a good amount of height on him, and I couldn't deny that the way he looked *up* at me, his tongue darting out to lick his lips, his bright blue eyes sparkling with mischief, made me feel as if I could melt into a puddle on his porch.

"Well, if we're going to do this, we should probably have a little fun with it. So, next time you want to stay out past your bedtime, Cinderella, give me a call," he said as he turned around, inserted his keys in the lock, and then left me standing there, hard and wanting in a state of blissful confusion as I stared at his number on my phone. Conveniently written in as *Eric Olsen* with a legit eggplant emoji.

What was the eggplant supposed to symbolize again?

CHAPTER 5

RILEY

"You definitely need to call him," Chris said, swiveling in my chair with his venti cold brew clutched in his fist. The scent of bitter coffee filled the room.

I stared at my phone on my desk in front of him, my arms crossed. "Yeah, but... what do I say?" I asked, my eyebrows furrowing.

Chris rolled his eyes. "You are hopeless, Riley, you know that right?" he said, bouncing his foot against his knee.

Glancing at the clock, I noted we had about fifteen minutes left for our lunch period. Fifteen minutes before a slew of seniors would traipse into my studio and destroy everything.

I swear high school kids are messier than the kindergartners.

"Tell me something I don't know," I huffed.

"Just ask him out for coffee or something. Surely you are capable of that, and if not, well, I can't help you there."

I nibbled at my fingernail, considering his words. Surely I could *text* a man to meet for coffee. It wasn't like I was asking him to marry me or something.

So why was I so fucking nervous?

"Yeah, coffee sounds good," I said, swallowing nervously.

Chris smirked at me. "You got a little crush, don't you?" he said with a laugh.

"I mean, yeah, I guess. He's attractive and..." I could feel myself heat as the memory of his dark voice, his bright blue eyes, pushed forth. "He's young," I settled on that word, whispering it into existence.

Chris's eyebrows furrowed. "How young?"

"Well, old enough to drink, for starters, but probably too young to know what a payphone is."

Chris laughed, shaking his head. "And he's got his own place in Jasper Springs Estates?" Chris whistled. "What is the guy a drug lord or something?"

It was my turn to roll my eyes. "God, I hope not," I said with a laugh.

"Maybe he's a high class escort," he said, wiggling his eyebrows.

"Or a mafia kingpin," I suggested with a laugh.

Chris shrugged. "Or a CEO of a Fortune 500 company who secretly owns a publishing company and a helicopter."

"He's not Christian Gray, Chris."

"You don't know that," he said as the bell rang. "All right, well, this has been fun but duty calls," he said as he pushed himself out of my chair.

The sounds of chattering teens filled the hallways, and I sighed, grabbing my phone and sliding it in my pocket.

"Keep me posted, Evans!" he said as he hit the doorframe with his palm on the way out.

"Yeah, yeah," I said with a wave, as students started to pour in.

CHAPTER 6

Eric

"Fifteen minutes to show time," I say to myself as I set my timer.

I hadn't slept the best the night before, and felt like I'd been dragging ass all day because of it.

But I guess Cinderella wasn't the only one who turned into a pumpkin after midnight.

I set about to setting my scene, making sure everything in my bedroom was clean. No photos on the nightstands, the covers freshly made and the pillows set just right.

I even made sure the floor was clear of any and all dust, and then I went about setting the lights by using an app on my phone. I didn't film in my room often, but like I said, I was dragging ass.

Plus my AC unit in the studio was on the fritz again, which meant until I got a replacement part installed, I'd be filming in my room since it had good lighting, and of course, a bed.

I crawled onto my bed, leaning back against the pillows for a moment, in nothing but my black boxer briefs. A quick glance at my phone told me I had ten minutes till I went live. Which was just enough time for me to get comfortable.

I closed my eyes, letting my mind wander in my daily prep ritual as I slid my hand over my soft cock, pulling and tugging as I controlled my breath.

I had a myriad of fantasies that usually did the trick, and I tried to keep my prep fantasies on a rotating basis.

Today, it was a tall, sexy man in glasses, wearing khakis and a button down, staring down at me, telling me the only way to pass his class was if I did some extra credit.

I'd had this fantasy since college, when I developed a crush on my Art History teacher.

He was straight though, so that extra credit would have landed me in the Dean's office, no doubt.

But a man *could* dream, right?"

I rubbed my chub through my briefs as the fantasy took hold. My viewers liked to be teased before the big reveal, and I noticed if I showed up with a visible tent first, prolonged the reveal a little, I got more likes and comments, which pushed the algorithm more.

Plus, I knew all my good angles.

I imagined Professor Hot Ass smacking his hand with a pointer stick, telling me if I didn't *beg* on my knees, he was going to strike me.

And then the strangest thing happened; Professor Hot Ass shifted in appearance.

In his place was Riley, the man who'd beat me at pool and nearly put an end to my money-maker last night.

Who apparently had a thing for kinky audio-books and needed a date to the school dance.

I mean... wedding.

But he did have that khaki wearing, studio professor vibe to him that I was totally into.

And he was kind of cute, if I was being honest. All flustered over the dirty words, all sincere and walking me to my door and shit.

His dark eyes filled my psyche, causing my cock to twitch, just as the alarm went off.

I let go of myself, opening my eyes as I glanced around the room, almost as if I expected to find him there, watching.

I shook off the weird thoughts as I watched

my computer load, waiting for the green light. Soon enough, I was live.

I waited momentarily for at least a few people to jump on before I addressed them.

I lowered my voice, rising to my knees as I made a show of lifting my cock, which was still quite hard and wanting.

Hearts bloomed across the screen as I leaned my head back, running my hand along my clothed shaft.

I carded my right hand through my hair as I used my left to continue stroking my cock. Turning to the side, I hunched over just enough to give a good side profile, enough to show the length and curve of my trapped cock, giving a good thrust to tease and titillate the viewers.

The tips came in quickly and I flashed them all a megawatt smile.

"I know what you guys really want," I said as someone commented, "Yes, Daddy, give it to me."

My mind decided that was the time to replay the smutty audio I'd heard in Riley's car, his blush filling his cheeks as he tried to shut it down.

You take this cock so good, baby... just like Daddy likes it.

My own cock throbbed at the word replay in my brain, and I had to suck in a breath.

"Take it off!" another commenter said as several more tips came in.

I sat back on my heels, sliding my underwear down just enough that my cock sprang free. I slid my hand back around my shaft, feeling its thickness and veins. I was *aching*.

And I was already sticky with precum.

What the hell?

I had masturbation down to a science. It was my job, after all. Usually, I opened up with a nice tease in my pants, let the cock bob free, maybe smack it around a bit before I started to go to town.

I didn't want to waste a minute though, being as my subscribers were paying for entertainment and not my own existential crisis.

So, I pushed through.

I spit directly onto my cock, covering my shaft in saliva and gathering the precum from the head, slathering it down my hardness. I closed my eyes and my head fell back as I built my rhythm, the *ding ding* of comments and tips like a melodic overture of chimes.

"You take this cock so good, baby," I groaned, a fresh sheen of sweat blanketing my skin as I fucked my slick hand.

I let my free hand wander, pinching my nipples, sliding it down to my navel.

Chime, chime, chime.

The sound of success.

Images flashed in my mind of Riley on my porch, looking at me with big old puppy dog eyes.

I let my mind wander further, imagining him falling to his knees on my porch, those big, beautiful eyes wide with lust as I pulled out my thick cock.

"Just like Daddy likes it," I groaned, my voice all gravelly and dark.

Chime, chime, chime. Ding, ding, ding.

My cock swelled, throbbing with need as the sounds of my wet palm slapping against my dick echoed in the air. I fell forward on my knees, my underwear sliding down a bit to reveal half of my ass. I glanced up at my screen, making eye contact with my subs as I rocked my hips forward, slowly pushing myself through my hand.

Riley looked up at me, mouth open and eyes wide as he waited for me to...

"Fuck!" I growled as I fell back on my heels, my cock spurting in the air like a damn geyser.

The sounds of chimes and dings on the computer echoed, one after another.

I blinked through the heat, my muscles contracting as I continued to pump my shaft. My hand was covered in my release, as was my bed, my abs...

Good lord, I couldn't remember the last time I came this hard and this much.

I let go of my cock, my gaze falling on the screen as I saw the comments.

All begging for my cum, my cock, and to be my good girl or good boy.

"Until next time, baby," I breathed, reaching forward to turn off the live recording manually like I always did.

When I was alone, I let out a deep breath, falling back onto my bed, my mind racing. I wiped my hand on the towel from my night-stand, trying to catch my breath.

I wasn't sure what happened. I hooked up with guys all the time, and I *never* once fantasized about them *during* a session. Or after we fucked in general. Most of them were mediocre at best.

Riley and I didn't even do anything!

My phone buzzed, and I moved to grab it, if only to put the ringer on silent, when I saw a notification that had nothing to do with my thirsty subs.

Would you like to have some fun tonight? Maybe grab some coffee?

The number was unknown, but I didn't have to be a private investigator to know who it was from.

Considering the emoji he'd sent was an eight ball.

Little shit.

I texted him back immediately with a pumpkin emoji.

You sure you won't turn into a pumpkin, Cinderella?

His response was instant.

Only if by pumpkin you mean pumpkin spice latte. Which in that case... yes.

A grin fell over my face.

What time? I asked.

Does 6 o'clock sound good? I work until 5.

I nodded, biting my bottom lip.

Sure. 6 sounds great.

When he texted me back with a thumbs up, I couldn't help but panic.

While I was excited to see the object of my fantastical performance, I was also terrified. Like most people, it seemed Riley had a regular 9-5 gig, and me...

A date to a wedding didn't mean we were getting hitched.

I didn't *have* to tell him what I did for a living right?

I looked at my closet, acutely aware that this impression was everything. I wanted him to like me.

I wanted him to *want* to take me to the wedding of his own accord.

Ugh, he must have wacked me harder in the

nuts than I thought. I can't remember ever mooning like this over... well, anyone.

Whatever, you're just having an off day, that's all.

At least, that was what I told myself as I shut down my bedroom studio, and headed to the bathroom for a shower.

CHAPTER 7

RILEY

I COULDN'T REMEMBER the last time I felt so nervous about just meeting someone for something as simple as coffee.

Though to be fair, Eric was right. If we were going to go to this wedding together, we should probably at least get to know one another a bit so it wouldn't be awkward. I'd given him the option to back out, but to my surprise he didn't.

Still, I felt like I was an awkward teenager all over again, waiting to meet my research partner at the library.

While secretly harboring a crush on said partner.

Which was insane. I barely even *knew* Eric.

"Hey," his voice pulled me from my spiraling thoughts, and I turned to see him standing in front of me.

His dark hair fell in his sparkling blue eyes, perfectly pouty lips on display. He was just wearing a tight-fitting pair of jeans and a pumpkin-colored ringed baseball tee, but he looked like he'd literally stepped out of a magazine.

Yeah, I'm definitely out of my fucking league here.

"Hey," I said, rising from my chair, clearing my throat.

"Thanks for coming on such short notice." I moved toward the counter, Eric following me.

"Uh... yeah, of course," He said, his smooth voice like cinnamon butter on a fresh bagel.

"I'll have a large coffee. Black, please," I said to the cashier, nodding at Eric. "What do you want?" I asked.

Eric looked around as if I could be talking to anyone else. "I, uh..."

"It's the least I can do to make up for yesterday," I said, my cheeks heating at the very memory of everything that went down yesterday.

The game, the audiobook... the fact I wanted to *kiss* him on his front porch.

I didn't go around kissing hot strangers. For God's sake, I didn't go around kissing anyone, if I was being honest.

So, the fact that Eric seemed to draw me in, the fact he made me want to do things I didn't usually do…

Yeah, I guess I had developed a crush.

Fuck me.

Eric smirked. "Well, if you insist, I'll have a large mocha latte with extra whip cream and sauce."

I watched as the cashier rang us up, handing the cups off to the barista as I paid.

By the time I was done, Eric had already grabbed our drinks and was waiting for me, looking just as hot as the damn beverages.

"I thought about what you said last night," I said as we took our seats.

Eric sat across from me, crossing his legs. The motion drew my attention to the definition of his form, the slender curve from thigh to knee, how his ankles tapered out into a larger foot.

I bet he would make a fantastic model to draw.

"You're going to have to be a little more specific, Cinderella. I said a lot of things," he teased, taking a sip of his drink. When he pulled back, I could see the faint hint of whip cream on his lip, and before I could say anything, his tongue darted out and swiped at it.

I wished I could say I wasn't so easy, but the truth of the matter was, I was as easy as pie.

The sight of him, licking any sort of frosted goodness off of those pouty lips was... sexy.

It made me think about him licking other... things...

I crossed my legs immediately as the image flitted through my mind, my cock twitching in agreement. I cleared my throat, burying myself in my own drink.

Pure, bitter, black coffee fixed everything. Especially unruly erections and existential crises.

"About having fun," I said, straightening my stature. I looked at him, his relaxed state, and I wished I could be like that.

Cool and sexy.

Instead, I was awkward at best where flirting was involved, and my life revolved around my job. Eric's suggestion that we actually hang out was intriguing to me not just because I wanted to get to know him, but also because I truly wanted to do something that was different. I didn't want to be a pumpkin anymore.

I wanted to be Cinderella at the ball, where she meets the prince of her dreams.

"Ah, I see. So, you thought you'd call me up and see what kind of trouble we could make together, is that it?" he said, flashing a grin, and

I got the feeling trouble to him was much more than staying out late on a school night.

"I mean, unless you have other plans," I said, biting my bottom lip.

I watched as Eric drank from his cup again, spreading more of that delicious white cream all over his perfect lips.

Now is not the time, Riley!

Eric let out a laugh, the sound just as smooth as hot fudge on a sundae.

"Tell me, Riley, what do you *wish* you could do? What do you like? And I swear to all that is holy, if you say *I don't know*, or *it's up to you*, you will eat those words." His tone was as aloof as it was dark, and I realized as his tongue darted out once more, sliding over his lips, that he was not just being cheeky. He was legit flirting with me.

Which made me even more self conscious.

"I, uh…" I cleared my throat again, trying to find the words. The truth was, I didn't know what I wanted to do.

Jasper Springs was a small town and there wasn't much to do there in general, and being as I didn't really spend my weekends traveling or visiting the city, I wasn't entirely sure what there was to do.

Or what normal folks did for fun.

My idea of fun involved getting messy with my canvas while I tuned out to my Spotify.

To just let go and... feel.

"Well, normally, I *like* to stay in and paint, but..."

"Painting, huh? Didn't peg you for an artist."

I knew I should have been offended by his comment, after all, artists didn't have a *look*. Everyone was an artist, the mediums just differed. Some were more literal, like me and paint with traditional tools, while others painted digitally in Photoshop, or with words when they wrote. Some painted with flour and butter and sweet frosting, and others painted with cotton swabs and microscopes and proteins.

Everyone was an artist, because we all created something.

But something about his words felt less accusatory.

"I am. I teach art, actually."

I watched Eric's eyes widen, as if he was genuinely surprised, a flush of scarlet grazing his perfect complexion.

"I, uh... that's... wow. Can't say I was expecting that, although I guess that explains some things."

Before I could ask what the hell he meant, Eric shook his head, that same charming air returning once more.

"Okay, so I'm thinking maybe something a little less... introspective."

"Like what?" I asked, leaning my hand on my chin as I watched him intently.

"Well, seeing as you owe me a rematch, I was thinking maybe we could play some games..." He said the words smoothly, the corners of his lips turning up in a smirk.

"I would think you would be too wounded to be beaten again," I teased him, realizing the moment I'd said the words, I hadn't thought twice about them.

Being around Eric seemed to be bad for my control.

It was like I just couldn't help myself.

Eric's gaze darkened. "You got Lucky, Riley. That's it. Pure and simple. But I wasn't thinking pool..." he said, flipping his hair out of his eyes.

"Oh yeah, then what kind of game did you want to play with me, Eric?"

Eric grinned. "How about I pick you up tomorrow night at eight o'clock, and you can find out."

Tomorrow night. Eight o'clock. My insides tightened and I panicked, since eight pm was usually when I started winding down to get ready for bed, but I also knew that was what I wanted.

I wanted to change things, and change started with adding a little more... *fun* to my life.

But if I was being honest, I would have

agreed to anything Eric proposed, even if it was a trip to Antarctica in the middle of January.

I bet he would look spectacular in a big puffy coat.

"Sounds good. I'll, uh, text you my address. Since I have your number and all," I said, blinking away the strange feeling that had settled over me, the nerves building in my stomach that screamed, "You're going to ruin this!"

I only hoped they weren't right.

CHAPTER 8

Be there in 5.

I stared at Eric's text, feeling the beginnings of sweat already to starting to form.

I'd gone through the entire day feeling nervous as all hell, and Chris's taunting didn't help. I knew he was just trying to ease my nerves, but I wasn't sure anything could take the edge off.

Nothing except probably a glass of wine, and I didn't think it was polite or good etiquette to drink *before* a date.

It's not a date.

It's just... hanging out.

With a really hot guy who you have a crush on and who's your plus one to a wedding.

As I delved further into a spiral of dread, my doorbell rang.

I took a deep breath, trying to calm my panic as I straightened my shoulders, heading toward the door. When I opened it, I had to focus on breathing.

For starters, Eric looked *divine.* Like sex on a freaking stick wearing a graphic tee that had some cartoon characters on it I had no idea who they were. But it was the ripped jeans, frayed at the knees, that *hugged* the man's thighs like a cradle and his shiny, perfectly spotless white tennis shoes that made him look like a polished magazine ad.

Mixed with his messy dark hair and bright blue eyes, and perfect jaw, I had to practically pick my mouth up off the floor.

It was a stark contrast to my dress pants and button down.

"Hi," he said, his voice like caramel, making my insides turn to molten lava again.

"Hey..." I said as I took in the sight of him from head to toe.

"You ready for a night out on the town, Professor?" Eric said with a darkness that made my blood rush. Eric looked around me, at the inside of my house, and a part of me wanted to abandon this façade altogether, grab him by the collar and pull him in here and lock the door.

Mine, mine, mine.

The realization, the feeling, was over-whelming and foreign. I couldn't ever remember feeling this way about anyone, let alone this soon.

I nodded, shaking away the odd thoughts and feelings, instead focusing on the next right thing.

Just like Ana in Frozen, when I played it during class last winter.

"Yes," I said as I grabbed my keys, stepping outside. I locked the door quickly, following Eric down my steps toward his... BMW?

Shit, maybe he really is a kingpin.

That's okay, he can kidnap me any day.

Eric stepped up to the car, unlocking it with the remote, and I had to admit I was impressed. I didn't have keyless entry.

Eric casually strolled past me to open my door, and it was then I noticed the shiny watch on his wrist, glinting off the sheen of the car, which was also pristine.

"Age before beauty," he snickered, his lips turning up in the corner to reveal a perfect, white canine. I practically sunk into the seat because if I didn't, I'd have melted into a damn puddle on the ground.

"Thanks," I said as he rounded to the driver's side and climbed in.

When he'd started the car, I'd finally gotten my bearings and spoke up.

"So, uh, how old are you anyway?" I asked, trying not to sound like a complete perv, but also because I needed to know for my own sanity.

Plus Chris told me I needed to ask *real* questions because those led to conversations. He didn't understand my conversation skills were sorely lacking when it came to being in the same room with Mr. Perfect.

"Twenty-eight, why?"

"No shit," I said, realizing the moment I said it I sounded like a complete asshole.

Eric put the car in drive and pulled out of the driveway. "What?" he asked.

"You just... I would have thought you were a lot younger than that," I said, quickly recovering with, "Not that that's a bad thing. I mean, looking young is great, like really great, but, uh—"

Eric shook his head, a smile overtaking his lips. "Age isn't nothing but a number, Riley. Especially when it comes to... certain things." He cleared his throat. "Which you should know, being as you're..."

I could tell by the tone of his voice he wasn't

offended. He was intrigued, and playing with me.

Which made me feel slightly more at ease, even if it was only a little.

"Thirty-eight," I squeaked.

Eric nodded in approval. "You look good for your age too, just so we're both on the same page," he said, letting out a dark chuckle. "But let's get something straight here, Riley Rabbit," he said, flashing me a smirk that made me warm all over. "Just because you're *older* doesn't make you wiser. And it certainly doesn't mean you're the one in charge," he said, taking his eyes off the road for a moment to cast a dirty look at me that brought my damn cock back to life.

No, no, no...

Not now!

"You understand?" he said, his voice dropping an octave, and I couldn't help the way I instantly responded, my voice full of desperation and need.

"Yes," I breathed.

Eric smirked, exposing that one perfect canine again, his shoulders squared, full of confidence.

"Yes, *Daddy*," he purred, and my entire being felt alive with electricity.

I don't know why I said the words.

It was like some spell, some invasion of the body snatchers bullshit.

My voice vomited the words of their own volition.

"Yes, Daddy," I said, with perfect dictation, my voice steady and strong.

"Good boy," Eric said as he turned back to the road, turning on the radio.

I internally chastised myself, my cock twitching at the thick tension in the BMW.

Fuck.

It's going to be a long night.

CHAPTER 9

Eric

I DIDN'T KNOW what came over me, but the need to press Riley's buttons was driving me crazy.

That little *'yes, Daddy,'* was so easy to pull out of him, it was practically like taking candy from a baby.

Not to mention it had me harder than a slab of fucking marble.

The man was damn near *salivating* for some heavy praise, someone to take control and just...

Take it easy, Eric.

You just met the guy.

If you want things to be different, you need to take it slow.

Otherwise, we might blow more than just Professor Good Boy's mind.

I pulled up to the parking lot of Wizard's Arcade & Grille, more than happy to have finally arrived. No sooner had I parked, was I out of the car.

I'd had every intention of opening Riley's door, like a fucking *gentlemen*, if only to show off that I too, could be prince charming.

I mean, my handle is Prince *Ayric*.

The slamming of the passenger door alerted me, and I nearly jumped, realizing he'd beaten me to it.

"An arcade?" he asked, almost as if he didn't believe it.

"Yeah... I mean, I did say we were going to be playing games," I said, noting the awe in his eyes.

I watched as Riley slid his hands into his pockets, turning toward me with a soft expression.

"I mean, I haven't been to an arcade since I was like, ten. I didn't even know these places still existed."

I nodded for him to follow me, feeling a bit pumped up at the moment that I'd chosen this place.

I had entertained the idea of taking him out to one of the many clubs in the city, but I wasn't sure how Mr. Perfect would react to shots and thumping bass for our first date, especially if he'd been on a strict curfew for awhile.

Not to mention, this isn't a date.

But even though I knew that, I couldn't help but let my fantasy build.

Maybe I wished it was.

God, I am so fucking off kilter today.

Well, technically ever since yesterday.

"Come on then, Cinderella. The ball awaits."

Inside Wizard's, the place was split into two sides. One side was lined with aqua leather booths and purple, mauve, and beige retro tables, white and mint green checkered floors giving the place a full on 50's meets 90's vibe. Combined with the sci-fi looking lamps and framed posters everywhere, it reminded me a lot of the mall I used to frequent as a kid.

On the other side of the grille was where all the fun happened. Rows and rows of arcade cabinets, pinball machines, and various dance machines brightly blinked and chirped, and there was even a console room with everything you could imagine if you wanted to have some more intimate one-on-one combat on the blow up neon furniture, or if you had a fantasy about getting caught with more than just your joystick in your hand.

I shook the dirty thoughts from my mind. I really was out of sorts.

I'd discovered this place when I did a photo-shoot with Jordan and Sticky for the Jasper Springs Hotties calendar a few years back. Sticky ended up sick, and so, naturally, he called me in as his replacement, which was fine. It wasn't like I had anything going on anyway.

All that aside though, I'd come to be a bit of a fan of the place, and tried to come as often as I could, just to get away from the bullshit. All the marketing, the promotion, the planning of content on TikTok as well as my OF, the varied side gigs—like calendars and online boutiques among other things—sometimes, it was just nice to leave all of that shit at the door and just play some fucking games and overdose on sugar.

"Wow," Riley said, freezing in his spot, his gaze darting around the room taking it all in.

"You know if you actually want to have fun, you're going to have to move past the entryway," I taunted him, but I couldn't help but feel a warmth in my body at the way his lips curled in happiness, or the way his eyes sparkled like Willy Wonka had just given him the damn golden ticket.

"Right, I'm sorry—"

"Hey," I said, grabbing him by the arm, pulling him toward me. Riley followed my lead without question, and I couldn't deny how nice it was, his implicit trust.

But I stilled my own desires, instead choosing to focus on the task—and the man—at hand.

"Don't apologize," I said, dropping his arm.

Riley's dark eyes gazed down at me as he pursed his lips, nodding.

"I get that this is all a lot probably, but just know as long as you're with me, you don't need to explain shit. Just do what feels natural. Have fucking *fun*, and don't over think shit, okay?"

I wanted to touch him, to grab his hips and settle my hand at his back, dig my fingers into his skin.

But I knew *I* needed to take things slow and easy. I didn't want things to be awkward between us, not this fast.

Because honestly, I *liked* him. Something about his Sunday School-Sweet-As-Pie Professor vibe was really fucking doing it for me, and I didn't just want to play with him like a pristine GI Joe.

I wanted him to like *me*. I wanted him to *want* to take me to the wedding, and maybe I wanted him to think I was more than just some guy he met in a bar who lost a bet. Maybe I wanted to be Cinderella, for once.

I couldn't explain where these strange ideas

or feelings were coming from, so instead of delving into a spiral, I gently pressed my hand to his back, urging him on.

"Well, big boy, it's your party, so pick the first game," I said as I queued up the QR code on my phone.

I'd been a VIP at Wizards for a little over two years and had accumulated way more credits than I'd ever use.

Guess I finally found a good use for them.

Riley walked through the aisles, and I followed, watching as the neon glow lit him up like some lost character from Tron.

Finally, after walking around for what felt like ten minutes, he stopped, pointing toward the center of the arcade room in the round robin.

"That one," he said nodding to the large, three paneled screen of Pac Man.

"Pac Man, really? That's what you're going with?" I asked, surprised he would have gone for the digital version and not the vintage cabinet a few rows over.

"What's—"

I shot him a glance, reminding him there was no apologies here.

"Yes, that *is* my choice," he said, like a petulant teenager.

His tone was so perfectly *bratty*, I had to put

my fist in my damn mouth just to still the twitch in my palm, the overwhelming desire to bend him over the player console and smack the attitude right out of him.

I bet he'd like it too.

"All right then," I said as I scanned my QR code for credit, and he took his stance.

"I'm going to get us some drinks," I said as he used the touch pad to make the little yellow guy chomp his way through the little blinking circles.

I watched the faint muscles in his forearm tighten as he tapped the buttons with precision and quickness.

"Sounds good," he said, flashing a smile as he focused on the screen.

CHAPTER 10

Eric

THIS SEEMS to be a pattern with us.

Riley fist bumped the air as he grinned widely. After two rounds of drinks, and more than enough games of Pac Man, I'd finally settled on my choice of challenge for the night.

Air Hockey.

"I'm starting to think you are just a sore loser," Riley chuckled.

I shot him a glare as I queued up my code for the scan credit.

"I've never been a fan of Pac Man, to tell you the truth. I'm much more of a Galaga guy."

Riley smirked as he took his stance on the

end of the table, the whizzing of the air from the puck spout pulling my attention.

"Are you even old enough to know Galaga?" he taunted, but the words carried a hint of insecurity.

"I'm old enough to kick your ass and make you beg for mercy," I said, slamming the puck down on the plastic field. I took my spot.

"I'd like to see you try," Riley said with a grin.

It was a blur of neon, a symphony of air and crashing goals as we both steadily kept up our defense.

Slam!

The sound of the puck and the loud buzzer sounded as my goal was scored.

"Yes!" I bit out. "I'm coming for you, baby," I said, a grin spreading on my face.

Riley only hunkered down more, his frame like a monster, his gaze hungry to *win*.

"Beginner's luck" he said, licking his lips.

The sight caused my cock to twitch as he slammed the puck down once more, whipping it toward me, directly into my goal.

"Fuck!" I growled, grabbing the puck as Riley *brattily* squared his shoulders, nodding to me cockily.

"You were saying?" he taunted.

I slid the puck back with force as he tried to

block me. But it was no use. This was my favorite game at Wizards, and I'd grown up playing it in my parent's basement.

There was no way I was going to let him beat me at my own game. My goal rang, and I smiled wickedly.

"I said, I am *coming for you*, Riley. Tonight, I will own you."

Riley aimed another shot, and I managed to block him. We were officially tied.

He grunted in annoyance, and I had to admit the change of tone, the undercurrent of *brat* on him was making me damn near salivate.

I whipped the puck back, angling from the side, and it slid in with ease.

Riley cursed, throwing his arms in the air. But we still had two points left until the game would be over.

The next shot from Riley was so fierce, the damn puck flew off the table. I caught it before it hit the ground.

"Nice try," I said, slamming it back down, hitting it with precision as it struck its goal, seamlessly.

"Fucking hell," he breathed, now visibly shaken. One point left, and he was mine.

"Should we sweeten the stakes?" I asked, licking my lips, knowing full well I had this in the bag.

"Really, Eric? *Now* you want to be all cute and cocky?" he said, slamming the puck down, setting his shuttle on top of it. His gaze bore into mine like a fire, imploring me to flinch. But flinch I would not.

"Winner chooses the next date," I said with a smile. A part of me wanted to immediately erase the word, which I hadn't meant to say, but before I could, Riley shot his puck directly into my goal.

Fuck!

I breathed in deep. This was it, the tie breaker. The moment of truth.

His steady gaze held mine, unwavering.

I let out a deep breath as I held his gaze, and took my shot.

Riley stopped it, slamming his shuttle on top of the puck and shucking it back at me from an angle. The puck bounced like a pinball off the sides, and I tried to stop it, its momentum building with each ricochet.

And just as I went to block, the contact and the air pushed it right into my goal.

Fuck!

Fury ignited me, heating my insides once more. I flashed my gaze up at him, to see the shock and awe on his face, watched as it spread into a grin that was somehow childish but also sexy as fuck.

I tossed the shuttle down as I stalked over to him, standing tall against his frame.

Riley smiled down at me smugly, touting the brattiest, "I win," I'd ever heard. He settled his hand on my hip, his lips turning up into a warm, victorious grin.

The feel of his palm against my hip, burning through the fabric of my shirt was damn near electric.

"Fuck you," I breathed, feeling overwhelmed by the sight of this man. Of his warm eyes, of his heated touch, of the way I wanted nothing more than to fall into him like a damn meteorite.

Riley leaned in a fraction, his lips inches away from mine.

"Eric..."

I didn't miss the way his Adam's apple bobbed, or the maddening hardness pressed against me. Instinctively, I slid my hand up his trim, solid chest, over his back. His pulse thrummed beneath my fingertips, and I found it hard to focus on anything except the one thought in my brain.

Kiss him.

CHAPTER 11

I COULDN'T REMEMBER the last time I had so much *fun*. Not only that, but I couldn't remember the last time I won anything on my own. I'd won several games of Pac Man, and defeated Eric at air hockey, which I had to admit was one hell of a game, but as I looked down at Eric, his hand settled on my hip, eyes ablaze, I felt like I was winning at far more than games.

And thanks to the drinks, I felt like for the first time, maybe I had something *fun* of my own to offer.

Eric seemed to bring out a part of me I didn't know existed, and I wanted more of that.

I wanted more of *him*.

Overwhelmed by his sparkling gaze, I knew all it would take, was one swift move and I could have him. He was so close.

My gaze dipped to his perfect mouth, the one that sounded so good talking shit, that was parted just the slightest.

Maybe it was the alcohol. Maybe it was the fact Eric looked hot as hell amid the neon glow of Wizard's.

Or maybe it was that I had lost my marbles completely.

I leaned in just a fraction, but our lips would never touch.

Because mere seconds later, someone was calling my name.

"Mr. Evans?"

Instantly, the spell was broken, and I dropped my hand, moving away from Eric, scanning the room to see who was calling my name, and where they were.

When my gaze finally settled on the culprit, my eyes widened.

Trent Klaypas, one of my students from Senior Painting, waved at me.

A quick glance at my watch told me it was only ten-thirty, which immediately set off my teacher brain.

What was he doing out so late on a school night?

Come to think of it, maybe we should get going.

"Hey..." I said nervously, feeling myself start to sweat.

"What are you doing all the way out here?" he asked, tugging on his backpack.

"I could ask you the same question, young man," I said, with a forced grin.

Trent laughed as he nodded to the bar. "I work in the kitchen. Dishwasher. Just on my way home," he said, looking back and forth between Eric and I.

"Oh, where are my manners?" I said, running a hand through my hair.

"Eric, this is Trent, one of my students. Senior Painting."

I watched as Eric's jaw tensed, his entire body stiffening. He held his hand out, and Trent took it. He appraised Eric like a specimen.

Did they know one another?

"Nice to meet you," Eric said politely, flashing a grin that was rather fake, but charming nonetheless.

"Yeah, *pleasure's* all mine," Trent said with a wink, and I watched as they dropped hands, and Eric shoved his in his pockets.

"Well, anyway, I'm heading out, I just wanted to say *hey*. See you in class tomorrow," he said, flashing a grin, and I waved.

When he was gone, I let out a sigh. "I know it's probably early for you, but—"

"Turning into a pumpkin already?" Eric said, his voice the same, smooth sound that made my insides melt, but something was off. He sounded... sad, almost.

Guilty.

But that was probably my imagination.

What would Eric have to feel guilty about?

"Yeah," I said, running a hand through my hair.

"I mean, it *is* a school night," I said sheepishly.

Eric nodded as he took the lead, and I followed.

The entire way home, he was quiet. The tension in the air was thick, and I was out of my mind wondering if I'd done something, said something.

If it was because we'd almost kissed.

If it was because we *hadn't* kissed.

For a moment, I thought I'd overreacted. Read too much into his attitude. His perfect lips...

"Well, Cinderella, better get you inside before the clock strikes twelve," he said finally as we pulled up to my house.

I nodded, letting out a sigh, the both of us quiet and still for a moment. Eric opened his door. I did the same.

"What are you doing?" I asked as I walked around in front of the BMW.

"Being a gentleman," Eric snapped, his tone slightly annoyed.

"You don't have to—"

"Yeah, well, maybe I want to," he said, his shoulders stiffening. "Maybe I want to be prince charming for once," he muttered.

Something about his words stirred something deep within me. Both a desire to placate and soothe as well as submit.

"Okay..." I said, much more breathlessly than I cared to admit.

Eric walked me to my door, and I fumbled with my keys. I didn't want him to leave, but...

The moment he turned away, to head back to his car, I couldn't help myself. I grabbed him by the arm, stopping him in his tracks. I decided at that moment, that I didn't want him to leave without knowing how I felt.

How he made me feel.

I'd been on a lot of dates in my life, but none had ever felt so... right.

"Eric," I started.

He turned, looking at me with bright blue eyes, full of wonder and dare I say hope?

"Yeah?" he breathed, his voice only shaking the slightest.

"I... I had a really great time tonight," I said, licking my lips. Sweat broke out on my forehead, and I could feel my insides swirling like a hurricane.

Eric swallowed, flashing me a genuine smile that was both endearing and wistful. And I was powerless to fight the feeling. I was powerless to fight the connection between us.

Eric fell into my space, and I fell into him with ease, pulling him close.

I slid my hand in his hair, tilting his face up to mine as I crushed my lips against his.

A part of me half expected him to pull away, but he didn't. Instead, he melted against me like warm butter on toast, groaning with a deep satisfaction that echoed in my mouth, bringing my cock back to life once more.

I gripped the edge of his hair with my fingers as I relaxed, relishing in the warmth of his skin against my palm, of his tongue in my mouth, caressing mine.

Eric kissed me like he was starving. Like he *needed* me as much as I needed him.

When he pulled away, I spoke. "I'd like to see you again. If... if that's okay, and you're free, I mean," I hurried, feeling a monumental weight as I said the words.

"I'd like that," Eric said, licking his pouty lips, which were beautifully swollen still from kissing me. His voice was like fudge, thick and rich. He walked away slowly.

"I mean, I did win the game," I said, smiling wide.

Eric appraised me with his gaze as he stopped halfway to the car.

"Right. Of course," he said, waving at me as he turned around.

I watched from my porch as he got in his sleek car, pulled out, and drove away.

Only once the door was locked, did I let out a breath of relief, a smile curling at the edges of my lips. I fist bumped the air like a total dork, like I too, was a teenager.

A teenager who'd gotten lucky with the hottest guy in school.

My mind was spinning, reeling from our night, our kiss.

One look at the clock on the stove told me it was nearing eleven thirty, and I knew I needed to get to bed soon.

Normally, I'd shower in the morning, but I was also usually in bed by now, so I knew it would be best to shower before bed so I could grab a few extra snoozes in the morning.

I undressed on my way to the bathroom, tossing my clothes in the hamper. Turning on the shower, I let the water run for a moment, waiting for it to warm. My cock throbbed, stiff as a board, and instinctively, I ran my hand along the length. Warm, sticky bits of precum lined my slit, and I let out a frustrated groan, remembering Eric's contented sound, his tongue in my mouth.

I let go of myself as I entered the warm spray, trying to push the images in my mind away. I needed to get cleaned up, needed to get to bed, so I could get up on time.

But the ache in my balls, and the solidness of my throbbing erection were too much, and I knew there was only one way to truly quiet my need.

I slid my wet hand over my shaft slowly, my hips thrusting of their own accord. Bracing myself against the wall with my free hand, I closed my eyes, focusing only on the feel of my hand, the motion. It'd been a long time since I felt *anyone* else's touch, and I'd grown content with that. At least, I thought I had.

But soon my mind filled with the memory of Eric once more, of my fingers in his hair, of his deep, throaty groans, of his warm tongue caressing mine.

Of his hardness pressed against me.

Slowly, I dragged myself out of my warm, wet palm, a deep groan escaping my throat.

I imagined we didn't stop there, on my porch.

I imagined my lips caressed that sweet corner of his mouth, the spot where his smirk sat as he gazed up at me. I imagined sliding my hands over his hips, along the curve of his ass in his sexy jeans, over his hardness.

I thrust myself through my fist once more, this time picking up the pace as I imagined the sounds he'd make beneath me, the way his hands would feel touching me the way I wanted to touch him.

I imagined the warmth of his needy mouth wrapped around my swollen cock, and letting out a frustrated groan.

My hips thrust harder, faster as the image of Eric before me—no, *beneath* me—perfect, pouty lips wrapped around me, sucking, licking...

"Fuck!" I growled as I came, hard.

My stomach muscles tightened as I hazily opened my eyes, watching my cock spray the wall with my release, with an intensity I'd never felt before.

I stroked myself slowly, trying to catch my breath as my release continued to spurt and I emptied myself. The water had gone cold when I'd finally gone soft, and I couldn't deny I felt different.

But it was a good sort of different.

Like everything was changing, and for once, I was looking forward to tomorrow.

CHAPTER 12

E RIC

W HAT THE HELL am I doing?

I tossed my keys on the counter.

Why do I always want things I can't fucking have?

Granted, I knew more than anyone that someone's job didn't define them, but I couldn't deny the panic that laced through me the moment Riley told me he was a fucking *high school* teacher.

No wonder he was the star of my professor fantasy.

College teacher?

Sure, I could handle that. College was a lot more lenient with shit than fucking high school, I knew that first hand.

I hadn't disclosed my occupation, and now I

was more worried than ever that discussing such a topic would more than likely torpedo everything. Cue *Bye Bye Bye* playing in the background and I'd never see Riley again.

I thought for sure I was going to lose my shit when his fucking *student* recognized me.

Which also made me feel guilty as hell.

Was he one of my regular subs or a casual lookie loo?

Was he even legal?

Christ, the night had gone from zero to sixty way too fucking fast.

There were a million questions floundering through my brain, and I needed to not think.

I needed to shower, and get the fuck to sleep and maybe then, in the morning when I was more clear, I'd be able to process how I was going to handle the situation. In the morning I could be the smart, better man.

But right now, all I could do was lick my lips, savoring the taste of Riley for just a moment longer.

Fuck me.

I removed my clothes, feeling all too constrained. My cock throbbed from the memory of his kiss, the taboo-ness of our situation.

I turned the shower on, making it as cold as

I could, if only to stifle the maddening erection I'd sprung.

The thought of *being caught* spiraled into being caught by my *hot professor date*, and cold water wasn't doing anything.

"Fuck!" I barked as I slammed my fist against the tile. I knew I needed to put Riley, and everything around him out of my mind, but the truth was I couldn't stop thinking about him. How much fun we'd had together, how sweet and... hot... it was when he grabbed me and kissed me like some Princess in a fairytale. Telling me he wanted to see me again.

My fleshlight mount rattled from my slamming the tile, and my gaze diverted to the answer.

Typically, I liked to edge myself a bit prior to my daily posts, if only because it made the experience and the filming more accurate, but that didn't mean I didn't pleasure myself off screen from time to time. Though my own self-love sessions had taken a stark backseat to my filmed ones, because it was easier to feel less alone with a thousand people watching me come. When it was just me, my hand, and a sea of subscribers, I could pretend better.

But alone, in my shower, with a cock harder than Thor's hammer, the overwhelming desire to *pretend* was irrefutable.

I slid my hand over my cock, spreading the water along the sensitive thickness of my shaft. The touch alone made my cock twitch, and I squeezed my head, running my thumb through my wet slit. My gaze focused on the mount in front of me, and I supposed I garnered it was a means to an end. It didn't *mean* anything.

Tomorrow, I'd deal with the truth, with destroying everything.

But now??

What would a little fantasy hurt, right?

I let go of my cock, smacking it just a bit to watch it bob back and forth. The need to *fuck* something was intense, especially with my favorite toy only inches away.

But it wasn't the warm, plush walls of my Fleshlight I really wanted. It was Professor Hot Stuff, on his fucking knees before me.

I closed my eyes as I let the image fill my brain, of him and his long legs tucked underneath him, hands flat on his thighs as he gazed up at *me*, begging *me*. Mouth open, waiting for my cock.

For me to fill his fucking mouth with my cum until it dripped out of the corners of his precious, fuckable mouth.

"That's it," I purred in the sanctity of my bathroom as I lined myself up, brushing my leaking head against the entrance of my toy.

I smacked it with my head, the wobbly texture of the Fleshlight jiggling as I did so, and I imagined it was his mouth, fighting for a taste.

"Open wide for Daddy," I murmured as I shoved myself in, letting the plush silicone walls encompass my aching cock. It didn't take long for me to build a rhythm. I braced both hands against the tile wall, picturing the way his lips wrapped around my thickness, letting my mind wander. The memory of feeling of his tongue against mine spurred thoughts of his tongue rolling around my head. I thrust harder, faster, needing to feel the warmth, his mouth sucking me, licking me.

God, it felt so fucking good.

Harder.

Faster.

I imagined him draining me of every last drop of cum I had, then teaching me a fucking lesson.

You're going to pay for that, he purred in my fantasy.

Another hard thrust, and my fucking mount slipped off as I pulled out, falling to the ground.

"Fuck!" I roared, my release so close I could taste it.

I knew it would take a minute to reposition everything, and I wasn't sure I had the focus or capacity to do so.

I needed to fucking come. I needed to put Professor Hot stuff out of my mind. I needed to fuck this out of my system.

I grabbed my Fleshlight from the ground, taking matters into my own hands once more.

Make me, I touted in my cerebral fantasy, the scent of my release prevalent in the air as he breathed his words into my ears. I turned over as I imagined him touching me, forcing me to give him my ass.

And then I came, hard and fast, my entire body spasming with release at the very *thought* of him punishing me.

Like the dirty little whore I was.

Daddy is a dirty little whore.

As soon as the relief came, so did the shame.

The guilt.

Because I knew it would only be a fantasy.

That's all it could ever be.

CHAPTER 13

RILEY

MY PHONE BUZZED INCESSANTLY as I stuffed down my first bite of my chicken salad. One glance at the screen showed it was my brother, Aaron.

Heads up we're heading out this weekend to check out a couple clubs for the bach party.

Shit!

I'd almost completely forgotten!

Technically, I was the best man and the bachelor party was my wheelhouse, but my brother and his friends all knew I was not the best choice when it came to partying, and I wanted my brother to have the best night, so we'd all agreed to choose a place after scouting out locations *together.* That way, I could oversee the finer details while also being sure that the place we picked was something up to Aaron's caliber.

Before I could answer, Chris came waltzing through the door, lifting himself to sit on my demo counter, swinging his legs back and forth as he giddily pressed me to tell him how my *date* went, so getting back to my brother would have to wait.

"It wasn't a date," I reminded him as I took another stab at my salad.

"Were you in bed before nine o clock?" he teased.

"No, of course not. I—"

"Did you have drinks? Flirt a little? Maybe even get a little first base action?" Chris challenged, using his hands to mold and grope the air like a seventh grader.

I couldn't help the heat that formed in my cheeks at his insinuation, and that was telling enough.

"Oh my God, you did!" he teased, and I threw down my fork in defense.

"It wasn't like that, it was... it was..."

"Riley and Mafia Man sitting in a tree—"

"Stop!" I said, unable to control my laughter.

Chris only wriggled his eyebrows at me

with a smile. "Hey, all I'm saying is you deserve to have a little fun you know," Chris said through his own laugh. "So where'd he take you?"

I smiled as I recalled the previous night. "Some arcade in the city, called Wizards."

Chris raised an eyebrow. "I know that place. They're like Dave and Busters on Pop Rocks."

It was my turn to raise an eyebrow. "Pop Rocks?"

Chris rolled his eyes, his tone mimicking the valley girl accent that perpetuated the films of our youth.

"Well, we *are* an anti-drug district, Mr. Evans, crack is wack. And so nineteen eighty."

I scoffed in return as I stabbed my salad.

"I, uh, actually ran into a student there," I admitted. "Wasn't sure what to say, you know, like how to introduce him or anything, so I just said like, hey this is my friend and this is one of my students... like a lame teacher."

Chris let out a laugh. "Hope you weren't in a compromising position," he teased.

Heat rushed my face again as I remembered being so close to Eric, wanting to kiss him right then and there.

I let my head fall onto my desk, hiding the flush I knew was covering my cheeks.

"I am so screwed," I murmured. I'd only

had a couple drinks, but the lord knew how teenagers talked.

It wasn't like I was completely in the closet, but I didn't really share my personal life with my students. Not that I had much of a social life to share to begin with, but still...

Most of the staff knew I was gay, but it wasn't like there was a neon sign outside my door.

"Looks like you won't be dancing on your own at the wedding after all," Chris said as my phone chimed again because I hadn't closed out the notification.

I lifted my head, if only to grab my phone and silence the notification.

"Lover boy texting you already? Wanting some of that grade A Evans di—"

"Oh my God, Chris, stop! No, it's my brother. We're doing the club scout this weekend. You know, where we're supposed to go into the city and find the perfect pen of debauchery or whatever..."

"You should invite Lover Boy. I bet he'd be down to get low or whatever it is the kids are calling it these days," Chris said, sticking his tongue out and making metal head signs with his fingers.

"I..."

I hadn't really thought about *inviting* anyone

because, truth be told, I hadn't *had* anyone to invite, until now.

Come to think of it, I *did* win the last game, and the winner got to pick the next date.

Certainly, my brother wouldn't object.

Just as I contemplated Chris's words, the lunch bell rang, and I realized I hadn't even finished my salad.

Damn it!

"Ah, well, that's my cue, Romeo. Catch up with you and that Grade A later," Chris called over his shoulder, his hand hitting the top of the door pane on his way out.

I sighed as the students filed into the room, vowing that during class time today I'd finish my lunch the way it was intended, and perhaps, I would take the initiative to invite Eric out this weekend.

CHAPTER 14

I casually sketched out a bust on my paper, if only because I needed to keep my hands busy while the rest of my students worked on their still-lifes.

I'd stared at the current set up of flowers and vases and reflective objects long enough, not to mention my brain kept replaying last night over and over. That moment on my porch, where Eric looked up at me with hope and wonder.

Like he could see *me*. And not just the me that towered over him, but the me I hadn't realized I'd lost.

Slowly, I shaded in the clavicle, adding

shadows to the neck and side of the head, cross-hatching the bust into more of a silhouette.

By the time the bell rang, I had Eric's facial features sketched in, albeit they were mostly visible via the shadows.

"Remember, your projects are due Friday!" I said, assuming my authority again as everyone started packing up.

"So, those of you who need art passes, make sure you see me no later than tomorrow morning!" I announced, though as usual, no one took me up on the offer.

I turned around to clean up the remains of my lunch, when a voice pulled me from my thoughts.

"Did you... uh... have a good time last night?" I turned around to see Trevor, tugging on his bookbag.

"Trevor, hey... I, uh... yeah, I had a great time. With... my... friend. My friend, Eric," I said awkwardly, almost word vomiting.

Trevor shook his head with a grin. "I know it's none of my business but, uh, it's just... I didn't think you were into guys..." he said hurriedly, recovering with, "Like Eric. I mean, it's cool if you are but, like, I just..."

"Trevor, I—"

"I mean, you seem like a really nice guy—for like, an old guy—"

Old guy?

I'm only thirty-eight for fucks sake!

I'm not dead!

"I'm thirty-eight!" I said in alarm. "I'm not—"

"I know. I mean, I don't know, but I know, I mean... ugh, why is this so hard?" Trevor said, his cheeks turning red.

I wasn't sure what Trevor was getting at it by his comment, and a part of me was surprised he'd confronted me in general. Though he was a great student with a lot of artistic potential, we didn't *talk* about his social interactions or things outside of school during his study hall sessions when he'd come in to work on his projects.

The flush on his cheeks, the chewing of the lip... the way he was dancing around the topic... Suddenly, I realized the subtext of what he was saying.

Trevor himself was gay. And likely hadn't told anyone.

"Trevor, if this is about what you think you saw... If you are feeling... some sort of way—"

"Oh God, no!" Trevor said shaking his head. "I mean, I like you, but not like that, obviously. Not that you're not attractive, or... Oh my God, what I mean is just..."

I swallowed harshly at his trail of compliments, because even as nice as they were, they were certainly misplaced.

"I just wanted to tell you to be careful, that's all. You seem like a good guy... I think, and I just don't want to see some asshole hurt you."

My heart sank at his words.

For starters, Eric was the furthest thing from an asshole, and why on earth would he hurt me?

"I appreciate your concern, Mr. Klaypas, but my personal life is just that. My *personal* life. There is a reason I don't share it. Because I value my privacy," I said as politely as I could.

"But if you need someone to talk to about anything, you know you can talk to me," I said as nicely as I could. I knew how hard it was growing up in this town; after all, I'd been a lot like Trevor once myself.

Trevor sighed, nodding. "Yeah, right of course, my bad. I just... I'm sorry, can... can we pretend this never happened?" he asked, his flush returning to normal. A part of me understood his desire to forgo the awkwardness, and clam up. Perhaps whatever was truly bothering him, he wasn't ready to divulge to himself.

"Of course," I said, for I too, wanted nothing more than to forget this equally embarrassing moment.

"Okay, well... um, in that case, I'm gonna go..."

I wrote him his art pass, sent him on his way, and tried to shake off the odd encounter.

Glancing at the clock, I knew I only had ten minutes left until the buses would clear out, which meant if I *wanted*, I could leave early.

I usually stayed around till at least six, working on curriculum and getting everything organized for my professional development and the upcoming field trip as well as organizing my things for next week's project. But as I looked out the window at the sun shining down on the pavement, as I watched the kids walking outside, goofing off, I felt a need to shirk my adult responsibilities and just do something fun.

Maybe I'd catch a movie—something I hadn't done in awhile—or swing by the cafe for a coffee, or even just go for a walk.

The world was full of endless possibilities, and so I didn't waste a moment as I grabbed my phone, my jacket, and headed out into the world anew.

CHAPTER 15

Eric

I stared at the text that read *Brunch?*

I hadn't seen Julie since the other night, when the guys and I met up at M's Place. The night I first met Riley.

Even though it was almost a week ago now, it felt like ages.

To be honest, I hadn't thought about much else except Riley, and the fact that I could feel myself falling into his quicksand.

It was hard not to like him, once you got past his Sunday School attire and his blushing cheeks.

And he does play a good game of air hockey.

I decided that maybe a good brunch was

what I needed to get my head right, to get myself back on track.

I needed to come clean to Riley about my job, about who I really was, if only because I knew it would come back to bite me in the ass if I didn't. I hated lying, and I wasn't ashamed of what I did.

But I worried that coming clean would be a deal breaker for Sunday's Best Professor, and I didn't want to think about the reality that my truth might push him away. Like it pushed others away.

So, instead of thinking about derailed fairy-tales, I answered Julie with a *sure*.

When I arrived at *Rose & Evelyn's*, Jasper Springs's "upscale" spot—which was about as upscale as a *Red Lobster*, Julie was already waiting, mimosa in hand.

"Good morning," she said with a grin, twirling her flute.

"Afternoon," I said, flashing her with a grin of my own. "It is eleven am, you're already drinking, and this is brunch, so I think we're well past morning."

Julie smiled as the waitress came by, and I put my coffee order in.

I barely had a look at the menu before Julie was off.

"It's five o'clock somewhere, darling," she said with a kissy face that made me roll my eyes.

"So, how did it go the other night?" she asked sweetly.

I peered up at her from my menu. "What?" I asked, feeling self-conscious all of a sudden. I hadn't mentioned to anyone about my date-not-date with Riley, but that didn't mean Julie couldn't have known. The woman had an uncanny knack for gossip and was often in the places you least expected her. It would be just like her to spot me in a compromising position, only to bring it up later.

"I mean, it's not every day someone beats you at a game of pool," she said, sipping her drink again.

Oh, of course... M's Place... the other night.

"Uh, yeah, I know. It's crazy, right?" I asked, breathing a sigh of relief. "It was fine. I guess. Riley gave me a ride home. Got all embarrassed when his smutty audiobook came on over the speakers. Was kind of funny actually." I chuckled at the memory.

"Shut up! He did not!" Julie exclaimed, her eyes wide, faced filled with excitement.

I shook my head, my own grin spreading across my face. It felt good to laugh, to just let out the things that had been rolling around in my head.

"We, uh, actually hung out the other night too. Had a good time."

Julie's face was practically glowing. "I knew it," she said, beaming with pride.

"What are you talking about?" I asked, and took a sip of my coffee.

"I knew you two would hit it off," she said as the waitress came by to take our orders.

After putting in for a tower of cinnamon spice pancakes, I did not relent.

"What the fuck are you talking about, Jules?"

Julie shrugged, smirking at me over her mimosa. "Oh nothing, just saying that's why I arranged the blind date in the first place. I had a feeling you two would get along," she shrugged.

What?

Is she saying...

"Riley... he was the guy you tried to set me up with? The one who blew me—"

"Well, not even fate could keep you two apart, it seemed. I mean, you did still both show up at M's Place—completely of your own accord, might I add—"

"I don't fucking believe this," I said, feeling a fresh wave of panic.

He was the guy who stood me up!

Julie dismissed my shock with a wave.

"Why didn't you say something the other night—"

Julie shrugged. "Maybe I just wanted to see how you two played out on your own."

"Un fucking believable," I said, downing my coffee.

"What?"

"You didn't think..." I said as I looked around, keeping my voice low. "You didn't think my job would be an issue?" I asked, raising my eyebrow at her.

"Why would it be?" she asked, cocking her head to the side. "I told him you worked in social media, that's not a lie."

"Oh, I don't know, Jules, maybe because I fucking get naked for a living and he melds the minds of today's youth," I growled.

Julie's eyebrows furrowed. "Since when has taking off your pants for a living bothered you? You're the one who's always saying—"

"It doesn't, but—"

"But what? Clearly something has your briefs all in a twist."

I sighed, just as the waitress dropped our food off. I stabbed my pancake much harder than I'd intended, the metal of the silverware chiming loudly off the plate.

"You of all people know how many people

have had an *issue* with what I do. And none of them were *teachers.*"

"So, no nude modeling then for the art class, got it," she teased.

I grunted in response as I stuffed some pancake in my mouth, the sickeningly sweet syrup thick on my tongue.

Julie's gaze softened. "I do know what you mean, you know. But I also know that Riley is one of the most accepting people on the planet. He's a good guy, Eric. I promise."

"Yeah, that's the fucking problem, Julie. He's *good.* And I'm..."

I couldn't finish my sentence, because I knew the truth that awaited. Riley was good, and I was a sin that would forever stain him, and the last thing I wanted was to ruin someone as perfect as him.

So I buried my heartache in my syrup and butter, because it was turning out to be quite a shitty morning.

CHAPTER 16

ERIC

AFTER THE BOMBSHELL Julie had dropped on me at brunch, I'd wanted nothing more than to put Riley out of my mind once and for all, but I couldn't stop thinking about the fact that he'd stood me up.

Not intentionally, I'm sure. Riley didn't seem the type to have a menacing bone in his body, but it still felt like a punch to the gut.

Another punch I wasn't prepared for.

It was like the universe was trying to push me toward the man when I was more than certain the truth would tear us apart.

Fuck, why is shit so damn complicated?

I decided instead to focus on my upcoming

daily post. For years, my job had been more of a comfort than a burden. In the beginning, it was just something I did for fun, for attention, and in some ways it still was, but somewhere along the line it became more than just fun, it became a habit, a job.

One that paid pretty well, and didn't require a lot.

And now, it was the only constant in my life. Every day, on the dot, I got to tap out of life, I got to forget.

Forget about my loneliness, about my non-existent relationships.

I adjusted my lights once more, making sure my bed was set up and I had everything I needed.

Lube.

Toys.

A well positioned camera.

It was the same every time, and I liked to be prepared, in case I wanted to switch things up. I lay back on my soft sheets, my head against the pile of pillows as I got comfortable. Palming my cock through my briefs, I tried my best to clear my mind.

I focused on the feel of my cock, solid beneath my briefs, the sensation of all the blood in my body finding its way to the center of me. I lazily rubbed my stiffness, biting my lip as I contemplated where I wanted this session to go. Where I needed it to go so I could forget.

The familiar sound alerted me that I'd started recording, but I didn't open my eyes yet. I formed a picture in my brain as I rubbed myself, thrusting my brief covered cock against my hand, and immediately pulled away.

Not yet.

I opened my eyes, making eye contact with the camera. I'd done this "oops you caught me" scenario more than once, and every time I did, the subs loved it. In the past, I'd gotten off on being watched, but now, getting off was just...

It didn't feel the same anymore. It felt empty, despite the fact thousands were watching me, waiting for me to come for them.

A quick glance at the comments coming in live only cemented the truth.

And for a moment, I wished he was watching.

Professor Hot Stuff.

What a show I could give him...

I knelt up on my knees, palming my briefs once more, making eye contact and asking them how bad they wanted to see my cock. How bad they wanted me to fuck their mouths, or their asses.

The resounding sound of tips and comments flooded along with my fantasy as I stared at the screen, pretending it wasn't me and a thousand people.

I looked into that camera, and despite my best efforts to do otherwise, I could only envision it was *him* watching me.

I slid my briefs down, letting my cock spring free. Arching my back for more thrusting, I let my hand trace over my thickness, feeling the sticky precum already coating my head.

I peered down at the screen, reading the comments. People said the most depraved, dirty things when they thought no one was watching.

One request caught my eye, and I garnered perhaps it would be better to let them lead me, so my fantasy didn't stray. If I was giving the viewers what they wanted, I could chalk it up to business.

What I wanted didn't factor in the equation, because what I wanted...

I pushed the thought out of my mind as I smirked for the camera, removing the rest of my underwear as I got off the bed, walking over to my nightstand with the toys.

I wasted no time picking out the thickest cock in my collection, along with some warming lube.

The request to watch me come while I got fucked wasn't an abnormal one, but it wasn't something I preferred to do for the cameras often.

Mostly because in love and in life, I was the one who preferred to do the fucking.

But I'd realized then that maybe it was what I needed to forget about Riley, forget about the things that would undoubtedly disappear the moment reality was back at hand.

I made a show of slathering the twelve inch *Big Daddy* cock in copious amounts of lube, slowly rubbing and squeezing my hands along the veiny silicone shaft I held beneath my leaking cock. I thrust my own against it, collecting some of the lube from the motion as more tips and comments came flooding in.

Leaning back on my bed, I spread my legs, positioning myself front and center so my audience could watch me fuck my fingers one at a time. Because I didn't do this often, I knew I needed to work myself up, which meant the video would be longer than my usual ten minutes, but I supposed once in a while a little variety was good, right?

My cock *ached*, throbbing with need as I slid my fingers out, positioning the giant cock at my wet, lubricated entrance. The tingling pressure as I inched the silicone shaft in was maddening, and I wanted to come almost immediately. I caught my breath, my eyes falling closed as I stretched myself to capacity.

Ungh.

So fucking full.

With a shaky hand, I let go, my balls and cock aching for release. I righted myself, going to my knees once more, which made the toy shoved in my ass bottom out completely. Letting out a slow breath, I carefully bent over in the slightest motion, rocking my hips against it, grabbing my slick cock with my free hand. With every thrust into my warm, wet hands, the dildo slid out of me just a hair. Back and forth, I built a slow, torturous rhythm.

In my brain, I imagined it was him.

Bending me over his desk, fucking me because once again I was *his* dirty little whore.

I needed to be punished by him, I needed to be *good*.

I came with a force that was unexpected, but welcome. I closed my eyes as I rode the wave of my orgasm, my insides contracting around the foreign invader as I continued the onslaught of my release, my stomach muscles and abs contracting with each pulse. For a moment, I felt like anything was possible.

With my eyes closed, I could pretend it was him fucking me into oblivion, wrapping those long arms and legs around me.

Holding me as he unloaded himself inside me, making me his.

But when I opened my eyes to see I'd cum not just all over myself, but on the bed, the incessant ringing of tips and comments, I felt a deeper ache than anything else I'd ever felt.

Because as good as I felt—and I felt *amazing*—I felt a wave of guilt that what I desired. What I wanted more than anything would never come to fruition. I felt *guilty*. Not just about what I'd done, but about who I was.

I wanted more than the emptiness I felt at that moment.

All the comments and the tips in the world would never feel as good as his kiss.

As his touch.

Nothing.

And so I wiped my sticky, cum-filled hand on my leg, dismounted my silicone friend, and turned off the camera. Tears threatened to break free, but I bit my tongue, stifling them down.

I'd just cleaned up my space when I saw the comments still flooding in on my phone. I almost pushed the thing away, but I didn't. Because one notification stood out among the rest.

A text message.

Are you busy Friday night?

Naked, I stood there, staring at a text message for the second time that day, only this one was more chilling, more frightening than a brunch invite.

Because every bone in my body wanted to say *yes*.

For you, I could be free even during an apocalypse.

I answered with a cool, *Yeah. Why, you want a rematch at that air hockey game?*

Best to sound nonchalant. I wouldn't want Sunday Best to get the wrong idea and think I'm just waiting on pins and needles for his call.

Even though that's exactly what I'd been doing.

Tempting, but... my brother and some of his friends and I are going to check out some clubs for the Bachelor party location. Was wondering if you wanted to be my plus one?

I knew better than most that the arcade wasn't actually a date, despite how much it felt like it was. It was just hanging out.

But this, deliberately asking me to join him and his family, a group of his friends, clubbing...

Friends are a big deal. It most certainly felt like a date.

I knew I should put an end to what was happening between us, what was happening to me, because every time I wound up around the man, I got soft. My walls started to crumble, and

I dared to dream, to hope maybe this time could be different, even though I knew it wouldn't' be. That was, if I told him the truth.

But I was a fool for Mr. Riley Evans, it seemed. And I didn't want to do the right thing.

I wanted to do very, very bad things. To him...

Yeah, that sounds fun. Where should I meet you?

I sat on the edge of my bed, the cool air of my bedroom contrasting with the fire in my blood, in my being, as I waited for his answer.

I'll pick you up around eight thirty.

After sending a thumbs up, I fell back on my bed, staring at the ceiling as the ominous truth loomed over me.

I knew what I needed to do, but perhaps there was nothing wrong with having a little fun first, right?

CHAPTER 17

RILEY

It's not a date.

Though my sweaty palms, flippant stomach, and nerves begged to differ.

I couldn't remember the last time I'd agonized this much over what to wear to an event that wasn't a fundraiser or a funeral.

The school was pretty laid back when it came to our attire, so most of the time I just wore my chinos and a polo to keep things comfortable and simple, and when I was home it was sweatpants and old t-shirts.

At the risk of my 'not getting properly laid', Chris had taken it upon himself to chaperone me after school on my trip to Kohls to make sure I was 'thirst trap material.

For a straight man, I had to admit, he did have a keen eye for fashion.

I'd settled on a shimmery chrome-like shirt that changed color with the light. The sleeves stopped at my elbow, to give the illusion of a rolled up sleeve, but really they were just cut that way.

Chris even talked me into getting a pair of black jeans to pair with the shirt. Jeans he said would really accentuate my *assets*, whatever that meant.

"Now, I expect a full report on Monday, and I don't want to hear none of that holding hands bullshit. You have one mission this weekend—"

"To find a location for my brother's bachelor party?" I drawled as I finished wiping down the blackboard.

"To get fucking laid," Chris said, miming a basketball shot into an imaginary hoop.

"Shhh. The kids are still here..."

Chris rolled his eyes. "Trust me, my foul mouth is not the worst thing these kids have heard on a Friday after school," he said with a laugh. "Don't change the subject. What's your mission?"

I sighed, knowing it was best to just go along with his antics. But also I supposed, given the fact he'd insisted on helping me at all, it was the least I could do.

"My mission is to have *fun* and..." I sighed, first checking to make sure no one else was in earshot before I breathed out, "Get laid."

Chris bit his knuckle, feigning a mother hen's look of approval. "God, they grow up so fast."

I rolled my eyes as I grabbed my blazer, heading for the door.

"Have fun on your date!" he hollered so loud I worried the damn office would hear. Even though they were more than a ten minute walk away.

"It's not a date!" I yelled back as I turned the corner, grinning ear to ear.

Date or no date, I meant what I'd said. Tonight was about having fun, and as far as I was concerned, that was my mission.

To drink, dance, and have fun with Eric, my brother, and our friends.

RILEY

I PULLED up to Eric's house at eight twenty on the nose. With the hurricane in my stomach still swirling, and the sweat starting to bead on my trim chest beneath the hot fabric of my shirt, I knew it was now or never. Just as I opened my phone to text him, I heard the door close.

I glanced up through my windshield to see Eric standing there in a pair of *leather* pants, with a hot pink shirt. With the sleeves rolled up to his elbow, nice and tight. His clothes were perfectly fitted to his form, showcasing his natural shape.

In my headlights, his skin looked pale, his eyes bright like sapphires, dark hair falling in his eyes like some cross between John Stamos in his

Uncle Jesse era and Ian Somerhalder in his Vampire Diaries era.

He was so fucking *hot*, and my cock more than agreed.

I barely noticed when he opened the door on his own, silently chastising myself that I should have just shut my mouth and met him on the porch, walked him to the car.

"I was going to text you," I said, like a dumbass.

"You're early," he said, licking his lips.

"You were waiting," I said, as I realized at that moment he'd been more than ready. I'd barely been in his driveway long enough to text, and he was out, locked up, and in my car.

He was *waiting* for me.

Like a date.

"I like to be on time, sue me." He shrugged, dismissing my comment. His tone was flirtatious, causing a smile to form on my lips as I waited until he'd put his seatbelt on before backing up.

The sounds of Miguel's *Sure Thing* graced the speakers, the smooth beats somewhat relaxing.

"No smutty audiobooks on our ride today?" Eric taunted.

Though the way he spoke, his voice was better than any audio narrator I'd ever heard.

"Oh, I'm done with that one," I said.

Eric relaxed in his seat, and I could feel his eyes on me. Like he was sizing me up or something, as the singer swooned on about being the reporter and the news.

"Too bad, I was hoping maybe I would get to see you all flustered by dirty words again," he said, leaning his arm along the window frame. "You, uh, you're kinda cute when you're all flustered."

His compliment went straight to my cock, then back up to my brain, making my cheeks redden along the way.

Did he just call me cute?

Then his tone softened as he shifted in his seat.

"Um, thanks, I think," I said, letting out a chuckle. I could feel his gaze on me, hot like fire.

"You know, you don't have to, like, be embarrassed about that shit. What you like is, what you like, you know? You don't have to feel weird about it. I just wanted to say that."

Truth was, I loved to read romance, but I'd never considered the things I read in my books as preferences or anything. Not that I had many people to test the waters with, anyway.

But something about Eric's words made me feel like maybe it was okay to be open about my preferences.

My desires.

Desires that might include him starring in my own personal show.

Maybe reading to me and then...

My cock stiffened at the thought, and I let out a sigh as I admitted to him, "I'm just not used to sharing my preferences or my taste in literature with other people." I swallowed harshly. "Especially other men.."

Yeah, men who I imagine taking the place of said fictional characters.

"You know there's, like, a wild ass community of people who are into smutty books, right?" he said seriously.

"Yeah, but how many guys do you know actually *listen* to gay romance?"

Eric's eyes sparkled for a moment as he smiled. "I think you'd be surprised."

His tone made me feel at ease, which was truly dangerous. Being around Eric, it was just so easy to be myself.

To talk, to play.

So, I didn't think twice before word vomiting out, "Are you? Into gay romance novels, I mean?"

Eric laughed, and I loved the sound.

That first night I'd seen him in the bar, playing pool, I'd assumed he was just a cocky asshole who didn't like to lose. Who thought he was all that and a bag of chips.

But in the days since then, I'd come to learn that while he most certainly did not like to lose, he wasn't some cocky asshole that was full of himself. If anything, I thought his cocky attitude was a front for covering up the person he really was, and that was something I could relate to. I wore a mask too.

Eric was funny, and easy to talk to. He was attractive, and mysterious, and I really liked being around him. I liked who *I* was around him.

Unapologetic.

Free.

Could this... could this serendipitous thing be something more?

More than just friends or a plus one type situation?

I dared to wonder what that would be like.

A lot of fucking fun, probably.

Eric shifted in his seat, propping his knee up as he got comfortable.

"Um, not quite novels, but I'm well versed in smut, you could say," he said, his voice dropping an octave to sound even *better* than my audio narrator.

Maybe he should be narrating audiobooks...

Well versed in smut.

The words alone made my cock twitch and my heart jump.

I was so out of my league.

"Well, good," I said, swallowing harshly. "Because I'm fairly certain I'm going to need your help tonight."

"For the bachelor party, you mean?" he asked.

I nodded. "It's kind of this unspoken thing between my brother and the other party members. They all think..." I started.

"They all think what?" Eric asked curiously.

The words were on the tip of my tongue. I knew what I wanted to say, but somehow saying it out loud made it a thousand times worse.

I looked at Eric, at his pristine blue eyes that coaxed me like a lamb to slaughter.

No embarrassment, no judgment.

"I know they think I'm going to make it lame. Like I don't know what's sexy, or what, you know, most guys are into."

Eric raised an eyebrow, in surprise. "How so?"

I looked at him as I huffed a sigh of annoyance.

Might as well just get it off my chest before I see everyone tonight.

"Because everyone thinks I'm some goody two shoes who can't let loose and have fucking fun." I sighed, as the words continued, flowing free of their own accord.

"And because I'm gay, like, they think I can't pick out good strippers or something. Hell if I know."

Eric laughed, and the sound was deep and sexy. It was infectious, and I couldn't help but laugh too.

Being with Eric was like that. Somehow, he found a way to infiltrate my fortresses and remind me who I was underneath it all.

Who I'd *forgotten* I was.

"But you're not, are you?" he asked inquisitively. "You're not the person everyone thinks you are."

"I mean, I'm gay, but I'm not blind," I bit out.

Eric chuckled once more.

My brother wouldn't come out and say such things, and I knew the other members of the party were not as organized, and no one was jumping at the bit to volunteer as tribute to plan a night of debauchery, but I could read between the lines.

I was fully intent on giving my brother the best bachelor party I could, because he deserved it. Even it meant I had to stomach a night of tits and ass that did not appeal to me.

It had to be perfect, and I knew between him, our friends, and Eric, I'd manage to make it the best.

"Is that why you invited me, Riley? To help you pick out strippers?" Eric chuckled.

The conversation was steering off the beaten path while I focused on the GPS telling me to turn onto Rodal Road, which meant we'd be at *Cheerleaders* in no time.

"I mean, can you blame me for wanting to bring along some personal eye candy?" I teased him.

Though his voice changed from playful, almost to sad.

"No, guess I can't."

A strange sort of tension fell between us, but I had no time to dwell on such things. I parked the car, just as my phone was ringing. It was my brother.

I opened the car door, sprinting around to get Eric's. His gaze met mine as I nodded with a smile, telling my brother we were there.

And when I finished up with him on the phone, I offered Eric my arm. I watched as he contemplated taking it, almost as if he were afraid.

"Are you ready to meet the rest of the party and have some fun?" I asked, my nerves starting to settle.

Eric flashed me a smile that made my stomach flip. "I thought you'd never ask."

CHAPTER 19

RILEY

THANKFULLY, the club district packed their buildings close together, and therefore we could easily hop from one place to the next. Our first stop of the night was *Cheerleaders*, and though I'd never stepped foot in a straight strip club before, I could see the appeal.

My brother and Eric toasted their shot glasses as the rest of the party, Lane, Grayson, Henry, and even Drew Axel—Giselle's rockstar buddy—and his boyfriend—the florist, Taylor—had come out for the event, and all were lined up at the bar, "testing" out the shots amid a myriad of fans who were taking selfies and getting their boobs signed by Drew.

"What are you waiting for? Christmas?" Grayson said as he came up beside me, holding out a shot.

I sniffed the concoction. It smelled like pumpkin-scented glass cleaner.

"What the hell is this, anyway?" I asked. I'd had two beers, which gave me an okay buzz, but I wasn't planning on getting drunk at the first place we checked out. I wanted to take note, observe the place and Aaron's reactions. Plus, shots weren't really my thing, but that was what everyone seemed to gravitate toward there.

Grayson smirked, and I could see the resemblance to his sister. They both had the same look of mischief.

"It's called a Pumpkinhead. Tastes like pumpkin pie."

"Gross," I said, as Grayson laughed.

"It's not so bad if you chuck it really fast," he teased.

"Yeah, that's the point, right? Fastest way to drunk is with a bunch of shots."

Grayson shrugged as he shot his in one swift motion, offering me the other.

"I prefer to get shitfaced on an exquisitely aged cab, but alas, straight men have the worst taste in drinks, I'm afraid."

I couldn't help but let out a chuckle as I shook my head. Thankfully, I wasn't the only gay man at the strip club tonight. Though Grayson, Henry, Drew, and Taylor looked far more comfortable with all the beautiful women surrounding our party than I felt at the moment. Even surrounded by the sights and sounds, they didn't seem to notice much more than their significant others.

In fact, as I surveyed the bar, I could see Drew and Taylor grinding on one another with smiles plastered all over their faces like lovesick teenagers.

I wished it were that easy for me. That I could have an ounce of sex appeal like Drew Axel, or the confidence of Grayson.

I took the shot from his hands, but my gaze was set on something else. Someone else. The object of my turmoil.

Ever since our car ride, something was different. I couldn't put my finger on it, but whatever it was, was driving me crazy. All I wanted to do was give the guy a hug and tell him I was sorry, for whatever it was I did, because clearly I was an idiot, and I'd done *something.*

I watched as Eric and my brother toasted another round of shots. I thought it was the third one.

Eric seemed to get along with my brother swimmingly. Granted, they'd met before, but we'd all been far too preoccupied with our game to properly make each other's acquaintances or get to know one another.

I watched as a woman in shorts and a bikini top sauntered over to my brother, squeezing between him and Eric.

She threw her arms around Eric, making a kissy face as she took a selfie with him. Though I couldn't blame her. In his hot pink shirt, tight black jeans, with his gorgeous face and the charisma that just rolled off of him every time he walked into a room.

"You know you are allowed to have fun too," Grayson said softly.

"I am having fun," I grumbled as I downed my shot.

Grayson twisted his lips. "Aaron is having fun. Your little boyfriend is having fun. You... you are *watching.* You're stalling."

I shot Grayson a raised eyebrow of my own. "For starters, Aaron is the one who should be having fun because this is about *him.* About the perfect bachelor party," I said with a sigh. "And Eric is *not* my boyfriend. I'm observing, you know, to take in the *ambiance* for scientific purposes," I drawled sarcastically.

Grayson shook his head, raising an eyebrow. "Really? I mean, you brought him, so I assumed..."

My gaze settled on Eric's bright smile as Aaron laughed at something he said.

"Plus, you've been staring at him for like ten minutes."

Grayson's words settled on me, stirring the hurricane inside of me again.

Had I really been staring that long?

Before I could say anything, Grayson's tone shifted. "Shit or get off the pot, Riley. Because if you don't make your move, I guarantee you someone else will."

I turned to him, raising my eyes. "Excuse me?" I said.

Grayson gestured with his gaze to the woman who was now *grinding* on Eric, bending over to twerk her ass against his crotch, her mouth at Aaron's waist level. Lane hooted and hollered as I watched Eric settle his hand on her jean-clad ass, and my blood boiled.

I realized as I meant to speak, I didn't know that Eric *wasn't* into women. Not every guy who liked dick hated pussy. Some preferred both.

Panic flooded me along with doubt. I'd been so focused on my own embarrassment, during our *preferences* conversation, it occurred to me I never asked if he had any preferences of his own.

Because I was nervous, and asking such things felt too intimate for friends.

But as the word settled in my brain—*friends* —I realized I didn't like the sound of it.

I didn't want to be *friends* with Eric.

I liked him. I liked him a whole hell of a lot, and as the realization struck me, I felt the air around me get thinner.

My gaze fixed on him as he danced with her, laughing with her, and I couldn't help but feel the pang of desire to be her.

To be the one held under his captivating gaze, to feel his hand on *my ass*, fingers grabbing *my* hips.

While I stuffed his mouth full of my cock.

My cock twitched at the thought, my heart beating faster with jealousy and desire, and I realized I wanted to know everything there was to know about Eric. I wanted to be the object of *his* desire. This wasn't about finding a date to my brother's wedding.

Not anymore.

I wanted to spend as much time as I could with the man who made me feel like I'd finally awakened from a long sleep.

But for all the strides I'd made, I was still sitting in the damn dugout, watching the game be played. Because I was scared.

I was scared that if I pushed too hard, Eric would run away.

Needy.

Desperate.

Stage five clinger.

The words my exes labeled me with rolled around in my brain.

How had things become so complicated?

Why couldn't I just walk over there, tell him how I felt, kiss him, and take him home?

I watched as Eric bent down, hands behind his back and sucked a shot from between her breasts, liquor running down his chin as Aaron fist bumped the air, the rest of the men at the bar cheering him on. He grabbed the shot glass from his mouth, slamming it down on the bar as everyone cheered. Aaron high-fived him. Watching him with my brother and the party, he fit in perfectly.

Like he *belonged* with them.

A fresh wave of jealousy rolled through me. Grayson's voice pulled me from my trance, and I realized he was still standing there beside me. Watching, observing.

"He's a pretty fish, but so are you. You're an Evans, for Christ sake. Own that shit. Stop staring and second-guessing yourself, and get the fuck over there. Blow his fucking mind. Make him forget everyone else," Grayson said, clapping me on the back. "That's what I did, and it worked for me." Grayson grinned before he headed toward Henry, who wrapped his arms around his boyfriend the moment he stepped into his proximity at the bar.

At that moment, I caught Eric's sapphire gaze, noting how the corners of his lips turned up in a smirk. Like he was truly *baiting* me.

And perhaps it was the shot, or the neon lights that danced over him, or the rage of jealousy, or Grayson's pep talk, but whatever it was, was enough.

Grayson was right. I wasn't a clam hiding under the mud, not anymore.

I was an *Evans.*

My brother may have been the sporty, pretty jock, but I was not without my charms. I could be commanding, and hot, and... and...

I found myself pulled into Eric's orbit once more as I slid between him and the pretty little tart who was downing another shot, this time with my brother and Lane.

The sounds of *Dirty Dancer* by Usher and Enrique came over the speakers, and in the distance, I could see a topless woman flipping herself upside down at the top of her pole, which was the only pole in the room to go from high vaulted ceiling to floor.

Okay, that's pretty impressive, to be honest.

"Having fun yet, Professorrr?" Eric said, slightly slurring his r's as he slammed down his shot glass.

"Not quite. Standing around doing shots isn't my idea of fun," I said as I slid the shot glass toward the barkeep, shaking my head to say we were done for the moment.

Aaron and Lane were laughing about something as one of the strippers tugged and pulled at Drew, begging him to take the stage with them.

Eric extended his arms along the bar, the motion drawing attention to his defined forearms. He blew some dark hair out of his eyes, with his pouty, perfect lips. He leaned back, crossing his legs, enticing me apathetically with his perfect pout, his bright blue eyes, and his flirtatious, sensual look.

His tone was cheerful, but his eyes didn't sparkle like they usually did.

"Awww, is the victor not enjoying his spoils?" Eric taunted, the alcohol making him sound huskier than usual.

"I'd enjoy it a lot more if I could pry you away from the bar... and handsy strippers," I said as my brother and his cohorts hooted and hollered yet again, chasing the pretty girl who was all over Eric moments ago, and Drew toward the stage.

"Oh, is that what you want...," Eric said, slowly taking a step toward me, his blue gaze full of sadness, despite the grin on his face. His dark hair fell in his face, and instinctively, I pushed it away, behind the shell of his ear.

"You want to whisk me away in your carriage off to your fucking castle, Cinderella?" he breathed out.

I settled my hand on his hips, captivated by his gaze, his hot breath on my skin.

"Like you're my knight in shining armor?"

"There are a lot of things I want to do with you," I whispered, letting my thumb trace his solid jawline.

Eric looked up at me, his gaze imploring mine. "Green's a good color on you, Riley," Eric purred, his fingers teasing the loops of my jeans.

"I'm not jealous," I huffed as the bartender slid me a shot. "I said—"

"This one's from the guy down there," he said, nodding to Grayson, who held up a shot, Henry wrapped around him like a coiled snake.

I took the shot, pursing my lips. After all, I didn't want to be impolite. I raised it, shot it, and slammed it back down on the bar. The burn of the pumpkin-flavored vanilla liquor was prevalent, and I sucked in a deep breath.

"I'm just testing out the product. Isn't that what you brought me here for?" Eric's breath against my neck was warm, and I leaned closer into him, his fingertips trailing lightly over my thigh, just next to my aching cock.

I stared down at him with a mixture of fury and desire, of jealousy and arousal. I wanted to kiss him. In this stupid room full of pert breasts and clapping cheeks, underneath the neon lights.

But I wanted *more* too.

I wanted to explore Eric's mysterious alleyways until I knew every corner and crevice of his mind, body, and soul.

"Dance with me," I breathed, my heart thudding loudly in my chest. It wasn't a request.

It was a *need.*

I needed to feel Eric's body pressed against me, needed to feel his lips on mine, his hardness against mine. The desire was overwhelming, especially this close, knowing we weren't truly alone.

Eric snickered, showcasing his pearly white canines in a way that was so undeniably *hot* it made me wonder if I had a fetish for sexy grins.

Or perhaps just a fetish for pretty boys with attitudes.

"Careful, Riley. You're starting to sound like a possessive asshole. All demanding and shit," Eric teased.

My cock stiffened in my tight pants, and a part of me worried someone—anyone —would see the burgeoning tent forming.

Seriously, how do guys wear pants this tight?

But as I looked into Eric's pristine eyes,

as the sounds of Enrique crooned about never being lonely, for the first time, I didn't care.

I *wanted* someone to see us. To see me with my hands on his hips, my lips on his.

Mine, mine, mine.

"I thought you weren't into strippers," I said, my voice dark and gravelly as he smirked back at me.

"Awww, is that what has your panties in a twist? Worried I'll trade you in for some pussy?" he drawled brattily.

The overwhelming desire to turn him around, bend him over the closest bar stool, and make him eat his words was a new feeling for me.

I wanted to erase anyone and everyone else from his mind, just like Grayson suggested.

"Careful, *Eric*, you're starting to sound like a petulant little cock tease," I said the words without thinking, emboldened by his behavior, the shots, and his gorgeous face.

The club music died out, and in it's place I heard Drew Axel crooning some rock version of Taylor Swift song.

Which one I had no clue, but the words resonated with me nonetheless.

I settled my hand on Eric's hip, gently tugging him closer. This close, his body against mine was warm, and I could feel the faint twitch of his cock against me.

Did he like this?

My own cock throbbed in response as I breathed him in, like he was oxygen.

As nervous as I was, it felt *good.*

Like I was breaking a barrier, jumping off a cliff.

Eric rolled his eyes, a dark chuckle escaping his throat.

"Let's get one thing straight here, Princess," he said as he walked his fingers up the buttons on my shirt, stopping as he grabbed me by my collar, yanking me *down* to his eye level.

His eyes burned like fire, and while a part of me was shocked at the touch, the *strength* and the force...

The rest of me was turned the hell *on.*

Fucking hell... This man...

"I am no cock tease. When I want something, I take it." His words were clear, not a slur to be heard in them.

He loosened his grip just the slightest, his fingertips brushing against my skin. At this level, his lips were inches away, ripe for the taking.

I didn't think twice. I only acted on impulse, on selfish need.

He didn't startle or jump, or try and push me away.

Instead, his fingers slid up my neck, into the edges of my hair at the nape of my neck, seeking purchase there. He let me take his kiss like a damn robbery, and that was where I realized I was drowning.

Eric wasn't just a pretty fish.

He was an elusive shark, and I was falling in love with him, hook, line, and sinker.

CHAPTER 20

RILEY

I LEANED against the leather couch in *Pleasure Dome,* the newest club on the block, which I'd heard was a bit more risqué than the others. Though there were at least four conjoined clubs on the strip here, we'd only made it to two.

The room was spinning, but I couldn't deny I didn't feel *good.*

Drew Axel fell beside me as I blinked, the neon lights blurring my vision.

I couldn't remember the last time I'd been this shitfaced.

Probably college.

"I booked us all a block at the Renaissance

across the street," Drew said, his voice much clearer than anyone else in our party.

"What?" I asked, trying to make sense of my surroundings. My gaze settled on Eric, who was on the dance floor, dancing on his own in the middle of the crowd. Aaron, Lane, Henry, Grayson, and Taylor were all strewn about the floor and bar. I had no idea what time it was, but the place was still thick with patrons, and strippers dressed in tight black latex outfits that were strategically cut out in all the right places.

"Tell them you're with Drew Axel. They'll hook you two up with a room."

I looked at him for a moment, his face slightly doubled.

"I'm so fucking drunk right now," I said, not giving a shit if I sounded like an idiot.

Drew laughed, shaking his head.

"I know, buddy. You're not the only one." He chuckled, clapping me on the shoulder.

"You?" I asked.

Drew shook his head as Taylor came to sit next to him.

"Not me. I'm the DD," he said as Taylor kissed him, stealing his attention for a moment. "Though I gotta say, your brother made it seem like you'd be the responsible one," he said with a laugh, wrapping his arm around his boyfriend. "But even the good guys need to go a little bad sometimes. Right, baby?" he cooed, placing a quick kiss on his boyfriend's lips.

Seeing them so comfortable with one another, so *in love*, made me jealous. But it also made me hopeful.

"I am re... re.. responsa-bb-le." I tried to say the words, but my wires were crossed, and it came out rather unintelligent.

Eric sauntered over toward us, his dark hair slick from the sweat of dancing as he leaned over, extending a hand to help me up.

"Drew says we should go hotel," I said, trying to make sense of my words.

"What?" Eric said. The music was loud, so I yelled what I'd said.

"Renaissance. Front desk, tell them Drew Axel Party," Drew's words echoed around us as I let Eric pull me off the leather couch. I stumbled into his arms, nearly knocking him over, but he held me steady.

My legs felt like Jell-O, and he smelled like sweat, liquor, and cedar cologne.

He smelled like pure sex, and my cock more than agreed.

"Yeah, okay," Eric said as he wrapped his arm around my waist. I liked how it felt there. "Probably not a bad idea..."

I leaned down, placing a kiss on his neck,

like Taylor had done only moments ago to his boyfriend.

Boyfriend...

Eric grunted a sound that went straight to my cock, my hands trailing over his chest. The thumping bass of the club echoed with my heartbeat, and I ground my cock against him.

"Uber's here," Eric said, his voice deep, gravelly.

"Okay," I whispered huskily as he steadied me.

"We'll walk you out," Drew said, leading the way.

The lights, the sounds, all of it was dizzying as we made our way through the crowds, outside to the black SUV waiting for us. Eric and I tumbled in the backseat as Drew closed the door.

My lips were on Eric's in a matter of seconds as I pulled him closer, into my lap. His kiss was wet and loose as his lips traveled over mine, along my jaw. My cock throbbed in my tight pants, and the need to take off my jeans and briefs was overwhelming.

"We're here," Eric slurred as the car came to a stop.

The door opened, and the cool air kissed my skin. Eric's fingers slid into mine as we walked into the bright lit lobby. I followed Eric to the desk, letting him lead.

It felt good to have someone else in charge for once.

"Drew Axel... Party," he said, his tone sounding much more crisp and clear than mine.

I watched as my vision sharpened slightly, as the woman presented us a card with a gold-embossed number seventeen.

Eric grabbed it with his free hand, never letting mine go.

I squeezed his hand, liking the feel of his warm palm against my own.

We wandered through the first floor, and thankfully, the room was close. Though it took a few tries to get the scanner to click, once it did, all bets were off.

No sooner than the door was locked was I unfastening my belt, angling to set my restrained cock free.

My back smacked against the wall as Eric's hands took over, his lips at my neck, biting, sucking.

"Fucking hell, I'm so hard," I murmured, the words falling out of my mouth without warning.

"Me too," Eric purred, his fingers sliding down my pants. I fumbled for his, my fingers making steady work of finding his buttons, and instead, my hand roved over his hardness, squeezing him through his jeans.

"Who's the cock tease, now?" he grumbled, thrusting himself against my palm.

I unbuttoned his leather pants, shoving them down with his underwear in one fell swoop.

I settled my hands on his warm, sweaty hips, over his ass, as I pulled him against me. His thick length against mine had me seeing stars, and I couldn't help the moan that left my mouth at the feel of precum sliding along my shaft.

Though I wasn't sure if it was mine or his...

"Fuck, Eric..." I closed my eyes as I wrapped my hand around our slick cocks, needing more. I slowly built a rhythm, pumping us both.

Eric leaned his head against my chest, his fingers working the buttons of my shirt as he thrust himself against me.

"I want you," I breathed.

"Oh, yeah?" he drawled, busting open my shirt, taking my nipple in his mouth. His teeth grazed the sensitive skin, making me cry out as a fresh blossom of precum coated me.

"How do you want me, *Professor*?" His voice was dark, full of things that made my stomach turn in knots, made my cock throb.

"I want..." I found it hard to think, let alone breathe as Eric laved his tongue across my chest, wrapping his mouth around my other nipple as I pumped our cocks slowly.

"I want *Daddy* to get on his knees," I purred, seeking his mouth with mine. His kiss was a rush of heat and he tasted like heaven.

I wanted to drown in his kiss, his touch.

Underneath him, I felt *alive.*

"So demanding," Eric touted as I let go of our cocks.

I made haste of unbuttoning his shirt, letting my hands explore his solid, hard chest.

In my hazy vision, he was a sight for sore eyes. Lips swollen from kissing me, blue eyes ablaze with lust, hair slicked back from sweat and heat.

I watched as he grabbed himself, running his thumb over his leaking cock.

"What will you do for me?" he breathed, and I couldn't help licking my lips.

Standing before me, naked, he was like a living wet dream.

I wanted everything.

Everything this perfect man was willing to give me.

"Whatever you want, *Daddy,*" I uttered. "I'm yours for the taking."

Eric pulled me from against the wall, leading me back through the room, and I followed him without hesitation. His lips caressed mine again as he pushed me down onto the bed. He nudged my legs open, and I leaned up on my elbows to look at him where he stood.

His cock gleamed in the bedroom light. He stood between my legs, gazing down at me as he *spit* directly onto my cock, making it throb once more. His gaze held mine as he slathered my cock in his saliva, breathing heavily.

"Whatever I want, huh?" he whispered, his voice dark and gravelly and filled with heat.

I nodded in response, my heart racing, waiting for his kiss, his touch, his mouth.

I needed release.

"Yes, yes... please..."

"Please, what?" he purred, dropping to his knees, licking me from base to tip slowly.

I arched my back, thrusting my cock at him, but he relented, teasing, taunting me.

"Please, Eric..." His name on my tongue was a mixture of pleasure, of pain, and of hope.

Please put me out of my misery, once and for all.

Eric's fingers dug into my ass cheeks as he *yanked* me off the bed, taking my cock into the back of his throat.

I took him into the back of my throat in one fell swoop until I couldn't breathe, his deep groan only making my own cock throb even more as he grabbed me by the back of my hair.

The words from my audiobook echoed in my drunken brain.

Eric groaned as he sucked me, fingers squeezing my flesh as my legs stiffened around his head.

"Oh fuck..." I could feel my orgasm on the edge, so close, yet so far away.

I sat up the best I could, but my upper half felt like Jell-O, and my lower half was hot, buzzing with anticipation as Eric licked and sucked me, hollowing his cheeks like I was a damn tootsie roll pop and his mission was discover how many licks it took to find the center.

"Eric..." I cried out, knowing I wasn't going to last.

I reached out, sliding my hand into his hair. I wanted to grab him, but I had no strength, no concentration. Everything pooled to my balls, my cock. I fought to lift my hips, to fuck his mouth like I had imagined when I thought of him in the confines of my shower.

But my grip was weak and my entire body shuddered as I came. I cried out in ecstasy, my words jumbling into an array of his name and some cursing. He didn't let go of me as my grip loosened in his hair, sucking down every bit of me until I was empty.

My legs and body were tingling with numbness like I was made of nothing but pure magic.

His cock slid against mine as he righted me, straddling my chest.

I looked up at him, dazed, watching as he held his thick, swollen cock above me.

"Open wide for Daddy, Professor," he commanded.

And I did.

I obeyed him without second thought.

I opened my mouth, watching as he threw his head back, pumping his shaft above me, fucking my mouth with rapid, heated thrusts, and within seconds, he erupted.

Though I would be remiss to say his aim was not the best, and neither was mine. He came on my chest, my face, and only partly in my mouth, but I didn't care.

Eric cursed as he fell back onto the bed beside me, the only sound our deep breaths, and contentment.

I curled next to him, throwing a hand over his hip as I fell into deep slumber, and I dreamed of wet, sloppy kisses and audiobooks, and dancing under the stars with the man of my dreams.

CHAPTER 21

MY HEAD WAS POUNDING, and I was sweltering beneath the sheets. Sheets that didn't feel like my own thousand thread count Egyptian cotton.

I blinked, my eyes adjusting to the bright light as I shielded myself from it. Once my vision sharpened, I realized I was certainly *not* at home.

And I was most certainly *naked*.

Fuck!

Before I could process my surroundings or how I'd ended up in a bed I didn't know, I heard the door open. I turned to see Riley, standing there in nothing but a white towel—his trim chest on display, the pale skin speckled with sparse, dark hair that swiftly led down his abdomen beneath the towel. Freshly showered dark hair hung in his eyes messily and panic spread within me.

I racked my brain, but I could not remember *anything* past Cheerleaders. I was drawing a literal blank at the moment.

Oh my God, did we—

"You're up," Riley said, as he took a slow step toward me.

My heart was running rampant as I tried to piece everything together, and I tried to remember just how badly I'd fucked up.

This is not how this was supposed to happen!

This was not supposed to happen at all!

"I'm so sorry..." I said, running a hand through my hair as shame and guilt built within me.

Riley stood before me, the fresh scent of hotel shampoo and body wash wafting off of him. My stomach flipped as I stared at the sight of him, looming over me, looking like absolute perfection at this hour. My cock twitched in response, and I felt as if I could barely breathe under his gaze.

"I'm not," he said, his voice soft, even.

His words washed over me, and I couldn't help but close my eyes, soaking them in.

God, I wished I could remember what happened.

"I don't... I must have blacked out. I... I don't remember what happened past Cheerleaders," I admitted, feeling embarrassed.

I couldn't remember the last time I legit blacked out. I usually liked to be in control of myself and the situation.

When I opened my eyes, I saw Riley's furrowed eyebrows as he took a seat beside me on the bed. The bed squeaked a little, and a fresh pounding assaulted my head, and I felt a bit uneasy.

"Is that what's bothering you?" he asked, his voice barely a whisper.

"I mean, this isn't my first rodeo, but..." I said, not wanting to sound like a whiny little bitch or something. Lord knew I'd had my share of scenarios just like this, only I was the one being regretted.

Did I regret what happened?

I wasn't so sure... and that only made my insides twist some more.

I pulled my knees up to my chest beneath the covers.

How had things gotten so complicated?

"How did we even get here?" I asked, running a hand over my face.

"Apparently Drew Axel reserved a block of

rooms for us, due to our... festivities going a bit overboard. He texted me just before I jumped in the shower. Checking to make sure we'd gotten in all right."

I dared to steal a glance at Riley, not wanting to ask but needing to know all the same.

"I, uh, don't normally do this sort of thing, you know."

I scoffed, refusing to look at him for the moment. I didn't want to see regret or pity in his eyes.

"What sort of thing?" I grumbled.

"Take attractive men home. I mean, I know this isn't home or anything..." he said hurriedly. I glanced at him from beneath my lashes.

"I usually don't drink so much either... I'm usually the responsible one, you know?" he asked, sighing.

The need, the desire to make him feel better, even when I was struggling for sanity myself was overwhelming.

"Do you remember what happened?" I asked.

Riley's gaze softened. "Bits and pieces, yes."

I attempted to soothe his own crisis at the moment, assuring him this wasn't what I usually did either.

Except, if I was being honest... I did do this sort of thing. Not often, but...

I didn't usually do it with people I had feelings for.

Did I have feelings for Riley?

I wanted to say no, but the truth was so much more complicated than that.

"I didn't mean to take advantage, of you I mean, I..." I breathed out a sigh as panic laced me. "I don't even know if you're..."

It was a stupid thing to say, to imply that I was panicking about whether or not Riley was clean, and it was even dumber to insist that was what was bothering me when I knew the truth. While I'd hooked up with guys via dating apps a couple times, I never performed with anyone, and I had a record that was spotless. I would have bet a million dollars Mr. Sunday Best was cleaner than a whistle.

Riley's shoulders fell, his lips pursed as he ran a hand through his hair.

"Oh my God, I didn't even think..."

"I'm clean," I blurted out, quickly hurrying through my confession if only to put it out in the open if it would help soothe Riley's nerves a fraction.

Hell, maybe it will even soothe my own.

"I mean, in case you, uh, were worried," I said, like an idiot.

"I mean, we probably should have had this

discussion before we..." I watched as his cheeks reddened.

"Fucked?" I asked hesitantly, the question hanging in the air.

My heart raced as I bit my lip, waiting for his confirmation.

"Actually, all I remember is you, um, on your knees..." he said, quickly recovering with, "And then I remember returning the favor, and then... I think we fell asleep because I had some weird dreams. We didn't, um, fuck," he said, and despite the redness in his cheeks, I couldn't deny the word on his tongue made my cock twitch.

A part of me was relieved, but also disappointed. Though there was no doubt in the world I wanted to drive the fine specimen next to me into next Tuesday with my cock, and I certainly wanted him to punish me with his.

I couldn't deny my attraction to Riley, but I also wanted to remember what he felt like, intimately. Images filled my brain of what felt like a far away memory... His lips ravaging my own, his tongue wrapped around my cock, him telling me...

I want you.

The words reverberated in my brain as hazy memory tried to surge forth. Of hands and heat, of hard cocks, and those three, little words spoken drunkenly, without thought or consequence. Spoken in truth.

I want you.

I wanted Riley Evans, but I knew I needed to tell him the truth.

I couldn't lie to him anymore. I wanted him to want *me* for me.

Not the me that everyone else got—*XxPrince-AyricxX*, the charismatic performer, Eric the eternal bachelor who knew how to have a good time. I wanted Riley to want me for the lost, childish idiot I was who couldn't breathe when he was in the same room.

My heart beat steadily in my chest as I squeezed my knees tight.

This was it, this was the downfall, I could feel it. I'd flown too close to the sun.

"I know you probably won't believe me, but I don't normally do this sort of thing either," I said, feeling on the spot.

Riley squinted his eyes before brushing some hair out of my eyes. The touch was gentle, and I hated how much I liked it.

I'd been in plenty of scenarios the morning after, both being the one to leave, and the one being left, and usually that was the end of things where I was concerned. But as I stared at Riley in that hotel bedroom, a part of me didn't want this to end.

A part of me wanted to believe that in the mistakes I had made, I could salvage a pure truth.

And that truth was that I was falling in love with Professor Riley Evans.

"Why wouldn't I believe you?" he asked curiously.

The words caused a lump to form in my throat.

"Because, Riley, I—"

But they'd never be spoken. They were lost the moment Riley swiftly caressed my jaw and planted the softest kiss I'd ever felt on my lips.

Riley kissed me like I meant something. Like I was truly *everything* to him, just the way I was.

And God forbid, I wanted to drown in that kiss.

I always dreamed a man would kiss me like that, but no one ever did. Not until that moment.

I kissed him back, not wanting the moment to end.

The vibrant spark between us.

"Shhh... it's okay," he whispered against my lips, brushing his thumb across my jaw.

"Riley..." I whined. Like a total bitch.

Riley's bitch.

Riley pulled me closer, and I fell into him like rain falls to the ground.

The impact, the feel of his warm, smooth chest against my own, his fingers in my hair... It all made me feel lightheaded.

I parted my lips, and he didn't miss a beat as we both fell back against the bed, my cock brushing against the damp, white towel separating us.

Riley slid his tongue in my mouth as his lips traveled over my jaw, down my neck, causing fresh fire to bloom in my blood. My head was pounding, my cock aching as his fingertips grazed my skin.

"Tell me..." he breathed as he draped his hand across my hip.

I allowed my hands to travel over his chest, down his abdomen, resting on the knot where he'd tied the towel closed, absentmindedly brushing my thumb over the bunched fabric.

Riley looked at me and in his eyes I could see he was scared too, though what he had to be scared of was beyond me.

"Tell me to stop," he whispered, letting his forehead fall gently to rest against mine. "Every time I'm near you, all I want to do is touch you..." he breathed, his voice thick with emotion and lust.

And something else I didn't dare acknowledge because I knew I would be doomed, if I did.

"And I know that makes me sound like a total creeper, but—"

I kissed him in return, my own demons clawing at me.

I knew I should have told him to stop. I should have ended things right there, and walked away.

But when Riley Evans kissed me, when he touched me... it felt like everything was perfect for once.

He made me *happy*.

And I didn't want that feeling to go away, so I said, "I don't want you to stop."

Riley kissed me wistfully, rolling me over so that I was on my back, my cock standing up straight with his own admission of excitement a tenting of the white of the towel.

As Riley leaned over me, his towel shifted, revealing his hip lines. The light of morning lit him up like a halo, as he pressed himself against me.

"I never want you to stop," I breathed desperately, imploring his gaze with mine.

Alarm bells sounded off all throughout my body, my brain.

Danger, Eric!

But I'd never felt so strongly about anyone in my life, and so I didn't know how to do anything else at the moment, except be the man Riley Evans wanted.

The man he wanted to kiss, to touch.

I wanted to be *his.*

Riley kissed me once more as he settled his fingers in my hair.

I slid my hands down his sides resting them on his hips.

The towel bunched in my grasp, and within seconds, I felt his hand covering mine.

"Tell me what you want," he purred, his voice full of tenderness as he slid his other hand down my chest. My cock throbbed as I arched my back off the bed, needing to feel his skin on mine.

My head was still pounding, pain mixing with pleasure.

Riley traced his fingertips lightly along my shaft, his touch electric as he mapped each swollen vein.

"Is this what you want?" he asked sweetly, running them up and down my dick.

I found it hard to focus, to breathe, due to the overwhelming feelings culminating in me. His lips pressed against my neck, right over my throbbing pulse, his tongue on my skin felt sweet and warm.

The moan that escaped me was unavoidable.

I wrapped my arms around him, seeking grounding as I pulled him closer. I thrust my engorged cock against his touch, needing more.

"Yes," I breathed, lost in his warmth.

Riley kissed me, his tongue caressing mine as he wrapped his hand around my cock, his palm warm and soft like velvet.

"Is this what *Daddy* wants?" he purred, his lips turning into a smile against mine as he slowly pumped me, brushing his thumb over my slit and through my sticky precum.

God, yes. I want this.

I want him... this man who makes me unable to think or see straight.

This man who drives me crazy.

"Yes," I cried out as my hands settled on his hips once more, which I noticed were now bare. I opened my eyes for a moment to see him above me, naked, his thick, beautiful cock also weeping with delight.

I let my hand slide lazily over his hip, cupping his ass as I looked up into his eyes.

Riley touched me with a reverence I'd never known. Like he truly felt my body was a *gift*.

Like nothing mattered but *this*.

Us.

Riley smirked as he withdrew his hand, sliding down and replacing it with his warm mouth. In one swift motion, he took me into the back of his throat, moaning and groaning as he labored his tongue around my engorged cock.

"Fuck..." I hissed as I fought against his hold. The desire to flip him and be on top, with my cock shoved down his throat was a natural reaction. I didn't like to be *anyone's* bottom.

Riley traced his fingers along my thighs until his hands were beneath my ass cheeks and he was gently lifting me off the bed. The edge of his thumb brushed against my entrance, teasing me, taunting me, and in his grip I was putty.

Resistance was futile, and the second he pressed the edge of his finger against my sensitive entrance, I cried out his name like a prayer.

And in some ways, perhaps that's what Riley was to me.

A prayer, a wish.

A chance to live happily ever after.

When my faculties returned, I turned to him, reaching for his cock.

Riley only smiled, shaking his head. "That's not necessary," he said softly, and he climbed off the bed.

Panic laced through me once again, that I'd done something wrong. Though Riley turned to look at me as he picked up his clothes, his gaze soft and inviting.

"But... I need to take care of you," I whined.

God, the things this man does to me, it's like I don't even know myself!

Riley slid his underwear on, my sight trained on him. He slid his briefs up over his cock, which looked to be softening.

"You already did," he said with a blush. "I'm, uh, going to find some breakfast," he said as he pulled on his shirt.

I watched him like a black and white movie; intently and with bated breath.

A part of me knew he wouldn't *leave* me, but anxiety and memory told me I'd been in this scenario too many times before to believe it would be different.

"Okay," I said shakily, watching him leave.

I hoped I was wrong.

CHAPTER 22

RILEY

THE RIDE back home was much quieter, probably due to the fact we were both more than spent.

Figuratively and physically.

I had meant what I said to Eric. I couldn't remember the last time I had gotten so drunk, or the last time I'd really let my walls down.

Which was most likely thanks to the alcohol.

I knew I should feel ashamed, guilty even, because I'd let myself have a little too much fun, and not only that... the liquid courage was more than to thank for my bold pursuance. For bringing Eric to bed.

But somehow, even though I knew I should be bothered by such things, I wasn't. In fact, I felt like we had turned a corner of sorts.

I had turned a corner of sorts.

For the first time in my life, I felt well and truly free. Like the sky was the limit.

Eric sipped his coffee as we pulled into his driveway, turning the car off. I immediately climbed out, going around to open his door before he could. Seeing the smirk on his face every time gave me a sense of satisfaction. I got the feeling it was hard for Eric to let someone else do things for him, probably because whatever it was he did—which we still hadn't confirmed he wasn't some mafia kingpin, though it was highly unlikely—he was probably the guy in charge, calling the shots. Which only made me like him more.

Just the very thought of him *commanding* me, like he had in our inebriated haze...

Fuck.

My cock stiffened as the memories tried to push forth, but I didn't want to walk down memory lane right now, no matter how nice it was.

I walked him leisurely up his sidewalk, the sun shining brighter than I'd ever noticed before. Eric's shoulders rose and then sunk as he slid his keys out of his pocket, as if he'd let out a huge sigh, though I didn't hear anything. He stood quietly, his lips pursed.

If I didn't know any better, I'd think something was wrong, or perhaps maybe I did something to sour his mood, but I knew from the way I felt—hungover and every bit my age—that he was likely feeling just as under the weather.

His gaze shot up to me, his voice tired. "Thanks for the breakfast, and the ride," he said firmly, though his tone seemed a bit off.

I wasn't too worried, though. Maybe like me, he just needed a couple Advil and a Netflix marathon.

I watched as he turned to open his door, and I couldn't help myself as I stopped him, setting my hand on his wrist.

"Are you busy later? Maybe we could hang out? Grab some dinner, or—"

Eric's shoulders rose and sunk once more, and he dropped his hand, his bright blue eyes looking almost glassy.

"I... I can't. I, uh, have plans this evening."

"Oh," I said, not at all hiding the disappointment in my voice.

"Yeah, I'm sorry, it's just... I have a lot to do on Saturdays, usually," he said, looking away.

"Catching up on stuff after the work week?"

I said, sliding my hands in my pockets as I gave him a soft smile.

"Something like that," he said, his eyes searching mine for something I couldn't quite put my finger on.

I took a step forward and he did not move back.

"When can I see you again?" I asked, my voice much huskier than I meant it to be.

Eric looked up at me like a lost puppy, eyes full of hope and wonder.

A part of me knew I was probably coming on too strong, but the rest of me didn't care.

In Eric's presence, I was bold, and unapologetic, and it felt *good* to be honest, to put myself out there.

"Tomorrow," he said, swallowing hurriedly. "I can meet you tomorrow, at the cafe?" His voice was somewhat soft, barely a whisper.

I smiled with a nod. "That sounds great," I said.

"Okay then, I'll see you tomorrow morning," he said as he turned from me, opening his door.

I waved to him softly with a smile on my face. Though a part of me wished he would invite me in, I knew it was probably best that I get home myself and catch up on things.

Starting with getting out of these tight ass pants and getting into my sweats and recuperating from my night out on the town.

But stupidly enough, the entire way home, I couldn't stop smiling.

Because I felt like for the first time, I was on cloud nine, and I realized that I didn't just *like* Eric and his sexy smirk, I didn't just want to hang out with him.

I was falling in love with him.

Suddenly, I was looking forward to my time off. Looking forward to spending time with him, just letting my guard down and having fun.

Not to mention I can barely keep my hands off of him, and who could blame me?

The man is like the literal embodiment of sex appeal.

He was perfect, and I knew at that moment, I'd made my decision. Tomorrow, at the cafe, I'd gather my bravery and be honest. I'd tell him how I felt. Because I didn't want to lie or hide my true feelings anymore.

I wanted to be with Eric, and the first step was admitting the truth to him. I hoped he would reciprocate. I hoped he'd say yes, to being mine.

My boyfriend.

When I finally made it into my house,

exhaustion hit. I pulled off my clothes, seeking the comfort of my lounge wear and the soft cushions of my couch, and I slept.

I slept better than I'd slept in a long time, and I knew it was because for the first time, I was *happy*. Nothing was going to ruin that

CHAPTER 23

RILEY

AFTER A GOOD LONG nap and a day spent actually relaxing, I felt better than I had in a while. My hangover was even dissipating.

I settled in on my couch with my computer around eight, the first time I'd really gone online all day.

Opening up my laptop, my first task was always checking my email, which was always packed not just with spam and promotional sign ups, but my students were also free to email me if they had questions, or if someone wanted to come in on Sunday afternoon during my set times and use the studio.

I'd gotten through most of my emails when I

came across one that was sent from an anonymous address, with the subject "Your boyfriend."

I immediately dismissed it, thinking it was spam or some porn bot initially, but then reality hit me.

My email was my *school email.* That email was filtered pretty good, and I'd never gotten anything remotely sexual on there.

Which only intrigued me more to click open.

There was nothing, but a link. No hello, no sincerely so-and-so, just a link to an Only Fans page.

The email itself was encrypted, and as far as I could tell there was no way to figure out who'd sent it.

Curiosity got the better of me, but I wished it hadn't at that moment. Because that was the moment everything changed.

I clicked the link.

Which brought me to an Only Fans page that was streaming live, and my blood ran straight to my cock as shame, guilt, and panic flooded me.

Eric's bright, beautiful blue eyes stared at me through the screen, his thick, swollen pink cock head sliding through his wet hands. He was naked, on his *bed*, stroking himself as he gazed into the camera, his deep, breathy voice cursing as he slathered his cock in precum, slowly thrusting himself into his hand.

My cock twitched as my blood rushed, my insides turning with arousal as much as panic.

Comments came flying in across the screen, talking about his *daily loads*, saying dirty things I'd only heard in my audiobooks.

I shut the lid of my computer, sucking in a deep breath.

My cock was as solid as marble, and I swallowed harshly as it twitched in my sweatpants.

"What the fuck?" I asked aloud to the empty room, panic lacing through me.

A part of me couldn't believe what I'd seen, thinking I must have imagined it.

My breathing hitched as my cock *throbbed* with need.

Catching my breath, I slowly opened the laptop once more, needing to know if I had indeed imagined it, or someone was playing a dumb prank on me or something.

The video picked up right where it left off, and sure enough, my eyes did not deceive me.

I watched Eric, or as a cursory glance down at his handle read, *XxPrinceAyricxX*, *smack* his cock before spitting on it. The memory of his hardness in my mouth only made the strain against my sweats more restrictive, and one glance at the wet spot forming made me feel guilty as all hell, but I knew what I needed to do to feel sane.

So that I could think clearly.

I settled the laptop down on my coffee table before shimmying out of my sweats. My cock sprang free, stiff as a steel pole. My cock head was already pretty wet from the friction of my pants, pressing against a fabric prison. Shakily, I cupped my head, my eyes closing for a brief moment as Eric's breathy moans filled the air.

"You want to watch me fuck my hand?" he purred, his voice through the speakers silky and smooth. It was almost like he was truly in the room with me.

I could hear the comments rolling in, like wind chimes.

"You want to watch me fuck my toy?" he groaned, and I pretended it was me he was talking to.

"Yes," I breathed out loud in the space of my living room, desperate for relief.

Make me your toy...

I watched as Eric smirked on camera, grabbing himself once more. His fingers slid through the sticky mix of precum and spit, and my own cock ached as I increased my pace.

I watched as Eric took some black, sleek contraption, sliding it over his cock. From the front, I watched it disappear, thrusting in tandem. He turned to his side, the view high-lighting his defined muscles, his hips and flexing abs as he thrust himself into the sleek toy, and I couldn't help how my mind wandered guiltily down a path I knew I shouldn't traverse.

Eric's voice screwed up as he cursed, groaning as his thrusts increased.

"Fuck!" he cried out as he pulled out, his release dripping down the silicone, spraying like a damn fountain as he dropped the toy to the floor, bracing himself against the bed.

"Oh fuck!" I cried out in unison as I came, watching his muscles contract as he continued to pump himself, his breath heavy, eyes shut in ecstasy as his release covered his abs.

"I'm sorry," he said, his voice a breathy whisper.

My own orgasm tortured me as I continued my own climax, filled with relief, but also guilt. I closed my eyes as reality set in, and the sound of the video cut out.

I looked at my cum-covered cock, at the black box on the computer screen, at his name in the lower corner.

XxPrinceAyricxX.

The banner at the top of the page listed a boatload of subscribers and I realized all at once, this was what he did.

Eric was a... what?

A stripper?

A porn star?

A... camboy?

My phone dinged, my gaze fixing on it like a laser beam.

I reached out to the arm of the couch where it lay, picking it up with shaky breath.

Is 10:00 am okay?

Eric's text stared at me from beneath the lit glass of my phone, calling me like a beacon.

My heart raced as I swallowed harshly, running my clean hand over the screen.

Sure.

I texted him back, feeling like the dirtiest human being on the planet. Knowing what he was doing only moments ago.

That I was *watching* him.

Eric sent back a thumbs up, and I dropped my phone as the sob came.

I breathed out a sigh of exasperation as my eyes filled with tears. My softening cock weeped its last bit of release, and I felt so fucking guilty.

This was a dangerous game I'd fallen into.

Eric was dangerous.

While I couldn't deny my attraction to Eric, I knew progressing further into a relationship *now* would be like walking on a tightrope.

If the wrong person recognized him...

I looked at the tab on my screen for my email, my heart sinking.

Perhaps someone already had.

A tear rolled down my face, because I knew what I needed to do.

But I didn't want to.

I really didn't fucking want to.

Because despite the shock, the guilt of what I'd done, what I'd seen...

Somehow I knew it wasn't *him.* Not really.

The Eric I knew was fun, and carefree, and a bit of a brat at times, and I was in love with him.

But I was scared. Scared of the uncertainty, of worrying about whether or not someone would talk, because they clearly knew.

I didn't want to wind up in the Principal's office or something.

No, I needed to do the right thing before things went too far.

They've already gone too far.

I wiped my tears with a shaky hand as I tucked my limp cock back in my pants, closing the lid to the laptop once and for all.

And when I showered that night, not even the hottest water could wash me clean.

CHAPTER 24

Eric

I stared at my set up, all the lights and equipment, as I hovered over my laptop, which I'd shut down abruptly.

It was like for the first time, they were foreign to me. Like they belonged to someone else.

Tears threatened the edges of my eyes as I slid to the floor, naked, drawing my knees to my chest.

Shame and guilt bloomed in the pit of my stomach.

I'd done my job. The same as I had the day before that, and the day before that.

What was different?

But I knew as I brushed away one of those burgeoning tears *exactly* what was different.

Because the entire time I performed, I was thinking about *him*. Closing my eyes, remembering *his* touch, *his* kiss, *his* smile. All of it.

I no longer derived pleasure from what I was doing, despite doing it well.

And the reality was, I hadn't really *enjoyed* myself the way I did when I was with Riley, or when I thought about him, in a long time.

I looked around my room, at the closet full of designer clothes, my comfortable 1000 count Egyptian cotton sheets.

I'd built this life for myself, by myself, using little more than my looks and sex appeal, and a part of me had always been proud of that. That I was able to make my dreams come true with a little lube and my big cock.

But that night, I felt my dreams shift. I felt myself emerging from some sort of cum-covered cocoon.

I reached for my phone on the ledge of my desk.

The comments were still pouring in, and each one made my heart ache.

I didn't want to hear strangers telling me how thirsty they were, or how they wished they could fuck me.

I wanted to hear *Riley* commanding me,

begging me, whispering sweet nothings in my fucking ear like a lovesick puppy.

I swiped up on my screen, brushing past all the comments and tips, bringing up my messenger.

Reaching out for my lifeline, the one person who I thought could calm my sudden hurricane before I spiraled too far out of control.

My fingers shook as I typed out my text, setting a time for tomorrow.

I knew I was reaching, that it wasn't what I really wanted to talk about.

I wanted to tell him the truth.

My fingers hovered over the keys as I thought about what to say, when his *okay* text came in.

I pursed my lips, staring at the text until another name came across my screen. One that didn't text me very often.

Jordan.

I tapped the notification immediately.

I have a proposition for you. If you're interested.

I twisted my lips. Not that I didn't trust Jordan, but I was not in the mood to be someone's stand in again, not right now.

But before I could answer, he texted me a damn novel.

Sticky and I have decided to start shifting our focus and look at more passive income streams. A friend of mine came to me with the idea of putting together a coaching course, kind of like a How-To on how to make bank on OF, but it wouldn't just be OF. She's looking for people who are good at content creation, and I thought maybe you might be interested in joining us. All the coaches are paid directly by her, so there's no middle man or anything. All you need to do is create your course, and once it starts selling on the platform, you get a percentage of the sales from every customer, and you only need to like... engage with them if they have questions.

I stared at the screen for a moment, trying to process his words.

An OF course?

Like... *teaching* someone?

I had to admit, the idea intrigued me.

Though I was also curious as to what caused my friends to *shift* focus.

Sticky's in? I asked.

Sticky's in. I'm sure he'll still do some posting, but I know he's been getting a little burned out as of late, trying to keep up with the demand of our subs.

I raised my eyebrow. Sticky's sex drive was higher than mine, so if he was considering *taking a break*, I knew it had to be something major.

Passive income *helping* others achieve what I did on my own without help.

I couldn't deny it sounded kind of nice, actually. Being able to spread my knowledge. Knowledge that wasn't necessarily tied to my performance skills. Using my brain for once instead of my cock.

I'll do it.

I didn't think twice, answering him. Moments ago, I had wondered if there was more to this, to what I was doing, and then suddenly I had my answer. A way out.

It was like the universe heard me and said, "Here you fucking go, kid."

The relief that washed over me with those three words was immense.

Cool. I'll send you details later.

With that, I was left, feeling like for the first time, maybe things *would* work out for once.

Maybe my luck was truly changing.

CHAPTER 25

I TOSSED and turned all night, because I couldn't stop thinking about the inevitable, and soon enough, it was time to head to the cafe.

Whereas in the past week or so I'd become accustomed to the butterflies in my stomach when I knew I was going to meet Eric, there were no butterflies this time.

Only anxiety and sadness.

When I got to the cafe, the place was already pretty busy. I took a seat, watching the customers smiling, laughing I took in the rich scent of coffee and pastries.

It wasn't all that long ago that I was supposed to meet my blind date here. But I'd been busy, and lost track of time, and I missed my shot. But fate intervened, it seemed, and that night I'd gone to M's Place to grab a drink with my brother and lick my wounds.

And that was the night I met Eric.

Almost as if he could read my mind, he waltzed in the door at that very moment, looking as divine as ever. Dressed in a pair of jeans and a black polo shirt, he looked positively sophisticated. His bright blue eyes sparkled like diamonds, and his dark hair was swept back, the light catching the gleam in his raven locks.

Gorgeous.

My stomach turned in knots as he looked at me, my blood rushing beneath the surface, straight to my cock.

He smirked at me, and then I remembered.

I remembered him staring at me through the computer screen, stroking himself and...

I shifted in my seat, if only to stifle my burgeoning erection, because now was certainly not the time to get all hot and bothered.

"Hey," he said as I rose, intending to head to the counter to order a drink.

I needed something to hold, to ground myself to, otherwise I would have sunk right through the floor.

"Hey," I said. I glanced at him as he leaned in toward me.

My heart raced, because I wanted nothing more than to give in and lean into him.

To kiss him like he had tried to kiss me.

But instead, I evaded him, making a beeline for the counter, and ordering a pumpkin spice latte immediately.

Eric didn't seem too bothered by my actions, instead just shrugging and he ordered himself a flat white latte.

When we'd placed our orders and had our drinks which Eric *insisted* he purchase for us, much to my disdain—there was no turning back.

"Something on your mind, Cinderella?" he drawled, and took a sip of his coffee.

"I just..." I said as I watched the muscles in his forearm tense and flex as he did so, and it only reminded me of the previous night, watching all of his muscles flex as he came.

Beautifully, I might add, but still.

I licked my lips, glancing away from him and sipping my own drink.

How the hell am I going to get through this?

I knew what I wanted to say, and a part of me figured I should just get out with it.

I saw you online, XxPrinceAyricxX.

I know what you do.

I think it might be in our best interest if we just...

But for some reason when I looked at him,

that's not what I said. Instead, I said, "It's just this wedding, I guess. We're close to the big day and things are just getting more stressful."

Eric reached out, setting his hand over top of mine. Instinctively, I wanted to pull back, but found it difficult to do so. Like my hand itself was made of iron.

I looked down to where he touched me, running his thumb along my knuckles.

"I mean, I get it. Weddings are a giant pain in the ass."

I scoffed at his remark. "Weddings are a time of love and joy," I said.

Eric let out a dark chuckle. "For some, sure."

"It's just... there are so many details. Things to get absolutely right," I grumbled.

"Isn't that like, the maid of honor's job or something?" Eric asked, raising a brow.

I pulled my hand back, all too aware that his touch was giving me goosebumps and causing my cock to twitch.

"Not everyone has a maid of honor, you know." I wrinkled my nose.

"I'm assuming the bride—"

"Giselle," I corrected.

"I'm assuming Giselle has, like, a ton of bridesmaids. I'm sure they have all the important shit taken care of. All you have to do is hold the rings, plan the party, and look pretty in a suit."

I pursed my lips as I sipped my coffee. This conversation was leaning farther away from what I wished.

Or perhaps, it wasn't, if I was being truthful.

Perhaps I was not the confidant, bold man I thought I was. Perhaps I was a coward who could not look this man in the eye and tell him, *I know.*

"You would know something about that, wouldn't you? Standing there, looking *pretty,* as you say?" I bit out, watching Eric's eyebrows furrow.

He left his hand on the table, leaning back in his chair languidly. The motion drew my attention to his groin, knowing full well in detail what he was packing beneath his tight, form-fitting pants.

But so did thousands of others.

Call it jealousy, call it petulance.

But I wished it was all for me and no one else, and that made my stomach flip once more.

"I know a thing or two about weddings, actually. I've been a groomsman, like, three times."

I blinked. "You never said..."

Eric shrugged. "You never asked."

Images flipped through my brain of Eric

looking pretty in a suit, of him and my brother and party members tossing back shots and dancing with strippers... To that of him wrestling his thick cock out of his suit pants, looking down at me like he looked at me through the computer screen, taunting me to take him into the back of my throat. My own cock twitched in response as my heart lifted, and I nearly jumped when my phone rang.

I didn't even have to look at the name to know who it was, since my brother had his own ringtone, after all.

"Excuse me a second, Eric," I said as I rose from my seat and headed outside, out of earshot.

"Hey, what's up?" I answered, trying to sound normal. The cool air outside the shop was like a balm to my flushed self, and I let out a small sigh of relief.

What sounded like a *sob* on the other end had me on high alert.

My brother *never* cried. Over anything, so the immediate sound was like a giant red flag.

"Aaron, what's wrong, are you okay? Do you need me to come get—"

"It's Giselle," he breathed, his voice heavy.

"Is Giselle okay?" I asked, panicking right along with him.

Giselle was his *world.* She had been ever

since they met in college, and I knew then the day he brought her home for Christmas break, there was no denying that one day they'd be the *it* couple of Jasper Springs.

A part of me was jealous, to hear him fall apart over her. I wished someone could love me like that.

With such intensity and depth, the world would stop for them when I walked into a room.

"She's fine, she's..." Another sob, and now I really was worried.

"What, Aaron, she's what?"

"Pregnant, Riley. Giselle is pregnant."

All the blood in my body chilled at those words, warmed only by the remaining ones, full of shock, awe, and happiness.

"I'm going to be a father, Riley. You're going to be an uncle."

I couldn't speak. I could barely process the words as he said them. Giselle was pregnant... and the wedding was only a few weeks away.

"We're not telling anyone, for... obvious reasons," he said, sniffling on the other end.

"Oh," I said, like an idiot, at a loss for words. I wanted to congratulate him, but suddenly the world seemed so vast, I could barely breathe.

I always figured they'd be all in on starting a family, but not this soon.

But I guess, some things don't come on schedule. Including babies.

I turned to look through the window, noticing Eric sitting there nonchalantly, browsing his phone.

For some reason, looking at him snapped me out of my daze, bringing me back to reality.

"Congratulations," I mustered, coming back to Earth.

"Thanks, I just... I needed to talk to someone, since, you know, this is kind of a big deal."

"I get it. Can't tell anyone, but you want to tell the world," I said, watching Eric mindlessly sip his latte, waiting for me to return.

To return and break his heart.

Was I capable of that?

Did I want that?

I wasn't so sure, as the very *thought* of not seeing Eric again made my heart palpitate.

"How... how do you feel about the news?" I asked, trying to focus on the subject. I tore my gaze away from Eric.

"I mean, marriage, kids, it's what I always wanted," Aaron said calmly.

"You say that like you're not sure," I spoke cautiously. If my brother was having second thoughts about the news, about the wedding...

"I mean, relationships aren't ever *easy*, you know. You just... when you love someone, you endure whatever you have to, because you know in the long run they're worth it."

I closed my eyes, feeling overwhelmed by the emotion in his voice.

"How do you know?" I asked quietly. "That they're worth it? The pain, the drama, the bullshit. How do you know that it's all going to work out?"

My brother sighed. "I don't. But I know I love Giselle, and I can't imagine my life without her. I can't imagine who I'd be without her, you know? And now..."

I listened as my brother got choked up, talking about his soon to be wife. The love in his voice was evident.

"God, if you would have told us when we were two college kids at a frat party that one day we'd be married with kids, I wouldn't have believed you. But now, all I can think about is seeing her face at that altar and wondering if this kid will have her eyes," he said, letting out a chuckle. "Our kid is going to be at our wedding, and no one is going to have any fucking clue."

I laughed with him, understanding the levity of this secret. Especially around our mother, who was notorious for sniffing out gossip.

With practically the entire town coming, it was really wild to think about.

I turned to look at Eric once more, catching

his gaze. He waved, and I couldn't help but do the same.

"Anyway, I got to go, I just... Thanks, man. Thanks for being you. And listening."

"Your secret is safe with me," I said, and the line went dead.

And as I looked at Eric in the light of the coffee shop, I wondered just how much my still-beating heart could endure.

CHAPTER 26

Eric

I watched as Riley came back inside the cafe, dressed in his white shirt and khaki's like some knight in Ralph Lauren.

Thankfully, his brief departure had given me much to think about, and I realized I couldn't do it. I couldn't tell him the truth, until I'd put it behind me.

I wanted to be respectable. I wanted to be *clean* for him.

Sunday Best, and all.

And I couldn't very well go diving headfirst into a relationship with Riley, no matter how bad I wanted it, without cleaning out my closet first.

I needed to go home, make my announcement, and then I could process my next steps.

The road to salvation wasn't going to be easy, but as Riley sat down, crossing his legs in front of me, I knew.

I knew that I was standing on the precipice of a new phase of life. The next phase of my life.

I'd been a groomsman, and I did know a thing or two about weddings, but I'd never considered the possibility of getting married myself. I'd only ever wanted a boyfriend, someone who I could be myself with, my *true* self.

Camming wasn't who I really was. *XxPrince-AyricxX* was someone I had become through guilt and loneliness, and because of that, others responded to him. Because perhaps, they were guilty and lonely too, and I could never begrudge them for that. After all, they made me who I was today.

I only hoped that they would understand that I was ready to move on.

I *needed* to move on.

"Hey, I, uh, I know I just got here but, uh, I have to head out. I have some stuff to take care of. Can we reconvene? Another day?" I asked, both nervous as all hell but also feeling a sense of disappointment.

How had things become so complicated?"

"Yeah, uh, that's probably a good idea. That was my brother, so I, uh, need to get going too."

"Okay, yeah. Cool. That works then. We'll be in touch?" I asked, hopeful.

"Of course," Riley said, smiling. But behind his smile I could tell something was bothering him, but I didn't want to press. Maybe it really was just stupid wedding drama. Been there, done that.

And with that, we parted ways. I climbed into my car and drove home. Walking through the door, I felt a sense of dread as well as relief. I knew what I needed to do.

CHAPTER 27

Eric

I sat on my bed, clothed. The lights around me were like a halo, and there wasn't a toy in sight. I didn't want anyone to get the wrong idea. Although my body was used to this, and as such looking at the camera made my cock twitch, I let it be.

Not now, not for everyone else.

I watched the timer as it ticked, the seconds like an eternity.

When I was live, I could see over a hundred people logging on, and I blew out a breath.

This was it.

I looked into the camera and I told them, my long-standing subscribers that there would be no more Daily Load. There would be no more *XxPrinceAyricxX*. I thanked them for their patronage, for their loyalty. For their praises and their tips, and for making a lonely guy feel a little less lonely for a while.

I told them that the years had been great, but it was time for me to simply move on and expand my talents elsewhere.

I told them that I'd met someone, and I wanted to really give it a shot.

The words as I said them were cathartic, and even though I knew I was talking to thousands of people, it didn't feel like I was talking to anyone but myself.

Saying it out loud was the hardest thing I'd ever done.

But the outpouring of *support* from my dirty talkers, my top tier and my bottom tier subs alike, was overwhelming.

Telling me like an old boss how much they'd miss me, but wishing me all the best. Joking at how they would have to find another cock to fantasize over, and praising me that whatever person—because I'd never disclosed my sexuality on my account openly—had my attention was the luckiest person on earth. Especially given what they knew about me, of course.

And when the live ended, I felt relieved. I

watched as my account updated, until it disappeared.

It was gone.

Several years worth of content, of comments, of memories. In the flash of a second, it was all gone.

There was no more *XxPrinceAyricxX*.

There was only me.

I breathed out a heavy sigh and tears prickled the edges of my eyes. The lights still shone on me, but there was no audience. There was no performance.

There was just me, my stiff cock, and my bed, for the first time in a long time.

I wiped my tears away as I thought about the levity of such a reality.

I palmed my cock through my pants, feeling a sense of guilt, but also a sense of freedom.

I slowly unzipped my pants, taking my time.

Shimmying out of them felt foreign, despite the fact I'd done it daily for years.

I didn't take my shirt off, or my socks, because I didn't feel like it.

Instead, I leaned back on my bed, my left arm behind my head, using my right to palm my cock slowly. Brushing my thumb over my slit, I relished in the shiver that went up my spine.

I'd been focused on the art of the cumshot

for so long, the motions so familiar and repeated, I hadn't truly engaged myself.

It's a strange sort of realization, to come to terms with the fact I *liked* my own touch. That I hadn't really given in to pleasing myself the way I wanted to, even though I thought I had.

My eyes fell closed as my hips bucked of their own accord.

My cock throbbed in my hand as I squeezed it lightly, the sensation causing a moan to escape my throat. Thick and swollen, I removed my hand from behind my head, letting my fingers travel down my abdomen to my base. I squeezed my balls with a light pressure that felt amazing, and my head pebbled with wetness.

I thought about Riley, and his perfect, silken lips wrapped around my cock. I thought about his tongue in my mouth, and his breath on my skin, and I thought about what he would feel like, the weight of him on top of me, pinning me down to the mattress, sliding his thickness inside of me.

My legs stiffened as my core muscles tensed, my veiny cock throbbing with release. I arched my back, my toes curling as my legs stiffened and I writhed in my bed, my hand pushing my cock toward my chest as I came with full force on my shirt.

The relief was euphoric as I lay there in my

bed, lazily stroking myself until I'd emptied myself completely, my shirt a sticky mess, my body flushed, and my heart full.

I didn't feel guilty about fantasizing about the man of my fucking dreams, and I didn't feel embarrassed or self conscious about my facial expressions or the way my toes curled or my body twitched when I naturally came.

I felt better than I had in a long time.

I vaguely remembered the phone going off with notifications as I drifted to sleep, peacefully.

And I dreamed of weddings and cafes, and pretty boys in suits who made me feel whole.

CHAPTER 28

RILEY

"WELL?" Chris's voice penetrated my thoughts as I realized I'd read the same line in my syllabus three times.

I blinked, turning to face my coworker and friend, as memory dawned on me.

"What's the verdict, Evans? Did you get the ass or not?" he taunted as he took a seat on my counter top. Though it was lunchtime, there were still kids around, and a part of me didn't care if they heard Chris's foul mouth.

I supposed it wasn't the worst thing they could hear.

I didn't really *want* to do the song and dance

with Chris. Especially given everything that had happened over the weekend.

But a sliver of me looked at the towering, sporty man who I considered the closest thing I had to a best friend, and I couldn't help myself.

"Please, please, tell me you got laid."

I nodded. "And then some. But..." I sighed, knowing it was best just to purge it all. Get it out in the open so I could grieve the perfection of *Prince Eric*.

Or however he spelled it.

"But?" Chris pressed.

"It's not the mafia. Or a drug dealer," I said calmly.

Chris raised an eyebrow. "Oh? Then what? Stripper?"

"Close. Only Fans. Cam Boy."

Chris's jaw was agape with my admission, a low whistle soon following. He didn't miss a beat. "And you're worried Mr. Only Fans might be bad for your reputation?"

My silence spoke volumes.

"You like this guy, don't you?" Chris's words were serious, all humor dissolved from his tone.

My own admission was harrowing, as I spoke it without thinking.

"I think I'm in love with him."

Chris offered me a soft smile.

"I'm not going to tell you it's not a

dangerous game. I'm sure you already know that," he said.

I sighed. "He doesn't know I know. I found out by accident."

"Browsing on your own?" Chris quietly asked.

"Sort of. Anonymous link in my email."

Chris raised his eyebrows in alarm. "Your school email?" he asked.

I nodded. "I tried to look into the sender, but it was encrypted. Believe me, I tried."

"Someone must've seen you two together," Chris said, stroking his chin.

I let out a deep sigh as reality hit me.

Of course, why didn't I think of that.

It could have been a colleague, while we were out partying, but I had a feeling it wasn't. I had a feeling, as I looked at the seat where Trevor Kleypas sat, exactly who'd dropped the bombshell.

He recognized Eric.

And was worried I was making a mistake.

I wasn't sure whether to be disgusted that he recognized Eric because I knew what that meant, despite the fact Trevor was one of the early eighteen year old students, so he was technically of legal age to view such content—or to feel a sense of gratitude that he felt strongly enough to look out for me, his teacher. His quiet, shy, *gay* teacher who was apparently out of touch with the dating world.

And all at once, I realized that I had felt the same way. Worried, concerned, that I was perhaps making a mistake.

But as I sat there in my office, talking to Chris, remembering what my brother had said, I knew that was one of those do or die moments.

If I cut things off with Eric for good, would I regret never *enduring*?

Would I always wonder what could have been, if I had put myself first, above my job?

"Yeah, maybe," I said, and Chris smirked.

"Sometimes, in football, there are really hard calls to make. Ones that you know will benefit the team, but might not benefit certain players individually," he said seriously. "Sometimes the risk pays off. And sometimes it doesn't."

I looked at him with my own seriousness and intensity.

"What play do you think I should make, coach?" I asked.

Chris dropped from the counter, standing tall as he slid his hands in his pants pockets.

"I can't tell you that, Evans. That's up to you. But I can tell you that you miss a hundred percent of the shots you don't take."

"Are you quoting The Office to me?" I asked, flashing him with a smile.

"Michael Scott had to get it from somewhere." He winked as the bell rang.

"Thanks, Chris," I said, feeling a little bit better.

"Mhmm," he said as he tapped the top of my glass like it was a basketball hoop, once more.

My brother, Chris... they were both right.

Eric was worth it.

We were worth it, weren't we?

CHAPTER 29

ERIC

"You what?" Julie gasped on the other end of the phone.

"You heard me," I said, tinkering with the cables in my studio as I unhooked my equipment.

Finally, the AC had been fixed, and with my sudden departure from my long-time job, I didn't think I needed *everything* anymore. Just keeping a ring light and a professional mic would be enough for recording my content now.

Jordan had introduced me via email to the founder of Only4U, a platform which housed more than just Jordan, Sticky, and I, and covered more than just Only Fans.

The owner, Paris, had intentions of launching her platform with courses that covered content creation on all platforms, including TikTok, Instagram, and more. Courses were curated and taught by those who were bigger names on their prospective platforms. Jordan, Sticky, and I were a team, our course content specifically geared toward creating different types of marketable OF content and how to get your content shown and in regular rotation with the algos—even if your content wasn't sex.

Most people tended to think of Only Fans as being a sort of porn hub, and while they wouldn't be incorrect, plenty of people have a variety of non-sexual accounts and content on there—and while sex may have been what we sold for a long time, I didn't start out that way, and neither had the boys.

"How do you feel about this transition?" she asked, surprise still evident in her voice.

"Good, I guess. I mean, maybe a change of pace is good for me. I'm not going to be young forever," I lamented. "Guess I really do work in social media now," I said with a chuckle.

Julie snickered. "Please, like there aren't thirty-something or fifty-something dudes out there making steamy *Daddy* content."

"And you would know this how, Jules?" I teased.

She snickered on the other end of the phone. "I might be taken, but I ain't dead, Eric."

I laughed a deep, rib-splitting laugh at her words. Julie was truly something else, and a part of me was glad to have a friend like her in my life.

Always supportive, and always a fucking hoot.

Then her tone shifted, changing like the chameleon she truly was.

"So what are you going to do now? About Riley?"

I nearly bumped my head on the desk at her words. I sat back on the floor, tangled in cords.

"I don't know, I haven't uh, really thought about it."

"You should tell him how you feel. Tell him the truth."

I sighed. "The truth is what I've been dying to tell him since I met him."

"What happened? Why didn't you?"

"Because I worried he'd just split, like everyone else. Because maybe I couldn't face the truth myself."

The silence was palpable between us as I listened to the sound of her soft breaths.

"You deserve to be happy, you know," she said seriously.

"I know, Jules. I just—" I swallowed harshly as I looked at my studio in disarray. "I think I'm on my way there, I just need to take care of some things first, you know."

"I know. I get it. But there's never going to be a right time, Eric. All you have is the here and now, so if you want him... go fucking get him. Tell him the truth, and if he can't see that you are an amazing person, beneath the sex appeal, he isn't for you."

I sighed at the weight of her words. "Do you think he is? For me, I mean."

"Shit, Eric I wouldn't have set you two up for a blind date if I thought you were bad for one another, you know that right? I mean, I like drama as much as the next girl, but I don't need to create any between my friends."

I smirked as I nodded in understanding. "You really think we're good for each other?" I asked, my voice small.

"I know you are. I think you know it too."

Just at that moment, Riley texted me. I swiped up, telling Julie I had to go, and she didn't press me.

Instead, she told me good luck, and hung up as I stared at Riley's text.

How about a do-over? Tomorrow night is bar bingo at M's Place...

I didn't hesitate to answer, *Yes, it's a date.*

CHAPTER 30

M's Place was always packed on Bar Bingo & Karaoke night. We'd agreed to meet up separately only because at the last minute, he had something work related to take care of via his Principal. A part of me was nervous, worried that somehow it had to do with me, or rather who I *was*, but I tried not to get too worked up.

Considering the fact I had shut down my online personal forty-eight hours ago.

Which also was the last time I—

"Hey."

Riley's smooth voice pulled me and my desperate cock from the grandeur of fantasy, and I had to do a double take. He stood in front of me like he had that first night we'd gone to the arcade together. Dressed down in dark jeans and a graphic tee shirt that sported some sort of dragon or something against heathered gray fabric. His light hair looked golden in the light of the bar, and my cock throbbed in time with my heart.

"Well, well, looks like Cinderella finally made it to the ball," I teased.

Riley looked a little worried, a little disheveled, running his hand through his hair. It wasn't a bad look on him, though.

I sipped my rum and coke, motioning for him to take a seat in front of the cards I placed in front of him, along with a bingo dabber.

One of the waitresses came by to take our drink order, or rather Riley's drink order, since I had started early. When she was gone, he looked at me with a slight expression of confusion.

"You got my cards," he mumbled, like some dazed teenager.

"I mean, it *is* bar bingo, and it's a game. You know how I like games. I think you like them too," I said, flashing him with a smirk.

The blush that crept onto his cheeks was my answer.

"I do. Like games, I mean, but... Eric..."

My eyebrows furrowed as his tone turned soft, worried.

"Is something wrong?" I asked, panic striking me.

Riley sighed, sliding his dabber up toward me. He tapped his long fingers on the table, biting his bottom lip before he said, "There's something I need to tell you."

"Actually, there's something I need to tell you too," I said, and took a sip of my drink.

"Really?" he asked, deadpan.

I nodded. "Yeah, but, uh, you first."

CHAPTER 31

IT WAS NOW OR NEVER.

"I, uh... came across something yesterday," I said, my entire body shaking like a leaf.

Eric's eyebrows furrowed with concern, and I let out a deep breath.

"I saw you. Online, I mean..." I said the words, and the moment they left my mouth I felt relief.

But that relief soon dissipated as I watched Eric's smile falter, as I watched his furrowing brows tighten, and his shoulders sink.

He didn't deny my words, or try to refute them.

But the sight of his sadness pulled at my heart and all I wanted to do was hug him.

But I was frozen in place, watching him.

"I can explain..." he said softly.

"I don't know if you need to, but..."

"I wanted to tell you, but I didn't know how. I worried that maybe—"

"What?" I asked, my voice faraway as I let myself get lost in his sapphire gaze, his youthful effervescence.

"I was worried you might... you know... want to stop whatever... this is."

"What is this?" I asked curiously, motioning between us. "Because ever since I met you, I haven't been able to define what this is. We're friends, I thought at first, but ever since the weekend, since the hotel, I—"

My words were jumbled in my brain as I tried to make sense of them, as emotion plagued me.

"I have friends. I don't feel a fraction for them, what I feel for you." I looked at him with a mixture of fear and hope.

Would he understand?

That he was worth it?

That despite the obstacles in our path—our jobs—that maybe this was fate?

"Say something," I pleaded, watching him bite his lip. "Say I'm crazy, and we can forget all of it. The games, the sex... Tell me you don't feel anything, and we can just be friends."

Eric's lips twitched at the words, his eyes sparkling with the beginnings of a somber mist.

"I don't want to be friends, Riley. I can't be friends with you," he said firmly.

"Oh," I said, feeling the worst rejection I think I'd ever felt in my life.

"I can't be friends with you when you're all I think about when I'm alone. Just me. I can't be friends with you when every time I'm near you I—"

He let out a deep sigh as my heart threatened to skip a beat.

"I should have told you the truth, about me. About what I *did*, but honestly, my experience in life taught me as soon as I did tell someone what I did, they peaced the fuck out, and I didn't want you to peace the fuck out," he said, twirling his straw in his glass. He looked at the cards, then at me as our waitress dropped off my beer.

"It was selfish, I know that. But when it comes to you I can't help my selfish desire. To be whoever you want me to be. To be wherever you are."

"Eric..." I breathed his name like the prayer it truly was.

"The other night, that was the last straw, just so you know. After I..."

The silence spoke volumes as we both caught one another's gaze, and he sucked in a breath.

"I'd been performing a long time before I met you, and I don't regret doing it for as long as I had. I only regret not ending it sooner, before I—"

"What?" I asked, leaning closer, hanging on his every breath, his every word.

Waiting for the words I dared to hope to hear.

"Before I fell in love with you." He said the words boldly, confidently, and my heart threatened to beat right up out of my chest.

I pushed away from the table, and rose to my feet. The look in his eyes killed me, because I knew he thought I was going to be like the others. I was going to walk away.

And in all reality and truth, I should have.

But I loved him too.

And love... it endures. It fights and it dances, and it wins and it loses.

But it always persists, even in the darkest of hours.

I moved toward him slowly, and he stood of his own accord, ready for an argument or defense, neither of which he'd need.

Because I knew as I looked at him, that he was more than what he displayed to the world.

I took his face in my hands, imploring his gaze with my own. I was well aware of our public display, and I didn't care.

I only wanted to soothe this man's worries, to show him I wasn't going to run.

I wanted to double down on our bets. Play the long game.

"What you do... it's not who you are. I know that better than anyone," I told him, rubbing my thumb along his jaw.

Eric looked up at me with glassy blue eyes. "You do?" he asked, his breath shaky. Vulnerable.

I nodded, letting my thumb brush over his lower lip. "You are a cocky, pain in the ass pretty boy who hates to lose," I said with a grin. "Whose voice is like velvet, and who I can't stop thinking about."

Eric parted his lips as a soft sigh escaped, settling his shaky hand on my hip.

"Besides, you still have yet to beat me at anything," I said with a smirk.

"Is that so?" Eric said, licking his lips.

I nodded. "I believe the score is Eric zero, Riley three."

Eric shook his head, grunting in response. "We'll see about that."

I swiftly tucked my finger under his chin, tilting his head up as I lowered mine, capturing his lips with my own.

Eric did not fight me, nor did he resist my advance.

I steadied him with my left hand as he sank against me, lifeless in my arms, under my ministrations. He parted his lips, and I desperately devoured his kiss, stroking his tongue with mine. My cock twitched, and he let out a small laugh.

"Maybe the score is Eric two , Riley three," he drawled against my lips.

"How so?" I asked as we broke away from each other's maddening kiss.

"Well, I certainly won where your cock is concerned. And perhaps your heart."

I smiled, shaking my head as he took his seat, crossing his legs like the cocky asshole he was.

And I took his bait.

I'd always take his bait, I realized. Because I loved playing with him just as much as he loved to rile me up.

"Yes, well, the night is still young. Perhaps there will be more victories in both of our cards."

Eric grinned wickedly. "Let's sweeten the stakes then. You win bingo, I'll sing like a canary for you and everyone here, whatever song you chose."

I shrugged. "Hmmm... I'm thinking Taylor Swift, or Axe 2 Grind..." I mused, flashing him with a grin of my own.

Eric rolled his eyes. "If I win bingo..." His voice was dark, inviting, and sinfully sweet. "If I win, you have to let me draw you like one of your French girls. And by that, I mean naked," he said with a shrug.

I raised an eyebrow at him. "Really Eric? You want to be the Jack Dawson to my Rose?" I laughed.

"Well, I wasn't sure you'd get the reference *old man*, but surely as a *professor of art*, you are well acquainted with the male form and how it is... inspiring, no?" he said, gleefully attempting a horrid French accent.

But all stereotypes aside, it was kind of funny, and I couldn't help but smile.

"Deal," I said as I took my seat and the MC took the stage to start calling numbers. But as far as I was concerned, I'd already won more than the game.

CHAPTER 32

Eric

We stood on my porch, like two awkward teenagers, as I fumbled with my keys.

"Do you want to come in?" I asked, feeling for the first time like I had nothing to hide.

Because we were both on the same page.

"Only if you're comfortable," Riley said sweetly, leaning down to deliver a quick kiss to my lip. "You are the one in charge here, and I am a gentleman, after all," he said, flashing me with a soft smile.

"Then yes," I breathed, not thinking twice. "Yes, I want you to come in."

Riley smiled, nodding as I opened the door

for him. He peered inside before taking a step in, and I followed.

My lights came on automatically as I shut the door.

A low whistle escaped his throat.

"Wow..." he said in awe, looking around my open concept living space.

"Wow as in good wow, or——"

Riley turned to face me as I slid my hands in my pockets, leaning against my sectional.

"Did... your job pay for this house?" he asked, though his tone was not judgmental as it was shocked.

I nodded, crossing my arms. "Yes. Took a while, because at first I didn't really know what I was doing, but once I figured out how to market, how to follow the algos, how to create engaging content, both sexual and non-sexual... I was able to finally monetize my content and buy a house. In a nice neighborhood, with nice neighbors, and..."

I realized I was rambling, and he was staring. He beamed at me with *pride*.

And it felt more than good to have someone look at me, the real me, and see the success I'd had, no matter how I'd come across it.

"That's amazing," he said as he stepped toward me and settled his hand on my waist.

"Like a Rubix Cube, so many intricate parts

make up who you are," he said, pulling me to him.

I slid my arms around his neck, looking up at him with so much love I could have been the heart eyes emoji.

"I'll never regret the things I did to get here, but I'm excited for this next chapter," I breathed against him.

Riley's eyebrows narrowed. "What's the next chapter?"

"I told you, after the other night, I closed my account. My friends slash coworkers, the guys from the pool game, we're going in as a team on a platform that teaches... well, anyone I guess who wants to know... about content creation and making a six figure business out of whatever it is you're passionate about, I guess."

Riley gleamed with pride. "That sounds amazing."

"Well, it kind of just happened to come at the right time, you know. I was ready to be done with performing because..."

My words disappeared as I looked at him, as I took in the sight of this man who inspired me to be the best version of myself I could be.

"I wanted *only* you," I whispered, pulling him into my kiss. "And I wanted you to be the only one who got me, all of me," I breathed, biting my lip as I let the words out, their finality like glass in the air between us.

Riley settled his hand on my collarbone, forcing me to look up at him as he nodded.

"You aren't the only one with selfish desires, Eric," he breathed as he slid his hands down my shirt to my waistband.

His fingers gently tugged at my belt, swiftly undoing the buckle, and my cock twitched. I looked into his eyes and knew, I'd never want anyone else.

Riley Evans was end game.

I settled my hands on his hips, tugging at the hem of his shirt. He let me remove it without question, and I had to stifle a groan as I laid eyes on his perfectly defined chest, lit up by the amber lighting of my sconces.

"Is that so?" I asked, raising a brow. "Why don't you tell me more about these... selfish desires?" I let my voice go dark and gravelly in the way I had learned most people liked.

Deep, sexy, with a tinge of growl.

Riley responded by shoving my pants and underwear to my ankles. My cock bobbed free, stiff as a board.

Desire was never a problem with Riley in mind.

He pulled me closer, his fingers curling in the hem of my shirt as he kissed my neck, right over my pulsing vein, before he removed my shirt, leaving me completely naked.

"Hmm... well, let's see... For starters..." He kissed my lips, his tongue hungry for mine as he squeezed my cock in his warm palm.

I groaned from the touch as he stroked me. I couldn't help but thrust my hand against him, seeking more, needing more.

More of his touch, more of his love.

More of *him.*

"I want to taste you," he breathed in my ear.

I was more than happy to oblige, picking up what he was throwing down.

"You want to choke on *Daddy*'s cock, huh? Want to wrap that hot little mouth around me until I come down your throat?" I taunted him.

He responded to my shift in demeanor, just as I knew he would, and I couldn't deny the way that simple shift, the way he just *obeyed* me as he dropped to his knees, eyes imploring mine, made me feel.

Like I truly was the king of this castle, like I was the king of his heart.

And his cock, which visibly strained against his jeans.

He reached for me, but I backed away.

"Ah, ah, I didn't say you could have this yet," I teased, assuming the role that was easiest for me, a role that I had a feeling was just what the professor needed.

Someone to take control of the situation, take control of *him.*

"Please," he said, licking his lips.

"Show Daddy how much you want this cock," I said as I approached him, letting my moistened tip brush the edge of his silky lips.

"Show me that pretty pink cock of yours," I commanded, and Riley did not hesitate. He removed his pants and boxers faster than I could blink.

"Sit on the couch," I ordered, and he did, leaning back against my gray cushions so I could take in the sight of him, all long legs and arms, toned and defined by the shadows the light was casting on him, his thick, pink cock standing at attention.

The last time we'd really gotten intimate, things were a blur. And then the next morning, when we'd gotten carried away, I'd walked away with my needs met, but Riley...

Riley had insisted he was fine, but I never got to reciprocate the pleasure like I'd wanted to.

As badly as I wanted this man's mouth on my cock, I wanted to please him, to make him feel as good as he made me feel.

I straddled his hips as I braced my knees on

the cushions, letting my cock brush against his. His arms stretched out like a trapeze along the back of my couch, his dark eyes gazing into mine with warmth and wonder.

"That's a good boy," I purred as I captured his lips with mine, rubbing myself against him. I pulled away for a moment, taking stock of his lustful gaze, smirking as I spit in my hand. His eyes widened.

"Is that what you want, Cinderella?" I asked as I slathered both of our cocks in my saliva.

I could feel the stickiness of precum mixing with the warmth of my spit. I slid my hand over his leaking head, gathering it as I coated myself in it. In *him.*

"Yes," he breathed, his fingernails digging into my ass.

I smirked, commanding him once more. "Then get on your knees, Princess."

Riley didn't waste a moment as he did as I asked, nearly knocking me to the floor as he did so. The moment his mouth wrapped around my cock, I felt like my entire body turned to liquid

Riley hollowed his cheeks, taking me to the back of his throat in one swift motion.

I grabbed his hair, letting out a deep growl, mixed with cursing as his tongue lapped at my head, pushing into my slit.

I pulled out, if only because I didn't want to

come yet, and I knew if Riley kept it up, I wouldn't last long.

I wanted to give him what he wanted, but I also wanted to take my time.

"Not yet, baby," I murmured huskily as he looked up at me, doe-eyed and needy.

"If you recall, I did win bar bingo. I need to collect my prize," I breathed out, trying to catch my breath.

Riley pursed his lips, nodding. "Oh… okay."

"Now, show me that fine ass I have had the pleasure of looking at all night," I commanded.

Riley blushed, but he did as I asked, bracing himself against the arm of my couch, propping out his ass for me like a nude model.

"I did say I wanted to draw you naked," I teased, tracing my fingers up his thighs, over the curve of his ass, in the dip of his back and up his spine.

Then I licked him where I'd touched him, watching as his thighs tightened and he thrust himself against my couch arm with need.

"I just didn't tell you my medium of choice would be my tongue," I whispered in his ear.

His skin was decorated with goosebumps as he shivered.

"Too much?" I asked, placing a kiss on his neck, beneath his silky hair. I could feel his pulse against my tongue, my cock aching for release.

"No, not enough," he breathed, his voice strained.

I slipped my hand beneath him, between the couch and his stomach, pulling him back against my raging cock as I grabbed his.

"We can stop if you want to, if you're not comfortable," I whispered.

Riley looked at me over his shoulder, arching his back as he brushed his ass against my stiffness, causing me to suck in a breath.

"I don't want to stop," he breathed, his eyes full of heat, and something else.

Love.

I smirked as he spread his legs apart, his gaze imploring mine.

"I need to hear you say it," I said, breaking character for a moment, if only because I was already so close to the edge, I didn't know if I would make it myself.

Riley parted his perfect lips, still swollen from kissing me.

"I want you, Eric." he breathed, my name full of so much love and wonder. "I want you to feel me... and in every thrust, every beat of my heart, I want you to know that it beats for you."

I kissed his shoulder softly, trailing kisses down his spine until I reached his ass. I spit on his hole as I gathered more wetness from his leaking cock in my other hand. In tandem, I worked both with my torturous fingers, taking my time as I slowly pumped his cock with one hand, working my way up to two fingers in his tight entrance. His thighs tightened, and he grit his teeth as I licked the puckered flesh before sliding a third in, and I didn't miss the way his cock twitched in my hand as I did so.

"Are you sure?" I asked, my lips trailing up his spine, assaulting his neck.

Riley nodded vehemently. "Yes," he said, his voice a hoarse whisper. "Make me come, Daddy." His voice was solid, unwavering, and his gaze spellbinding as he looked at me.

I would give this man anything and everything he asked for, now and forever.

I grinned wickedly, capturing his gaze and never dropping it as I quickly slid a condom down my shaft. I watched as his pupils enlarged, as his jaw tensed, as his eyebrows furrowed. I watched his mouth form a tiny 'o' as I breached him, felt his entire body tense.

"Just breathe," I said, though I wasn't sure who I was talking to, myself or him.

Slowly, I fit myself inside him and his body welcomed me like a glove. And for a moment, we stood there, unmoving, connected in the most basic, most primal of ways.

His cock throbbed in my hand as his breath shook.

"I love you," he whispered, his lips planting a soft kiss on mine.

Three words.

Those three words I never thought would bring me such peace, were my undoing.

I thrust my hips slowly against him. In my mouth, he groaned as I slid myself out, slowly inching in again until we'd both accustomed ourselves to the feel of one another. Slow and steady, we rocked together, my cock in his warm, tight ass and his cock in my warm, tight hand.

It felt like hours, but in reality it was probably mere minutes. When I broke away from his kiss, I buried my face in his hair, unable to hold off any longer. I gritted my release out through my teeth, stilling inside him as he let out his own moan of ecstasy, coating my hand in thick, warm release, until we both collapsed against the couch, spent and sated.

"I love you too," I whispered against his neck, feeling overwhelmed with happiness.

EPILOGUE

RILEY

I KNEW the closer I got to the wedding, the more stressed I'd be. But at least I didn't have to worry about finding a plus one.

"So, what really is there left to do?" Eric asked, sipping on his drink.

"What is there left to do?" Giselle looked like she was about to pop a vein.

"The girls still need to pick up their dresses, the guys need their tuxes, I need to finalize with the caterer..."

"Who's your caterer?" Eric asked as Aaron supportively stroked his wife and mother-to-be's shoulders.

No one had made a comment about

Giselle's sudden shift in drinks, which led me to believe they also knew and had been sworn to secrecy, or perhaps they weren't that observant.

"Penn's Bakery..." she said. "Why?"

Eric pointed over to the jukebox. "Like, Penn Barrett?"

Giselle opened her mouth as Eric shrugged. "He's over there, talking to Mitchell. You do know, Mitchell, like, Jasper Springs's fucking paparazzi?"

Giselle let out a deep breath, fixing her expression.

"I do. Mitchell is my photographer, actually."

Eric smiled. "Well, it must be your lucky day, because they're both in some heated discussion over there. Probably should go break it up before hands are thrown," he said with a chuckle.

"Standing over there with the that sexy vet and Weston Rhodes."

Lane laughed as Grayson rolled his eyes.

"You know Weston Rhodes?" Lacey asked, surprised.

"Yeah, he's my neighbor."

The looks from the party were shocked.

"You live in Jasper Springs Estates?" Henry perked up.

"Yeah, been there since I was like, I don't know, twenty-two."

"What the hell are you? The next Paris Hilton?" Aaron said as Giselle headed over to talk to the boys.

"More like, if I told you I'd have to kill you," Eric said with a wink.

"Ah, the pretty ones are always either gay or criminals, alas." Lacey sighed.

"Or argumentive photographers," Grayson mewled, as everyone else chuckled.

"What's so funny?" Henry asked.

Julie made a sour face as she pushed her Mai Tai toward Eric. "Ugh, this is way too sweet for me, please take this."

Eric shrugged, taking a sip, puckering his lips. "Yeah, that's tart," he said.

"Mitchell is quite an opinionated man," Grayson shrugged. "I don't think there's a soul in Jasper Springs he hasn't pissed off."

"Isn't that, like, bad for a photographer? Don't you want, like, a good reputation?" Henry asked curiously.

"I mean, we don't actually know what happened. All we know is the gossip that gets spread, and in my experience, gossip is only like thirty percent true." Eric chortled.

"True," Julie agreed as we all watched Aaron

and Lacey head over to where the boys were standing.

That was the moment the crowd roared with excitement as Jasper Springs's favorite musician rolled into the bar.

"Nice of you to make it, Drew," Julie said as she hugged Taylor and his rockstar beau.

"You know I wouldn't miss this wedding for the world," he teased. "Besides, I'm kinda digging this place," he said, flashing a megawatt smile.

"It does have its charms," Eric said as he raised his glass, and everyone else at the table agreed, raising theirs in response.

"I can't believe we're only one week away," I whined. "Which reminds me..."

Eric looked up from his drink.

"Have you found suitable *attire* for the wedding yet?" I asked, knowing full well the man in question had a closet full of suits.

But I wasn't asking about his daytime attire.

With Eric officially as my plus one—and with the title of *boyfriend*—I too had turned a corner.

While I might have been shy, quiet, and reserved in my day to day life out of preservation, even before I'd met the man, there was a sense of freedom that I was now able to explore parts of myself I'd hidden for far too long.

And with the freedom and support from my boyfriend, I was starting to feel comfortable with myself and my *preferences* in a way I'd never vocalized until now.

Because I'd never been *comfortable* with anyone, the way I was with Eric. He didn't judge me for the literature I'd consumed, or the fantasies I held, and he certainly didn't judge me when I wanted to shut the world out and have some drinks and play some games.

And I'd also learned, that my *Daddy* liked to give up control once in a while himself. Something that was as foreign to him as taking control was to me.

Both of us were learning how to explore the parts of ourselves we'd kept hidden, and there was a contentness in sharing that experience.

Being with Eric was the easiest thing I'd ever done. He fit into my life, into my heart like the glass slipper fit Cinderella.

"I think I've found some *sufficient* accessories, yes," he replied, not missing a beat, smirking devilishly.

"I hope they aren't too uncomfortable," I said, heat filling my cheeks, as I knew what we were talking about was exclusive to us.

Eric twisted his hands together, his fingertips feathering over the skin of his wrists, where he still sported a little rope burn beneath his watch.

"Not at all," he said, his eyes sparkling. "But you will have to wait until the wedding to see my full ensemble," he said, his tone cocky and full of attitude, making my cock twitch once more.

"Some things are worth the wait," I said coolly, brushing him off, knowing all the while it would drive him mad.

And as I sipped my beer, laughing with my friends, my arm around my boyfriend's shoulders, I couldn't help but think the best was yet to come.

Thank you for reading Eric and Riley's story.

If you enjoyed this book, please return to your favorite retailer and leave a review. Even a few words could mean the world to an author.

Continue the series with Mitch's story, Book 6 in Jasper Springs!

MITCH

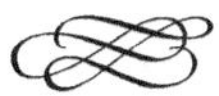

AN MM GAY AWAKENING ROMANCE

Mitch
An MM Gay Awakening Romance
Jasper Springs
Book Six

Copyright © 2024
Evie Riley
Second Edition
ISBN: 978-1-77357-721-0
Published by Naughty Nights Press LLC
Cover Art By Willsin Rowe

MITCH

**A perpetual bachelor.
A sweet, tempting baker.
A chance to heal a wounded heart.**

Mitchell DeVille knows a piece of art when he sees it. After all, he's the hottest photographer in Jasper Springs. When Mitch discovers a fresh face at the wedding of the season, he can't turn away. And when his Pretty Boy muse offers him the chance to work together, he can't refuse.

Mitch soon discovers that the object of his desires is struggling with his newfound attraction, and he knows he shouldn't play with fire.

Penn Baker dreams of finding the perfect... someone. With a string of ex-girlfriends and one-night stands, he isn't sure there is anyone out there for a shy golden boy like him. Until he discovers a sexy, confident, photographer, that is.

As unusual feelings and desires rise in Penn, he finds himself falling fast for the charm of the man behind the camera.

Can Mitch be honest with himself about what he wants? Or will his high-built walls keep out more than just his fear of rejection?

Readers seeking a gay awakening romance set in a cozy little town may find this story checks those boxes. While Mitch and Penn may have cameos in other stories, each book in this series can be read as a standalone.

CHAPTER 1

Mitch

"ALL RIGHT, just turn to your right a little more,"
I coaxed, practically holding my spine in the
most unnatural position known to man. I arched
myself like some sea serpent, back as far as I
could go, just to get the one perfect shot.

Giselle's lips turned up into a perfect smile as
she took my direction. A little more to my left,
and the sun lit her up like an angel as her groom
gazed upon her.

Click!

The fast clicks of the shutter echoed in the
air, capturing the moment in time, preserving it
forever.

"Okay, I think I got what I need, thanks," I

said as I forced my body back into an upright, natural position.

Aaron and Giselle scampered off hand in hand toward the doors of the Paradise Hotel, where everyone was gallivanting around on the terrace during cocktail hour.

I watched as the two of them ran off like two kids, snapping a few more candids as they did so.

But I couldn't deny my jealousy.

I loved my job, truly. Being a part of my clients' special occasions was something I didn't take lightly. I loved capturing the love between people, the stolen moments. Put simply, I loved love. I just wish it loved *me*.

My family couldn't understand how someone so entrenched in the business of love and weddings was a perpetual bachelor. It was a choice, I guess. Or at least that was what I told myself for years. It's a lot easier to run a self-employed business when you're the only one you have to answer to.

But lately, working weddings hadn't felt the same.

I still loved photographing my clients but...

At the time, I had found myself feeling slighted by the over-presence of love in my life that had nothing to do with me.

I wanted those things, too, but it just didn't

seem like it was going to happen. I'd been on dates, sure, but nothing ever really worked out. Not to mention the dating pool for an openly gay dude in Jasper Springs was practically nonexistent. When you lived in a small town like Jasper Springs, knowing everyone wasn't all it was cracked up to be. When you were the premier photographer for the county, and everyone knew your name and your business, it was even worse. Knowing everyone can have its advantages sure, but it made dating a fucking bitch.

I followed behind the happy couple, strolling up the expanse of the perfectly manicured green knoll, toward the marble steps of the Paradise's swanky terrace.

The guests were starting to arrive in full force, and so I made my rounds photographing candids of the guests and all the little details. The charcuterie boards, the champagne fountain, the gold foil etchings on the napkin.

Slipping past a group of black-tie suited guests, I made my way indoors to the Paradise's grand ballroom. The outside of the hotel was gorgeous, as architecturally it was practically something out of Gone With The Wind.

But inside?

It dripped opulence, with its sparkling chandeliers, white marble floors, and ornate, high vaulted ceilings.

I'd done a lot of weddings in Jasper Springs and the surrounding areas, but I had to admit, Giselle and Aaron's wedding took the cake. I was honestly surprised the fucking Pope didn't show up with the amount of people that turned out for their wedding.

Thankfully, both Giselle and Aaron's families were quite well off, so renting out the entirety of Jasper Springs's most sought after venue was nothing to them.

I sauntered around the inside, taking my detail photos, my candids of the arriving guests. Soon enough, it would be time for dinner, and I was fucking starving.

My stomach grumbled, and I silently cursed myself. If I hadn't have been so rushed that morning because I overslept, I would have had time to eat more than a pop tart and a mocha Double Shot.

The breakfast of photographers everywhere.

I found my way over to the elaborately deco-rated wedding cake, which was all of five tiers. Though, I guess it fit right in with Giselle's style, the layers of ivory cream speckled with gold leaf and deep, burgundy flowers cascading down the side.

I set up my camera, working the angles of

the giant cake, noting the smoothness of the icing. I'd seen a lot of cakes in my years, but this one was absolutely perfect. It almost didn't look real.

A part of me was impressed, knowing the disasters that could happen when transporting a cake, especially one that big.

After taking my shots, I turned to do some crowd photos, noticing as I scanned the room, someone I most certainly didn't recognize.

He was dressed far more casual than the rest of the guests, which told me he was likely hired help.

Perhaps he was with the catering or the Paradise event staff?

I settled my lens as I looked through, noticing his side profile. With the zoom on and the lens I was using, the chandeliers and background blurred into bokeh—a soft, out-of-focus background with faded glittery spots—as Pretty Boy and his side profile became the focus.

From the angle, his blond hair caught flecks of gold from the chandeliers, his pale blue eyes standing out in stark contrast against his fair complexion and dark lashes.

He casually cocked his head in thought, his wistful gaze set on someone or something, but that didn't matter to me.

Snap!

I watched through my lens as he licked his lips, as his eyebrows furrowed, and something in my chest snapped at the same time as the shutter.

I understood that look of longing.

That look of wishful thinking.

I lowered my camera, if only for a moment, gazing at Pretty Boy in his lavender button down, looking at a couple dancing. The look of heartbreak on his face was unmistakable, and I had the craziest feeling, that I wanted to go over there and *hug* him. Maybe even ask him to dance, if only to take his mind off something that was causing him such evident pain. Despite the fact I didn't know how to dance like half the people were on the dance floor to whatever cocktail hour shit was being played.

Surely such a thing was crazy, right?

I didn't even know the guy.

"Mitch! There you are!" Grayson said, his bright Colgate-smile tearing me away from the nameless Pretty Boy.

I gazed up at the bride's brother, dressed to the nines, of course, in his flashy tux, with a martini in hand.

"Something I can do for you, Grayson?" I asked, glancing back to see mystery pretty boy had disappeared.

"Actually, there is," he said, flashing me a grin.

CHAPTER 2

Penn

I THOUGHT BEING BACK in Jasper Springs would be a good thing, but as I looked around the Paradise, I wondered if perhaps I'd been out of the Jasper Springs loop for far too long.

Four years *was* a long time when you came from a small town like Jasper Springs.

Where everyone knew everyone, and everything was always picture perfect.

Take the bride of this wedding, for example, Giselle.

Her family was one of the most well known in Jasper Springs, and her husband also came from another well known, wealthy family in the area. Their families were involved in everything, just like the Rhodes, and loved by nearly *all* of Jasper Springs for their philanthropy, their parties and soirees.

Even Giselle's brother, Grayson—who was the talk of the town years ago for his *scandalous* tryst with his sister's ex, of all things—seemed to have the *perfect* life with his new boyfriend.

I wished I could have that.

The ease of self, the happy ever after.

I thought the change of scenery was what I needed, when I left for pastry school, but sadly, my life was not a Jasper Springs success story.

Aside from a few one night stands that ended awkwardly with the girls leaving me to stew in mortification, a couple girlfriends, and my too close parents constantly trying to play matchmaker, I'd practically given up on dating.

Maybe I was just meant to be alone.

So, instead of going out and meeting people like my mother suggested, like a normal twenty-three year old, I turned to the one thing I knew I could do well.

Bake.

My parents had owned Penn's Bakery—affectionately named after their only child, me—since I was in middle school. While they weren't the only bakery in Jasper Springs, they were pretty well known in the county. My mother's macaroons are *to die for.* I swore she could compete on Great British Bake Off with those things.

Who cares if she hasn't been home to London in twenty years.

No, as usual, instead of socializing like a normal twenty-three year old, I locked myself in my parent's bakery—my birthright as my father would say—and took out my perpetual singledom and emo woes on the giant five tier spectacle Giselle had ordered for her wedding. I got lost in the flowers, brushing and smoothing the buttercream on each individual tier. Every little detail was a welcome relief as I strategically placed each flower and accent.

I'd always loved weddings, and had fond memories of my mom baking for weddings and parties growing up. Our small house was overtaken by mom's cake and cookie orders, since in those early days before they opened the shop she'd work from home.

And when I'd ultimately ended up at home on a Friday night, because I was the awkward kid who didn't fit in anywhere, she'd always let me help.

Though now, I was doing more than helping. Now that I had my certifications, my degree, I could finally take on more responsibility with the shop.

My dad wouldn't admit it, and I knew my

mom would say otherwise, but I was no fool. I knew that they were looking at retirement, just *waiting* for the right moment. Waiting for me to graduate, move home, and take over the family business. I knew what my future looked like.

But I also knew I wanted to love more than just my job.

I wanted to share my life with someone the way my mom and dad did.

But no matter how many women they set me up with, or how many times someone swiped right on me...

Nothing ever felt right.

And then I came to the Paradise, on a job, and I saw *him.*

Over in the corner by my masterpiece.

He was tall, dark, and handsome like the men in the fairytales always were. A little rogue-ish looking, which told me he was definitely *not* a guest. The wedding was a black-tie affair, but my mom assured me my button down and slacks would be enough. After all, I came home a week earlier, due to a glitch in the computer system regarding my train ticket, so it wasn't like I was planning on going to a fancy wedding.

Not to mention the closest suit shop was in the city, and I *hated* going into the city. All those people, the traffic...

Mr. Tall, Dark, and Handsome leaned

against the table, looking like he was bored to tears.

I swallowed harshly, feeling strangely hot, like I was going to get caught with my hand in the cookie jar or something.

Which was an odd way to feel about some stranger, some man who looked like something right out of a romance novel or something.

A part of me felt compelled by his apathetic expression, the way he *sexily* leaned against the table like he was the King of the castle or something.

But I was frozen in place, scared to move, to even *breathe* in his vicinity.

What the hell?

My cock twitched in my pants, and a maddening blush crept up my cheeks.

Now was certainly not an appropriate time for an erection!

My brain was a bit slow to process, and that's when I felt more embarrassed than ever. Not because of where I was, but because...

What the fuck?

I'd never been attracted to men before, like *at all.*

I thought surely, something must be off, maybe I got a whiff of some perfume, or maybe I, too, was suffering from boredom.

Or maybe it's because I haven't jacked off since I came home.

I shoved the weird and inappropriate thoughts out of my mind though, because my *mother*, of all people, broke my concentration.

"Penn, sweetheart, I've been looking everywhere for you."

"Huh?" I shook my head, dispelling the strange moment. I turned back to look in the direction of the hot stranger, noticing he was gone. Maybe I'd imagined it. Maybe he was some sort of sex-deprived mirage.

Could dry spells cause hallucinations?

I wasn't sure.

"Our work here is done," she said, taking in the sea of people as the bride and groom made their way around the tables to socialize.

I scanned the crowd once more for my mirage, but he truly was nowhere to be seen.

That's it, I'm definitely losing my marbles.

"Penn..." she said, snapping her fingers, pulling my attention back to her once more.

"Okay," I said, swatting at her hand, her perfectly manicured nails smacking my palm.

"We're heading out, come on," she said, looping her arm in my mine, leading me out of the Paradise Hotel.

CHAPTER 3

Penn

I⊤ should have been a downright shame that I was at home, in my boxers and under my blue flannel comforter before nine thirty.

My parents were usually in bed by eight, what with keeping baker's hours my entire life.

Aside from a few times my classmates and I went out, I was mostly the same.

There was a simplicity to my routine, but that night I couldn't get comfortable, despite feeling practically exhausted from a long work day.

The house was quiet, and I knew I was the only one awake, which didn't help matters.

My mind was strangely alert, but then again,

doomscrolling social media probably wasn't helping matters.

I wasn't the jealous type by any means, but if I had a nickel for every post I saw of a classmate getting married or having kids, I swore I could open my own bakery.

I'd never really thought about getting married or having kids in the sense that I imagined myself with my exes making cheesy and annoying posts like that.

I'd always known I would get married and have kids someday, much like a kid knows Christmas is coming. You don't question it, but the day itself varies and the gifts aren't always the same.

When I thought about what I wanted in my future, that's what came to mind, but I hadn't met anyone I could envision my cookie cutter Hallmark Happy Ending with just yet.

I continued to scroll as I thought about the wedding.

About all the couples dancing, the bride and groom smiling ear to ear.

The hot stranger standing by my cake.

Instantly, my cock twitched in my boxers, reminding me of my embarrassment from earlier. Except, there was nothing to be embarrassed about in the privacy of my own bedroom.

Maybe I really did just need to bust out a good nut.

Nonchalantly, I slid my hand in between my boxers, gently pulling and brushing my thumb over my head as I set my phone down with my free hand.

I eased into my pillows, beneath my covers, building a slow rhythm. I closed my eyes, clearing my mind to focus on the feel of my hand, the thrust as I tightened my grip.

Steadily, I increased my pace, my palm already wet from the precum soaking my head. It was warm, sticky, and for some reason, it turned me on a lot more than it usually did.

I gripped my shaft, squeezing as my breath hitched. I stopped only for a moment, to spit in my hand, to get myself *real* wet and slippery. I slid my boxers off, needing the freedom of movement. Underneath the covers, I throbbed with need. I grabbed myself once more, lathering my cock in my spit.

The touch of my hand against my rock hard cock, my thumb brushing over my rigid veins felt *so good.*

And then the strangest thought popped into my brain.

A hot, wet tongue licking my shaft, from my balls to my head, taking me into the back of his *throat, while he cupped my balls, squeezing them until I—*

Before I could even process such an anomaly of thought, I came.

"Oh fuck..." I cursed under my breath, scrambling to cover the spewing geyser that was my cock, if only because I didn't want dried jizz on the inside of my comforter.

My body shook as my cock pulsed, coating my hand, and my entire body practically melted into the mattress.

"Everyone has an off day, Penn, that's all it is," I told myself, swallowing harshly as the thought dissipated in my brain.

"It doesn't mean anything," I said, reaching in my drawer for a towel with my free, clean hand.

I took my time cleaning up, trying to focus on *anything* but the weird image my mind had formed to get me off.

What was my deal today?

First that hot stranger, now this?

Maybe my lack of a sex life really was affecting my mental state. I should probably look into that.

Pulling my underwear back on, I settled into bed once more, but a harsh object poked me in the back.

"Ow!" I yelped as I reached behind me, pulling out my phone.

Of course, how could I have forgotten.

Just as I went to plug it in, I noticed I'd been tagged. Or more or less, the bakery had been tagged. The bakery's Facebook page saw more action than my personal one, which was just another reason I'd given up on socializing.

I scrolled through the images of the wedding, coming across some beautiful images of the cake. Truly, I'd never seen images like them before. The angles, the detail. I wondered if I could use said pictures for my cake portfolio.

I clicked my way around until I found the name of the photographer.

De*Vil Photography was the name of the company. Clicking on the page, I noted their tagline was *the devil's in the details,* pasted across a collage of artfully done black and white images that captured people in various states. Silhouettes of brides, little kid hands inside of their parents holding flowers, even an image of two men embracing on Main Street under the streetlights, the light refracting off the puddles of rain.

I squinted as I tried to make out their dark features. One of them looked like that Rhodes guy, the one who was always in the paper. Weston or Westley or something or other.

Scrolling down the page, I looked for their information, fully intent on emailing them to ask if I could use their photos, when an idea popped into my head.

As I clicked through their portfolio, it was apparent that they were really good at what they did, not just by the photos they'd posted of the wedding tonight already, but in every wedding album, the photographs of the cakes, the cookies.

I knew mom and dad had no clue when it came to social media, or digital content.

I'd started an Instagram in college for the bakery as a side project, but until recently I hadn't focused on it at all, being as I wasn't home.

I'd showed my mom numerous times how to take a picture with her phone and upload it, but clearly she wasn't as invested in the technological advances of business nowadays.

But that was my job, wasn't it?

To take over the operations?

To bring Penn's bakery into the twenty-first century?

Which was why I didn't think twice about messaging Mr. De*Vil about the use of his photos of my masterpiece, as well as potentially collaborating on a social media campaign for the bakery.

I figured it couldn't hurt to reach out, right?

CHAPTER 4

I SAT BACK in my editing chair, watching as the loading page did its thing, taking forever for my post to actually post.

While it would take me a while to really cull through and edit the wedding of the century, I needed to at least post a couple candids or favorites to keep both my clients and my followers clicking.

After getting home so early, I had more than enough time to hand edit a few shots of the details to keep everyone satisfied while I worked on the main attraction, the bride and groom.

So, I'd opted to showcase the Paradise in all its matrimonial glory, from the sparkling chandelier to the spectacular cake, the overflowing charcuterie board and towers of champagne.

Finally, the post went through.

I looked at the clock on my computer, which read nine thirty. I debated if I should keep going as I swiveled back and forth in my chair.

Staying up late editing photos wasn't my favorite way to spend a Saturday night, but it wasn't like I had anything else going on.

Which was pretty pathetic, if you asked me.

God is this like the pre-thirty jitters or something?

What the fuck is wrong with me?

Just as I moved to close out my browser, I saw the familiar little red notification letting me know I had a message.

I groaned, wondering for a moment if I should ignore the message and get back to whoever it was in the morning, but I couldn't help myself, and checked it out.

When I saw the photograph in the icon, next to the name Penn Baker, I sat up straighter. I clicked the photo, viewing his profile instantly.

Despite it being set to private, I could see enough photographs to confirm my sudden shock.

Pretty Boy had a name, and apparently the star Baker was a... baker?

How on point can you get when your last name is your profession?

Then again, I had no room to talk because my family literally owned *M's Place*, the local watering hole, and had named the bar after all three of us. My brother Miguel, myself, and my younger sister, Max, and not to mention, my photography business was a play on my last name, DeVille.

I couldn't help myself as I scrolled through the available information, which showed Pretty Boy's most recent profile picture of him standing outside Penn's Bakery on Charleston Street.

I'd been to the place a dozen times, mostly when I needed to grab something to bring to a potluck or a holiday gathering, but still.

The photograph showed him dressed in blue jeans and red and white converse that matched his red and white striped shirt. A bright, wide smile that reached his eyes gazed back at me, his toasted marshmallow colored hair blowing in the breeze like he was doing a photoshoot for the Disney Channel or something.

God, he was fucking *adorable*.

I smirked as I came back to my inbox, glancing over his message, the light of the computer bathing me in artificial anonymity.

I read over his message, asking about using the images of the cake for the bakery's social media page, followed by an *inquiry* about working together. It wouldn't be the first time someone asked to partner up with me for my services, but it was definitely the first time I wanted to say *yes*, without even a second thought.

Even if it's only because the little cinnamon roll looks positively delicious.

I typed back with a smirk on my face.

All right, Penn, I'll bite. I could use a little sugar in my portfolio. Let's meet up and discuss our... partnership over coffee. Say tomorrow afternoon, if you're free?

I hit send, leaning back in my chair, grinning like a little kid.

Was it unprofessional of me to flirt with a potential client?

Probably.

But the perks of working for myself was I could do whatever the fuck I wanted to do. I was the HR department, baby.

Penn responded rather quickly, which only fueled my confidence more.

What's your favorite sugary snack? I can bring something if you like.

Oh, he made this too easy.

Sweet little cinnamon rolls who message me at nine thirty at night.

Maybe I had no shame, but a part of me didn't really care what people thought of me. Either Penn would find my personality fun and easy, or he would get his little tighty whities up in a twist and turn the other way, which was possible.

But honestly, if he was *that* uptight with his masculinity that he couldn't take some light flirting or teasing, I didn't want to work with a stick in the mud.

To my chagrin, he responded with, *I'm more of a cream puff, actually.*

A dark chuckle escaped my throat.

Alrighty then, game on, Penn Baker.

Fluffy, delicious, and full of sweet cream. Just the way I like.

For a moment, even I thought I'd gone too far. Light teasing and flirting was one thing, but the squirrel in my brain who was my HR department flashed a very large *WARNING!* in my brain.

Thankfully, Penn's response didn't call me a fucking perv.

Instead, it was the opposite.

What time should we meet up?

I chuckled, noting how he hadn't responded to my obvious overstep, but the fact he still wanted to meet up, even after my faux pas told me he was interested perhaps in more than just photographs.

Pretty Boy wants to play hard to get, that's fine.

How does twelve thirty sound, Cream Puff? I messaged.

Penn responded quickly.

Sounds good to me, Cupcake.

I let out an actual laugh at his words as I messaged him back, telling him I'd see his sweet ass tomorrow afternoon.

CHAPTER 5

Mitch

THE CAFE WAS ALWAYS BUSTLING at lunchtime, but honestly, I preferred the crowd. It provided me with a multitude of entertainment. I always noticed the little things no one else did. The barista behind the counter who couldn't stop staring at the dishwasher's ass, the teacher running late to his class because he was deep in doomscrolling TikTok, the feuding couple in the corner who were practically vibrating with sexual tension as they drank their coffees in silence.

I leaned back in my chair, my gaze sweeping over the room, watching to see what small town excitement was afoot today, when the door jingled. I turned to see Penn, carrying a pink box, dressed like he was going to the fucking Science Fair. He wore pale khakis and a deep blue button down with pale blue dots all over it, his golden-brown hair swept to the side like Justin Bieber in his *Baby Baby* era.

Which should have been off-putting, but for some reason it wasn't.

My cock twitched as my stomach growled.

Delectable, indeed.

"Well, I'll be damned, if those are really cream puffs in there, I might kiss you," I teased as he took a seat, setting down the package.

I didn't miss the blush spreading across his fair cheeks, and my cock twitched again, my mind immediately thinking about other parts of Pretty Boy's body that would look *so nice* with a little pink tint.

"Well, a deal is a deal, right?" he said, tucking some stray hair behind his ear as he pushed the box toward me.

I smirked as I pushed the lid open, my eyes widening when I saw about a dozen cream puffs stuffed to the brim, their thick pastry cream seeping out of their tiny holes. The scent of vanilla cream and strawberries made my stomach growl again, and my mouth was practically salivating as I took in the sight of the cupcake in the center. The icing was whipped, sprinkled with bits of strawberries and red syrupy sauce that dripped down the sides. Even though it was in a cardboard box, the presentation was still gorgeous.

I glanced up at Penn, who was watching me intently. I pulled out a cream puff, plopping it into my mouth, if only to quiet my stomach and my damn erection.

It was fucking amazing.

"Mmmmm." I groaned as the sweetness of the pastry cream hit my tongue.

"Glad to see I can please your sweet tooth," he said with a shy smile.

I went for another cream puff, because sue me, they were delicious.

"Too bad I left my camera at home. Your little tableau is quite creative."

I watched as his smile spread wide from the praise, and that didn't help the matter of my unruly erection one bit.

It would appear my little Cream Puff likes praise. Well noted.

"Oh, I, uh, the cupcake was a last minute thing. I wasn't sure if you were a vanilla guy, or—"

"Oh, I assure you, Penn, I am not vanilla in any shape of the word," I said with a smirk, wiping some stray cream off of my lips.

I watched with interest as Penn's entire face

turned a shade of red I'd only ever seen on fire hydrants, and he physically *squirmed* in his seat.

He cleared his throat, and I couldn't help but grin.

Oh, this is going to be fun.

"Penn? Penn Baker, is that you?" a saccharine voice disturbed our bubble.

I watched as the color drained from Penn's face and his eyes widened in fear.

"A... Amy... Hi..." he said as he crossed his legs, his entire body *tensing* at the sight of her. He looked up at her, swallowing harshly.

She was average height with short blonde hair, a round face, and deep brown eyes. She was also dressed in a tight, low-cut red dress and black boots, and looked like she could pass as Penn's Disney Channel co-star.

She looked familiar, but I couldn't place her. Then again, in my line of work, sometimes people just blended together.

Amy tucked her hair behind her ear as she coyly made eyes at my Cream Puff, and a spark of jealousy fired inside of me.

Which was irrational, right?

I barely even *knew* the guy...

"Amy, this is..."

"Mitchell DeVille. I know who you are," she said with a giggle.

I leaned back casually in my seat, catching her gaze.

"And you would be..." I drawled.

"Penn and I dated for a semester in college."

I looked from her to him, watching as he chewed his lip.

Oh.

Oh... shit.

Was I wrong?

Was Pretty Boy not who I thought he was?

At that exact moment as I questioned my gaydar, I saw him steal a glance at me.

And it was enough for me to understand, that this... This was uncharted territory for my little Cream Puff.

That should have been enough to deter me. I'd been in the game long enough, and I was open about my sexuality.

But Penn clearly was not.

Though I wasn't sure if it was just a case of being in the closet, or if I genuinely had a bi or gay awakening on my hands.

I knew I should have walked away then. Said thanks for the cream puffs and called it a day, and given him a license to use the photos from the wedding for his promotional needs.

But I liked a *challenge*. Both in my work, and in my personal life.

I smiled, nodding at Penn, if only to try and quell his panic.

Don't worry, baby, I won't spill your secrets.

"Penn and I are colleagues, isn't that right, Penn?" I said, giving him the floor, the chance to control the narrative.

I knew firsthand how important that was when you were trying to figure it all out. When you didn't have the answers yet.

Penn's shoulders loosened as he looked at me with a soft smile, and I knew.

The man was going to ruin me.

But maybe I like a little destruction.

"Yeah, colleagues. Mitch is, uh, doing some work for me. For the bakery."

Amy teetered back and forth as she looked between us.

"Oh, of course, duh! Mitchell is like *the best* photographer. I'm sure whatever he's doing for you, will be so worth it."

Penn smiled, but it wasn't genuine. Beneath the sparkle in his eyes, I could still see the panic.

"Totally," he said, running his hand through his hair.

"I thought you were still up north," she said.

Penn shook his head, tapping his fingers on the table. His gaze fixed on her face, never once venturing below to her prominent cleavage or the way she twirled her hair.

Watching her flirt with him made me angry, jealous, even though I knew that was insane.

I watched intently as he settled his hands in his lap.

"I was... but I graduated, so I'm home now."

"Oh that's awesome! Congratulations!" she said as she clasped her hands together in front of her bountiful cleavage.

I raised my eyebrow in disgust.

Oh honey, you are barking up the wrong tree, clearly.

"Thanks," he said sheepishly.

"I hate to interrupt this little High School Reunion, but we are kind of in the middle of a meeting, *Amy*," I said.

The tone of command and possession in my voice was not missed, even to me.

Penn eased in his seat as Amy focused on me instead.

"Oh, I'm so sorry! I didn't mean to be rude, I just wanted to say *hey*!" she said, waving. "I'll leave you two to talk business, but Penn..." She sighed, chewing her lip.

"Hmmm?" he asked, looking up, his expression pained.

"We should hang out sometime."

Yeah, I bet her idea of hanging out is Netflix and Chill. Sans the Netflix.

Penn nodded. "Mhmm. Totally," he said hurriedly.

I watched as she teetered off out the door, turning my attention back to Penn.

"She's... cute," I said, deadpan.

Penn slid down in his chair, running his hand through his golden locks.

"I mean, I guess," he said softly.

"Seems like a nice girl."

Penn sighed, his voice full of disappointment. "She is."

"But?" I asked calmly.

"I mean, you know how it is... I just didn't see us going anywhere," he murmured.

I bet you didn't, Cream Puff.

I popped another cream puff into my mouth.

"And where is it *you* want to go, Penn?" I asked.

I was only busting his balls, to try and lighten the mood, but a part of me wanted to know the answer.

What *did* Penn Baker want, really?

Penn sighed, sitting up straighter.

"It doesn't matter. You're a busy guy, and so am I, so I won't take up too much more of your time with my personal drama," he said, his shoulders falling as he pursed his lips.

"Ah, yes... this is the part where you sell your soul to me," I said, flashing him with a smirk.

I watched as the corner of Penn's mouth

started to rise, the hint of a smile fighting its way out from the frown on his adorable, sweet face.

"One week in general should be sufficient, I think. You can come to the bakery, see how we operate, take some candids as well as still life shots."

I raised my brow. "Still life, huh? You minor in art *up north*?" I asked.

Penn shook his head.

"No. Pastry, but... my dad paints in his spare time."

"Usually, I charge by the hour, but—"

"I'll pay you whatever it is you want," he blurted out, and I couldn't help but smile at his desperation.

He was so cute, I couldn't stand it. I just wanted him to ease up, to feel better.

"I was going to say… but, for you, I can do a flat rate of six hundred for the week, and this next part is the most important part of the nego-tiation," I said, leaning closer.

Penn leaned in without hesitation, putting his face inches away from mine. He smelled like sugar, spice, and untapped desire.

I gently pulled the box of goodies toward me as I whispered, "I'm going to need another box of cream puffs, and maybe a sweet, spicy, cinnamon roll. As terms of the payment, of course," I said, flashing him a grin.

Penn's gaze fell to my lips, and I watched him swallow harshly, his Adam's apple bobbing as a soft *sigh* escaped him.

This is a bad idea.

Penn looked up at me with glassy, turquoise eyes, biting his bottom lip, and my cock twitched once more from the sight.

"Deal," he said.

My gaze dropped to his lips. Pink, pouty, and perfect.

Fuck.

If he had been any other man, I would've just gone for it. I would've closed the gap and kissed him, but somehow I knew I needed to take my time with Penn.

I knew kissing him like this, now, would only push him away. So, for the moment, I stowed my desire, my sudden attraction, in favor of being *professional* and giving my Cream Puff the space he needed to process everything that had just happened.

"I'll start Monday," I said, pulling back.

CHAPTER 6

Mitch

"What's with the face?" Dawson asked, poking me in the side like a juvenile.

I took a sip of my beer as Weston flirted relentlessly with his boyfriend, my oldest friend, Cade.

Dawson and Cade were probably the closest thing I had to what one would call a *best friend*. Cade and I had hung out since middle school, and after he and Dawson broke up, the guy refused to leave. But with that being said, I actually enjoyed his idiocy most of the time.

When I was in a better mood that was.

"What face?" I deadpanned as Nolan came back to the table with a handful of drinks. True to his white knight nature, Cade immediately moved to help him, abandoning whatever Weston was going on about.

"Thanks," Nolan said, his glasses sliding down his nose in the process as the liquid sloshed around in the glasses. Miraculously, nothing spilled as Cade helped pass out drinks.

"The constipated face you're currently making," Dawson nipped. "I would think you'd still be smiling from ear to ear from the wedding. I know I am," he said, grinning like the Cheshire Cat for added idiot effect.

Dawson was like that.

Like a big, dumb golden retriever. Most of the time, I didn't mind.

But Dawson was right, I was in a mood, and I had been ever since Amy showed up to crash my date—no, *meeting*—with Penn.

It wasn't like I thought Cream Puff and I were going to run off into the sunset after one box of baked goods and some stupid flirting, so why did it bother me so much?

"Yeah, well, you don't have over three thousand images to cull for editing either," I snapped back.

Weston took a sip of his drink before wrapping his arm around Cade *again*, for like the fifth time since they'd arrived only an hour ago, which was also irritating me.

Fuck, maybe I just need to get shitfaced to forget about this weird ass day... Go home and work on some photos.

"No, that's not it," Weston mulled, his tone accusatory.

I shot him a glare.

Since he'd started dating Cade, he made it his business to know *everything* about our little group.

Who was crushing on who, what social gala was I photographing next, was everyone free for Poker on Sunday?

It was nice to have someone in the group to take over organizing shit, but it also got on my nerves.

Aside from my jobs, I didn't schedule shit. I liked the spontaneity of life and *not* knowing what was going to happen or where I was going to end up.

I looked at my friends, canoodling with their boyfriends like some gay version of the Stepford Wives, and it only pissed me off even more.

"Weston's right, something else is on your mind. I can tell." Dawson poked me in the ribs again, and I smacked his hand.

"Come on, Mitch, let it out. I promise you'll feel better," Dawson teased.

Nolan rolled his eyes. "If he doesn't want to talk about it, leave the guy alone."

I shot an appreciative glance at Nolan, the newest addition to the group. A part of me had to give the guy props, for being Dawson's other half couldn't have been easy.

And from what I'd seen, Nolan might be the only person on the planet who could actually get Dawson to *stop* and sit still, to be quiet, with just a damn *look*.

Knowing Dawson, it was probably some sort of sex role-play thing, but I liked to think underneath all of that steam, it was more than that.

I saw the way he *looked* at the pencil pusher.

I'd give my left nut for some pretty boy to look at me like that.

Pretty Boy...

I sighed, figuring fighting the truth was moot.

Besides, I was on my second beer of the night, and I hadn't even gotten to karaoke yet.

"Nothing. I just have, like, the worst gaydar on the planet sometimes."

A resounding, "Oh," followed from Dawson, louder than it should have been.

"Rejected by a straight man?" Weston nonchalantly drawled.

"Worse," I admitted as Nolan pushed Dawson in the chest, the two of them play-fighting over something.

"Worse?" Cade asked, his eyebrows

furrowing as his baby blues fixated their concerned gaze on me.

"I think I have a fucking awakening on my hands."

Nolan let out a, "Fuck," while Weston only shrugged.

"I don't see the problem," Weston said as I took another sip of my own drink.

"Yeah, well, you may be the type to just roll in and command shit, Wes, but some of us actually have to play by the rules. Especially when it involves our jobs," I snarled.

"So, you're working with him?" Nolan pressed.

I sighed, figuring there was no use denying it.

"Sort of. We met today to go over the job. Some social media campaign stuff, and..."

"And what?" Dawson pressed as I scanned the room.

At that moment, just as I opened my mouth, I saw him. He'd just walked in, alone, with another one of those pink boxes, looking like a lost kitten.

My heart lurched in my chest as I swatted at Dawson, excusing myself from the table.

"Fine, it's my turn to sing anyway," Dawson touted from behind me, but his voice was white noise.

CHAPTER 7

PENN

"ALL RIGHT, Miguel said he has his sister corralled in the stock room, so we have, like, ten minutes tops to get this shit set up," Archie, my best friend slash co-worker, said as we entered the bar.

The DeVille siblings who owned and worked at the bar were notorious for their over the top birthday battle. According to my mom, they'd been one-upping each other for a decade now. But I never paid attention to stuff like that.

I was always just focused on studying, or baking. I was never the kid who went out and socialized, even when I did live here.

I had to admit though, as an only child a

part of me was always envious when I heard stories about siblings having fun at one another's expense.

It was a small window to get set up, but it was a window still, so instead of dreaming about siblings I'd never have, I focused on the task at hand.

Archie and I could work pretty fast. We'd set up much more elaborate tables than a cake and cupcake bar on the fly.

Will, the DJ, saw us and immediately came over to help Archie and I with our boxes while some patron wailed out to Nickelback on stage.

Seriously, dude should not quit his day job.

"I know, I know," I said as I gingerly pulled out the cake, setting it on a high top in the corner by the Love-Meter machine.

That's when I saw him. Across the room, sitting with a group of guys, who were all over one another.

A blush crept up my cheeks.

M's Place was well known for it's queer-friendly atmosphere, but I couldn't say I spent a lot of time there. Not because knowing that freaked me out, I just...

Somewhere in my DNA, I missed the link that made me able to engage in situations like this.

I wanted to go out and party, and karaoke...

but I was always working, or studying. The few times I *did* go out, only ended with one night stands where the girls ran out the morning after anyway, so I didn't have the best track record or experience with bar culture.

Hell, who was I kidding, I didn't have the best experience with *people*, period.

I was better off frosting cakes for people who actually *knew* how to have fun.

But something about Mitchell DeVille called to the little voice inside of me, begging me to let go.

To have *fun*.

I swallowed as I watched his friends smiling, kissing one another, and being unabashedly public about their affections.

Then reality hit me like a sack of flour as I put two and two together.

His flirting online and at the cafe, his *very* PDA friendly friends, the way he was currently looking at me... like he wanted to *devour* me whole...

Oh fuck...

"What's got you all in a twist? Hot young thing? Ex-girlfriend? Hot ex-girlfriend with another hot ex-girlfriend?" Archie snarked as he set down the boxes of cookies and cupcakes, popping the lids.

"Nothing. I —"

But it was no use; Archie's radar was laser sharp. He'd laid eyes on Mitchell, who was now getting up from his seat, and walking toward the bar.

"Oh... so... hot guy then. Hmmm," he said with a shrug as my entire body heated from his words.

"Archie!"

"That is not nothing," Archie jabbed.

"Oh my God, Archie, it's not like that. He's a—"

What could I say?

Friend didn't seem like the right word, but we weren't strangers either, right?

"He's a... work... friend."

Archie raised his eyebrows. "Mhmmm. Sure. I have to say I'm kind of surprised, though," he said, shaking his head as I fought to refute his insinuations.

"Didn't think guys did it for you," he teased.

"They don't... I mean—"

How could I explain something I barely understood myself?

I was not sure *anyone* really did it for me. It wasn't like I had a ton of experience with people in general. I'd dated a few girls, and while I didn't *mind* fucking, especially from behind, I would have rather ingested a year old cake than go down on a girl.

Does that mean I'm gay?

"You're blushing like a whore in church, Penn. Besides, that man has more flames than a bag of Hot Cheetos. You can't hide that shit."

My stomach twisted in knots as I tried *not* to look at the tall, dark, cocky photographer.

And damn, was it a fight not to look.

"He's right you know," Will said as the last notes of the song played out. "You're about as subtle as a hurricane."

"He's coming over here," Archie said giddily. "Be cool, be cool... You gotta make a man work for it, baby."

Mortification spread across my cheeks, through my veins, and caused my stomach to flip.

"What? No, Archie, I swear... I—"

Archie smirked as I tried to find some sort of escape route, but between the tables with Max's goodies, the bar, and the crowd, I was stuck.

"I can't do this right now, I have to—" Panic crept up my neck with the maddening heat of a blush I couldn't seem to quiet if my life depended on it.

Will laughed as he turned away from us, calling out over his microphone that he needed the patrons' *assistance* to wish Max a happy birthday.

"Miguel said five minutes, Penn," Archie whispered, just as Mitchell made it to the bar.

I felt him before I saw him, as I tried to focus and busy myself with arranging the cupcakes around the cake.

"Hey," he said nonchalantly, leaning on the edge of the bar.

"Hey..." I said, like an absolute idiot as I turned around to get a look at him. Under the pink and blue lights of the bar, Mitchell looked stunning. Like some actor on an HBO show or something.

My cock more than agreed with the assessment, which made me acutely aware that whatever was happening to me, I was in over my head.

Never in my life had I looked at any woman, even the ones I'd dated, and formed an *instant* boner.

Panic flooded me as I shifted my body toward the table, if only to hide my inappropriate erection.

What the fuck?

Under his steely neon gaze, I felt like I couldn't breathe. I couldn't process all the stimuli assaulting me at once.

"What brings you to this hole in the wall?" he asked, shifting his stance as he focused his gaze on me.

I felt like I was going to spontaneously combust.

I swallowed harshly as I turned away from him, needing air.

Why was *talking* to him so difficult?

I talked to lots of people!

"I mean... it's your sister's birthday."

Mitchell raised one eyebrow. "So?"

I motioned to the cake. "Birthdays are kind of my job."

"That sounds horrible," he said with a grin.

"It's not so bad... sometimes, I guess," I said, running a hand through my hair, if only because I was feeling more on the spot than if I'd have had to karaoke in front of this entire damn room.

"I can't say I'm surprised. This has Miguel written all over it," Mitchell said, nodding to the cake. "Does that say... Happy Birthday *Bitch*?"

I blushed at his curse. Something about the way his voice sounded when he swore made my damn blood rush and my cock twitch.

Please, just kill me now.

"It was requested," I replied, but because I was nervous, I started rambling.

So unprofessional.

"I made a cake that said Merry Fucking Christmas once. My classmate and I piped on some bare assed elves. It was a hit at his Christmas party."

Why the fuck did I say that?

Mitchell smirked, his eyes alight with mischief.

"What's the dirtiest cake you've made, Cream Puff?"

My cheeks heated from his cocky tone, and before I could answer, thankfully, I was saved by the bell.

Or rather, Archie strong-arming his way to light the candles on the cake.

"S'cuse me," he said, knocking me into Mitchell. Because of the tight space, I nearly fell over, but Mitchell caught me by the arms.

I was acutely aware of his warm palms against my skin, making the rest of my body heat like an oven. Instinctively, I reached out to steady myself, my hands settling on his hips as I cursed from the shove, both mortified beyond all belief, and the slightest bit pissed that Archie would be so careless.

Someone could have gotten seriously hurt!

"What the Hell, Archie?" I growled as I removed my sweaty hands from Mitchell's hips, fidgeting with my shirt and pants, if only to quell the burgeoning hardness that would not relent.

The last thing I needed was Mitchell noticing such things.

A strange sort of thought presented itself as I had to acknowledge a part of me that wondered what his reaction would be if...

I forced the thought down, moving away from Mitchell for the moment as Will called out for everyone to sing Happy Birthday.

My focus was pulled to the end of the bar, as Miguel forced Max along the hallway out into the open bar area.

The shock on her face was evident, and I could see she was cursing him up and down, but despite that, there was a light in her eyes that could not be mistaken when she set gaze on her cake.

A two-tiered cake trimmed in white and pink fondant, with small liquor bottles and fondant bulldog faces.

I didn't understand the reference, but then again, I didn't need to. Whatever language they had as siblings was understood, and that was all that mattered.

The look of happiness on her face made me smile, too. It settled all my nerves, and made me feel a thousand times better, because that one look...

That look of sheer delight was why I loved baking.

Bringing joy to the little moments in life, not just the big ones, was what I loved most about baking and designing.

The sounds of off-key and off-timed renditions of Happy Birthday filled the air, and I couldn't help but join in as I moved aside, making room for Max and Miguel.

Max stood in front of her cake, and as the last notes of the out of sync bar hummed her birthday serenade, she took a moment to pause.

To make a wish.

I wondered for a moment what she wished for, and then watched as she blew out each flame one by one.

Watched as one candle flickered back to life as the bar roared with laughter and "oohs" and "awwws" filled the space.

"Happy Birthday, Max," Mitchell said, flashing his sister with a smile.

"Happy Birthday to my favorite bitch," Miguel said as he hugged her.

"You fucking assholes," Max said, laughing as she fell into her brother's hug. "All right, enough sentimental shit, I need to get back to work."

"Henry volunteered to take care of the bar for the next hour, so sit your ass down," Miguel said as Archie cut the cake.

"But, but..."

"No buts, missy. You heard the man, sit your ass down and enjoy yourself for once," Mitchell said, before settling his gaze back on me.

"Same goes for you, Cream Puff."

"What? Oh, I'm not staying, I—"

"Let me buy you a drink."

Archie's backside as he moved around the high top knocked me into Mitchell's space again, and I was starting to get pissed.

"I—" I panicked, trying to think of anything, any sort of excuse to escape this situation. Because between my cock and the heat from embarrassment, and a rather tight space, I was afraid I might literally expire.

"Come on, it's my sister's birthday, and with her in time out, I can guarantee you the drinks will actually be good."

"Fuck you, Mitch!" Maxine bit out, but there was no venom in her voice. Only the sarcasm of an annoyed older sibling.

Mitchell slid his hand behind my back, his palm settling at the dip above my ass, and I felt like I was going to pass out.

"Ar... Archie and I are on the clock," I said, swallowing nervously.

"No, we aren't," Archie quipped. "This was the last job for the day. The shop's already closed up."

Mitchell grinned, and the sight was like hot, melted chocolate ganache over sponge cake.

Fuck.

"Sounds to me like you're pretty free," he said smoothly. "Besides, we do have something to celebrate."

I tried to focus on not melting into a puddle on the floor because everything was converging on me at once.

"I guess..." I said, biting my lip, if only to quell the sudden urge to curse out of panic. "Wait... We do?" I asked. I didn't miss the light stroke of his fingertips along my spine, sending a shiver throughout my entire body.

It was as soothing as it was new.

Different.

I looked at Mitchell, under the bright neon, and something in his dark gaze settled my anxiety.

"Yeah, our partnership," he said, flashing me with a smirk.

"Partnership..." I said the words like I didn't know how to speak English, which was insane.

I could technically speak two languages. English and French.

But under Mitchell's gaze, I could barely speak Caveman.

Mitchell gently pushed against my back, coaxing me to follow him.

I needed to get out of this tight space. I needed to breathe.

"Uh... I guess, one drink wouldn't hurt."

CHAPTER 8

Mitch

"Hey, Mitch, what can I get ya?" Henry drawled from behind the bar.

I'd pulled a couple shifts myself over the years, but I wasn't technically on the M's Place payroll.

But I had to admit, watching Henry sling drinks with ease made me miss the craziness of the weekends, not to mention the tips.

But I didn't miss the drunk assholes throwing up all over the bathroom.

"Going to switch it up from my warm up beer to a rum and coke," I said as I turned toward Penn.

"What about you, Cream Puff? What's your poison?"

Watching Penn's cheeks flush like a freshly steamed tomato every time I called him such only fueled my desire to keep doing it.

He looked pretty fucking cute all flustered, and maybe I was a glutton for punishment.

"I, um, I don't really drink a lot, so I'm not sure—"

"You are old enough to drink, right?" I asked, momentarily wondering if maybe I'd assumed too much, but Penn only blew some fluffy, golden-hued hair out of his eyes with a bratty little huff.

"Of course, I'm old enough. I'm twenty-three."

I smiled as Henry chimed in.

"Can I make a recommendation?" Henry asked as he worked on pouring three beers and passing them out to their owners.

Penn blinked, licking his lips as he turned from me toward Henry.

"That, uh, that would be great."

"If you've got a sweet tooth, the cotton candy martini or the Chateau Ste. Michelle is pretty good. We've also got Angry Orchard Cider, and if you're really not into cocktails, wine, or beer, there's always White Claw."

I watched as Penn twisted his lips, trying to

figure out what he'd go after. My guess was White Claw, so I was surprised when he went for the cider instead.

"Good choice," I said as Henry set about fixing our drinks.

"I think I had it once, but I can't remember what it tasted like," he said with another blush.

"Let me guess, you were one of those guys who blacked out after one crazy hangover-style night and haven't touched the stuff since?"

Penn smirked. "I've never really *blacked* out, even when I have been drunk."

Henry passed us our drinks.

Penn took a sip, puckering his lips.

"When is the last time you were drunk? Or... out in general?" I asked as I stirred my drink first.

Penn shrugged. "I don't know. Toward the end of school, I kinda lost interest. Well, and my friends, too, I guess. But that's to be expected when you break up with someone, I suppose. You become the pariah."

He took a long drink and I noticed his shoulders loosened only a fraction. When he pulled the bottle away, some juice trickled down his lip, to his chin.

My cock twitched immediately at the sight and I let out a grunt of my own as I fought the desire to brush it away with my thumb. So instead, I took a sip of my drink, turning my body slightly away, if only to quiet my cock.

Don't get any bright ideas yet, buddy.

"Fuck 'em," I said, shrugging.

Penn looked at me with surprise. "What?"

"If those people bailed on you because you weren't fucking their friend anymore, they weren't your friends to begin with. I don't know you that well, but from what I do know, I know that you're way better than those kind of superficial assholes."

Penn's eyebrows furrowed as his gaze softened. "Thanks, I think," he said, his voice dropping an octave.

I raised my glass to him. "To new friends. And new experiences."

I watched as he raised his bottle, a smile forming on his perfect lips.

"I'll cheers to that," he said as our glasses clinked, my knuckles brushing against the edges of his fingertips.

CHAPTER 9

Mitch

THE KARAOKE HAD RESUMED, and I could see Miguel forcing our sister up on stage as the crowd roared.

"Drink up, Cream Puff. Because class starts now."

"Come on, Penn, you have to take a turn!" Archie, Penn's friend, begged.

"Absolutely not," Penn said, shaking his head, his cheeks rosy and his smile damn near contagious.

Nolan chimed in with his rescuing stance, as usual. "Guys, if he doesn't want to, leave him alone."

I had to admit, the pencil pusher was a nice

addition to the group. Like Cade, he was a natural empath.

"Thank you," Penn said as Dawson rolled his eyes.

We'd gravitated toward my friends, if only because Cade and company didn't seem to take kindly to me keeping Cream Puff all to myself.

They are worse than a throng of teenage girls.

But there was a part of me that felt like maybe Penn *could* fit in here.

With us.

With *me.*

I watched him drain his third Angry Orchard, his pretty blue eyes sparkling with the glaze of good old-fashioned drunkenness.

At that moment, Will called him to the stage.

Penn's eyes widened in shock, and Archie grinned.

"Archie... No..."

"And leave your adoring fans waiting?" he said with a dismissing wave.

I watched Penn bite his lip, weighing what to do.

I didn't know his friend well—hell, I didn't know Penn well—but from the little I did know, I had a feeling he was just trying to push Penn out of his comfort zone.

New experiences and all.

"I'll go with you," I said definitively, setting my drink on the table.

Penn's gaze shot to me.

"What—"

"Just... let me do the singing, okay. You can just stand there and look pretty."

I watched the blush spread on his cheeks as Archie grinned.

"I—"

"What are you waiting for, get up there!" Archie laughed, taking a sip of his beer as I headed up to take the stage.

I half expected even in my drunken state, that Penn would sit it out and let me take over, so I was thoroughly surprised when I heard his footsteps on the platform behind me.

"All right what did Archie Comics pick out for you to sing?" I drawled as I squinted at the teleprompter as Will queued the song up.

Into The Groove by Madonna.

I cast Penn a glance, raising my eyebrow. "Didn't peg you for a Madonna fan."

But there wasn't enough time for him to answer me. Not when the first few notes came across, and I had to speak into the microphone, "You can dance."

I glanced at Penn, watching his glassy eyes focus on me and then the mic. Deciding if he wanted to be a pretty standby or part of the show.

I continued my first few lines, watching him with intent.

I sang on about getting into the groove, and how a boy had to prove his love.

Penn licked his lips, his gaze flashing from my eyes to my mic. The vibration of the stage and the loud speakers drowned out everything else.

Everything but *him*.

Just focus on me, Cream Puff, you'll be fine.

Suddenly, I wasn't sure if I was convincing him or myself.

Will shouldered him, drawing his attention away as I continued to sing, turning to face the crowd.

Over the bright lights, I could see Cade smiling, Weston's arm slung around his neck.

Dawson and Nolan were fighting at the table, while Archie hollered and screamed.

And then I felt a nudge against my arm. I turned, facing bright blue eyes and rosy cheeks that gazed into mine like I had the answers to *everything*.

He sang, his voice clear and strong as he belted out the lyrics about feeling free only when dancing.

I watched as he swallowed harshly, closing

his eyes and I picked up where he left off. I lit out the words about locking the door and no one else seeing, watching as Penn opened his eyes and he moved back and forth, finding the rhythm. The groove, as Madonna would say, I guess.

He sang about being tired of dancing by himself, licking his lips as he focused on me.

A smirk spread across my face as I leaned into him, my microphone between us.

I sprang forward with the next line and focused in on his bright blue eyes.

The rest was a blur.

As far as I was concerned, there was no one else in the room but Penn.

We sang in tandem like that, building off of one another until the music faded.

I grabbed him by the back of the neck, pulling him to me as I whispered in his ear, "Good job, Penn." I slapped him on the back appreciatively before handing Will my microphone.

I exited the stage, my body feeling flushed from the heat of our proximity mixed with the harsh stage lights, and my own building desire.

Penn followed after me, calling my name.

"Huh?" I turned around, just as his foot caught on the last step, causing him to pitch forward like a clumsy little lamb.

Despite my inebriation, I reacted first.

I leaned forward, catching him in my arms, preventing his fine ass from complete embarrassment.

The heat that blossomed between us was like an inferno as he looked up at me, eyes glazed with liquor and something else I couldn't place.

His fingertips sank into my heated flesh as he steadied himself.

"Lightweight," I teased as I righted him, but I didn't remove my hands from his hips, and he made no move to stop his fingers from clutching my biceps.

Looking at him in my arms, feeling his grip...

Fuck, I could get used to that look.

My cock twitched as a grunt escaped my throat, mingling with a soft sigh that escaped his.

"Uh, yeah. Guess I'm a mess, huh?" he said wistfully.

I steadied his frame as I shifted us further into the shadows of the empty pool room to let the next contestant—a woman I didn't know—up on the stage.

The shift pulled us into the low-lit corridor adjacent to the game room, which lead toward one of the three emergency exits.

It was close enough to hear the woman

wailing on her rendition of Carrie Underwood's *Before He Cheats*, but not so close that we didn't have a modicum of privacy for the moment.

"You're having fun. Fun can be messy sometimes," I said, licking my lips as I focused my gaze on his perfect pout.

I wanted to kiss him.

I wanted to tell him that messy or not, he deserved to have a good time.

I wanted to be the one to show him just all the fun *we* could have.

Together, if he'd give me the chance.

Somewhere in my mind, I knew it was a bad idea. For starters, he was technically a client, and pursuing any sort of romance was unprofessional.

Then there was the whole question about whether or not Penn was even remotely into the idea of any sort of romance or relationship with someone like me.

Because I wasn't a tall, tanned, pretty blonde woman.

I was the furthest thing from that.

But caught up in the shadows, with Penn in my arms, looking like a bedazzled wedding cake with his plush lips and rosy cheeks and glittering eyes...

I couldn't resist.

The words fell out of my mouth without warning.

"I want to kiss you right now," I whispered, my voice catching in my throat.

Penn stood upright, his entire body stiff as a rod.

"I think... I think I want to kiss you, too... but..."

I reached out, sliding my hand through his damp, sweaty hair.

"But what?" I asked, trying to breathe.

"I've never kissed someone like you... before," he admitted.

In my drunken stupor, I stupidly asked what I already knew. But perhaps I just wanted to hear him say it.

Out loud.

"Like me?" I drawled. "I think I need you to elaborate, Cream Puff."

Penn squeezed my side as his breath shook.

"I mean... I've never kissed a guy," he whispered, licking his lips as he swallowed harshly.

"There's a first time for everything," I said, ignoring all the alarm bells sounding in my head.

I ran my hand down his neck, cradling the back of his head as I used my thumb to nudge his chin up.

Penn fell into me with ease as I brought my mouth to his.

Like he'd been waiting for my kiss all his life.

His lips against mine were soft and lush, and as sweet as a literal cream puff.

A deep groan escaped him, igniting me like a firework on the fourth of July.

I took his groan as permission to go further, slipping my tongue into his mouth as I pulled him by his hips, moving him closer, brushing my hardness against him.

"Fuck," I whispered, feeling lightheaded as his tongue responded in unison.

The sounds of Will announcing last call rang out, and shattered everything.

Penn broke away, his eyelashes fluttering as he opened his eyes and immediately stiffened once more, pushing away from me.

"Oh fuck, I'm so sorry. I—"

"It's okay, I—"

"I have to go," he blurted, anxiety taking over.

Fuck!

I pushed too hard, I—

"Penn..."

"I... I'm sorry. Thank you for the drinks, but I need to go. I need to go..." he said, and then he took off like a bat out of hell.

All I could do was watch as he found Archie, and then they headed out the door.

"Fucking asshole!" I snarled, chastising myself as I punched the damn Love Meter machine. It went off with a whir, buzzing and vibrating.

"Shut the fuck up!" I snapped as the meter sounded off, hitting the "Scorching" setting.

"There you are," Cade said as he found me nursing my sore fist.

"Wes and I are headed out. Was wondering if you needed a ride home? I know you came by yourself, but I don't think your brother will care if you leave the car here overnight," he said softly.

I cursed silently, feeling the effects of my alcohol and my shame.

"Yeah, I could use a ride," I said as he settled his hand on my shoulder.

"And maybe while you're at it, you can dig my fucking grave, too."

PENN

My head was killing me.

I guessed when you didn't go out drinking all that much to begin with though, it was probably ten times worse than you remembered.

Archie, however, was absolutely fine. Or at least, he appeared to be as he waltzed into the shop with a carrier of sweet-smelling coffee.

"Good Morning, Pennington," he sing-songed, making my headache throb and my eye twitch.

"What's so good about it?" I grumbled as he set the carrier down behind the counter before heading to grab his apron.

While I'd been away at school, Archie and

my dad opened the shop most days, but now that I was home, my dad had taken a step back. He and my mom usually came in later now, around mid-morning. Which meant, for the time being, Archie and I had the shop to ourselves.

Archie pulled out a coffee cup and handed it to me with a raised eyebrow.

"Feeling the hair of the dog, eh?" he poked, flashing me with a smirk.

I grabbed the coffee, breathing in its delicious cinnamon-vanilla scent.

Cinnamon Dolce Lattes fix everything.

Except drunken shenanigans.

I popped open the plastic lid, diving into the frothy cream on top, letting the sweetness coat my tongue and soothe my frayed nerves for a moment.

"More like hungover and full of regret," I mewled. "Now I remember why I don't drink."

Archie grabbed his coffee as he leaned back against the back prep counter, imploring me with his steely amber gaze. His naturally tanned skin stood out like fresh-baked gingerbread against the cool marble and cobalt blue.

The sun was only starting to come up, and as such, lit up the inside of the bakery like the gates of heaven.

"Why? Because you get all flirty and handsy when you're drunk?" he teased.

My cheeks flushed with heat at his words, and the memory of last night pushed forth all over again.

Mitchell's hand on my back, his fingertips brushing against mine.

His tongue in my mouth.

My cock awakened at the thought and I gritted my teeth as I focused on breathing.

"It's not like that. I—"

I've never been kissed by any of my girlfriends like... that.

Archie smiled, shaking his head. "You know what they say? Drunk words are sober thoughts. Maybe your actions are more in tune with what you want than you think."

"I'm not... gay, or... or bisexual!" I shouted, feeling on the spot. "I'm straight!"

Some of my cream sloshed over the side of my cup from my sudden vibration, my voice echoing off the bakery walls.

Even as I said the words through, I felt like something had shifted. Like a volcano erupts or a glacier breaks away, floating apart from its foundation.

Archie *was* gay. Loud, out, and proud gay, and so was Mitchell DeVille. I knew that now, and there was no denying it.

But me... surely I would *know* if I was bi or gay. I mean, a person just knows, right?

I'd *looked* at lots of girls, and found them attractive. But never had I ever popped an instant boner looking at *anyone*.

At least, that was up until I'd seen Mitchell at that wedding.

Or until last night... after we *sang* together... when I fell, and he caught me.

"You trying to convince me, Penn, or yourself?" Archie asked curiously.

"I... I've only ever been attracted to women. I have had, like—"

"Three or four girlfriends? Yeah, how did those relationships work out for you?" Archie asked.

I turned around and instead of looking at him, I focused on stacking the cooler display.

"That has nothing to do with—"

"It has *everything* to do with it," Archie insisted. "The dick wants what it wants. It does not lie."

"It's not that simple," I refuted.

Archie shrugged as he set to making a fresh batch of cinnamon rolls, the first item on today's calendar prep.

"Don't believe me, watch some porn. You'll figure it out pretty quick."

I huffed in annoyance. "Are you serious? I don't watch porn, like, at all."

Archie snickered. "Then what do you have to lose? Consider it research. If you find yourself all keyed up over tits and ass and tight pussy, then by all means, I will leave you alone about this forever. I'll take your steamy drunk dude make out to my fucking grave," Archie said.

I turned to look at him with a raised eyebrow of my own. "Promise?"

Archie held his hand over his heart. "Promise. But I have a feeling you aren't as straight as you think," he said, turning to roll out the dough, and leaving me to my own devices, just as my parents came in through the door.

What the hell?

They never come in this early anymore.

"Hey, Mom, Dad... Is everything okay?" I asked, suddenly alarmed.

"We need to talk about last night," my dad said, his voice stern, and gruff.

"What?" The blood in my veins ran as cold as a frozen croissant.

A part of me was worried they'd heard us talking, or worse someone might have said something to them. That they might have somehow seen me and my suddenly shifting morals, and that I'd somehow embarrassed not just myself, but my family.

"Well, it's not often you come home so late, and you *did* leave all the lights on," my mom said with a smile as she headed over to grab an apron while my dad settled his arms on the counter.

"The event last night must have been quite a night," he said with a grin, winking at me.

My cheeks reddened again as I stammered.

"Oh, I can assure you, Mr. Baker, it was," Archie said with a giggle.

I shot him a glare. I watched as my mother rolled the dough smoothly, passing it to Archie to cut and roll.

"What time is the photographer coming today?" she asked, and once again my blood chilled.

I was a popsicle of fear, embarrassment, and curious desire.

It was Monday.

Mitchell would be coming in *today*.

Today, the day after I stupidly got drunk and...

Kissed him.

I kissed a boy, and I—

My cock twitched as the memory filled my brain. Of his warm, soft lips moving hungrily against my own, of the way my entire body— especially my damn cock—responded to his mouth, the sounds he was making.

The hardness I vaguely remember in my pants.

"Um, uh, I think..." I tried to focus on my words, but I felt like I was slowly slipping beneath choppy waves. "I think Mr. DeVille is arriving around noon," I finally said.

Archie snickered in the background, and I turned away.

"Splendid!" my mother said with excitement.

"I can't wait to see what you two come up with," my father chimed in.

The hours on the clock were like an eternity. Especially, those last fifteen minutes. A part of me wondered if perhaps he wouldn't show. Maybe he, too, was nursing a hangover, and would want to reschedule.

Did I want him to reschedule?

A part of me wanted to avoid looking the man I'd kissed in the eyes, while the other part of me—a larger part—was curious to see him again. Maybe I could apologize, clear the air.

Away from my parents and Archie, of course, which wouldn't be too difficult if I could somehow come up with a guise to get Mitchell alone that wasn't suspicious.

I'd almost sweated myself out of my clothes by the point he actually showed up.

Dressed in tight burgundy jeans and a zebra print button down, his dark hair was gelled back, the lights of the bakery casting a shimmering sheen on his dark locks. Slung across his back was a tripod, and he carried what looked like two giant suitcases. He looked like he was going on a trip to Key West and not a small town bakery to photograph desserts.

Without thinking, I headed toward the door, if only to help him drag in his equipment.

"Hey..." I said as I swooped in to grab the suitcase he gripped in his right hand. "Let me help you with that."

Mitchell smirked, his dark eyes full of mischief and excitement.

"It's good to see you, too, Cream Puff," he said, his voice dark and... *sexy*.

I swallowed harshly as I tried to focus on the task at hand, and not the weird things his deep rumble was doing to me.

For God's sake, my parents are here!

"You must be Mitchell," my father said as he came up beside me, extending his hand. "I'm Samuel Baker, co-owner of Penn's Bakery."

Mitchell's smirk shifted into a much more *polite* smile, his entire demeanor shifting like a chameleon.

"So nice to meet you, Mr. Baker," Mitchell said as he extended his hand.

Panic laced its way through me.

"And this is my wife, and co-owner, Marissa." He introduced my mom who shook his hand, smiling ear to ear.

"Nice to meet you both," Mitchell said, his voice as saccharine as the buttercream frosting Archie was whipping up for this afternoon's orders.

I forced my legs to move, if only because I needed to get as far away from the Twilight Zone as possible, or I thought I might legit pass out.

Thankfully, my parents had sequestered Mitchell for the moment so I could breathe behind the counter. I dropped his suitcase in front of the display case, figuring it was a good spot. I'd been working on the display practically all day to settle my nerves about this very moment.

Archie smirked at me.

"What's so funny?" I bit out as the oven timer went off for the three tier cake we were working on for Gloria Tanen's fiftieth.

The smell of fresh baked vanilla rounds swept through the air, soothing my senses just a fraction.

"Nothing, nothing at all," Archie snickered as he slid me the buttercream.

I shot him a glare as I kept my back to my

parents and Mitchell, deciding instead to get lost in frosting the cake rounds.

The rest of the day—which was only about four hours or so—I spent avoiding Mitchell.

Which wasn't an easy feat, given the size of our shop. But somehow, I managed to busy myself with Miss Tanen's cake, and spent the last hour doing dishes.

My parents had taken off, and it was just Archie and I. At least, I *thought* it was just Archie and I, until I came around the corner and ran smack into Mitchell, camera still in hand, taking pictures of the marble and cobalt tile, of the back of the counter. He pitched forward a moment, the snap of the shutter going off as he cursed, finding his grounding.

I looked back and forth, expecting to see Archie, but he wasn't in the front.

He never usually left without saying good-bye, so I knew he had to be there somewhere.

Hiding in the freezer maybe?

"Oh, I'm so sorry, I thought you left," I said, startled.

Mitchell set his camera down on the clean counter, raising an eyebrow.

"How could I leave without proper payment?" he said, flashing me a grin.

My cheeks flushed at his insinuation, and I

wasn't sure if I should have been offended or not.

"P—payment?" I swallowed, my mind thinking of his plush lips, his tongue in my mouth...

"I believe you *did* say there would be desserts involved in this gig," he said teasingly.

Of course!

I felt like an absolute idiot. He'd offered his services at a discount because I had promised to pitch in some bake shop goodies.

"Yeah... yeah, of course. Uh, so, what, uh, what would you like to take home?" I asked as I slowly ambled backward, away from him.

Mitchell leaned against the back counter, spreading his arms along the ledge. He'd rolled up his zebra print sleeves to the elbow, and the first two buttons on his shirt had been popped.

With the way his dark hair fell in his eyes, and the smirk on his face, I couldn't deny he looked divine.

Just as delicious as any dessert in my display case.

I cleared my throat as I headed toward the case, grabbing a cardboard box and putting it together.

"I can think of one thing that isn't in that case, that I'd *love* to take home," he toyed shamelessly.

I turned from him, my cheeks heating from his words.

What the hell was wrong with me?

Granted, I'd never been the best when it came to flirting, and I usually despised guys who were so cheesy in their pick up lines when it came to women.

No one had ever flirted with me like Mitchell did.

Man or woman.

Something about that made my entire body heat like a bonfire.

Is that what I want?

I wasn't really sure *what* I wanted. I liked Mitchell's words. I thought he was pretty hot, even in a pink zebra print shirt that totally clashed with our clean and crisp aesthetic.

And I had to admit, drunk or not, I liked it when he kissed me.

No, I liked *how* he kissed me. Because no one had ever kissed me like I was some princess in a fairytale.

Like a dragon-slaying knight in shining armor.

"I highly suggest the cinnamon rolls. We make them fresh every day," I said, ignoring his blatant flirtations.

Mitchell didn't press me. He only hummed

in understanding as he responded, "Whatever you say, Cream Puff."

I turned around, incensed by the moniker he'd gifted me that first night we'd spoke.

It was hard to believe it had only been a few days ago.

I'd messaged him, and he'd been flirty then, too. I'd just assumed at the time we were joking around, but if I was being honest, it felt easy then, too, talking to him. Letting my guard down.

It was the Internet.

Who didn't say things they wouldn't in person on the Internet?

It didn't mean anything.

It was just... fun, right?

Yet, I couldn't deny every time he called me *Cream Puff*, I actually found I kind of... liked it.

No one had ever really given me a pet name before.

Pet names are for people in relationships, Penn.

You are most certainly not *in a relationship with this... man. Photographer.*

The photographer you hired *to help the bakery get some more focus.*

Has the buttercream gone to your head?

"That's not my name," I touted with annoyance, before turning back to the display to fill the box with half a dozen cinnamon rolls.

Where the fuck was Archie?

Why hasn't he broken the case down yet?

Mitchell laughed. "I know. But you make it so easy with those rosy cheeks and those pretty rolling eyes of yours every time I do it," he said.

I rolled my eyes, but he couldn't see me.

At least, I hoped.

"I take it you got everything you needed for the day?" I asked as I set the last cinnamon roll in the box, sealing it.

I turned with the box in my hand to see him zipping up his camera bag and slinging it over his shoulder.

"For the most part, yes. I'll go home, download everything, and start culling and editing. I should have a couple teasers for you by tomorrow," he said, his tone changing from the flirtatious, sexy one to the much more cut, dry, professional one.

The tone he probably used for all his clients.

Because that's what I was.

A client.

Mortification coursed through me once more as I remembered our kiss.

God, he must think I'm a total basket case.

Or a total slut.

Which would be the farthest thing from the truth, but I couldn't deny that the thought—the wonder about what *he* thought about that kiss, about me—was just as nerve wracking as the memory itself.

But I also wasn't the kind of guy who just got drunk and made out with people.

I liked to take things *slow*. Meet someone for coffee, get to know them, go out on a nice, romantic date, and then, if the moment was right, then I'd kiss them.

And sex?

I didn't even like to fuck until at least three or four dates in, if we even got that far to begin with!

Most of the girls I'd seriously dated never made it past second base, except maybe Amy, and I didn't like to think about the one night stands that left me feeling like a total loser.

Like I'd been used and discarded like a napkin without so much as a companion for breakfast.

The thought of my ill-fated love life left me feeling more than on the spot.

"Oh. Okay. Thanks," I said, clutching the pink box of goodies as I watched him turn his back to me, zipping up his remaining suitcases of equipment.

Mitchell turned to face me, his naturally dark eyes kind, and endearing.

"Of course," he said, his tone softer "I'll see you tomorrow, Penn."

And with that, he took the goodie box, and headed out the door, leaving me both breathless and feeling guilty as all hell.

How the hell was I going to get through a week of this?

CHAPTER 11

IT WAS NEARING NINE THIRTY, and I knew I should go to sleep, but I'd been tossing and turning for at least an hour and couldn't get comfortable.

Partially because I had gone over the past twenty-four hours in great detail. From my arrival at M's Place, to that *kiss*, to Mitchell showing up today, to that weird, charged moment between us before he left.

Including Archie's words.

Maybe you're not as straight as you think, Penn.

I turned on my right side, my gaze falling on my laptop, its screensaver lighting up the darkness of my room like a salacious beacon.

It wasn't that I had anything *against* porn, it just wasn't something I ever experimented with. Mostly because I was afraid my parents would somehow find out and I'd get in trouble. Even when I went away to college, on my own, there was still that veil of taboo-ness that I couldn't shake. I never considered myself a prude by any means, but suddenly, after that kiss, I was questioning a lot more than I ever thought I would.

Maybe, I was overreacting.

Maybe, I was just all keyed up because I was back home in Jasper Springs. Maybe, I was going through some early twenties crisis or something now that I had graduated or something.

Whatever it was, I felt this curious spark inside of me building, cresting with anxiety.

I was twenty-three years old. Surely, I could just watch a little porn. Prove Archie and his speculations wrong.

I crept over to my desk quietly, even though I knew both my parents were out like a light, and there was no way *anyone* would hear me. Anxiety swelled as I stuffed down the part of me who wanted to turn around and just say we did...

But I was an honest person, if anything, and maybe I was *a little* curious. Being someone who had no idea what the fuck they were doing, I fired up Google like any curious person would do, I'm sure, and googled "where to watch porn" like the complete idiot I was.

I randomly picked a link, hoping it would work.

Immediately, my vision was accosted with women on their knees, cum-stained mouths full of cock, and I shut the lid almost on contact.

Not because it turned me on, because I thought it was kind of gross, actually, but because I had started to wonder if it was a good idea.

"Jesus Christ, Penn, you're a fucking adult, not some hornball teenager. It's research, man, just skim a few videos and call it a night," I said to myself, taking a deep breath before I opened the computer again.

I clicked on the first video again, letting it play as I leaned back in my chair. I didn't *dislike* watching the big, beefy guy shove his cock down the woman's throat, but I wasn't really into her over-acting moans and her sticking her tongue out.

I watched intently as the man's hands slid over his cock, his thumb brushing over the tip of his swollen head. God, the guy was enormous.

Was all porn like that?

Surely, there had to be some regular sized guys out there, right?

Noticing my thoughts were straying, I decided to try something else. A few seconds later, I was viewing a woman being bent over a countertop, with another large, muscled man fucking her from behind.

My cock twitched, as I watched him fist his hand in her hair, watched his slick, thick cock disappear into her ass. I licked my lips, sliding my own hand down beneath my boxers, feeling the smooth skin of my shaft against my palm.

See, Archie, totally straight.

I rubbed and tugged slowly, hardening as I continued to watch the man's veins in his arms tighten with every grip of her hair, with every thrust of his cock against her ass. But then it was over in an instant as he pulled out, only to cum all over her, and...

And I was still no closer to coming myself than I had been when I started to watch.

This is ridiculous.

No one actually likes this stuff.

I had half a mind to just close it out, until I saw a gif on the side, something starring a bigger guy, with dark hair and deep eyes, who literally called to me and made me click.

I don't know why or how, and I couldn't even put it into words, but it was like I was just drawn to his aesthetic. He was hot, all tan muscles and wild hair, fiery eyes.

The video that came up on my computer showed him in the shower, the water running down his defined chest in rivulets and my cock sprang to attention.

There he was, standing there alone, running his large hands over his chest, through dark, chestnut hair, down his abdomen. The curve of his golden-skinned ass, the definition of his muscles... I watched as he tilted his head back, running his hand down to his...

I swallowed, hard, as I watched him grip his thick, pink cock, tugging at his length as he *groaned.*

It was like a train wreck. I literally could not pull my gaze away, and I didn't *want* to.

I licked my lips again as I pulled at my own cock, feeling myself harden again with renewed vigor.

I watched him lean his hand against the tile, thrusting into his hand slowly.

Watched as his cock disappeared into his slippery, wet hand.

Then he looked up. The sound of the shower door opened, and I tensed. I don't know what I was expecting, but an average sized, blond male, who looked to be about in his early twenties, stepped in. His body wasn't as defined as the tall, dark, and handsome man pleasuring himself in the shower.

In fact, golden boy's body kind of reminded me of my own. Soft around the edges, but trim enough that I had *some* shadow of a six pack.

Okay, well, technically, I had fallen off the workout train after I broke up with Amy, on account her friends were gym rats who practically lived at the university rec center.

I watched in curiosity as the smaller man came up behind the star of the show, who never broke character or turned around. I watched as golden boy lathered his hands up and down the man's body, fingers splayed across muscles. Something in the way he touched him, smoothly, lazily, caused my cock to twitch as I watched him trail his lips over the other man's neck, his fingers brushing along the other man's hand.

My own hand built its rhythm as I felt my orgasm building deep in my balls, my cock stiff as a slab of marble. A fresh bead of precum dribbled from my slit and spread along my fingers. I let out a shaky breath as understanding dawned on me.

I liked what I saw.

For the first time in a long time, I felt connected to myself. I was enjoying something I often thought of as a nuisance or a chore.

My breathing hitched as I watched the golden boy drop to his knees, parting the man's legs as he ran his *tongue* along the man's ass, and then...

His fingernails dug into the man's flesh as deep groans left his throat, and the man he was accosting—no, *eating out*—came without warning.

And so did I.

My breath shook as I cursed, my release coating the inside of my hand and my boxers. My cock pulsed, and my head fell back against the back of the chair, my eyes fluttering closed as I rode out the waves of the most *intense* orgasm I'd ever felt.

And when it was over, I opened my eyes, and the truth hit me like a ton of bricks.

Archie was right.

Maybe I wasn't as straight as I thought.

And that changed everything.

CHAPTER 12

MITCH

MY ALARM WENT OFF FAR TOO EARLY for my taste. Especially, since I'd been up until at least one in the morning working on Giselle and Aaron's massive photo cull and edits.

I had promised Penn that I would have some teasers, or at least some good raw images for him to check out, but I'd completely forgotten about the wedding of the century sitting at home on my computer.

But I was a man of my word, and come hell or high water, I was *not* going to show up to Penn's Bakery without *something* for my little Cream Puff to view. After all, he *did* send me home with some delicious cinnamon rolls.

I slammed my hand against the incessant alarm on my phone, groaning as I tumbled out of bed. Penn's parents had informed me that Penn and his friend slash co-worker, Archie, usually opened the shop around five am, which wasn't my favorite time to get up, but being as the sunrises in Jasper Springs always looked best first thing in the morning, for the shot I wanted to get, I knew I was going to have to be an early riser.

If only I would have quit on time last night, instead of going through pictures from the bakery.

I'd managed to capture a few of Penn, as well as Archie and his parents doing their thing.

I couldn't help as I culled and edited the good stuff, that I let myself get a little lost in the details. When you're a photographer, you see everything. People's flaws, the scar on their left cheek from when they fell when they were six, the wrinkles at the corners of their eyes, even the tiniest frayed and static hair. Part of my job is to cover up those flaws. But in contrast to that, my job isn't so much about making someone beautiful with an airbrush. It's about finding the beauty in the things that already exist.

And let me tell you, zoomed in at 400%, there was not a flaw on Mr. Perfect as far as my trained eyes could see.

I got lost in the smoothness of his skin, the thickness of his eyelashes. The look of utter concentration on his face as he worked diligently on his cake and avoided me like the plague.

I'd thought maybe he regretted what happened between us. That I'd been an idiot and pushed where I shouldn't have.

But then when we were all alone, with no one else to be seen, he seemed less cold.

It was almost as if he *wanted* to open up, wanted to explore whatever was forming between us.

And as much as I knew it was probably a bad idea, I couldn't deny I wanted to explore the unknown, too, even though I knew it might hurt me in the long run.

I jumped in the shower, letting the hot water soothe my sore muscles. Most people didn't think about the physical demands of my job.

I didn't have an assistant, and I never had. I was a one man show, and as such, only I was responsible for my equipment, my car, my happy clients.

But I'd be lying if I said it didn't come with its own set of problems, too.

Including the sore back and muscles.

God, I'm not even thirty yet, what the fuck?

I lathered up the soap, taking my time to

wash up, if only because I was tired and hated early mornings.

I ran my hands along my body, working up a good layer of suds. I wasn't the bulkiest guy at the gym by any means, but I was no stick either. After all, you've got to possess some strength to carry heavy ass equipment to weddings and what not.

As my hands made their way to my balls, I closed my eyes and breathed in the relaxing citrus and pine scent. My cock twitched against the back of my hand, and I knew it was better to just take care of myself rather than wait for my damn erection to die down on its own.

I took my cock in my hand like I normally did, pulling and tugging on my shaft until I found the rhythm that I wanted.

Usually, I can just rub one out without too much thought, but for some reason, my brain wanted to cause me more problems.

Because instantly, as I thrust my cock in my hands, *his* image came to mind.

Bad idea, Mitch.

Don't go there.

I knew I shouldn't.

But it was just a fantasy, and I was alone, so what did it matter?

At least that was what I told myself, at the time.

Instead of fighting what felt natural, I let the thoughts bloom.

The memory of his tongue in my mouth, the deep groan that escaped his lips when he kissed me.

His hardness against mine.

Fuck!

Sticky moisture beaded at my slit, and my hips picked up their pace. I knew it wouldn't be long.

The thoughts mingled with the memories as I imagined his soft, plush lips along my heated skin, his warm tongue licking me along my shaft, until he wrapped his lips around my swollen head, and...

"Fuck!" I barked as I fell forward against the tile, bracing myself as I came suddenly.

My stomach muscles spasmed as my cock pulsed and I tried to catch my breath, watching my release circle the drain. I tugged my cock, working to empty the remains as my muscles started to soften, leaving me with a sense of euphoria.

Fuck, how the hell am I going to make it through seven days of this, if I can barely handle twenty-four hours?

CHAPTER 13

Mitch

When I finally arrived at Penn's Bakery at six oh three in the morning, I was feeling much more relaxed.

I'd stopped at the Starbucks on the way, fully intent to grab myself a coffee, but decided to on a whim grab Penn one, too.

After all, what was a day spent with baked goods without a proper cup of coffee?

I didn't know the guy all that well, but given he worked with sugar, and considered himself a cream puff man, I'd opted to get him a Cinnamon Dolce Latte. Then, because I'm not a complete asshole, I tossed on a Chai Tea Latte for Archie. I remembered him going on about how he was obsessed with them the other night at M's Place.

It seemed like a good idea.

I walked across the street, nodding at the daylight warriors who were also leaving their cars and the others who were starting to filter in on the street to park and head to their jobs.

I opened the door to see Archie stocking the case, Penn behind the counter, wiping everything down.

"Good Morning!" I called out, catching his attention.

Penn looked up, his eyes widening in shock as if it was Groundhog Day or something.

I approached him, carrying the carrier of drinks in one hand, dragging my suitcase with my tripod strapped to my back. I'd taken to wearing the camera around my neck for the moment.

I'm sure I looked every bit the weary traveler at that time of morning.

"Here, let me help you with that," Penn said as he threw down his rag, exiting from behind the counter to come around to my aid.

I couldn't help but smile at his actions. He truly was just as sweet as the delicacies he carried in his shop.

"I come bearing gifts," I said as he grabbed the suitcase.

"Gifts?" he said, raising an eyebrow.

With my spare hand, I checked the labels, before handing him his drink.

"Cinnamon Dolce Latte for the Cream Puff, Chai Tea Latte for the pain in the ass, and Tuxedo Mocha with an extra shot of espresso for the photographer," I said, flashing a grin.

Archie came around to receive his drink, smiling. "Thanks, man," he said as I nodded.

"Yeah, don't get too used it. I needed the caffeine and my mama didn't raise an asshole." I flashed him a grin.

Penn chuckled as he took a sip of his drink, his eyelashes fluttering as he moaned in satisfaction.

The sound went straight to my cock, and the memory of my fantasy this morning resurfaced.

Not now!

"God, I swear these things will fix anything," Penn said as Archie nonchalantly grabbed the suitcase, whistling as he pulled it back behind the counter to put it in the office no doubt, like he had yesterday.

Which left Penn and I alone for the moment.

"It's like six am, Penn. What do you need to fix already? The day hasn't even started."

Penn sighed, running his fingers along the heated cardboard.

"If you only knew..." His voice was wistful, yet sarcastic.

Clearly whatever was bothering him was stressing him out.

"Try me."

Penn sipped his drink again, twisting his lips as he gazed up at me as if contemplating what to say.

Or rather, *how* to say it. But he thought better of it.

He sighed, shaking his head as he murmured. "Stupid fucking porn."

The adult in me knew I should probably leave it alone, whatever it was clearly was none of my business.

But the immature asshole in me could not very well leave well enough alone, and of course, I steamrolled through that admission like I was scoring a touchdown.

"Really, Cream Puff? Your panties all in a bunch because the WiFi cut you off too early or something?" I teased.

"Oh my God! I didn't just say that out loud! Oh my God!" His cheeks turned pink, and I couldn't help but laugh.

I reached out, setting my free hand on his shoulder. "It's okay, sweetheart, it happens to the best of us," I taunted him, flashing him a wink.

His cheeks reddened as he groaned. "I am so

fucking bad at this!" he said, turning around, and practically *running the other way.*

"Bad at what?" I called out, as he huffed, scampering behind the counter.

I swung my tripod off my shoulders, setting my coffee down on one of the tables in front of the big bakery window. The sun had started to peek up and I knew I didn't have much time to get the shot I wanted.

"Nothing!" he called out from behind the counter, and I couldn't help but smile, hearing the embarrassment in his voice.

He looked so damn cute when he blushed like that.

I unzipped the tripod, hurrying to set it up to get my shot. I'd just gotten everything set up when the light hit the window, like a firework. I knew once I got the photos downloaded for the day, seeing those bright blue letters amidst the sparkling sunrise, it would be stunning.

And just like most things in life, it was over in a literal flash. I'd stopped the moment, even if only for a fraction, embedded in photography forever.

As I disassembled the camera from the tripod stand, I had to wonder if that wasn't some weird metaphor for my life.

I was always waiting for the right moment to

capture, but in doing so what had slipped through my fingers?

I turned to look at Archie and Penn, working in unison to one another as the first customer came through the door.

"Good Morning!" Penn said cheerily, his smile stretching from ear to ear.

"Oh, Penn, you're home!" The woman squealed as she ran up to the counter to give him a hug.

I knew most people in town, and she did look familiar, but that was also the rough part of this job. Everyone looked familiar, but rarely anyone stood out.

Not like Penn does, with his bright eyes and pretty smile, and his golden boy aura.

I instinctively framed them in my viewfinder, zooming in as she hugged him tightly. The smile on his face was genuine, soft, and caring.

This woman wasn't just a customer to him.

She was family.

Click, snap, click.

His gaze flashed up at me a second later, noticing my observation.

And for a moment, I thought he smiled at me, too, but that would be crazy, right?

I lowered my camera as he held out his arms, sliding his right one around her back.

"Got in last week, Miss Reynolds, and I've just been playing catch up. You know how it is."

I watched as he helped her to the counter and Archie popping in with a, "Hey, Miss R!"

"Archibald, it is always a pleasure," she said with a chuckle.

"What can I get you this morning, ma'am?" Penn drawled, the saccharine sound of his voice like something out a romance movie.

He really was prince fucking charming.

"Oh, I'll just have an order of those amazing cinnamon rolls for the boys at the office. You know how men love their sweets! Can't get 'em to work without a little food motivation," she said, flashing a grin.

I couldn't help but chuckle at her words as I continued to watch the event unfold through my camera. This was going to be gold for his campaign, no doubt.

An idea shot through me, and I decided to file it away, with the hope that it may help later, after I'd gotten things edited, and after I finished the wedding of the century.

CHAPTER 14

Mitch

The day had been more than eventful. Not only was the bakery packed from seven am until at least three, but the phone was continuously ringing off the hook with orders.

I'd just zipped up my suitcase, when Penn came around the corner, wiping his hands on his apron.

"Oh, I'm sorry, I didn't realize you were in here," he said, moving to turn around.

"If you have a minute, I can show you those teasers from yesterday?" I asked, unzipping the front flap where I stored my USB drive.

"Oh... I.... I mean, you don't *have* to. I—"

"I promise I won't bite," I said with a smirk,

noting how Penn's shoulders loosened, how his eyes dipped to my lips as he licked his own. "Unless you want me to, that is," I teased, testing him out.

I turned the USB in my hand nervously, watching his face, holding my breath.

Pen nodded with a sigh.

"Right, I mean, it's just pictures."

"Right, just... photos," I said as I plugged my USB drive in, bringing up the set of four images I'd worked on last night.

Penn slowly took a few steps forward, his shoulder brushing mine in the small office.

That close I could smell the spray or body wash he'd used. Cinnamon and cloves, mixed with cedar and pine. I fought to breathe him in, acutely aware of his proximity.

I pulled up the first image, one of him and his mom working on a cake.

"Wow, this is really great," he said softly. "My mom's going to love this."

A soft smile played at my lips. "Can totally see the resemblance."

I watched Penn's cheeks tinge pink, making my heart skip a beat.

"You don't take compliments very well, do you?"

Pen flashed his pretty blue eyes at me. "Why do you say that?"

I watched as he tucked some stray blond hair behind his ear.

"Well, for starters, you blush every time I give you one."

Penn's gaze flashed to mine once more as he chewed his lip.

"I guess I'm just not used to good looking guys complimenting *me*. Usually, I'm the one dishing out sweet nothings, you know," he said, his voice small.

I wanted more than anything to wrap my arms around him and pull him into my lap, tell him to hell with everyone else.

As far as I was concerned, he was damn perfect.

But the sincerity in his voice called to something much deeper than my need to worship and adore Prince Charming.

What Penn *needed* was acceptance. He needed the space to feel safe and comfortable in who he was, in figuring it all out.

Maybe I wasn't cut out for *this*.

Maybe I was just playing with fire.

But as I looked at Penn's bright blue eyes, the computer monitor shining an ethereal light on him, I knew it didn't matter what I wanted.

I'd be whatever Penn needed me to be.

"That's because most men are afraid saying nice things means they're soft."

Or gay, but we all know niceness and penchant for dick are not mutually exclusive.

"Thanks," he said, a ghost of a smile on his lips.

"You're welcome, Cream Puff," I said with a grin as I cycled to the next photo. I didn't miss the way his eyes lit up when I did so, and that was all I needed.

For the moment, anyway.

"I love the angle of this," he said as he illustrated with his long, lithe fingers toward the cake on screen. "It looks like something that should be in a magazine," he drawled, turning to me once more. "You're really good, you know that?"

Unlike Penn, I could take a compliment, but when it involved my work, I was my worst critic. But as I looked at the image, at the awe on his face, I felt seen in a way I hadn't before.

"I mean, a good photographer should be able to photograph anything within ten feet of their vision, so..."

"Really?" Penn said, his tone much lighter.

I nodded, swiveling in the chair as he crossed his arms, raising an eyebrow at me.

"Yeah. Really. That's, like, photography 101."

"What would you photograph here?" he said, twisting his lips.

The bakery office was pretty tight, and the

shelves were stacked with supplies, the desk full of binders and paperwork among knick-knacks. Even the chairs, including the one I was sitting in, were dated. Much more so than the outside of the bakery.

But as far as I was concerned, there was only one thing worth photographing in my vision.

And he was a lot closer than ten feet.

I smirked as I leaned back in the chair, spreading my legs as I cast him a dark glance.

While I may have had my own awkward moments in middle and high school with my sexuality, as an adult, I felt like I had a good handle on my own sex appeal.

And judging by the way Penn's pupils dilated, I knew he was susceptible.

"You," I said confidently.

Penn swallowed harshly. "Me? Seriously? I'm a mess."

I chuckled at his golden hair, all disheveled, at the apron covered in cake batter, dried icing, and chocolate.

At those perfect, pristine blue eyes, and pouty lips.

God, he was so fucking *pretty*.

"It's the little details of imperfection that make things perfect."

I could tell we were starting to venture into flirty, heated tension territory, and I didn't want to overwhelm the guy too much, so I quickly said, "What about you? Cream Puff? What would you photograph?"

Penn furrowed his eyebrows as he looked around the space, taking it all in, thinking.

It was cute as all hell.

He framed his fingers like a lens, looking at me through them.

"You," he said firmly. "All spread out like a GQ model."

It was my turn to blush, the heat rising in my cheeks even as I let out a dark chuckle.

"Only, I'd add some chocolate, and some cheesy tagline, like..."

"One bite and you'll be on your knees?" I offered, with a laugh.

Penn's eyebrows shot up as his cheeks flushed scarlet, and he laughed.

"I mean, that is a pretty solid tagline," he said.

"Oh, and for shits and giggles, we could add a tub of chocolate frosting in between my legs." I laughed.

Penn chuckled, shaking his head. "Are you always this... this..."

"What?" I asked through my laugh.

"Scandalous?" he said grinning.

"Oh, Penn, this isn't scandalous. This is me being polite."

Penn bit his lip, looking me over for a moment before speaking.

"We make a good team, don't we?" he asked softly.

I cocked my head to the side. "I think we do."

Silence befell us, and I was certain we weren't talking about cakes and goodies anymore.

I waited for a moment to see what he would do. If he would act on whatever desire or thoughts he was having, but he only stood there, stiff as a board.

Afraid.

How can I show you that you don't have to be afraid, Penn Baker?

That was the moment his father decided to come into the already tight office space.

"Dad! I thought you and mom left..."

"Your mother forgot her sweater," Mr. Baker said, rolling his chocolate eyes.

In the office, up close to Penn, I could see similarities, but Penn looked more like his mother with his complexion, his golden hair, and his ocean blue eyes. His father was a pretty large and bulky framed man with olive skin and jet-black hair. It was like night and day, though Penn shared the same jaw-line, the same thick eyelashes, and the same shape of mouth.

He truly was the best of both of his parents. A beautiful subject.

"There it is!" his father said as he moved to grab the sweater draped over the chair I was sitting in.

"Oh, I'm sorry!" I said as I grabbed it, handing it to the man.

Penn looked more than flushed. He looked like he was going to pass out.

Of course, he must be worried his dad saw something...

"Penn and I were just going over some photos I took yesterday, if you'd like to take a look," I offered, speaking as professionally and curtly as possible.

Penn caught my glance and I tried to shoot him a reassuring smile.

It's okay, I got this. Your secret is safe with me.

"Oh, that's all right, I can look at them later. We're headed out for the night to visit our friends in the city, and we really need to get going."

"Fair enough. Have a lovely evening!" I said sweetly as his dad slung the sweater over his shoulder, hugged his son, and made his way out of the office.

When I was certain he was gone, I spoke, pulling Penn from his frozen state.

"When's your next event?" I asked, deciding

to change the subject so my little Cream Puff could breathe easier.

"What?" he said, blinking, shaking his head. Coming back down to Earth from where his thoughts had taken him...

God only knew what was going through his mind.

"Your next big event? You know, like a wedding, or a party, or..."

"Oh, uh..."

"I was hoping I could get some shots of you and Archie out in the field," I said as I pulled the USB out of the computer.

Penn moved next to me once more, checking the calendar on the wall beside me. That close, I could feel the heat rolling off of him.

He was practically sweating.

The motion pulled his shirt up on the side, exposing the sliver of perfect, golden skin, making my cock twitch.

Fuck, now is really not the time!

"Purely business related, Penn," I said, hoping it would settle his anxiety, and also to quiet my damn cock with a mind of its own.

It wasn't like I was asking him on a date or anything. It was just... business.

Right?

"Right..." he said, licking his lips. "I, uh,

have an event tomorrow night. Near the city," he said quietly.

"Time?"

"Six."

"Cool. If it's okay with you, I can meet you and Archie at the event?"

I watched his eyebrows furrow. "You mean, you wouldn't be coming into the shop tomorrow morning?"

I didn't miss the hint of disappointment there, but I didn't want to read into it. No, I couldn't afford to get hopeful.

Even though I wanted to believe it was because he wanted to see *me*.

"Well, if you have an event, those are usually a couple hours, right?"

Penn nodded. "Yeah, I guess so."

"I'll need time to edit what I took today, plus I still have a boatload of photos to go through from Giselle and Aaron's wedding."

"Right, right. I'm not your only gig, I get it," he said, and I frowned.

I hadn't wanted him to think I was brushing him off, or that I didn't care about this gig.

"Penn..."

"No, it's fine, I get it. Uh, yeah, you can meet me at The Robin. Six o'clock."

I nodded in response as I packed up the USB once more, and grabbed my suitcase.

"It's a date. See you tomorrow, Penn."

CHAPTER 15

Penn

I'D BEEN to The Robin a couple times in my life, mostly for events. My parents said in the past it used to be a little local style tavern, but after it changed hands with new owners, they completely redesigned the space to have a more modern feel. Though some of the original design was still intact, such as the deep, mahogany walls and the blue tile floor with the specks of silver all throughout.

Archie and I took turns unloading the van. While weddings were our bread and butter, I personally loved the special occasion or milestone parties like this one, for Tracy Lewis's fiftieth. There was just something that pulled at my heartstrings about having a big birthday party with your closest friends, all decked out.

When her friend called to place the order for the cake, I was given a few suggestions. Black, gold, and silver was the color scheme, and they asked that the cake have a "Gatsby vibe".

So of course, I went all out on the theme, adding little silver painted champagne bottles that spilled out large edible pearls and jimmies, cascading down the three tiers.

Just as I gripped my hand around the box, I slipped.

"Fuck!" I said, thanking my lucky stars I didn't drop the cake.

"Need a hand?" a familiar voice asked.

I looked over my shoulder to see Mitchell, once again dressed in some flashy island print shirt, his dark hair gelled back to expose his flawless olive skin.

My gaze roved over him, down to his tight, black jeans, and my cock twitched in my own.

Fucking hell.

"Uh... yeah..." I stammered, like an absolute idiot.

How was it that every time this guy walked in the room, my brain took a vacation?

Mitchell slung his camera around his neck around to his back as he helped lift the other end of the box.

"Okay, go slow," I said.

Mitchell smirked. "Always."

Thankfully, I could hide my blush behind the box as my insides twisted at the tone of his voice.

I'd never really appreciated anyone's voice before. But there was something about the way Mitchell spoke, even when he was being flirty as all hell that was just... soothing. Relaxing.

I could fall asleep to that voice.

Mitchell led me in through the door, pausing to ask if I was okay every few steps, until we'd reached our destination in the reserved room.

The place was decorated with Gatsby-twenties style decorations, and all the mingling party-goers were dressed in costume.

"Shit, I feel overdressed as fuck," Mitchell said as we set the cake box down.

"I mean, I knew there was a theme, but they didn't mention there would be costumes," I said as I worked closely on separating the box from the cake itself.

I could hear Mitchell clicking away. Compared to my black button down and dark jeans, he definitely looked better than I did.

Seriously, I wished I could wear prints like that, but I'd just look like a reject from the eighties. Mitchell looked like some smooth model from South Beach.

"Looks good," Archie said as he started to unfasten the tape on the box. We still had one more box to get—the box of sheet cake that would be in the back for traying up and serving the party.

Most of our three-tier cakes had a real top layer, but the bottoms were fake. Partially to keep down on the amount of cake related incidents in transport, but also because of cost. It was a lot cheaper for our clients to order what was essentially a small cake for the guest of honor and a large sheet cake that could feed a hundred people easier and for less.

"There's still the sheet cake..." I started as Archie waved me off.

"I got this. Why don't you go grab something to eat. I know you've got to be starving."

My shoulders loosened as my stomach rumbled. He was right, I was hungry. Mostly because I'd spent all day sweating over tonight.

It was weird to walk into the shop that morning, without seeing Mitchell. Even after just a few days, I'd gotten used to his being around, and I kind of missed him.

"Are you sure?" I protested, but Archie only glared at me.

"Go. We've got plenty of time before we have to tie this up and get it ready."

Mitchell shrugged. "You don't have to tell

me twice," he said as he cocked his head toward the main dining room, near the bar. "I haven't had more than a cup of coffee and a cinnamon roll today," he said as I reluctantly followed and Archie headed for the doors.

"Busy day for you, too, I take it?" I asked, glancing around the dining room. It wasn't packed by any means, but there was a good handful of people dining, and sitting at the bar. Mitchell walked up and grabbed a menu off the bar, taking a seat at one of the open stools.

I followed suit, if only because I didn't know what else to do.

"Yeah, weddings are usually a lot in general. Just hours and hours of adjusting lighting and cropping out family members making weird faces and... This is probably boring the shit out of you."

I shook my head. "No, not at all. I think it's interesting. I mean, I get that talent only gets you so far. The rest is just hard work, right?"

Mitchell smirked. "It's not work if it's something you love."

"No, it's still work," I said with a laugh. "But it's a *labor* of love."

Mitchell passed me the menu as he asked, "Did you always want to be a baker?"

I scanned the menu, my gaze settling on an

appetizer platter full of hot wings, fried cheese sticks, and potato skins, and my mouth watered.

I shrugged as I set the menu down. The bartender came over, took our orders—my platter, Mitchell's steak flatbread, and two cokes—just as Archie came in with the giant box.

"Hold on, let me—"

"I got it, Penn!" Archie touted as he wobbled around the corner.

Mitchell reached out to steady him.

"Tell you what, you wait here for our food, and I'll help Archie get this back to the kitchen, okay?" Mitchell offered, getting up from his stool.

I wanted to protest, but the look he shot me had my cock twitching and my ass frozen to the seat.

No one had ever looked at me like *that*.

"Uh... okay..." I stuttered as Archie and Mitchell walked off.

"What the hell am I doing?" I asked myself out loud, when they were out of earshot. The bartender slid our cokes to me, his gaze judgmental.

I guess I'd be judgy of a guy sitting at the bar talking to himself, too.

Everything felt so different.

I'd been out with Archie, and my ex-girlfriends, plenty of times. It wasn't like I didn't *know* how to go out *once in a while*, have a little fun.

But something about Mitchell felt different than it had with everyone else. I knew we were working, technically, but there was an ease about him, that I just wanted nothing more than to sit down, eat some junk food, and have a beer and *laugh*.

When he returned, he smiled. "Good job holding the fort down," he said with a wink.

"Please, all I did was watch the bartender pour the coke from the fountain."

"The party should be arriving in like twenty, Archie said. So we've got more than enough time to eat and work."

I scooted toward him, if only because I wanted to get closer to the bar.

"I kinda always knew I'd be a baker. My mom, she was always baking at home, letting me help her. When she opened the shop, I just knew it was where I'd end up. It was my home away from home."

"That must have been amazing. Sharing the passion with someone else who gets it."

"Your family doesn't get photography?" I asked quizzically.

Mitchell laughed. "No, they do not. I mean, the hospitality and restaurant business is way different. I'm basically self-employed, so I *am* my business. If I'm not chasing the clients, posting on all the channels, doing the thing and keeping my name in the forefront... then I'm not working."

I guess I never really thought about how hard that would be, being as I've basically been brought up and raised to take over the family business. I could only imagine how scary it was to *be* your business. A one man show.

"Still, you're like the *top* photographer in Jasper Springs. You're practically small town famous."

"Not as famous as Dawson Richards, Mr. March," he joked.

I didn't remember much of my conversations with Mitchell's friends from the other night, including the firefighter, but I did recall they all seemed pretty chill and cool.

I wouldn't mind us all hanging out together again in the future.

Somewhere in my gut, I knew that was some sort of sign.

Some inkling of destiny, but at the time I fought to ignore it.

"I don't know, I think you're pretty hot," I said, realizing the instant I said it, that I didn't just *think* it.

My cheeks burned like a five alarm fire as

embarrassment flooded me and I hid my face in my hands.

"Oh my God, I am so sorry. I can't believe I—"

Mitchell let out the deepest laugh, and within seconds I felt, warm, soft hands pulling at mine. The touch sent a shiver up my spine.

It felt... different.

His warm palm against my skin was smooth, relaxing, and surprisingly gentle.

He pulled my hands down slowly, his dark gaze holding mine. I was acutely aware of the tension between us, and the fact that I couldn't take my eyes off his lips.

Lips I remembered just how they felt against my own.

"Penn, listen..."

Oh God, this is the part where I completely fuck everything up.

This is my early life crisis.

"Uh..."

"You don't have to be afraid of what you feel. With me, I mean. I'm not going to judge you. I..."

I watched as he swallowed, his gaze softening as he set my hands in my lap, his thumb brushing over my knuckles faintly, as if he too were afraid.

And for some reason, that made me feel better. More at ease.

"I know how... *confusing*... things can be when you're trying to figure it all out."

My blood chilled as I prepared for his rejection.

Why did I care if he rejected me?

It's not like this was a date, and he wasn't my—

Wait, did I want him to be my—

"I know what it feels like to question things and second guess yourself. But I need you to know it's okay to feel what you feel. To be who you are. If that's a guy who likes tall, pretty blondes..."

I frowned, the memory of Amy interrupting us at the coffee shop resurfacing.

Mitchell smirked. "Or a guy who likes..."

"Tall, dark, and handsome photographers?" I gulped, feeling strangely emboldened by his words.

I watched the grin on his face widen, and his own cheeks tinge pink.

"I like you, Penn. But I don't want you to think I'm pushing or being too forward or..."

"I just... this is all new for me. I like you, too, I think. I just—"

Mitchell's thumb ran rhythmically over my

knuckles, making me feel like everything was going to be okay.

Somehow, this bright, new world of feeling and attraction didn't seem so scary.

Because when I looked at him, I felt *seen*.

Like for the first time in my life, someone *got me*.

My gaze dipped to his lips, then his dark, fiery eyes.

"What is it?" he asked.

"I..." I swallowed, wondering if I really *could* be honest with him.

And myself.

Saying it out loud meant it was real.

That the reality I once knew was over.

I'd shatter my own glass ceiling, but maybe... maybe that's what I needed.

To emerge from my cocoon and embrace the unknown.

I squeezed his hand as I took a deep breath.

It was now or never.

I scooted closer, the motion putting me right between his legs. "I kind of want to kiss you," I whispered.

Mitchell smiled, and it was soft. Sweet.

His eyes glittered in the amber light of the bar. "Then kiss me," he said, his voice dark and gravelly. "I won't stop you."

My entire body felt alive with fear, desire,

and curiosity. It wouldn't be the first kiss we shared, but up until that moment, I'd rationed it was the alcohol that pushed me to act so brazenly the last time.

But there was no denying the truth, when without an ounce of alcohol in either of our systems, the desire was just as maddening, just as overwhelming as it had been before.

And that changed everything.

I slowly leaned into his space, my breath shaking as I did so.

Mitchell met me halfway, cocking his head to the side, his breath low and heavy as he whispered, "I'll never stop you."

I closed the distance between us, ghosting my lips against his, closing them against his bottom lip. His lips were soft against mine, not rough or harsh, and he stayed still as a statue, waiting.

Waiting for me to make the jump.

I settled my free hand on his neck, feeling his pulse beneath my fingertips, the rush of blood and warmth. I moved my lips slowly against him, acclimating to the taste and feel of him. When I was drunk, all I could remember was the *heat*. His tongue accosting mine, the deep groans that left our throats, and our raging alcohol-fueled boners.

But this kiss wasn't like that at all. I gripped

his neck a little tighter, sliding my fingers back in his hair as I probed his lips with my tongue.

And then the throat clearing "ahem" of the bartender with our food reminded me where we were, and what we were really doing. I broke away, heat flushing my cheeks.

"Hungry?" he asked with the sexiest grin I think I've ever seen.

"Um... starving," I said as I turned back in my chair toward my leaning tower of appetizers, feeling a new sort of hunger that had nothing to do with wings and mozzarella sticks.

CHAPTER 16

PENN

"I KNOW this probably sound cliché, but... I had a really good time tonight," I said as I helped Mitchell finish packing up his equipment in his truck.

I didn't miss the smirk on his lips, or the way my cock responded.

I was *so* out of my league.

"I had a good time, too, Cream Puff. In fact, that's probably the most fun I've had at work in a long time."

The smile that formed on my face was irrefutable.

"Really?" I managed to squeak out, my cheeks heating.

Mitchell nodded. "You know," he started as he tossed his tripod in the trunk of his black Jeep Cherokee. "We could do this again. Outside of work, I mean."

His tone was even, careful. Almost as if he was afraid he'd say the wrong thing.

My eyebrows furrowed as I realized what he was asking.

"You mean, like a... date?" I said cautiously.

Mitchell nodded. "Well, unless you just want it to be a friendly hangout. It can be whatever you want it to be."

His voice was solid, unwavering.

And I think that was the moment I realized I was in over my head.

Because the idea of going on a *date* with Mitchell sounded like a really good idea.

So I sucked in a deep breath, and said, "Yes." I nodded, tasting the word on my tongue. "Yes, I think I'd like that. To go on a... date. With you."

If my cheeks were pink before, I could tell by the heat ransacking my body, they were probably tomato red now. I had never felt so on the spot in my life, waiting for someone to respond. Anxiety and panic flooded me. But the grin that spread on Mitchell's face soothed all of that.

"How does after work tomorrow sound?"

CHAPTER 17

Penn

THE WHOLE DAY I felt like I was on pins and needles. For starters, with Mitchell nearly ten feet away most of the day, it was hard to ignore our impending...

Date.

I'd agreed to go on a date with a guy, and I'd be lying if I said I wasn't nervous. Not because I'd never hung out one on one with another man before, but because I didn't know what the protocol was. I knew I wasn't like most guys in general when it came to the women I'd dated, but then again, Mitchell didn't seem like most guys either.

There was something about him, something I couldn't quite put my finger on.

"You're going to run a hole in the ground, Penn," Archie said, cornering me in the stock room. "What is up with you today?"

I avoided his gaze, if only because I needed to focus on taking stock, but Archie was not phased.

"Nothing," I lied.

"Bullshit. Did something happen yesterday? You've been acting weird ever since the drive home."

I sighed in exasperation once more, figuring resistance was moot.

Besides, I didn't really have anyone else to ask about this sort of thing, so I swallowed my fear.

If I couldn't talk to Archie, who could I talk to?

"Mitchell asked me out."

Archie's eyes widened in surprise. "And you're bothered by that?"

"I said yes." I squealed as I fell back against one of the racks, knocking some boxes loose.

"Oh... I see," Archie said slowly, nodding. "You're freaking out because you said *yes*."

I stared at the floor, twisting my lips. "I'm freaking out because I don't know how to do this with another guy. I mean, I never considered myself a bad date before, but I don't have the best track record when it comes to relationships."

Archie held my gaze as he locked the stock room door.

"What are you doing?" I asked, panicking.

"Giving us some privacy for the moment," he said seriously.

My blood ran cold at his seriousness.

Archie pulled up a stool, imploring me with his gaze.

"I'm going to ask you something, and I want your one hundred percent honest answer," Archie said, his gaze freezing me in place as much as his tone.

"Okay..."

"Do you like him?" he asked.

It was a simple question that required a simple answer, but somehow it was... complicated.

"I..."

"It's just me, Penn. You can be honest with me."

I thought about his question. About my answer, because I knew the moment I said it out loud, it would be one more break in my glass ceiling.

"I think so."

Archie chuckled. "Pretty sure you wouldn't

have said *yes* to a date if you needed persuading."

Something about Archie's tone, his laugh, his ease, made me relax.

I pulled up a stool of my own, my shoulders sinking as I sat down and ran my hands over my face.

"I'm so fucked," I grumbled.

Archie patted me on the back. "Welcome to the club."

His pat turned to a slow rub, that made me sigh.

"What are you so nervous about?"

I sat up straighter, letting my hands fall in my lap as his fell from my shoulders.

"I don't know. Like, historically, I've always been kind of boring on dates in general."

Archie nodded. "So you're worried you'll be a boring date, is that it? Worried you won't make a good impression?"

I shrugged. "Maybe?"

"He asked *you* out, right?" Archie said, crossing his arms.

"Yeah."

"Then I'm pretty sure you have nothing to worry about." Archie said, flashing me with a smile as he got up.

I sighed, hoping he was right.

CHAPTER 18

PENN

I STARED at myself in my bathroom mirror.

I'd mulled over my appearance, my outfit for the last twenty minutes, and time was dwindling down. Mitchell had offered to pick me up at my house, probably to give us both time to get ready after being in the bakery all day, but I'd spent the last half hour fussing over what to wear and if I could really do this.

It's just a date, you've been on plenty of them.

He asked you *out, you have nothing to worry about.*

Just be cool.

The text on my phone chimed, and I checked it immediately.

Here.

Shit!

He was here!

I let out a deep breath, slicking my hand through my hair one final time, and hoped that things would go smoothly.

It's just hanging out, having dinner.

We did that the other night, while working and everything was fine.

Well, until I ended up kissing him like some swoon-worthy damsel in distress.

But if I was being honest, I *liked* kissing Mitchell.

I wasn't sure if it was him and his suave, smooth air, or if it was just the newness of kissing someone of the same sex, but either way, I couldn't deny that it *did* something for me.

In a way kissing Amy or my exes never did.

Who gets turned on from a *kiss?*

Me, apparently, because just the thought of kissing Mitchell was enough to get me off after I'd gotten home that night.

I pushed the thoughts from my brain, if only because I didn't want to keep my *date* waiting.

I grabbed my wallet, slid it in my pocket along with my cell phone, and was out the door.

"Where are you off to?" my father asked, peering over his newspaper.

I stopped dead in my tracks. I hadn't said anything outright to my parents, mostly because I was still in the *coming home* phase where we hadn't really set boundaries yet, but I was also twenty-three years old. I didn't need my parents' permission to do anything.

But still, it felt weird. Like somehow, some way, they just had parental radar that told them "he's going on a date with a guy!"

I swallowed nervously, turning to face him.

"I'm, uh, just hanging out with Mitchell."

"The photographer?" My dad raised his eyebrow.

I nodded. "Yeah, we're, uh, going to grab a bite to eat. I'll be home late, so don't wait up."

My dad twisted his lips, and I thought he was going to throw a monkey wrench into my evening, call me out or something.

But he only said, "It's nice to see you making friends, Penn. Have fun."

Friends.

Why did that word cut me to the core like a ceramic knife?

I didn't have time to process such things, so I just nodded and headed out the door to see Mitchell leaning against his car, looking absolutely *smokin'.*

His dark hair was gelled back in his usual appearance, and I noted he'd expertly trimmed his facial hair, which made the dark color stand out all the more pronounced against his tanned skin.

He was wearing another one of his flashy shirts, this one bright pink with neon palm trees and aqua inner tubes. Coupled with his black ripped jeans, he looked like Surfer Ken, if Surfer Ken shopped at Hot Topic.

I looked at him, feeling more out of my league than ever.

Especially in my dark wash jeans, my black converse, and a *nice* pale blue polo.

God, I am such a freaking dork!

I knew I should have worn a button down!

Mitchell's gaze roved over me from head to toe and back again, meeting mine.

"Well, aren't you as pretty as a picture," he said, flashing me a grin as he walked around to open my door.

Instantly, his words caused my blood to rush to my cheeks, but I didn't turn away.

"Thanks," I said with a soft smile, trying to ease my own nerves.

When I was buckled in, and Mitchell had started the car, I realized I was shaking with nerves. I only hoped he couldn't tell.

"So, what did you have in mind tonight?" I asked as he pulled out of the driveway.

"If I told you, I'd have to kill you," he retorted, his voice thick with sarcasm.

I leaned back in the passenger seat, taking a look at his profile.

His pronounced jawline, his sleek, shiny hair.

The fine hair he'd trimmed along said perfect jawline. His skin down over his throat looked so smooth, and I felt an innate desire to run my fingertips along the freshly shaved surface.

God, he was so fucking hot.

Yup, totally out of my league here.

"I think I already died, so what's the difference," I mewled, trying to quiet my twitching cock.

A startling thought coursed through me as I adjusted myself.

What if...

What if Mitchell, like, expects certain things...

I wasn't the type to fuck around on a first date in general; usually, I waited until I at least had some inkling the other person wasn't going to run off immediately.

But just the *thought* of touching someone else's dick made me feel rather conflicted.

The thought of touching *Mitchell's* dick, however...

My cock twitched once again, and I felt a stray sweat break out.

Think unsexy thoughts!

"You okay, Cream Puff?" Mitchell asked, pulling me from my momentary lapse of sanity.

I crossed my legs, squeezing my cock between my thighs to try and break the spell of desire that had managed to infiltrate my walls.

"Yeah, totally fine. Everything's fine."

Mitchell took a quick side-glance at me.

"You don't have to be nervous, you know. This doesn't *have* to be a date. It can be whatever you want it to be."

I looked at him, thinking about Archie's words.

I swallowed harshly as I nodded.

"I agreed to a date. It's a... date."

Mitchell smiled. "Fair enough."

The rest of the way to our location—which happened to be an outdoor food festival in the city—wasn't as awkward. Then again, when you're listening to the radio and singing carpool karaoke, I suppose it lets off some steam.

I pulled my knees to my chest, wrapping my arms around them as Mitchell disposed of our food.

The park was packed with food trucks lining the streets, but there was ample greenery to sit on and watch the fireworks show Mitchell had mentioned was tonight.

To be honest, I was having a good time.

Sharing food, kicking back with a beer, and listening to the bands who were playing was more fun than I thought it would be, and a rather nice surprise.

I'd just set my beer down when Mitchell returned.

The sun had gone down, the sky painted shades of orange sherbet and cotton candy pink with hints of pale blue, and set against its backdrop, Mitchell looked absolutely beautiful.

He was handsome, sure, but his features were dark and stunning.

And I realized at that moment, I didn't just *like* Mitchell DeVille.

I realized I was falling in love with him.

"You ready for some fireworks?" he asked, raising his brow.

I nodded, at a loss for words as the reality hit me. "Uh huh."

His eyebrows furrowed, his arm brushing against mine.

I gazed into his dark eyes and felt like I was treading water in a vast, dark sea.

But I had a feeling that Mitchell would not let me drown.

His gaze dipped to where our arms touched, and I could see he was holding back.

"Are you nervous?" I asked.

Mitchell shrugged. "I told you, you're the

one running the show this evening," he said softly.

I chewed my bottom lip.

"I don't want you to hold back because of me," I said, feeling slightly upset that he would even think to do such a thing.

Mitchell's gaze flashed to mine. "I just don't want you to feel like I'm pushing you."

"Because you like me?" It wasn't a question as much as a statement, but when I said the words, I could see the way his entire body relaxed.

"Yeah, Cream Puff. I like you. A lot, actually."

I turned toward him, angling my body closer. I could feel the warmth between us, a cozy fire of our own making.

Archie's words reverberated in my brain. The question I'd been afraid to answer before, wasn't as scary now when I looked at Mitchell.

Instinctively, I reached out, letting my fingertips feel the silkiness of his throat and the freshly shaved skin there. I'd been dying to touch it all evening. The smoothness beneath my fingers was warm and it felt... right.

He felt right.

"I like you, too. A lot," I said, my voice barely a whisper.

I watched as Mitchell closed his eyes,

rubbing his cheek against my palm, some of his coarse facial hair scratching my skin.

It wasn't an unpleasant feeling at all, and I found myself wanting to run my fingers over the rough texture lining his jaw.

Wanting to run my fingertips over his lips, into his hair...

I didn't think twice about pulling him to me, about kissing him.

Mitchell groaned in my mouth as my lips moved slowly against his, and I let go just as the first *boom* hit the sky, echoing above us.

When I broke away, I could see the sun had disappeared, dusk taking over and changing the world into something different, something new.

And when I looked in Mitchell's dark eyes, I could see the sparkle like a northern star as the fireworks crackled behind him.

He slid his hand over my neck, his fingers playing with the edges of my hair at the nape of my neck as he pulled me in for another searing kiss.

This...

This is what love is supposed to feel like.

And as we made out underneath the fireworks, I came alive for the very first time.

CHAPTER 19

Mitch

I parked the car in the parking lot, glancing over at Penn as I contemplated just taking him home. It would have been the gentlemanly thing to do, since I already felt like I was pushing the envelope with him.

But truth was, I liked being around the guy and his golden aura. His sweet disposition, his blushing cheeks. He was fun to mess with, and fun to instigate, and...

He was a really good kisser.

A part of me couldn't believe he'd agreed to a date in the first place—after all, I knew better than anyone as far as *we* were concerned, this whole *thing* was new for him.

I'd dated my share of men in Jasper Springs, so I understood wholeheartedly the caution of jumping into a relationship with some boy next door like Penn.

But I didn't want to let him go.

Ever.

"Are you okay?" he asked, pulling me from my thoughts.

"What?"

"I mean, we've been parked for five minutes and you, like, zoned out," he said, his eyebrows furrowing together with concern.

"Right, sorry," I said as I looked at him. "You don't *have* to come in, if you don't want to. I can take you home, if you want."

Penn's lips pressed a thin line as he shook his head.

"No, I... want to. Come in. With... you."

"Okay," I said, not wanting to give him a chance to change his mind.

I opened my door and quickly made my way to open his, my heart in my throat. I knew whatever happened, it could still go south. There was a big difference between making out in the park and making out on my couch.

There was the possibility that he'd get scared and run off, and I'd ruin everything.

"I just want you to know that you're still in charge. We don't have to do anything you don't want to do. We can just watch a movie or something."

I needed him to understand I wasn't pressuring him into anything, and his comfort was my top priority.

Penn nodded as he looked up at me. "I know."

His soft smile tugged at my heart, making it thud so loudly I could hear it in my own ears.

"I just like spending time with you," he admitted.

I nodded, sliding my hand into his. There was no hesitation when he squeezed mine back.

"I think a movie sounds nice."

"All right then," I said as I pulled him down the hall toward my apartment on the bottom floor.

As I stood in front of my door, sucking in a few breaths, I realized just how nervous *I* was.

I opened the door and waved him in, turning on the lights. Once he was in, I closed the door quietly.

"Wow, It's..."

I'd never felt so on the spot before, showing a man my apartment.

Technically, most men didn't make it to see anything past my couch or my bed, so this was new territory for me, too.

"A disaster?" I said, running my hand

through my hair as I headed toward the couch, turning on television and queuing up Netflix.

"I was going to say it's pretty chill, actually," he said as he walked around my kitchen, looking like a deer lost in the headlights.

My heart thumped away as I watched him, committing his image in my kitchen to memory.

He looked perfect, standing there, in the light.

I slowly slid my phone out of my pocket and snapped a picture.

"What was that?" he said, startling.

"Nothing, what, uh, what's on your mind? Rom-com, drama? Cartoons?"

Penn chortled at my cartoon comment, and I couldn't help but smile. He was so easy to tease, and I loved it.

My heart echoed as reality hit me like a punch to the gut.

I was falling in love with Penn Baker.

I knew it at that moment as he casually strolled toward me, the golden light of my kitchen lighting him up from behind like an angelic halo.

"Mmm... have you seen Home Again? With Reese Witherspoon?"

I shook my head, dispelling the weird sort of aura that had blanketed me, making me lose my damn mind.

"No, can't say that I have," I said as I sat down, letting the cushions break my fall.

Penn gingerly sat next to me, leaving a modicum of space between us.

I started up the movie.

"Oh, it's a hoot. Reese is a total gem. I used to love Legally Blonde growing up. It was one of my mom's favorites."

I shifted my weight, trying not to appear too desperate, when the truth was all I wanted was to wrap my arm around him, and...

Penn slid across the sliver of space, putting his body flush against mine. I looked down at him, at his perfect, kissable lips, then back to his pretty blue eyes.

"Penn..."

He settled into the open space of my arm, which was stretched along the back of my couch. He shifted his weight, making my body dip toward him, and I was acutely aware of my burgeoning stiffness coming to life.

He leaned in closer, resting his head on my arm as he looked at me with glassy, blue eyes.

"Yeah?" he asked, his eyebrows knitting together with worry.

"Do you have any idea how badly I want to kiss you right now?"

Penn's cheeks flushed and his eyes sparkled with mischief.

"Maybe."

So he wants to play.

I can play.

"I don't think you do."

"Well, what are you waiting for?" he asked, his gaze dipping to my lips.

I hooked my knuckle under his chin, forcing him to look at me. I needed him to hear my words, really hear them.

His body relaxed under my touch, and my cock twitched with anticipation.

"I want... I *need* to hear you say it," I said, my voice coming out dark and husky. "I need to know what *you* want." I licked my lips. "I need your permission."

"I want..." I watched his pupils dilate, his lips part. Involuntarily, he leaned into me, threading his leg through mine, his hand resting on my knee. He swallowed nervously, but he didn't break my gaze. "I want you to kiss me."

"Is that so?" I asked, hanging on his every word.

He nodded.

So, I kissed him. Softly, my lips caressed his as I let my tongue slip in through the cracks, and he slid his hand around my waist. I could feel the tremble in his touch, but I could also feel the curiosity as he slowly traced his fingers along my hip.

I sucked at his bottom lip as he let out a groan, grabbing me, pulling me closer. I settled my hand on his hip and he leaned into me like a falling star.

His body pressed against mine was indescribable. My cock twitched as I recognized the similar feeling of his hardness against mine, and I knew I needed to slow down.

But I didn't *want* to slow down. I wanted to make Penn feel as wild and untamed as he made me feel.

I broke apart from him, gazing down at his perfect mouth, lips still swollen from my kiss.

"Is that what you want, Cream Puff?" I asked, tracing my thumb over his bottom lip. "You want to play Netflix & Chill?" I teased.

Penn grinned. "I... I don't know. I just know I want..." His eyebrows furrowed again, as his cheeks flushed.

"Use your words, Penn. I told you, you can be honest with me."

"I just know that I've never felt this... hard from just *kissing* someone."

Well, if that wasn't a boost for my ego, I didn't know what was.

I couldn't help the smile on my face.

His hand on my hip slid down a fraction from our shifted weight, right over my solid erection.

Fuck.

Penn's eyes widened as he yanked his hand back, like he'd just touched hot iron.

But he didn't move away from me. Instead, his glassy eyes held mine as he let out a shaky breath.

"We can stick to kissing, if you want," I said as I adjusted myself.

Which was when I noticed his legs were pressed together rather tightly, and his face was pink with...

Embarrassment.

Of course, this was all a new sensation for him, and he was probably confused as all hell.

Real smooth, Mitch.

I gently pulled his hand out of his lap, giving it a reassuring squeeze.

"We don't have to—"

"No. I *want* to, I just..."

"Are you sure?" I asked, worried I'd somehow thrown a grenade into an otherwise perfect evening.

Penn nodded. "Usually this is like... third or fourth date material for me. And even then, it's not... I don't feel like... *this.*"

It was my turn to be confused.

"Like what?"

Penn sighed, his cheeks going red. "Like I'm

going to fucking explode in my pants like a damn teenager."

I let out a laugh, because it was funny, but also because as funny as it was, it was also maddening.

"Well, we can't have that," I teased, letting go of his hand.

Penn settled against me once more, curling into me like I was a teddy bear. He reached up, his fingertips trailing over my jaw as he bit his lip.

"And usually there's a discussion about, you know... former partners and all first..."

I watched as he chewed his lip, waiting for my response.

"I can assure you as far as former partners go, I'm clean, Penn. If that's what you're worried about."

His eyes widened as he let out a breath.

"I mean, that's good. Uh... I've only ever been with, like, three people, and uh, I'm good. Nothing to worry about," he said awkwardly.

I brought my lips to his, trying to reassure him this was okay.

Talking about things was normal. Communication was key when it came to relationships, new or old.

He relaxed in my hold, breaking my kiss for only a moment as he let out a breath.

"Good to know," I breathed against his lips.

"Just... go slow, okay?" he said shakily.

I nodded, grasping his hand in mine. "Always," I promised, and he kissed me once more.

I let him lead this time.

Penn's mouth against mine was a torturous sort of desire. He pulled me closer, his hand sliding through my hair and soon, he was beneath me, his breath labored as his kiss transformed into something much more passionate, much more heated than before.

I straddled his hips with my legs, bringing my swollen cock flush against his abdomen. I could feel his erection below me, twitching with interest. I breathed deep as I broke our kiss.

Penn's hands slid over my hip to my front, and he grazed his fingertips over my jean-clad erection.

It was a curious, light touch, and I fought the instinct to grind myself against his palm. I settled against him, my hands on his hips, holding on for dear life.

"Do you like this?" he asked, his voice curious as he looked up at me.

I nodded, kissing him once more. "Yes, Penn. I like making out with you. I like it when you touch me," I said the words plainly, with as much levity as I could.

He needed to know this was okay. That I liked this as much as he did.

That I liked *him*.

Penn swallowed as he held my gaze, *squeezing* my sensitive cock in his hand.

"Fuck," I cursed, trying to hold back.

"Yeah?" he breathed, his breath hot on my skin.

"Fuck, yes," I said, my breath shaky as excitement laced through me.

Penn kissed me once more, letting his thumb rub over the fabric of my jeans where I could feel moisture already pebbling at my slit.

I groaned in defeat as he *thrust* himself against me, whimpering in my mouth with unrelenting truth.

Heat ransacked my body from his explorative touch.

"Tell me what you want, Cream Puff. Tell me and I'll give you *anything* you want." I could hear the desperation in my voice. I'd never begged *anyone* like this before.

The multitude of that was not lost on me, but I felt like I would truly expire if he stopped touching me.

Penn pulled away, letting out a deep breath as he spoke his desires. "I want to see it," he said, his voice dark and full of curiosity.

A smile curved on my lips. "Are you sure?" I

asked, grinding myself against his hardness, making my already weeping cock sob all the more.

Penn looked me dead in the eyes, and said, "Yes, I'm sure."

I leaned back on the couch, unfastening my belt and shaking my jeans to the ground along with my boxers. My cock sprang free, precum bathing my tip and glinting in the light. I wrapped my hand around my cock, watching as his gaze dipped to my engorged dick.

Penn sucked in a breath, grabbing himself as he let out his own curse.

"Fucking cherries on top," he murmured.

"What?" I asked, feeling like maybe I'd gone too far. Maybe this was a terrible idea.

"Archie was so right."

Before I could ask what he meant, Penn *rubbed* himself through his pants, and all senses left me.

Because the sight of him *touching* himself because of me was like a balm to my soul, like a match to my flame.

I stroked myself, noting the way his breath hitched as I did so.

The way his pupils dilated, and his cheeks flushed.

The enormous tent in *his* pants.

I slid my thumb through my precum,

coating my pink, swollen head, and Penn groaned in defeat. His gaze practically glued to my cock.

"Like what you see?" I asked, feeling a grin spread on my face.

Penn nodded slowly. "Better than the porn I watched, that's for sure."

I laughed, leaning back as I cocked my head to the side, giving a good thrust into my palm.

Penn cursed under his breath, but he didn't break his gaze.

"Is that what you want, Cream Puff? You want to watch?"

I wanted to go slow because I wanted him to feel comfortable, but I'd be lying if I said I didn't want to explore every inch of Penn's body just to see how he'd react.

Penn's gaze flashed to mine.

"No... I mean, yes. I mean... Fuck, why is this so difficult," he huffed. "Yes. I want to watch you."

I thrust against my palm again, sliding my hand against my shaft.

"But what about you?" he asked, his eyes widening.

"What about me?" I asked, building a slow rhythm as I stroked and pulled my hardness.

"What do you want?"

I grinned wholeheartedly.

"I want whatever you are comfortable with, Penn. I told you, you're running the show."

I half-expected him to just sit there and to continue rubbing himself through his pants, and that would have been just fine for me.

Knowing I turned him on, just with my kiss, seeing his growth as he watched *me* would have been enough to get me off right there.

"Do you like what *you* see?" he asked, his voice taking on a more seductive tone. The curiousness behind it told me he'd likely never tried it before, which gave me another ego boost.

Because he sounded so damn sexy, it was a crime.

Somewhere in the background, the movie droned out and the music played, but it was white noise.

"God, yes, Penn. Can't you see what you do to me? You are killing me," I said as I watched him slide his hand over his giant, jean-clad erection, rubbing himself. "You're the prettiest thing I've ever seen."

Penn slowly slid his hand up and over his covered cock, his head hitting the back of my couch as his eyes closed.

"Fuck," he said, his voice all screwed up. "I don't know if I can do this."

"You're doing such a good job, baby," I said reassuringly, watching as he squeezed his cock, the sound of another whimpering cry escaping his throat.

"Look how well you handle your cock. I bet you'd handle mine just as nice," I purred, stroking myself.

The heat, the tension, my own dark and desperate voice mixing with Penn's soft cries was like a firework all on its own.

"Mitch..." he whimpered, his voice all screwed up.

Hearing my name uttered from his lips like that was enough.

I couldn't hold back any longer, my balls tightening and my cock pulsing as the words left me.

"Fuck, I'm coming," my voice strained as I hurried to shift my shirt, giving myself enough of a space to unload on my abs, but I sorely missed, and rope after rope of my cum clung to the satin like Velcro.

I pulled at my buttons, shifting out of my shirt and crumpling it up. Using it to wipe up the last remains of my release, it wasn't until Penn let out a strangled sound that I remembered exactly who I was with, and what had transpired.

I tossed my shirt to the floor, pulling up my jeans as I set my sight on Penn, who looked to be in pain.

I rushed over to him, noting his hand was still squeezing his cock tightly through his pants.

He breathed deeply. His gaze fixed on the ceiling.

"Are you okay?" I asked, concern flooding me.

"I'm so hard it hurts," he muttered.

"Tell me what you need, Penn." I swallowed nervously.

"There's nothing to be embarrassed about here. If you want some privacy or—"

He lifted his head from the couch, his glassy blue eyes full of awe and excitement, and... fear.

"No," he shook his head, his gaze imploring mine.

I ran my hand across his collarbone, letting my fingers find the edges of his hair.

He licked his lips, his entire body relaxing under that one, small touch.

For Penn, this was it.

There was no going back after this.

"I want *you* to make me come."

CHAPTER 20

PENN

I WANT you to make me come.

The moment the words left my mouth, I felt lighter, but there was still the overwhelming desire that made it hard to breathe.

I'd never felt for anyone what I felt for Mitchell.

It was truly like I'd been going through the motions, doing what I was *supposed* to be doing, living blindly.

But kissing Mitchell, touching him, feeling his warmth, hearing his *praise*, I knew everything, and everyone before him had been a *lie*.

I'd been living a lie.

In the span of only a few hours, I'd gone on a date, made out with, and watched my hot date blow his load from *watching me.*

If there was any question or any sliver of a chance that I was straight, it had been blown to smithereens now.

Because no one had ever kissed me, flirted with me, or touched me like Mitchell.

No one ever felt this right.

A thousand things came to mind when he asked me what I wanted. I wasn't sure about anything. None of my ex-girlfriends ever really asked what I wanted, and the one night stands didn't really focus on my needs.

I wasn't the type to keep asking either. If my partner didn't want to suck my dick, I wasn't going to push her about it.

My mind was a blur as I tried to process for the first time what it was I wanted, and the decision was as overwhelming as the reality of my throbbing cock pulsing in my hands, the wetness forming at my head, spreading against my boxers.

I just knew I needed to come before I went blind with ecstasy.

"Permission to touch?" Mitch's voice asked, bringing me back down to earth, down to reality.

"Fuck, yes! Please, just make it—"

The *need* to feel his warm palms heating me through my shirt, to feel his fingertips graze over my sensitive skin, was something I'd never experienced with anyone before.

But I wanted more of it. I wanted more of *him.*

The warmth of his hand around mine was like water after a drought.

His hand brushed over my sensitive, strained cock, before gently, swiftly sliding up to unbutton my pants.

Somewhere in my brain, I knew this was it.

Once I let him touch my cock, I knew it would be over.

There was no going back from that.

Almost as if he could sense my turmoil, he spoke.

"If you want me to stop, just say stop, okay?" he breathed, his voice shaking as his hand hovered over my zipper, warming my cock where he had stopped.

My cock *ached* beneath the heat from his palm, separated by metal and denim.

I couldn't help but submit to the desire to thrust myself against his touch, seeking the friction.

Seeking release

"I don't want you to stop," I breathed, knowing this was my death.

But it was also a sort of rebirth, too.

Because I knew at that moment, I was *his*.

I was completely and utterly at his mercy.

Mitchell held all that I was in the palm of his hand.

I breathed a sigh of relief as he slowly unzipped my pants. Lifting my hips to help him, I let go of the remaining threads of my old self, letting my jeans fall to the ground.

Mitchell gently tugged at the waistband of my underwear, sliding them down just enough to expose me. The minute my cock was free, it was a relief. No more pain as I strained against constricting fabric.

"Fuck," Mitchell cursed, but it wasn't dark and seductive like before.

It was awe-struck.

It was *lovely*.

"You are fucking beautiful," he murmured, the edge of his fingertips brushing against my balls, sliding slowly, achingly slow, against my shaft.

I whimpered in defeat as he closed his hand around my cock.

Mitchell settled next to me, sliding his arm behind me, shifting my body on its side, bringing me closer. I stared at him, shirtless, his dark eyes full of something softer than the lust I felt was consuming me.

His dark hair fell in his eyes, his lips still swollen from kissing me, and he was the sexiest thing I'd ever seen.

And he was slowly, torturously rubbing my cock, and it felt... good.

Better than good, actually.

He kissed me slowly, distracting me from my euphoria for the moment as he slid his tongue in my mouth, and instinctively, I bucked my hips against his hand.

His palm was warm. But his mouth was warmer, and at that moment, I knew exactly what I wanted, and for the first time, I didn't feel awkward, at all. I felt invigorated.

"Mitch," I tried to speak, my linguistics all off-kilter. All I could do was breathe, all my attention pulled to the sensation of his touch as he stroked me, coaxing me closer and closer to the edge as his fingers spread my precum over my shaft like it was freaking lube.

God that feels amazing.

"Yes, baby?" he purred into my mouth, his voice dark, sexy, and absolutely perfect.

He just called me baby.

I think I really might die.

"What does my Cream Puff want, hmm?"

" Please... " I cried. I was so close. I needed to feel his mouth, his tongue on me.

"I like you like this. All needy, and responsive."

A tortured groan escaped me as I thrust myself in his hands, using my own to slide my fingers into his messy, dark hair, to run my fingertips over his rough facial hair, down through the coarse hair on his chest. I let my fingers slide through it, gripping it and committing the touch to memory.

I *liked* how it felt beneath my fingertips.

"Mitch..." I moaned as his mouth accosted mine again. In that kiss, I knew I could do anything.

Mitchell had given me so much already, and I knew all I had to do was ask.

And for the first time in my life, I didn't feel *guilty* about asking for what I wanted. This was it, the final straw, and knowing that made me feel braver, actually.

So, I didn't think twice about what I said next.

"I want you to suck my cock," I breathed, my entire body heating like a flame.

At the reality I'd actually spoken my desires out loud, I added a well placed, "Please."

I didn't want to sound demanding, after all.

Mitchell took my lips again, nipping at my

bottom lip as he spread my precum along my already sticky shaft as he slowly pumped me.

"Are you sure, baby?" he murmured, positioning me back on the couch so I was partially laying down, moving his body between my legs.

His fingertips slid up my exposed thighs as my underwear moved down to my knees. I shifted my body, and he gently pulled them down my calves, past my ankles, until they were discarded on the floor, leaving me fully naked from the waist down. I looked down at his face between my thighs, his dark eyes, and hair falling across his temple.

He was stunning, and he was kneeling before me, ready to take whatever I was willing to give.

And something about that realization gave me the courage to reach down, thread my fingers through his hair and push him toward my cock.

Mitchell didn't miss a beat.

He wrapped his lips around my swollen head, and the relief was instant.

His warm mouth felt so fucking good.

He rolled his tongue around my shaft, grazing over my engorged veins, over my slit, and I couldn't help the groan that escaped me.

I watched as he hollowed his cheeks, groaning with his own ecstasy as he built his rhythm. I let out a guttural moan as my hips rocked of their own accord. I gripped his hair with my fingers and I rode his face, shoving my cock down his throat without a second thought. His tongue lapped at my shaft as deep moans escaped him, throwing me over the edge.

It didn't take long at all. Three licks, and he'd found the center of my proverbial tootsie roll pop as I moaned in ecstatic defeat, coming down his throat with a force I'd never felt.

Somewhere in the back of my mind I worried he might not be able to breathe—after all, most of my experience with women had taught me they could only take so much before they literally choked—but such was not the case with Mitchell, who swallowed every drop like my release was nothing more than his favorite drink.

I don't know how long I stayed there, in absolute bliss, but eventually I came back down to earth when I felt Mitchell shift me once more.

"Feel better?" Mitchell asked, his voice tinged with sarcasm.

I curled my half-naked self against him, throwing my arm across his hip as I *cuddled* him.

He was soft and warm, and safe.

And he made everything feel undeniably *perfect.*

"Mhmmm," I said dreamily.

Perhaps I still was dreaming. I closed my

eyes, taking in a deep breath. His facial hair scratched my forehead as his lips pressed a soft kiss to my skin.

"Good. Now get dressed so I can get you home before midnight. I know you need the rest."

"I don't want to go home," I murmured sleepily.

There was a moment of silence, but it wasn't awkward or strange.

It felt comfortable. Because I knew he was there.

"I don't want you to go home either," he whispered. And for the moment that was enough.

The room was silent and I zoned out to the ramblings of the movie and Mitchell's steady heartbeat.

Mine beat in unison with his, and I knew I was a goner.

I was one hundred percent gay for Mitchell DeVille, and I was absolutely head over heels in love with him.

Patient, sarcastic, and sexy as all hell.

I wanted *him*.

"When's your next event?" he asked, pulling me from my swoon-worthy thoughts.

"What?"

"Your next event. So I can photograph it?"

Oh, yeah. That.

I'd almost forgotten Mitchell was technically working for me for the moment.

"Tomorrow night," I yawned. "Engagement party, five o'clock."

"I'll be there."

CHAPTER 21

PENN

I WALKED into the shop and it felt like the sun was shining *everywhere*, despite it being dark and gloomy out. But even as happy as I felt, there was still the nagging bit of my psyche that was still coming to terms with just how far Mitchell and I had gone on our date.

Usually, I preferred to keep things PG until the third or fourth date, partially out of respect, but also because, prior to Mitchell, it took a while for me to build up the desire to *want* to be intimate with my partners.

Which probably should have been my first clue.

And there I was, on my first date with a

dude, with my dick down his throat by the end of the night.

Did that make me a slut?

Archie came in at that exact moment as my existential crisis hit.

"I'm doing a half day today, leaving around ten."

"What?" I said, blinking, trying to dispel my thoughts.

"I told you yesterday, it's my cousin's birthday."

"Right," I said, trying to remember.

Archie came over to me, approaching me like a wary animal.

"Yikes? Was it that bad?" he asked, his eyebrows furrowing with concern, his words pulling me from my thoughts.

"What?"

"You're grimacing. Either it's a cake disaster or your date tanked."

"My date... Yeah, uh, about that..."

Archie grabbed an apron, tying it around his waist as I ran my hands over my face.

"What happened?"

"Things, uh, might've gotten a little hot and heavy last night." I chewed my lips, avoiding his gaze.

Archie yelped with excitement. "Yes! That's awesome! It is awesome, right? Or did it suck?"

His choice of words made my cheeks flush with heat, and before I could say anything, he slapped me on the back.

"They grow up so fast," he said approvingly.

"No, it didn't suck. It was probably the best blowjob I've ever had, to be honest."

Archie smirked. "Of course it was. So what's the problem then? Why the long face?"

I let out a deep breath as I grabbed the rag and cleaner to polish up the counter.

"I mean, I've never done anything like that on a first date before," I admitted.

Archie picked up what I was throwing down.

"Ahh, I see. So you think he's going to think you're easy, is that it?"

I bit my lip, my jaw tensing. "I mean, I don't want him to think that's all I'm about, or what I'm after, you know?"

Archie sighed. "Did you feel pressured?"

"No," I said, turning around, shaking my head. "Not at all."

"Who made the move?" Archie asked. My cheeks heated once more.

"What do you mean?"

"Did he offer? Or did you ask?"

My cock twitched at the memory of the words leaving my mouth, of the memory of his warm tongue wrapped around my aching cock.

"I asked," I whispered, even though at this hour there was no one here but us.

Mitchell was meeting me after work for the event, and my parents were only doing the orders today, so they'd be in and out by noon. Which meant, for the majority of the day, I'd be here by myself, prepping cupcakes for tonight's event.

"And you asked because *you wanted it*, right? Not because you thought you had to?" Archie pressed.

"Well, yeah, I mean, it just felt right at the time, I guess."

Archie smiled softly. "If it feels right, it's right, Penn. No matter who it is, or when it happens."

Something about his words settled something inside of me, and I sighed.

"I guess that makes sense."

Archie nodded. "Don't over think everything. You'll drive yourself crazy. Just do what feels right. Listen to your heart and shit."

I shook my head, a light laugh escaping me. "Is that what you do? Listen to your heart?" I teased.

Archie smirked. "I listen to my dick, but one day when my heart speaks up, I'll know."

"How do you know I'm not listening to my dick?" I taunted him.

"Oh, I know you're listening to your dick," he drawled, both of us laughing. "But I also know that you're not the type to casually get intimate either. Your heart pumps blood to your brain and your dick. They all work together you know."

"I know. I was the one who actually passed Biology, remember?" I said as I went about my cleaning.

"All I'm saying, is you don't do anything half-assed. Give yourself a little more credit, Penn. Trust yourself."

I nodded in understanding. Archie was right. I did need to give myself more credit. I knew my worth, and I had a feeling Mitchell knew it, too.

CHAPTER 22

MITCH

I KNEW we didn't have to be at the event until four thirty, but I couldn't stop thinking about Penn, and what had happened between us.

It seemed wild to me that I'd barely known the guy a little more than a week, and somehow, some way, I'd become a total simp for the man.

I wasn't usually the type to get attached so quickly, and while I loved where things were going with us, I was also scared of how quickly Penn had stolen my heart.

Because the truth of the matter was, I loved the guy.

I loved the sparkle in his pretty blue eyes, the

way he blushed, the way he *teased* me, the kind-ness of his heart, the gentleness of his soul.

And I really, really loved kissing him.

I loved the way he brought out a side of me that no one else had ever been able to access.

Which is probably why I'd convinced myself to show up early to the shop.

Penn looked up from behind the counter as the door jingled.

"Hey," he said, surprised.

"Afternoon," I said, sauntering in with just my camera bag. Today, I wanted to shoot Penn in his element freehand, capture a more candid feel for this set of images.

And after combing over wedding photos all morning, I couldn't deny Penn in his little white, cake-stained apron, blond hair shimmering in the light, was like a breath of fresh air.

My own personal Cream Puff.

"I thought we were meeting up at the event," he said, and he turned to the back counter, which I could see was covered in cupcake trays, not all of them full.

With his back turned to me, I quietly brought out my camera, zooming in on the lineup.

"I thought I'd come in and get some solo shots of you," I said, clicking away.

Penn headed to the bowl of batter on the

steel table in the corner, grabbing a large bowl and scoop.

Click.

"Where's Archie at?"

Penn shrugged, letting out a sigh as I went behind the counter, tucking myself into a corner as I watched him.

"Uh, he had a thing, I guess. Took a half day."

I framed the trays as I watched him scoop some batter into the first tray.

"And your parents?"

Penn chortled. "They've got a more active social life now that I'm home, working. They left this afternoon to go stay with some friends for the weekend in the city."

"So, it's just you running the ship today? And you have an event?"

Penn sighed once more. "Yeah, I guess it looks that way."

"You've been working every day this week. Don't you get a day off?"

Penn shrugged. "I mean, I've been gone for months, so I'm making up for lost time, I guess."

"Still, you're human. Humans need rest."

Penn hurriedly set his bowl down, turning around and looking for something, a confused look on his face.

I set my camera down. "Looking for something?"

"Uh, yeah, the cupcake liners. They're...."

I noticed them out of the corner of my eye, behind my camera. I picked them up, heading over to Penn, who reached for them. I pulled them out of his reach.

"Mitch, come on..."

"You scoop, I'll line."

Penn pursed his lips. "You don't have to—"

"Maybe I want to."

I watched as his eyebrows furrowed, and his shoulders relaxed.

"I'm not used to help. I mean, Archie has his own duties, and my parents, well, when they're here everything is pretty much done already, and I—"

I hip-checked him, nudging him toward his bowl as I started to peel the liners out of the stack, placing them in each muffin cup in their prospective trays.

"You've already helped me so much, it feels like I'm taking advantage. I wish there was something I could do to show my thanks," he said softly, taking the hint and grabbing his bowl of batter, following behind my lining.

I chuckled darkly. "I could definitely think of a few ways you could show your gratitude," I teased.

Like I expected, Penn's cheeks blushed with that perfect pink tint.

"Mitch!" he squealed, but it wasn't angry or worried. It was tinged with laughter, and only a hint of embarrassment.

"What? I told you when we first met, I like sugar. And cream."

Penn shook his head as he moved down the line to fill more of the lined cups as I added, "And you *did* promise me sweet, sugary goodness."

I turned toward him as I reached the end of the line. Penn grasped the bowl tightly as he glanced up at me, rosy cheeks and glassy eyes making my damn cock twitch and my heart beat faster.

"Would dinner suffice?" he asked, raising an eyebrow.

His bowl of batter was practically empty, and I couldn't help myself. I ran my finger along the inside of the rim, collected a small amount of the creamy goodness on the tip, and took a lick of the batter.

Penn licked his lips, tightening his grip on the bowl.

"You know there is raw egg in that?" he warned.

I licked the batter off my finger with a moan of delight.

Vanilla cream.

Fucking delicious.

"Yeah, and it's delicious."

"Help me put these in the ovens," he said, averting his gaze as he picked up the first tray with one hand, popping open the top and bottom oven doors.

I gladly grabbed two trays and followed suit, loading them in.

Penn grabbed the last tray and put it on the bottom rack, closing the doors.

"To answer your question, where did you have in mind? For dinner, I mean."

Penn cleaned up his dishes, setting out new things. A piping bag, a bucket of frosting.

I glanced at the label, to see the frosting was also vanilla.

I picked up my camera once more, watching as he separated the vanilla frosting into two separate bowls, coloring the one with red food coloring.

Snap! Click!

"I was thinking maybe since, uh, my parents are out of town, you could, you know, come over to my place and I could *make* dinner? Unless of course, you'd rather go somewhere, or—"

My heart skipped a beat as I realized he was asking me over to his place.

On his terms.

And he wanted to make me dinner.

The excitement coursing through me was unimaginable.

I never said yes so fast in all my life.

Granted, I knew I still had lots of work to do on both his images and the wedding, but there was nothing I wanted to do more than spend time with Penn Baker.

"I'd like that," I said as the oven timer went off.

Penn tossed me some oven mitts, hitting me square in the chest.

"So bossy," I said as I set my camera down, dressing my hands with the bright blue oven mitts.

Within seconds, Penn had the first two trays, and I had the rest, setting them down on the steel table in the center of the kitchen.

They smelled heavenly.

Once set, Penn pulled his mitts off and I did the same, following him as he loaded up his icing into piping bags.

"You said you wanted to help..."

I smiled at his *whine*. I swore there wasn't anything I wouldn't do for my little Cream Puff, if he asked so nicely.

Hell, who was I kidding?

I'd do anything for him if he looked at me

with those pretty blue eyes and those perfect, kissable lips.

Penn tied off the end, and handed one to me.

"I'll do these two, you do those two, okay?" he said, nodding to the trays in front of me.

"Yes, boss," I teased him, watching the smile form on his face from my words.

I watched Penn out of the corner of my eye, his focus on his cupcakes stern.

Unbreakable almost, which gave me an idea.

"Hey, Penn," I called his attention and he looked up, and I squeezed a dab of icing right on his cute little nose.

"Gotcha," I said with a grin.

Penn huffed as he swiped the frosting off his face. "Asshole," he teased, but his voice was full and light.

"You just looked so serious," I said, heading back to my cupcakes.

"I was concentrating," he defended.

"Uh huh," I said as I focused back on my last tray.

"Hey, Mitch..." he called, nonchalantly.

"Yeah?" I looked up, and was met with a *smattering* of icing across my face as his fingertips slid across my cheek.

"You little..." I cursed as Penn jumped back, holding up his bag of frosting like a sword.

"Not so funny when you're the target, is it?" he teased.

I grabbed my own bag in defense. "I'm going to get you for that."

Penn's smile was infectious, his pristine blue eyes sparkling like diamonds in the afternoon light.

"I'd like to see you try," he said, giggling as he took off, and I chased after him.

We ran through the bakery, spraying pink and white vanilla frosting at one another in retaliation, and the sounds of our combined laughter filled the air.

Penn hurriedly flipped the sign from open to closed, all while dodging me as I tried to catch him like a wild gingerbread man.

When I finally did catch him, it was just as he was coming around the front counter, and I grabbed him by his apron ties, pulling him backward and into my arms.

We were both covered in frosting, panting from our chase. The light from the windows behind him lit him up, showcasing the stark white cream all over his cheeks, his neck.

His lips.

I didn't think twice about pressing him against the wall and licking the sweet cream off of his gorgeous face. As I did so, I could feel his cock hard against my own, and he wrapped his arms around me, the tip of his piping bag poking me in the back as he held it.

I licked the frosting from his lips, biting gently at his bottom one.

The throaty moan that left his throat went straight to my cock.

Penn kissed me back, melting into me once more, before he squeezed himself out from under me, heading back to the last tray of cupcakes.

I didn't miss the smile on his face as he finished decorating, or the words that were caught in my throat.

Those three little words I'd almost said out loud.

"We've got less than an hour to finish these and get to the party," he said, pulling my attention once more.

"Right," I said, shaking my head.

CHAPTER 23

PENN

I COULDN'T EXPLAIN IT, but it was like ever since the night before, when we'd gone on our date, when I let Mitchell touch me, when I asked him to suck my damn dick, it was like a switch had been flipped.

I couldn't stop thinking about him. About his talent, about his smirk, about his sexy voice. About how he was always giving *me* the reins to control where we were going.

Because deep underneath all the vibrant shirts and sarcasm, Mitchell *cared* about my needs, my comfort.

After my conversation with Archie, I thought

a lot about what he said. About things just feeling right.

About how I'd *asked* for Mitchell to bring me my release.

About how my fingers gripping his hair while he did so and how it was the purest ecstasy I'd ever felt.

And I guess you could say I was curious if I was capable of providing Mitchell with the same amount of pleasure he gave me.

I tossed my chicken in the pan, feeling Mitchell's gaze on my backside, and the instinct to blush took over once more.

Even though I couldn't see him, I could feel his appreciation, how he studied me.

Plus, I could hear the faint sound of a shutter clicking every few moments.

"You really didn't have to do this, you know," he said.

I gave the chicken another toss as the pasta continued to boil on the stove. I turned to look at him, sitting there at the counter and the nerves came rushing back.

Could I do this?

Was I absolutely, certifiably insane?

Most of my relationships, the serious ones anyway, didn't last long. I was with Amy for all of eight months, and that was my longest relationship.

I'd made dinner for her a few times, but it was still awkward after.

Sex with Amy wasn't *bad*, but it wasn't anywhere near the amount of rapture I experienced with Mitchell.

I looked at him sitting there in my kitchen, and my heart skipped a beat.

"The way to a man's heart is through his stomach," I said, flashing him with a nervous grin.

I had this grand idea that we'd have dinner, then maybe we could make dessert, together, and then...

My cheeks flushed with heat as the thought I'd been keeping at bay all day crept into my brain.

I swallowed harshly, turning away from Mitchell to avoid giving away my embarrassment at my wayward thoughts.

"Well, you had me hook line and sinker with those cream puffs. And the cinnamon rolls."

I turned off the burner for the pasta, drained it and moved about my kitchen with precision.

"I mean, those were part of the agreement. This..."

I realized within seconds Mitchell was behind me. Setting his hand just above my ass.

He leaned in closer, his lips close to my ear.

"Is not part of the agreement, I know," he murmured, his breath hot on my neck.

I quickly added the pasta to the oversized skillet with the chicken and cream sauce, then I turned to look at him. His dark hair fell in his eyes seductively, and all the nerves that had been making my stomach flip all day dissipated.

I was without a doubt, in love with Mitchell DeVille.

The world around me fell away when he looked at *me.*

When he touched me.

When he kissed me.

"No, it wasn't," I breathed, my gaze dipping to his lips. I didn't think twice about pressing my lips to his.

As far as I was concerned, I could kiss Mitchell forever and ever.

I could feel his grin at the corner of his mouth as he slipped his tongue between my parted lips.

My entire body eased from his touch and I let my hand rest on his hip for a brief moment.

A soft laugh erupted from my throat as I reluctantly pulled away from him, and fumbled for the knob to turn off the skillet.

Looking back at him over my shoulder as he pressed himself up behind me, I knew this was it for me.

I'd looked and looked for the right person, but I had been looking in the wrong places.

There was a reason my previous relationships hadn't been successful.

Because they were one-sided, and they weren't *him.*

I wasn't sure how to define myself just yet, but I knew without a doubt I was one hundred percent gay for Mitchell.

Probably only *Mitchell.*

I broke away, my entire body warm as a grin spread over my face.

"You are so distracting, you know that?" I teased.

Mitchell hummed lowly, the sound dark and inviting and going straight to my cock.

Which did not help matters as the fantasy I'd been brushing off all day came back full force.

"I like distracting you. You get all flustered, and it's fucking adorable," he purred, his voice gruff and filled with a seductive tone.

I rolled my eyes as I gingerly pushed against his chest. "Sit down, please. I need to plate *your* dinner."

Mitchell tugged my hips closer, putting me right against his rigid erection. "Penn..."

"Dinner first," I said kissing him chastely. "Then dessert."

Mitchell sighed, but relented, and I hated

the feeling when he removed his palm from my waist.

CHAPTER 24

"OH MY GOD, is there anything you don't do?" Mitchell groaned as he made his way through his second bowl of pasta.

I shrugged, twisting the noodles around my fork. "Well, there are a couple things..." I said nonchalantly.

I was still nervous because as the night drew on, we were getting closer and closer to my big plan.

Would I chicken out?

Would I get up close and personal with Mitchell's cock and run the other way?

Or would I be able to stomach it in my mouth?

What if I was *terrible* at sucking dick?

Worse?

What if I couldn't take it?

"I really appreciate your helping out with the campaign and all," I said, shifting the conversation to one that wasn't going to give me a heart attack.

I took a bite of my pasta, finishing my plate.

Mitchell got up and brought his dish to the sink, and I followed suit.

"I'm glad to do it, you know. It's definitely something different for me. Usually, I'm stuck photographing weddings and engagements, and corporate events. This is a nice change, something I can add to my portfolio," he said.

I nodded for him to follow me to the living room. Our house wasn't huge by any means, but before my mom had the shop, my dad had blown out the original wall separating the kitchen and living room and turned it into an open concept, which helped in those days because mom was always baking up a storm. A few card tables and TV trays in conjunction with the counters was basically her operating bakery.

"You don't like shooting weddings or engagements?" I asked as we took a seat on the couch. Mitchell settled in easily as I reached for the remote, fully intending to actually *watch* a movie while our food settled and then we could make dessert.

I'd planned for something simple; a peach crisp, topped with some vanilla bean ice cream.

But we wouldn't get that far.

"I don't dislike it, but..." Mitchell sighed, looking away from me. His voice softened. "A lot of the time I can just focus on the job, but sometimes... sometimes it just hits different, you know?"

I did know.

My heart sank as I watched his jaw tense, his body sinking into my couch.

I knew exactly what it felt like sometimes to watch two people, so in love, celebrate their bright future together when you were single.

When all you wanted was someone who would look at you the way they looked at each other.

I reached for him, pulling him toward me to settle my arm around him, like he had with me.

Looking into his eyes, I was overwhelmed with emotion and fantasy, with love and anxiety.

"I know exactly what you mean, Mitch," I said, hoping he could understand.

How could I make him understand what I barely comprehended myself?

"Penn..."

I leaned in, capturing his lips with mine.

Mitchell melted against me, a deep satisfying groan leaving his throat.

I slid my hands down the expanse of his chest, feeling the solidness through the fabric of his banana print silk shirt. The image of him shirtless before me replayed in my brain and I slid my hand beneath the hem of his shirt. I trailed my fingers over his warm skin, against the waistband of his jeans.

His hand found mine as he gently pushed me away.

"Penn…" he whispered my name, and I couldn't deny I liked the way it sounded.

I took his bottom lip into my mouth as I grabbed his hip, pulling him closer, my cock straining against my jeans once more.

Fuck dessert.

Mitchell is all I want.

Mitchell's body loosened as I leaned forward, backing him up against the armrest, settling my body between his legs, his hardness pressing against me causing an influx of heat to my entire body.

Mitchell pushed me away, breaking our kiss. "Penn, hold on."

Panic and anxiety flooded me.

Had I done something wrong?

Had he changed his mind about me?

About us?

I looked up at him, his lips still swollen from kissing me, his dark eyes glassy.

"What's wrong?" I asked, realizing that perhaps this *wasn't* about me.

I sat up straighter, reaching for his hand. I hated to see anything but excitement and mischief in those eyes.

"I just... You don't *need* to do this, you know," he said, swallowing hard. "I don't want you to feel like you *have* to because of..."

I shook my head.

This again.

"When are you going to realize that I *want* this? I want *you*," I said.

The sigh of relief that left him was indescribable.

I slid my fingers in between his, squeezing as I continued. "I get that you're trying to give me space to figure things out, and I appreciate that more than you know. But you..."

I swallowed nervously as the words made their way out of my throat. "You feel right. This... feels right. Doesn't it?" I asked, afraid of his answer.

Because, with one word, Mitchell DeVille could bring it all to a halt.

And that terrified me more than anything else. Because I didn't want my time with him to end when this job did.

He'd wedged himself into my heart and my life, and I didn't want to go back to the way things were before I met him.

When I was just existing. Without knowing who I was.

Without knowing him.

Without knowing what *right* felt like.

And when the words left me, they were the truest ones I'd ever said.

"When it's right, it's right. No matter who it is."

CHAPTER 25

Mitch

Something settled in my heart the moment Penn said those words. He felt like I was *right.*

That this connection, this fire between us, was right. That despite how it happened, it had happened, and the only one preventing us from moving forward was me.

Because I was scared he'd burn through me and leave me in a pile of ash to seek out better dick because that's what everyone else did.

I was scared that he'd wake up one day and realize this was just some experiment, and not anything *real.*

But as I looked at Penn Baker's pretty blue eyes, I knew.

This was more than just real.

This was *it*.

Penn was everything I'd ever wanted, and everything I thought I could never have.

I leaned into him without thinking, crashing my lips to his. His smooth, plush lips slowly moved against my own as I slid my fingers into the edges of his hair, and he slid his hands down my side, moving one to settle over my straining cock. His hand stayed there for a moment, rubbing and teasing me over my jeans.

I couldn't help the moan that escaped my mouth as my cock twitched, automatically pressing up toward the heat of his hand.

Penn slid his tongue in my mouth as he settled between my legs once more, his lips finding their way to the corner of my mouth, along my jaw, my neck.

H explored me with his lips as he shifted my body beneath him, backing me up against the arm of the sofa.

I closed my eyes in ecstasy as his lips trailed over my skin, one hand pulling at my collar while the other slowly unbuttoned my jeans.

I wanted to protest. To throw up my walls of protection and give him the out.

He must have felt my hesitation, because he whispered into my ear, "Tell me to stop and I'll stop."

I shook my head, burying my lips in his hair, at the shell of his ear.

"I don't want you to stop, Cream Puff."

Penn yanked on my zipper, and I grunted as he fumbled with my jeans, shifting us both as I arched my hips off the cushion to give him better access. His hands did not shake, and there was no tremble in his voice, in his kiss, or his touch.

Penn ran his warm palm over my sheathed cock, gabbing me through my boxers, squeezing me.

Fucking hell.

"Penn..." I groaned.

"Yeah?" he whispered, his thumb separating the thin opening.

"I—"

My words died on my tongue as he pulled my cock through the opening of my boxers, the cool air kissing my shaft like a balm.

He wrapped his hand around me, slowly stroking me into muteness.

I couldn't speak, nor could I process anything except his slow, curious touch.

He settled himself between my legs, using one hand to cup my balls while the other slowly stroked me. I could feel the moisture pebbling at my head. I expected him to continue with this new exploration, touching, rubbing, maybe even grinding, but...

The last thing I expected was to feel a hot, wet mouth wrap around my cock.

"Fuck!" I cried out as my cock hit the back of his throat.

I grit the curse through my teeth as the wind was knocked out of me.

Within seconds, Penn was off of me, leaving my cock wet, throbbing, and aching for *more*.

"Are you okay? Did I hurt you?" he asked, his eyebrows furrowing with concern.

A laugh erupted from my chest.

"No, you didn't hurt me. Just took me by surprise is all," I said, looking at his swollen lips, his bright eyes focused on me.

His lips were so close to my cock. I bucked my hips, brushing my wet tip against his lips and he smirked. I wondered if this breath of fresh air would deter him, but it didn't.

I watched as his tongue darted out to lick the drop of precum off my tip, and he didn't gag or convulse or even make a disgusted face.

He grabbed me by the base with one hand, his other still cupping and massaging my balls as he swallowed and dived back in.

"Fuck, I was right. You take my cock so fucking well." I groaned.

A contented sound escaped his throat as he

massaged my balls, using his other hand to stroke me while he licked and sucked, groaning with his own euphoria.

"Your mouth feels so good." I moaned, letting my fingers find the back of his head as I gently guided him forward to take more of me.

Penn picked up my request, once again, taking me to the back of his throat without warning.

"Fucking hell, Penn... I'm going to—"

Penn hollowed his cheeks, sucking, licking, and groaning around my cock like I was his favorite dessert, and I couldn't contain myself.

My back arched off the cushions as my balls tightened, my spine tingled, and the onslaught of my orgasm ricocheted through me. My cock pulsed as I came, hard and fast.

I half expected Penn to jump back at the first taste, but he only gripped me tighter.

Swallowing every bit of my release down his throat like my cock was a damn keg at a frat party.

And when I was done, he released me, leaning back on his heels as he *wiped* some of the remains of my cum from his swollen, perfect lips, and I couldn't contain myself.

I lunged forward, tearing his pants off.

Penn's cock sprang forth, bobbing in the air.

His head was slick with precum, his veins thick and pronounced.

"Did you like that, my little Cream Puff?" I purred, Penn's eyes widening at my gruff tone, his golden hair all disheveled, sticking out from the static of the couch cushions that cradled his head.

He licked his pouty lips, his gaze heated and dark with lust.

It was like something flipped inside of me the minute he said those three words.

I want you.

Like the veil had been lifted, and suddenly, we were both in uncharted territory.

Penn grabbed himself, his gaze fixed on mine as he nodded. "Yes," he said the word firmly. It was not a whisper.

It was an admission.

I grabbed his hand, pulling it away as I settled on my elbows between his legs.

His voice softened for a moment as he leaned himself up on his elbows, looking down at me with curiosity and asked, "I did good, right?"

I nodded my head, a dark chuckle leaving my throat.

"So good, baby," I praised, licking him from shaft to head, watching him shiver with excitement. "Like you were made to suck *my cock.*"

I watched his cheeks tint that wondrous shade of pink, watched him bite his lip at my praise.

"God, you are so fucking beautiful, you know that, right?" I said, staring at him for a moment, taking in the sight of him before me like this.

Messy blond hair, bright blue eyes, and a thick, gleaming cock bouncing free, just waiting to be devoured.

A perfect specimen waiting to be worshipped.

I ran my tongue up his shaft, taking pleasure in the way Penn squirmed under my attention, and I couldn't deny I loved him like that.

Desperate.

Needy.

He thrust his cock at me, hips bucking of their own accord, and I grabbed him by the base. I ran my tongue over his leaking head and he cursed.

"Mitch..." he begged.

I nipped and sucked at his head, groaning in response. "Yes, Cream Puff?"

"Please...." he begged, his voice getting all screwed up again.

A salacious smile curved on my lips.

God, I loved this man.

"Please, what?" I taunted as I settled one

hand underneath his ass cheek, digging my fingernails in as I pulled my attention away from his cock for a moment to watch the look on his face. His dilated pupils met my gaze, and in his eyes I could see the need, the trust.

"Please make me come," he voiced his words with boldness, with confidence this time, and I couldn't help but smile.

I would give this man anything he asked for.

"You are so pretty when you beg," I praised.

Penn whimpered in defeat, his chest heaving with breath.

"Fucking hell." His head fell back. "You are killing me…"

"How could I tell you no?" I murmured, and I took his cock in my mouth, lavishing his thickness with my tongue as I squeezed his ass.

"Oh my God… Mitch… I—" Penn's legs squeezed the sides of my face as his voice strained.

He was so close.

So fucking close.

"God, I fucking love you," I murmured the words without thinking.

Fuck!

"Wh… what?" he asked, nearly breathless.

It wasn't untrue, I did love him, but the last thing I wanted to do was push him away with such an admittance. Nothing *killed* the mood quite like an unrequited admission of love in my experience.

So instead, I did the only thing I could think of to distract us both from said admission.

I took Penn into the back of my throat, groaning my appreciation around his cock, my tongue sliding over his thick veins, and brought him the release he begged for. The pleasure he more than deserved.

"Oh my God," he mewled, thrusting his cock in my mouth as he emptied himself, hot and creamy, down my throat.

When his body went limp, I let go, and reality blanketed us once more. I settled back on my heels as I watched his chest heave with his breaths, watched his pupils slowly return to normal.

Ecstasy had been replaced with anxiety as his eyebrows furrowed, and he looked me over.

I'd fucked up.

Shit.

"Mitch..." he breathed through labored breaths.

I grabbed my pants, pulling them back up around my legs as I stood, collecting the shards of myself I'd just laid bare for Penn to see.

Fuck.

I need to get out of here before disaster hits.

Before I break apart at the seams

"I'm sorry," I said as I zipped my zipper, buttoning my pants. "I should go..."

Penn stood, dressing himself. There was only a modicum of space between us, but it felt like a canyon.

I needed air.

I needed to preserve what dignity I had left, because surely I'd just ruined everything.

"Mitch..." his voice softened, and I hated it. The sadness, the disappointment.

I grabbed him, kissing him with all that I was, hoping he could feel my truth. Hoping it would be enough to make him forget my words, no matter how true they were.

"I'm sorry, Penn," I said. "I'll see you tomorrow afternoon."

CHAPTER 26

Penn

I watched him leave and I just stood there.

Frozen, like an ice cube.

Mitchell said he loved me.

Granted, it was with my cock down his throat, but the admission itself struck me in the chest like Cupid's arrow.

Time moved slowly and all at once as I tried to grasp onto those words, tried to keep them alive and in the air.

God, I fucking love you.

I'd never told anyone I loved them.

But at that moment, I wanted to say *yes.* Yes, I love you, too.

But then I was distracted by Mitchell's

expert tongue and my impending orgasm, and the world around me disappeared.

Once again, I was at the mercy of Mitchell DeVille, and there was nothing I could do except ride out the bliss until I'd fallen back to earth.

I reached for him. I needed to touch him, to know he was real. I needed to tell him how I felt, but I was scared.

Everything was just happening so fast.

I could barely keep up with my own emotions, let alone the ones Mitchell had obviously buried.

I wanted to soothe him, to tell him it was okay.

I loved him, too.

But the world around me slowed to a crawl as he dressed himself, kissed me, and left.

And I just let him.

Because I was afraid of chasing after him.

I was afraid he was running *away from me.*

I absentmindedly colorized my five bowls of frosting, numb to the world around me. I barely heard Archie when he spoke.

"What is with you today? Earth to Penn?" he said, waving a spatula in my face.

"This wouldn't have anything to do with that photographer boy would it?" my mom's voice cut through, bursting my bubble, as Archie screeched, "What?"

My Mom set down the tray of sugar cookies, which I needed to ice for the Pride Fundraiser we were working tonight.

She did not look at all phased.

"I mean, you two have been attached at the hip lately in a... non-friendly way."

My cheeks heated immediately. "Mom!"

Archie laughed, but my mother only crossed her arms as I loaded the piping bags.

"What? A mother *knows* when her son is in love."

I wasn't sure how to proceed with her insinuation, but figured honesty was the best policy.

Even if it was uncomfortable.

"Yeah, well, it's a bit more complicated than that."

My mother grabbed the red piping bag to start working on a tray.

It reminded me of Mitchell, who'd just shoved his way into helping me just the other day, and I felt sick all over again.

What if I'd fucked up because I didn't say anything?

Because I didn't go after him?

What if he never wanted to see me again?

"Anything worthwhile isn't easy."

"Your mom is right. Whatever happened, I'm sure it can be fixed," Archie said.

I chewed my lips as I lined the cookies my mom passed down to me with blue lines.

"I just... should have told him the truth. But I didn't."

My mom settled her arm around me. "So tell him now. There's no expiry on telling someone how you feel."

I glanced up at her, feeling my heart catch in my throat as she rubbed my shoulders like she used to do when I was afraid. When I was a kid.

My voice shook as I fell apart under my mom's gaze.

"Even if it's a guy?"

My mom pulled me in close, wrapping me in a tight embrace and I hugged her, my shoulders loosening and my head buried in her apron.

"Baby, I wouldn't care if he was an alien from Mars. As long as he makes *you* happy, that's all that matters."

I could feel Archie's hand on my back as he softly spoke, too. "When it's right, it's right, no matter who it's with."

Something inside me clicked, knowing that I had their support. That I wasn't doing this alone, and as scary as it was, I had back up.

I had people who understood me and supported me.

And that included Mitchell.

The man I loved.

"Thanks, Mom," I said as she broke our hug to return to her piping.

"You don't have to thank me, sweetheart," she said, and with that I knew exactly what I needed to do.

CHAPTER 27

Mitch

I wasn't the biggest fan of the Jasper Springs Pizza, but I was feeling like a damn asshole, and I guess the cheese blanketed the guilt enough.

"What's your deal today? You look like someone stole the last cookie from the cookie jar," Dawson nipped.

Cade sipped his drink before chiming in. "Dawson's right. You seem more sullen than usual. Does this have anything to do with that guy from karaoke? Pete, was it?"

"Penn," I said his name, feeling it echo in every part of my being.

Nolan tapped away on his phone, but I didn't miss his glance.

I sighed, picking at my crust.

"I mean, kind of, yeah."

"Do you want to talk about it?" Weston asked cautiously.

I sighed, knowing it was best to just get it over with. Maybe then they'd let me eat my feelings in peace.

"He's new. To, you know, guys."

"Ah," Dawson said. "So you're worried he doesn't really like *you*."

Penn had told me he did, but I guess old habits died hard.

"And you really like him," Cade chimed.

I didn't even have to answer them. Instead, I just groaned in defeat.

"Yeah, and on top of all of that, I said I love you. By accident."

Dawson smirked. "So you really like him, then."

"Yes, Dawson. I fucking love him okay, are you happy? Is that what you want me to say?" I snapped.

Cade sighed. "He didn't say it back, obviously."

I huffed in annoyance. "Obviously. But that's probably because his dick was down my throat."

Nolan laughed.

"What's so funny Pencil-Pusher?"

Nolan set his phone down. "Nothing."

"So let me get this straight, you're worried you fucked shit up because you were *honest* about your feelings?" Weston asked seriously.

Well, when he put it that way...

"I mean, I don't even know *what* I am to him, but—"

"What is he to you?" Cade asked.

Everything.

My lack of response was probably telling enough.

"How did this become so fucking complicated?" I asked, running a hand over my face.

Dawson piped in, his tone serious. "Don't tell me to fuck off, but I want your honest answer."

I shot him a glare, and he continued.

"Did you give him a *chance* to talk about it?"

Dawson giving me relationship advice was the equivalent of hell freezing over. The man was notorious for his lack of commitment.

At least, he was until he met Nolan.

I'd replayed the moment over and over in my mind, but suddenly I saw it with startling clarity.

I'd *avoided* Penn because *I* was afraid he was going to clam up and avoid me because of what I'd said.

So I beat him to the punch.

I left before he could hurt me.

I didn't give him a chance, because I couldn't even give myself the chance to be vulnerable for once in my life.

I'd *really* fucked up.

"No," I said, my shoulders sinking.

"When's your next event?" Cade asked.

I looked at my phone, noting the Pride kickoff was our last event.

Tonight, that was my shot.

My chance to make things right.

To set the record straight.

Once and for all.

CHAPTER 28

PENN

"ALL RIGHT, I think that's everything," Archie said as we loaded the empty boxes into the dumpster out back behind the firehouse.

The annual Jasper Springs Pride Show was always one of our biggest events. Most of the businesses took part in it, each with a table that boasted their wares or business brochures.

The firehouse always sold their calendars, the pet hospital usually had animals that were up for adoption out to meet, and all the restaurants and food services usually donated food or sold snacks.

I'd always loved the event, because I loved making the cookies and desserts in bright colors, something different than our usual bear claws and croissants or wedding cakes.

Although this year, I felt like it was an entirely new experience.

I surveyed the crowd, searching for Mitchell. I knew he would be here as we'd discussed all my events ahead of time, and both had agreed this event would be the last, and the biggest, and since the Show usually happened the Friday before the Pride Parade, Mitchell had promised to have something ready for the social media page that we could use.

But that wasn't why I was looking for him.

I needed to tell him the truth.

I wanted to be with him, and while I knew the road of a relationship would be full of uncertainty, I knew that was what I wanted because I loved him, and that was enough for me.

I only hoped it would be enough for him.

"I'm going to grab some grub from the taco truck. You want anything?" Archie asked as I adjusted the plate of cookies at the bakery table.

"No, I'm good," I said.

Archie nodded. "Your mom said she and your dad would be here around four to relieve us."

I nodded. I was nervous, still unsure of how my dad would take the news his son had turned a new gay leaf, but I supposed there were harder things to deal with.

Like saying out loud, "I love you, and I want to be your boyfriend."

Archie sped off, leaving me to man the ship myself.

I still hadn't seen Mitchell, but that didn't mean he wasn't there. Being the most popular photographer in town, I was sure he was snapping more than just my cakes and cookies today.

"Hey, Penn!" Amy's voice broke my train of thought, and I tensed immediately.

I turned to see her, standing there in a bright pink mini dress, her gold curls bouncing against her shoulders. She looked like the epitome of Elle Woods in Legally Blonde.

She smiled brightly, standing next to a woman who was adorned in a white tank top, jean jacket with an array of pins, and a rainbow belt.

The woman's dark hair was braided with glitter, her green eyes standing out against all the bright colors. She was beautiful.

"Amy..." I said, feeling my blood freeze.

"Fancy meeting you here," she said.

I shrugged. "My family's bakery works this every year," I said, hoping to dodge any invitations.

"That's cool. I've never been. This is my first Pride, like, in general since..."

I watched as her cheeks blushed, and her friend smiled softly.

The world slowed to a standstill.

"Oh, Jesus, I totally spaced, uh... Molly, this is Penn. My ex-boyfriend," she said the words sweetly, almost endearingly.

Molly smiled, nodding as she looked me up and down. "I see," she said.

I never felt so judged in all my life. Seriously.

"Hi," I said awkwardly.

Amy giggled. "Penn, this is Molly. My girlfriend."

Girlfriend.

The bubble popped as understanding dawned on me.

Amy reached down, grabbing her *girlfriend*'s hand, smiling from ear to ear.

"You're..."

"Bi," she said with a smile. "Though, I'm still kind of new to the whole... *dating* girls part."

"Huh," I said, at a loss for words, blinking furiously.

"That's why I wanted to talk..." she said softly. "I know we weren't, like, end game or anything, but I didn't want you to hear it from someone else. I—"

My shoulders loosened as her words hit me.

"I know we had our ups and downs, but I always felt like we were good friends, you know?"

I did know. Throughout our relationship, talking to Amy was one of the easier parts. The sex wasn't bad, but it wasn't great either, and felt like it was just part of what we were *supposed* to do.

Which made a lot of sense as I looked at her *ease* with her girlfriend. I never made her smile like that.

The sight made me think about Mitchell.

"How did you know?" I asked.

Amy blinked. "Know what? That I was bi?"

I shook my head. "No. How did you know it was going to work out... with... your girlfriend?"

Molly shrugged, her green eyes lit up with amusement. "Because I'm a total catch, obviously."

Amy rolled her eyes, shoving her playfully. "And humble, too."

I watched as Amy smiled, flipping some hair over her shoulder. "Honestly, the thought of being without her was worse than the thought of what could have been."

I smiled genuinely. I understood her words one hundred percent.

The thought of being without Mitchell made my entire body tense.

Wondering what we could be if I was open to a *real relationship*. The possibilities made me want to try.

Maybe I could be happy, too, like Amy and Molly.

I didn't want to live a lie anymore. I wanted to be genuine, and that started with my feelings.

That started with Mitchell.

The rest of it, I'd figure out.

"I'm happy for you. Both of you," I said, grabbing a tray of sugar cookie rainbows, offering it to them.

"Thanks, Penn," Amy said, and she bit into the cookie, her eyes rolling back with satisfaction. Molly and I both laughed.

"It was really nice meeting you," Molly said as she pulled her girlfriend along.

"We should totally get together sometime!" Amy said through a mouthful of cookie as I waved at her.

"Absolutely," I said with a smile, just as Archie came back with a container full of tacos.

"Who was that?" he asked.

"My ex-girlfriend," I said, with a smirk. "Who apparently likes pussy way more than I do."

Archie laughed, popping open his container. "Mitchell's over at the Jasper Springs Pet Hospital table hanging out with his friends."

Archie's words settled on me.

He was here.

Just across the road.

"Go," Archie said, waving me off. "Go get your man and all that," he said, biting into his taco, crunching away.

I didn't have to be told twice.

Mitch

I clicked away on my camera while Cade and Weston handed some kittens over to a group of girls.

"You're stalling," Dawson said, nudging me in the shoulder.

"Don't you have to go wash a fire truck or something?" I nipped, watching the look on Cade's face as he placed the kitten in the arms of a woman with vibrant blue hair.

"Today is your lucky day. I'm off duty."

"You're about to need a medic if you don't get off my ass," I quipped.

"All I'm saying is, this is your last event together, right? You got here early. And you haven't left Cade's side since you arrived. I know he's your emotional support animal and shit, but come on, Mitch."

I lowered my camera, turning to glare at Dawson, who had the audacity to look perturbed.

At me!

Didn't he know he was the resident pain in the ass?

"I'm just—"

"You say it's complicated, I will punch you," Dawson grumbled.

"I'm working!"

Dawson hummed annoyingly. "Mhm. Well, here he comes, so buck up, Buttercup."

"What?" I asked, turning to see Penn walking across the street, right toward us, his hands stuffed in his jean pockets.

His bright blue polo shirt stood out against his pale skin, blond hair blowing in the wind. I half expected to hear some Bananarama playing behind me, or for someone to offer him a bottle of shampoo.

Fuck, he was so pretty.

My gaze caught his, and the smile that spread across his face was enough to melt an iceberg.

Instinctively, I snapped a photo.

"Hey," he said as he approached my lens.

I slowly lowered it, my heart catching in my throat. Behind me, I could hear Dawson humming away annoyingly.

"Hey," I replied, at a loss for words.

Up close, he smelled like sugar and cinnamon, like whipped vanilla frosting.

Like a fucking cream puff, making my mouth water.

I noticed the tiny rainbow flag pinned on his shirt, and couldn't help but smile.

"I, uh, can we talk? Somewhere?" he asked, running a hand through his golden locks.

Cade nodded at me from my side, clearly telling me I should leave.

But a part of me was certain this was it.

The inevitable crash and burn where Penn was going to tell me he didn't feel the same way.

That he just wanted to be *friends*, or worse.

Friends who sucked each other's cocks.

Which wouldn't have been a bad arrangement, if I didn't want more.

And with Penn, I'd always want more.

I'd want to wake up in bed with him curled around me. I'd want to have impromptu dinners in his kitchen, and cupcake frosting fights, and drunken karaoke make outs.

I'd always want him in a way I could never have him, if we were just *friends who fucked around*.

"Yeah, sure," I said, gripping my camera

strap. I followed him across the street to one of the park benches in the small park, which was crawling with overflow traffic from the show.

Couples and groups of friends were littered all across the lawn, and it sort of reminded me of our date.

Where we'd watched a bunch of cover bands and made out under the fireworks on the lawn.

"What, uh, what's up?" I said, trying to sound nonchalant. Stoic.

I knew what was coming, and there was no avoiding it.

"I, uh, I've been thinking about... stuff," Penn stammered, biting his bottom lip.

I sighed.

"About... us, I mean," he said the words softly, and it was like a knife to my heart.

Here it comes.

"What are we?" he asked the words curiously. "Because I saw you at that wedding, and we were strangers. Then, we talked online, and you were someone I hired, and then we hung out, and you were my friend, and then we went on a date and you were...." His voice trailed off, and he closed his eyes. "You weren't a friend, anymore, but I wasn't sure what you were. What you are, to me."

"I get it, Penn. You don't have to... Fuck, we don't have to do this. I just..."

"No, I need to do this. I need you to hear this," he said firmly, and I sighed deeply, my palms sweaty against my strap.

"I know I don't always know what I'm doing. Hell, I'll be the first to tell you I have no realm of experience here. I've never felt for anyone what I feel for you."

I looked into his glassy blue eyes and saw the fear there.

The unknown.

Instantly, my panic melted, my nerves fraying at the edges.

I reached out to wipe a tear from his face, shoving my own fear aside as curiosity got the best of me.

"What do you feel, Penn?" I dared to hope he felt the same.

That somehow, some way, I hadn't lost him.

"I—" he stammered, biting his lip. "I think I'm totally in love with you, Mitch."

My heart leaped at his words. I blinked, wondering if I'd imagined them. If I'd lost my marbles completely and gone full on insane.

"Penn..."

Penn slid his hand over mine, chewing his lip once more.

"I know I'm not the best boyfriend, period. I

don't always know the right thing to say, or the right thing to do. But I know when I'm with you... I *want* to be the best boyfriend."

He licked his lips, his glassy eyes sparkling with truth as my heart swelled with pride, with joy.

"I want to be *your* boyfriend," he said the words, and they pierced my heart, lighting me up with the brightest, fullest feeling in the word.

Love.

"Yes," I murmured, pulling him toward me, claiming his lips with my own. "Fuck, yes," I whispered, and he kissed me. I could feel his lips turning up in the corner with a smile as his hand settled on my hip, his tongue sliding into my mouth.

I kissed him back deeply, with all the love I could. When we broke apart, we both breathed heavy sighs, his palms hot against my thigh.

"So... that's a yes?" he asked sweetly, flashing his bright eyes up at me.

"Yes, Penn. I want to be your boyfriend, too." My heart soared.

CHAPTER 30

Penn

My heart beat so loudly in my chest, I wondered if Mitchell could hear it.

I wiped some stray confetti from my shoulder as he opened the door to his apartment. We'd been here before, only days ago, but somehow it felt like a lifetime.

After my parents had shown up to take over for the remainder of the event, I was excited to just be a part of the event.

With my boyfriend.

Well, and his friends, of course. We even ran into Amy and Molly again, and then Mitchell asked if I wanted to come over to his place and actually watch a movie and just hang out.

I settled against him, appreciating the warmth of his arm around me and I couldn't stop smiling.

I stared at the half-empty box of pizza on the table as Ace Ventura did his best parrot impression. I didn't get the movie, but watching Mitchell laugh his ass off, was enjoyment enough.

"What?" he asked, glancing down at me. "Do I have pizza on my face?"

My heart beat away in my chest as I turned my head and took in the sight of him.

"I just... a lot has happened since we were here last," I said.

Mitchell leaned in, giving me a sweet, quick kiss, and I melted once more, kissing him back.

"One of these days, we're going to make it through an entire movie," he whispered, his grin making his eyes light up with mischief.

I slid my fingers against the hair at the nape of his neck, slipping my tongue into his mouth with a confidence I hadn't possessed the last time I'd been here.

I slid my hands down his frame, wiggling them underneath the hem of his shirt.

Mitchell laughed against my kiss.

"Today is not that day," I whispered against his lips as I ran my hand over his abs, up over his solid chest.

Mitchell cursed, sighing deeply as he pulled his shirt off.

"There's always tomorrow," he said, shaking his head, running his hand through his hair.

I leaned forward, kissing him once more, letting my hands explore his bare chest, fingertips running over his nipples.

My cock throbbed in my pants, and I wondered how I'd ever lived without this.

Without *him.*

As if he could read my mind, he tugged at my shirt, and I let him remove it.

We both sat there, on his couch, shirtless, visibly aroused, and exposed in a way that had nothing to do with skin.

Mitchell stood up, holding his hand out to me.

I didn't think twice about taking it.

He pulled me close, into an embrace that was as tender as it was strong, melting my heart. His lips moved slowly against mine as he breathed deep. His hand settled on the flesh of my hip, warm and solid.

"I love you," he said. "I thought today, at the show, when you asked to talk, I thought..."

I searched his gaze, noting the glimmer of fear.

I knew it well, because up until recently, I'd also been afraid.

But as I stood there, shirtless, in *my boyfriend's* living room, I knew there was finally nothing to be afraid of.

Not when we were together.

"I know," I whispered, my heart in my throat. I leaned in, capturing his lips with mine once more. I settled one hand on his waistband, the other on his neck. His pulse thrummed beneath my palm, beating in time with my heart.

"I wanted to tell you I loved you, yesterday, but you ran off."

Mitchell gently pulled away from me, walking toward the hall. He stopped, his shoulders dropping as he breathed, "I ran off because I thought I'd scare you away."

He turned to me, his dark gaze glistening with promise.

With a vulnerability that hadn't existed yesterday.

I took slow steps toward him, my cock twitching with need. I didn't feel embarrassed about grabbing myself, and I didn't feel embarrassed about the way his gaze fell to my hand, or the way he looked at me.

Like I was truly *his.*

I stopped in front of him, reaching out to brace myself against the wall with one hand, picking up his hand with the other.

I let out a deep breath as I placed it over my heart. His palm was warm against my chest and I liked how it felt there.

Mitchell smirked as I said, "I'm not scared of what I feel when I'm with you."

His gaze softened as I leaned in closer, bringing our bodies together. His fingers slid over my pec, taking my nipple in between his thumb and forefinger as he pinched and pulled, causing my cock to twitch, and me to stifle a moan.

"Not anymore," I said, moving my hands to gingerly unbutton his jeans, unzip his zipper.

Mitchell shook his head as he let out a dark chuckle. "Is this what you want, Cream Puff?" he taunted, sliding his hand down over my stomach, to cup my cock through my jeans. "You want to be the prince charming?"

His thumb rubbed my cockhead through my jeans, and I pushed his pants down to the floor. I gazed at him up and down, taking in the sight of his nakedness in its entirety. Amidst the dark shadows and the amber light, he was by far the hottest thing I'd ever laid eyes on.

And he was *mine.*

The truth coupled with my desire was a heady cocktail, and I thought about all the times he'd been patient with me and my insecurities.

A world of possibilities and unclaimed

moments lay ahead of us, and I, for one, was more than excited to venture into the unknown with him.

I took a step back, watching as he stood there patiently waiting.

Waiting for *me* to call the shots, to tell him what to do, I realized.

I slowly unbuttoned my own jeans, divesting what was left of my clothes. Mitchell's heated gaze fixed on me, trailing over me with lust and love.

So much love, it was like a sugar high.

I grabbed my cock, sliding my hand along my shaft as I gazed at him.

Mitchell praised me constantly, and I couldn't deny I liked it, how his words made me feel.

So, I took a page out of his book as I closed the distance between us, catching his gaze as I let go of my cock, bracing my hands on the wall, pinning him beneath me. His gaze glistened with excitement as I pressed myself and my leaking cock against him.

"You are, without a doubt, the hottest thing I've ever seen," I said, finding my voice.

"Oh yeah? Is that so?" he drawled, grabbing *both* our cocks together in his hand.

Instinctively, I thrust myself against him, but it was no use, I needed more.

Mitchell moved his hand slowly up and down as he jacked us both, and I captured his lips with mine.

A thousand thoughts ran through my brain, a thousand wants, a thousand *needs.*

The foremost being one I never thought I'd dream in a million years, but that felt more right than anything else.

Tuned into me like he was, he only whispered, "Tell me what you want, Cream Puff."

I let my hand drop along his body, pulling him away from the wall. I slid my fingers over the supple flesh of his ass, my heart in my throat as my fingertips slid over his seam.

Mitchell groaned from the touch, which only fed my desire more.

"I want you," I said, letting my fingernails dig into the skin of his cheeks. The lust in my voice was foreign, but somehow it felt so undeniably true I couldn't refute it.

The need to be inside of him, possessing him, was both scary and exhilarating because I'd never *wanted* anyone as badly as I wanted Mitchell.

"How do you want me, baby?" Mitchell teased, using his thumb to spread our combined wetness along my shaft.

I swallowed harshly as the words fell out of

my mouth. My heart thumped in my chest as I held his gaze, like a blazing fire.

"I want to fuck you."

Mitchell smiled the sexiest grin I thought I'd ever seen, his dark hair falling in his eyes as he leaned up to nibble my lip.

"Is that so?" he purred, pushing me gently as he dipped toward the shadows. I followed him like a moth to a flame.

Toward his bedroom.

Bedroom.

A part of me felt scared as he turned on the light, keeping it low enough to see, but not bright enough to be distracting. I watched as he sauntered toward his bed, the dark black and gold geometric comforter standing out against the black, padded headboard.

There was something exhilarating about standing in his bedroom, feasting my eyes on his amber-lit flesh. My cock throbbed as the air kissed my moist skin, and I had to wrap my hand around my cock to quiet the need for touch.

Mitchell gazed at me over his shoulder as he opened his bedside table drawer.

I took one step closer, watching his shoulders knit as the sound of a cap popping echoed in the space. Then I took another step, then another, until I was in front of him.

I braced my fingers on his shoulder, letting them travel over his skin and I wrapped my arms around him, pulling his body flush against me.

Mitchell turned in my arms, and I leaned forward, kissing him with all that I was.

And what I was, was a ball of nerves, of sensation, of fear and love, and excitement and uncertainty.

But underneath his touch, underneath his kiss, I was safe.

I could just be... me.

"Yes," I breathed against his lips, stepping forward, nudging his legs apart with my knee.

Mitchell fell back against the bed with ease, and I tumbled with him. He shifted us both back, wrapping his leg around my hip, our cocks brushing together, hard and wet.

I couldn't help the moan that escaped my lips. A cool wetness kissed the edge of my cock, familiar but also foreign.

One glance to his nightstand, and I noticed the open bottle of lube, which was like a splash of cold water to my system.

I wanted this, wanted him.

But it had also been a while since I'd had sex —let alone anal—with anyone.

And I'd certainly never done it with a *guy*.

My nerves threatened to upend me, but

Mitchell only slid his fingers through my hair, pulling my lips to his.

"You're in charge here, Penn. If you want to stop…"

I shook my head, crushing my lips to his, his words giving me the strength they always did.

Letting me know it was okay to not be okay.

That it was okay to be nervous.

I slid my hand over his thigh as I ground myself against the cool wetness of his puckered opening, his cock sliding against my stomach, leaving wet trails of precum along my skin.

And when I looked in his eyes, seeing the desire, the love there, I forgot all about my nerves.

I kissed him softly, letting my tongue caress his, and I slowly tilted his hips up with one hand, gripping myself with the other, lining myself up. My breath hitched as the head of my cock pressed against his slick, lubricated entrance, and the rest of the world around me blurred.

For a moment, we lay there, intertwined, panting against one another as I inched my way inside his heat, breaching the tight ring of muscle. Mitchell's cock was solid and wet against my abs, throbbing as I kissed him. I grabbed his hardness in my hands as instinct took over, and my cock throbbed in the tight space and I started to move.

Mitchell rocked his hips in unison with my thrusts as I built a rhythm, slow and steady.

His insides clenched me tightly, driving me absolutely mad.

I didn't want to stop.

Not now, not ever.

"Fucking hell, Penn..." Mitchell grunted, wrapping his other leg around my hip, pulling me deeper, until I'd completely bottomed out.

"Mitch..." I grunted, my words starting to disappear, my linguistics systems taking a siesta again.

Words were hard to form when I felt *this* good.

His cock throbbed in my hand as I brushed my fingertip over his slit, wet and sticky precum coating both my hand and his shaft as I quickened my pace. There was nothing but the sounds of our breath, of wet skin slapping together, of guttural grunts and whispered curses as the flames consumed us both.

CHAPTER 31

Mitch

I wasn't partial to topping or bottoming, but underneath Penn, I became someone else entirely.

I became the one who was needy, desperate for release.

I became the one begging for mercy as he caressed my cock while filling me to the brim.

Penn slid his thumb over my weeping cock, his lips hot against my neck as he breathed against my ear. "Tell me what you want, Cupcake."

I wish I could have laughed at his choice of endearment, but the way he spoke, his voice deep with desire and command, I would have answered to fucking Princess.

I'd held Penn beneath me plenty of times now, and I'd coaxed him, guided him to tell me explicitly what it was he desired, both because I needed to hear it, but also because I liked hearing him *beg*.

Now the tables had turned, and I was desperate for *his touch*.

"I want you to make me come, baby," I breathed as I bit his lower lip. His cock throbbed inside of me, spurring me to grind my aching, wet cock against him once more.

"Please," I added, just to be a smartass.

Penn quickened his thrusts, nailing my prostate over and over, and it didn't take long for either of us, really. The minute my blinding orgasm came, I felt a sudden rush of warmth, followed by Penn practically collapsing on me, his breath labored as he squeezed my cock tighter while I came.

I didn't know how long we lay there, connected. Penn curled against me, buried to the hilt as I softened against him. Our legs intertwined together, him wrapped in my arms.

I kissed his temple as he sighed contentedly. "I love you," I said with a smile.

Penn buried his face in my hair as we both

rolled over onto our sides, the motion causing him to slip out, as well as his release.

Penn looked up at me with bright eyes full of wonder and hope.

And when he told me he loved me, I knew I'd finally found the person who made me whole.

CHAPTER 32

MITCH

I OPENED Penn's passenger door, my camera bag slung over my shoulder.

While he slept, I stayed up to work on photos, mostly because I couldn't sleep after being so wound up over what had happened.

We'd fucked.

Well, technically, I was the one who'd given it up, and I was okay with that. If that was what my little Cream Puff wanted, I'd gladly let him fuck me six ways from Sunday.

Because, to be honest, Penn made a pretty good top.

Who would have thought the shy, quiet, boy

next door baker would be so fucking *hot* in the bedroom?

It's always the quiet ones.

Penn climbed out of the car, grinning like a kid on Christmas.

It was after ten, and I had to admit it was weird to see someone else open the shop.

"Hey, Penn!" Archie called out, waving at us both. "Mitchell..."

"I hope you had fun time last night," Penn's mother said, flashing a smile as she pulled her son in for a hug. I headed for the office, stopping in my tracks when she said, "I meant you, too, Mitchell."

I turned to see Penn blushing as his mom held him close.

"I have a feeling we'll be seeing a lot more of one another," she said.

I looked from Penn to his mother, raising an eyebrow at Penn, who looked like he wanted to disappear completely.

That was the moment his dad came out of the office.

"Mitchell, so nice to see you. I hope you have those photos from the show ready. I really want to start getting some posts circulating this week. It's a big week you know."

"Uh huh. Actually, I, uh, have the files right here. Stayed up almost all night finishing them."

Penn broke away from his mother as he came to my side.

"You didn't have to—"

"I wanted to," I said, flashing him with a smile. I caught his father's judgmental gaze as he looked from his son to me, half expecting him to yell, or cuss me out, or something.

But he only vacated his chair, looming in the doorway as he said, "There better be some actual pictures of baked goods and not just candids of my son."

Frozen, I attempted to speak as his mother hit her husband in the stomach.

"Leave the boy alone, you're embarrassing him," she chastised, flashing me a smile.

Penn turned an adorable shade of pink as his father narrowed his eyes, moving to let me into the office.

Penn entered first, as I stood in the alcove, staring up at his father. As I brushed past him, he whispered to me.

"Break his heart, I'll break your bones. Got it?"

I looked up at him, the obvious love and the genuine acceptance making me feel as if I could perish right there on the bakery room floor.

"Yes, sir," I said, entering the office, setting my gaze on the most perfect man in all of Jasper Springs.

If Penn and I could survive our own selves, surely we could survive anything else the world threw at us.

Including overprotective fathers.

I sat in the office chair, hooking up my external drive, and bringing up the photos as his father left the office, replaced by an excited Archie.

"All right, Mitchell, let's get this show on the road," Archie said, slapping his hands together.

One by one, I cycled through the photos. Cakes, cookies, prep work, well-lit signs, customers.

I was always proud of my work, but these were certainly stand outs in my portfolio. From the smoothness of the buttercream, to the employees, I was more than proud of the shots I'd captured.

Because the bakery wasn't just a business to Penn or his parents, or even Archie.

They were a family, a community, a place to relax, and indulge.

"These are phenomenal, Mitch," Penn said in awe.

His mother smiled. "I agree. Do you do prints? I might want to order some of those portraits of my pride an joy you took," she said sweetly.

Penn blushed, and I couldn't help but smile.

"I think that can definitely be arranged," I said.

Archie smirked. "Maybe I'll grab some for my profile," he said, preening like the pain in the ass he was.

But nothing could sour my mood, not even Archie.

And when Penn smiled, rolling his eyes, too, I knew this was only the beginning.

EPILOGUE

THREE MONTHS LATER…

Penn

"Okay, this time you're actually singing solo," Archie touted at me over his beer.

I rolled my eyes as I leaned on the high top, sipping my Angry Orchard. "I believe it's your turn to embarrass yourself on stage this evening," I bit back.

"Cream Puff's right. You managed to fly under the radar last time, but tonight is your penance," Mitchell drawled as Cade made his way down from the stage.

I checked my phone once more, waiting for Amy's text. I'd finally taken her up on her invitation to hang out, which wasn't terrible. In fact, once we both actually started talking, it was more cathartic than anything. I even told her about Mitchell, and she suggested we all hang out.

So, I invited her to our monthly karaoke hang out with Mitchell's friends.

"She'll be here, don't worry," Mitchell said, nudging my arm.

I glanced at him, feeling instantly at ease. No matter what was bothering me, Mitchell always seemed to have a way to soothe my nerves.

"All right, next up we have... Archie? Is there an Archie in the house?" Will, the DJ, called out.

I smiled smugly as I watched Archie's jaw tense.

"You..." he hissed out.

"Your audience awaits," I teased, taking another sip of my drink, just as a familiar voice pulled me from my victory.

"Hey, Penn!" Amy sing-songed, sliding between Mitchell and I for a hug.

And when I hugged her back, it didn't feel awkward or unwelcome.

Amy smiled as I gave a quick hug to Molly, too.

"Amy these are my... friends, Cade, Weston, Dawson, and Nolan. Guys this is... my... friend, Amy, and her girlfriend, Molly."

A resounding hello and polite introductions

were made as Henry came to our table, dropping off our drink refills. On his heels was none other than Grayson, his boyfriend, and...

I turned to see the newlyweds with their bridal party in tow, sidling up to a high top two spots over.

Archie belted out the worst rendition of Mariah Carey's *Heartbreaker* I'd ever heard, while Giselle all but skipped over to our table.

"Hey!" she said with excitement, hugging Mitchell. He kindly returned the favor as she leaned back, setting her hand on her newly formed bump.

Archie finished his set as Mitchell and Giselle dived into a discussion about baby photos as Drew Axel took the stage with his boyfriend, Taylor.

"How long is Drew in town?" I asked, cutting into their discussion.

"Wait, you know him?" Amy pressed.

I shook my head. "I don't *know* him, know him. But I've met him like once. He has a house here, I think."

Grayson nodded, sliding his arm around Henry. "He does. Comes and goes though, guess that's the life of a rockstar."

Drew and Taylor's rendition of Taylor Swift's *Love Story* was a much better performance than Archie's screeching.

I think Dawson was actually better than him, and that was saying something.

"Giselle!" Aaron called from across the way, waving her over to the table where her bridesmaids slash friends, Julie and Mia were sitting, as well as a man who looked very familiar, but I couldn't place.

Though he kind of looked like the guy in the porn I watched all those months ago.

But I'm sure that was just my mind playing tricks on me.

"You karaoke?" Dawson asked, nodding at Amy.

"Who me?" she asked, looking around confused.

Dawson nodded.

"Oh, uh, I mean, not usually..."

I caught Molly's gaze, and we shared a knowing look. Amy was a natural carpool karaoke fan.

As Drew and Taylor wrapped up their star performance, I couldn't help but think about just how much my life had changed in the course of three months.

I'd come home from college lost. Single, alone, and wishing that I could find someone to love, someone to share my passions with.

And as I sat in M's Place, surrounded by

drinks and laughter, I felt like I'd finally found everything I was looking for.

I found the man of my dreams, but I'd also found a family.

A place where I finally fit in.

I raised my glass, looking at Mitchell.

"To new friends, and new beginnings," I said with a smile, as the beginning of a classic Freddie Mercury song sounded across the stage.

"To new friends and new beginnings," Mitchell said, clinking his glass with my bottle, and one by one everyone chimed in.

"I'll drink to that," Dawson said.

"Me too," Cade said as he raised his glass.

And when we all brought our drinks back down, I shot my boyfriend a glance.

"So you want to catch a movie after this?" I smirked.

Mitchell picked up my cue without missing a beat.

"That depends. Are we going to actually watch the movie, or are you just trying to get in my pants?"

"That depends on your choice of movie, Cupcake."

Mitchell sipped his drink, his dark gaze full of mischief as he shrugged.

"One day, Cream Puff."

I settled my hand on his hip, casting him a

devilish smirk of my own. "Today is not that day," I said as I pressed my lips to his.

Mitchell melted into my kiss as the sounds of Amy crooning out Whitney Houston's *Higher Love* sounded in the space around us.

"There's always tomorrow," I whispered against his lips.

Mitchell gripped my hips as he kissed me.

And as we made out in the middle of M's Place, surrounded by laughter and drinks, and friends, and love, I looked forward to what tomorrow would bring.

THANK you for reading Mitch and Penn's story. If you enjoyed this book, please leave a review. Even a few words means so much to me.

THANK YOU!
~*Evie Riley*

Federal Protection Agency

Mason

Rafe

Ryzen

Cooper

Noah

Damien

Sebastian

Gabe

Logan

Ruthless Empire

Courting Danger

Chasing Danger

Kissing Danger

Smokejumpers

Hawke

Cyrus

Jase

Gage

Jackson

Xavier

Jasper Springs

Cade

Dawson

Drew

Grayson

Riley

Mitch

From The Edge

Shattered

Runaway

Jaded

Rescue

Hidden

Tormented

Gray Vale Pack

His Fated Mate

His Wounded Warrior

His Healing Heart

FOLLOW EVIE

Facebook Author Page
https://www.facebook.com/AuthorEvieRiley

Blog/Website
https://authoreveriley.blogspot.com/

Goodreads
https://www.goodreads.com/author/show/39018597.
Evie_Riley

Bookbub
https://www.bookbub.com/authors/evie-riley

Instagram
https://www.instagram.com/authorevieriley/

LGBTQ+ Romance Books ARC Team
https://booksprout.co/author/25823/lgbtq-romance-
books

ABOUT THE AUTHOR

Evie Riley is a prolific, neurodivergent author known for her captivating MM romance novels. She has gained a significant following and topped the LGBT+ action and adventure best-seller charts with her series.

Evie's writing style often explores dark and gritty themes where her men must overcome difficult obstacles in their search for love, but she has also ventured into sweeter small-town romances, incorporating tropes like enemies-to-lovers, friends-to-lovers, age-gap, and forced proximity. She is known for crafting engaging romantic suspense novels and has a knack for creating interconnected series worlds that keep readers invested.

Outside of writing, she enjoys spending time at the beach and has a quirky personality, described by her partner as ranging from cute to deadly, depending on her blood-chocolate levels.

Evie spends her nights writing bad boys in love,
and her days wrangling the sweet boys she loves.

www.ingramcontent.com/pod-product-compliance
Lightning Source LLC
Chambersburg PA
CBHW070521220726
48294CB00019B/7